PASSION'S CHAINS

"Ah, Ria." He smiled devilishly and she took a step back. "You have an unfortunate knack for making me forget any good intentions I might ever have had."

She saw the sudden flare of renewed passion in his eyes. "I—"

"Are you going to tell me you hate me? Don't. It's a waste of energy you're going to need for other things."

"You may do what you want tonight," she said furiously, "but tomorrow will come. I will leave your ship."

"Ria"—his voice was firm now—"tomorrow you will be as much mine as you are tonight . . . and will be for a long time."

Before she could answer he bent his head and covered her lips with his, slowly destroying the barriers she had had very little time to raise.

"You are a hypocrite, my sweet. You and I both know that no matter what enemies we might be, there is still this . . . and there will always be this."

What good is it to protest? she thought. All he had to do was stroke her flesh and the core of defiance in her would melt, leaving her powerless to prevent him from doing as he pleased. . . .

SYLVIE F. SOMMERFIELD

Elusive Swan

ZEBRA BOOKS
KENSINGTON PUBLISHING CORP.

ZEBRA BOOKS

are published by

Kensington Publishing Corp.
475 Park Avenue South
New York, NY 10016

First printing: May 1987

Printed in the United States of America

Dedicated To

Cynthia Swanson

As a warm welcome and even warmer thanks for the contribution of the hard work it took to put this book together.

Acknowledgments

I would like to give special thanks to Phoebe Voyer, of Lowell, Massachusetts for her invaluable contribution of historical material used in this book and her aid in discovering other sources.

I would also like to thank the St. Augustine Historical Society for taking the time and interest to forward some wonderful material.

I would also like to extend my gratitude to Connie Richardson and Jacqueline Fretwell, from St. Augustine for making that extra effort to help me in my search for material.

Ad Finem

On the white throat of the useless passion
   That scorched my soul with its burning breath
I clutched my fingers in murderous fashion,
   And gathered them close in a grip of death;
For why should I fan, or feed with fuel,
   A love that showed me but blank despair?
So my hold was firm, and my grasp was cruel—
   I meant to strangle it then and there!

I thought it was dead. But with no warning,
   It rose from its grave last night, and came
And stood by my bed till the early morning.
   And over and over it spoke your name.
Its throat was red where my hands had held it;
   It burned my brow with its scorching breath;
And I said the moment my eyes beheld it,
   "A love like this can know no death."

For just one kiss that our lips have given
   In the lost and beautiful past to me,
I would gladly barter my hopes of Heaven
   And all the bliss of Eternity.
For never a joy are the angels' keeping,
   To lay at my feet in Paradise,
Like that of into your strong arms, creeping,
   And looking into your love-lit eyes.

I know, in the way that sins are reckoned,
  This thought is a sin of the deepest dye;
But I know, too, if an angel beckoned,
  Standing close by the Throne on High,
And you, adown by the gates infernal,
  Should open your loving arms and smile,
I would turn my back on things supernal,
  To lie on your breast a little while.

To know for an hour you were mine completely—
  Mine in body and soul, my own—
I would bear unending tortures sweetly,
  With not a murmur and not a moan.
A lighter sin or lesser error
  Might change through hope or fear divine;
But there is no fear, and hell has no terror,
  To change or alter a love like mine.

Prologue

Off the Carolina Coast—1786

The ship limped toward the harbor, spars broken, canvas ripped. Men were wounded and this, too, slowed her progress for few of her crew manned her. The *White Bird* was one of the many ships owned by Charles Maine and Son of South Carolina. It was also one of the many that had been struck by a swift pirate vessel, and left damaged and stripped of valuable cargo.

Once docked, the captain of the *White Bird* saw to his crew's medical care and his ship's repairs; then, anger in his dark eyes, he hired a buggy to take him to the office of the Maine shipping line. Charles Maine listened to his report of the encounter with a heavy heart. It was similar to the reports he had heard from three of his captains within the past six months. Maine was nearing sixty, yet was as erect and sturdy as he had been when he'd started the Maine shipping line. His figure was lean and strong, and his face was still handsome. His thick, snow-white hair contrasted with the dark tufts that winged over his deep amber eyes, and at this moment those eyes glowed with an anger that surpassed that of the beleaguered captain.

"Again the same damned rascal!" Captain Peters said. "One need only compare the reports to see it is the same ship."

"Yes, Captain Peters," Charles agreed. "This is getting beyond endurance. There must be some way to catch the blackguard, but for the life of me I cannot think of what to do outside of sending an escort ship with every merchant vessel. However, that is going to raise the cost of shipping to a point I fear the merchants can ill afford."

"I do not see any other alternative," Captain Peters responded in a resigned voice.

"Well, see to your ship and your men, Captain, and I will arrange a new cargo when the *Bird* is ready for sea again."

Captain Peters stood up and extended his hand to Charles Maine, who took it in a firm grip.

"I'm truly sorry about this, sir."

"Yes, Captain, so am I. Now I must think of a way to stop the piracy."

"I'll report to you when my ship is ready."

"Very good, Captain . . . good day, sir."

"Good day, Mr. Maine."

Charles Maine watched the captain leave; then he slumped into his chair. He worried more than he would let the world know. The piracies were responsible for heavy losses that he would have a difficult time recouping. He thought of his son and daughter to whom he wanted to leave a successful shipping line. He'd planned to build a dynasty around the Maine name, but now one defeat seemed to be followed by another.

This brought to mind his son Lucas who seemed totally disinclined toward the idea of marriage.

Charles knew the handsome young rake was loved by many acceptable women, yet offered his name to none. Charles was fast reaching the end of his patience; even Lucas could never push him too far.

He picked up a letter that he had been reading when the captain had arrived. It was from an old and dear friend, and Charles was determined it would put an end to Lucas's roaming and settle him down, for it contained an acceptance of the marriage between Lucas Maine and his old friend's daughter, Arianne St. Thomas.

Charles set his jaw firmly, then folded the letter and put it into his pocket. He left the office and walked home, determined to settle at least one of his problems.

Chapter 1

Charles's face was mottled with rage as he glared at his son Lucas across the dinner table. Lucas wore a patronizing smile which infuriated Charles even further.

"Is it not enough that I have one ship after another sacked by that damned pirate, must I have a son who does not take this family's fortune seriously!"

"Now, Father, that's not so," Lucas replied. "I most certainly take what happens to our ships seriously."

"Arrogant young puppy!" Charles snapped. "I did not say my concern was only for our ships."

Knowing what was coming, since it was an ancient refrain, Lucas remained quiet. But his silence provoked Charles to rise and pound his closed fist against the table.

"I mean an heir damn it. Why must you continue to ignore every pretty woman of any social standing?"

"I don't think Lucas ignores many of them."

The words came from Lucas's sister, Cristine, who sat across the table from him. Her amber eyes, in which danced flecks of gold, now sparkled with mischief.

"In fact, Papa"—she giggled—"he pays a lot of attention to them all."

Lucas's glare stilled her laughter, but did nothing to stop the fun she was having at his expense.

"That's just it, why must you flit from one to another? Why can you not choose one? Will I be dead and buried before I can know there are other Maines to inherit what I worked so hard to build?"

"Father, for God's sake." Lucas groaned. "Can you tell me that someone forced you into marriage with Mother? From what I've seen over the years it was your choice to wed her, because you loved her and wanted to marry her."

Andrea Maine, the mother and wife in question, forced herself to refrain from laughter as did Cristine, although it was a struggle for both to do so and neither Charles nor Lucas missed the effort.

Charles was now a step beyond rage. He glared at his wife who remained totally calm in the face of anger she had long ago learned to ignore.

"I will see you in my study, young man," he said coldly to Lucas. With squared shoulders, he left the room and soon the sound of a not-too-gentle close of the study door came to them.

Lucas rose reluctantly, and again Andrea had to restrain herself. She tried to achieve a sympathetic expression, but was not successful.

"Mother, I'm sure you and Cristine find this amusing, but for God's sake I'm nearly thirty. I believe I'm capable of choosing a wife."

"Quite capable from what I hear," Cristine said wickedly.

"And you," Lucas said, his patience growing thin. "I'm going to give you a swat on your backside so you won't be sitting for a week."

"Lucas, your sister is just teasing," Andrea put in.

14

"But your father is right. You should settle down."

Lucas smiled at her. "When I find someone like you I shall certainly do that, but I fear Father has gotten the only such woman in the world."

Andrea smiled, though she was not fooled by his charm for a moment. "Quite complimentary, my son, but I suggest you go and try some of the famous Lucas Maine charm on your father."

Lucas chuckled and walked around the table. He pulled a wayward curl of his sister's hair as he passed her, then bent to kiss his mother's cheek. He sighed deeply, knowing what he was to face, and walked toward the study. After knocking on the study door, he entered to find his father pouring brandy from a decanter. Charles handed one glass of it to Lucas.

"Sit down, son, I have to discuss some things with you. I'm not sure you will approve, but there are very few choices left."

"Choices . . . between what?"

"The last ship . . . the *White Bird* . . . I'm afraid its loss has put my back to the wall."

"Are you serious, Father? Is it truly that bad?"

"I find myself with only one alternative. I must ask you to do something for me. Something I know you will find difficult."

"You know there is nothing I wouldn't do for you."

Except marry and provide grandchildren, Charles thought, but this time he was clever enough to keep silent. "The biggest losses to my line are the shipments made by Sir Reginald St. Thomas."

"Sir Reginald St. Thomas . . . I don't know him do I?"

"No . . . no. He is an old friend of mine from London. Quite wealthy and always ready to ship with me . . . until now."

"And?"

"I need to recoup my losses. I have lost clients, and some are waiting to see what Sir Reginald will do."

"Then what is the difficulty? Convince him to ship with you and the problems will be over."

"I thought it would be simple and did as you suggested just now."

"And?"

"And I received a letter from him."

"He agreed?"

"With a condition. Oh, a very subtle suggestion, but if one reads between the lines it is a condition."

"What is this condition?"

"Sir Reginald has a daughter, Arianne . . . very pretty from what I'm told."

Lucas was already getting suspicious. "A daughter?"

"Lucas"—his father's voice lowered—"if you do not agree to an arrangement of marriage between our families, St. Thomas will refuse to ship with me again. If that happens we are completely lost."

"Marriage!" Lucas was the one who was angry now. "What is the matter with this girl that her father has to buy a husband for her . . . and what the hell kind of father goes about buying a husband? For God's sake, Father, you haven't agreed to this?"

"No, son, I haven't," Charles replied in a well-controlled tone. Nonetheless, defeat was in his voice. "I will write and say no, but I feel I must prepare you, your mother, and your sister for the loss of a great deal of what we have."

Lucas digested this slowly. Charles knew very well how much Lucas's family meant to him so he had deliberately planned to touch his son's loyalty.

"There . . . there's no alternative?"

"None. We must just . . . adjust."

16

"But Mother and Cristine—"

"Will have to learn to do without. I shall try to build again, but it will take time."

Lucas went to the brandy and poured another. Charles remained silent, suppressing the smile that sought to touch his lips. He knew his son so well.

"Then," Lucas said softly, "I suggest you agree and make the arrangement."

"Son, I'm not asking—"

Lucas laughed. He felt he needed to console his father now.

"Don't worry about it, Father. After all you were just saying you wanted me to marry. I guess Arianne St. Thomas will make as good a wife as any other."

"It might not be so bad, son. I've been told she's lovely and well educated, and has a sweet disposition."

"A paragon of virtue," Lucas quipped. "Hardly a girl a father would have to buy a husband for."

"Lucas . . . maybe we can manage—"

"I won't have my mother and sister destitute. Make the arrangements." He gulped down one more drink and left the study.

Charles sat in silence for a few minutes, then lifted his brandy glass to drink.

"So, my son, you are to marry, and I shall urge your beautiful bride to come quickly. Maybe she will be more than you bargained for."

From his pocket he took a small oval locket. It had been sent to him by his best friend Reginald. Within was a picture of Arianne St. Thomas, and Charles was quick to see that she was beautiful. He hoped his son would recognize her beauty.

In his own room Lucas raged against fate until he

17

was exhausted. Then he sat down and gave the matter some considered thought. After a long while he began to smile. It was good that Charles could not see him then, for the smile turned into a deep and very pleased laugh.

Within two weeks Charles came to Lucas to inform him that the arrangements had been made and that he was to sail for England within three days. Lucas seemed to agree, and Charles was relieved.

Lucas then left the house and went to a tavern where he met with two young men who would be likely to do what he wanted done. One was Christian Martin and the other was Scott Fitzgerald. Chris and Scott were Lucas's closest friends. The three had been almost inseparable since they were boys. They were much alike in values and temperament, but entirely different in looks.

Chris, the darkest of them, had deep brown hair and large expressive hazel eyes, and he tended to keep his emotions under control. He usually examined situations closely and cautiously, except when he was with Lucas and Scott. Then he tended to relax and indulge in some of their fun-loving ways.

He was nearly as tall as Lucas, but much less solid in build. Whereas Lucas gave the appearance of overpowering strength, Chris seemed lean and wiry. His face was square and open, dominated by large intense eyes and a broad mouth that smiled easily.

Scott was closer to Chris in height and closer to Lucas in temperament. His sandy hair was a shade between that of Chris and Lucas. In fact he often seemed to be a part of each of them. He was light-hearted, apt to leap into anything, especially if he felt needed by one of his friends. His loyalty to the values he'd acquired was often surprising, yet both Chris and Lucas knew they could always depend on him in any situation.

Lucas ordered tankards of ale for the three of them, and they sat down to talk.

"So old man"—Scott laughed—"what's this urgent meeting about?"

"Yes, Lucas," Christian added, "and so mysterious too."

"Drink your ale, gentlemen, because I have a bargain to make with both of you."

"Speak up," Scott declared. "I'm in the mood for something exciting."

"Well, for you, Scott my friend," Lucas stated firmly, "I have something very special. You are going to be my proxy at my wedding."

"Proxy . . . wedding . . . me?" Scott stammered.

"Explain," Chris urged.

"All right. My father has arranged my marriage with an English lord's daughter. Seems the lord was an old friend of his. Anyway, I'm going to be entirely too busy to go, nor would I be inclined to go if I weren't. The lady will have a bought husband, but one she'll never see. You go as my proxy, and I'll send a letter with you. You will have a nice purse to spend and a lot of pretty ladies to help you. What do you say, Scott?"

"I say it sounds like great fun. I deliver your note, stand in for you at the wedding, and then enjoy myself on your money."

"That's about right."

"Then I agree."

"Good, you sail on the *Blue Mist* day after tomorrow. Scott, I don't want my family to know a thing about this."

"I sense you're up to a little more?"

"I am . . . Chris and I are going to go catch a pirate."

"Ah, now it gets more interesting," Chris replied. "What do you have planned?"

"I'll arrange the ship. We'll leave the same day Scott does so my parents won't be suspicious. Scott goes to England and we go pirate hunting. We will pretend to be pirates ourselves in order to find out just who is preying on the Maine shipping line and why. Then we'll deal with him and rid my father of the problem. After that"—Lucas sat back and smiled—"a divorce can be gotten."

"How?" Scott questioned.

"Why, my friend"—Lucas laughed—"I have no intention of consummating this marriage. I intend to have it annulled."

"You've got this all figured out." Scott laughed now.

"I have. Just because Lord St. Thomas wants to buy a husband for his daughter doesn't mean I have to be that docile, ever-obedient, and well-paid-for husband. We'll comply, but Lord St. Thomas and his homely little daughter are going to get one hell of a surprise." Lucas's voice grew harsh and his anger was momentarily obvious. "I'll be damned if I'll be bought. When I take a wife, it will be one of my own choosing."

Scott had been watching Lucas closely as he spoke, noting that his friend's amber eyes danced with tiny gold flecks as he became more emotional. Since childhood, Scott had admired Lucas, first for his mental and physical strength, later for his ability to succeed with just about any woman he chose.

Lucas was tall, standing three inches over six feet. The breadth of his shoulders and the lean hardness of his body attracted women like a honey pot attracts bees. His hair was sun-touched gold, a deep contrast to his whiskey-colored eyes.

20

"Lucas." Chris spoke the name inquisitively. "How are you going to arrange this sleight of hand? Surely your father is going to be at the dock to see you off, or"—he laughed—"just to make sure you're really going."

"Oh, he'll do that all right. He's certainly not a man to be fooled easily. We're all going to leave on the *Mist*, but Chris and I will be put ashore down the coast a ways, where I already have another ship waiting."

"Sounds like this is going to be fun," Chris said.

"Maybe Chris," Lucas declared seriously. "Maybe it's going to be a little dangerous too. I don't like to think of what might happen if one of those cutthroats finds out who we really are. I'm afraid there would be no journey home and my new wife would end up a widow."

The three young men were silent for a moment as the full impact of what they were about to do became clearer—much clearer.

"Well, anyway"—Lucas raised his tankard—"let's have a toast to the success of this venture. We can't afford to fail so we won't think about that. Scott, kiss my new bride for me and deliver my message. That should put an end to any desire she might have to meet me until I can solve this mystery. When this is all over the three of us will celebrate, for we will have ridden the seas of a pirate, given my father's ships the freedom to rebuild, and freed me to choose my own bride. To us," he said, then laughed buoyantly.

They clicked their glasses together and drank.

That night Lucas sat at his desk and penned a letter meant to arouse enough annoyance in his bride to keep her away from him, yet to be too polite to anger her family. He gave it a great deal of thought, trying to keep his sense of humor under control as he did.

My dear Arianne,

I take the liberty to address you by your given name before our marriage is one of fact. I regret that I must send a proxy to attend to the details of our wedding, but our ships are plagued by piracy which has regrettably curtailed their mobility. These attacks are also cause for worry in my part.

I suggest firmly that you harbor no thoughts of coming to the Colonies at this time. The seas are alive with pirates, and the Colonies themselves are unsettled. Furthermore, a woman of your delicate background would find it quite impossible to bear the hardships of such a journey. I will take it upon myself to come for you when I feel the times are more stable.

Until then, I assume our future will be bright, and hope the wedding is pleasant despite my absence.

Your obedient servant and husband,
Lucas Maine

He looked at the letter in satisfaction. If he received such a letter he knew he would be happy to keep as much distance between himself and the writer as possible. He was quite sure his new bride would not take well to the proxy, to the idea that she was much too delicate to travel, or to the thinly veiled suggestion that he had no time to think of her and did not really care to see her in the near future.

He smiled, then folded the letter and made ready to give it to Scott who would have to face the lady's distress without him.

When the ship left the harbor Charles was on the pier to wish his son Godspeed. He and Andrea stood with Cristine and waved goodbye.

Lucas was forced to laugh when Scott's voice came from behind him.

"I don't think your father would look so pleased if he had any idea of what you were up to."

"You can count on that," Lucas replied. "He would have my head on a platter. But, he need never know. Once I bring him back the scoundrel who's been robbing him blind he'll be ready to listen to my arguments about an annulment."

"I hope you're right."

"You sound unsure."

"I've just got a feeling. . . ." Scott shrugged.

"Getting premonitions like an old woman?"

"I suspect this little adventure is going to be more than we think it will be."

"Nonsense, it's very simple. Next year at this time it will give us something to laugh about."

"I hope you're right," Scott muttered under his breath.

Several miles down the coast another ship lay at anchor waiting for the arrival of its owner who would be captaining it on a unique adventure. Lucas had chosen her crew well. All the men were loyal to him, and had the ability to keep quiet about the project.

After Lucas and Chris were rowed to that vessel, they stood at the rail and watched the *Mist* sail away.

"Do you know exactly where our destination will be?" Chris asked as the last of the *Mist*'s sails faded over the horizon.

"After I give the word to be underway, I'll take you down and show you the maps. I can't say we know the exact spot, but I've got a pretty good idea."

"We just sort of feel around 'til we find him?"

"No. We just announce that we are the best sailors, the most feared, and the most successful pirates on the sea." Lucas grinned. "Then we let them find us. I don't think a captain as arrogant as that pirate is going to let such a challenge go unmet."

"Trying to get us killed I take it," Chris said wryly.

"Now, Chris"—Lucas shrugged—"aren't we the best?"

"Speaking of arrogance," Chris replied with a laugh.

"Let's go below and decide a couple of things over a drink."

"What? Decide what?"

"Our course and what we are going to name our ship."

"It's already named."

"Now, Chris"—Lucas chuckled—"does any self-respecting pirate sail about in a ship named *Lady Jane?*"

"I guess not. What do you have in mind?"

"Oh . . . I don't know. What about *Shady Lady?*" Lucas laughed.

Caught up in the humor of the situation, they called out names that were equally unusable, equally suggestible.

"Seriously, what do you say to the name *Black Angel?*" Lucas finally asked.

"Sounds good."

"Then *Black Angel* it is."

"That's settled, but you certainly can't be Lucas Maine, nor can I be Chris Martin."

"You're right. I hadn't thought of a name for myself."

"Well, it has to be equally . . . piratical."

"Equally piratical . . . hmm . . . what about Black Beard?"

"I'm afraid there's already been one. I suggest Gabriel Blanc."

"Why Gabriel Blanc?"

"Well, Gabriel was an angel . . . and *blanc* means white, so you'd be the white angel captaining the Black Angel—very original and poetic if I do say so myself."

"You are brilliant. I agree. So, we set sail. The *Black Angel* under the hand of Captain Blanc . . . terror of the seas."

"Terror of the seas," Chris scoffed. "If it comes to proving it just what are you going to do?"

"I'll cross that bridge when I get to it."

"I hope this works."

"It will as long as we keep our heads."

"That's what's worrying me, keeping my head. If they get wind of who we are, our heads might be hunting for our bodies at the bottom of the ocean."

"I'm not going to think about that." Lucas rose from his seat and went to a huge chest. He took from it clothing that brought a smile from Chris—black pants, a white shirt with full ruffle-edged sleeves, and a wide red sash.

"You're going to wear that?"

"To be a pirate one must look like one—excite the imagination. One look and I will be the object of respect and fear."

"Whose?"

"Well . . . the ladies at least. Part of this adventure should be fun."

"Do you have more of those fancy clothes?"

"I do." Lucas motioned to the chest. "Help yourself."

They amused themselves by dressing as pirates and then going on deck, where they were subject to a few ribald remarks by the crew. When Lucas finally had the men quieted down, he explained in more detail what he expected to accomplish.

"I know this is amusing now," he said, "but I want you to understand just what we're up against. Where we're going there's no one to protect us, no law. The strongest win. We must be the strongest. If we make a slip, one slip, it is going to cost us our lives."

"We don't expect to make a slip, Captain." The tall sailor who had spoken laughed.

"Right, Captain," another crewman put in. "We'll show the bastard who's been takin' your ships that it's not smart to steal from those who can steal back."

"Well, men, I'd like to teach them that little lesson, so the sooner we get under way the better. Mason!"

"Yes, sir!"

"Let's get her sails up!"

Huge squares of white canvas were unrolled from spars, and quickly filled by the breeze.

"Head her out to sea," Lucas commanded.

Men climbed about the rigging, securing the white sails, and as the breeze lifted the ship, she began to ease toward the open sea.

Late that night, Chris walked the deck and allowed his thoughts free rein. He was unsure . . . but he was loyal. He would follow Lucas Maine to the end of the earth if asked.

Below, Lucas lay on his bunk. He was excited about the adventure, but it was not predominant in his thoughts. As he folded his hand behind his head, he contemplated just what Arianne St. Thomas might be doing at the moment. He also wondered just how she was going to react when Scott and his letter arrived.

He could just see her—thin, pale, and quite unattractive. Probably a woman who preferred books to anything else, a woman whose father thought he had bought a husband.

"Well"—he chuckled to himself—"there's a long reach between the buying and the owning. So, my little wife, you can just forget me . . . because it will never be. I choose my own bride . . . and I didn't choose you." Lucas laughed softly.

Chapter 2

Arianne had been angry—had wept, threatened, and pleaded—but her father had been adamant. She had been promised in marriage to a man she had never seen and had no inclination to see.

"A colonial!" she had cried. "Some ignorant savage who probably never wore shoes or ate at a table."

Her words brought no change in her father's benign expression.

"He is not a savage, and I dare say he is as educated as you."

"Father, how could you! How could you!"

"Good heavens, Arianne, listen to reason."

"Reason! When you ask me to marry a man I have never seen!"

"Lucas Maine is the son of my very dear friend Charles Maine who I have not seen in many years. As a young man Charles was quite handsome, the catch any woman would want. I dare say his son has taken after him."

"I will not marry him!" she cried. "I will not."

Reginald St. Thomas could match his anger against any man's, but now he had reached the end of his rope.

"You will!" he shouted, his face red and filled with fury. "You will . . . I have given my word and we have made the arrangements. When that young man comes you will show some of the good breeding I have tried to instill in you. You will be a lady by damn." He slammed his hand on the table to emphasize his words. "If I have to tie you to the bed!"

Arianne had seen her father angry but never in quite such a rage as this.

She began to think more rationally. If she kept calm, maybe she could handle the situation better.

"I'm sorry, Father," she said in as contrite a voice as she could manage.

"Arianne," St. Thomas began, "you have been frittering your life away with your horses and your gallivanting about like a boy. If I had wanted another boy I would have had another child. Your brother Brian and you are enough. One boy, one girl—your mother and I were pleased with you. But . . . why must you insist on following your brother about and attempting to jump your horses as he does? You must resign yourself, my girl, you are a woman and this kind of thing must cease. Marriage will be the cure for it."

Her thoughts were as far from his as possible, but she controlled her reactions. She had no intention of marrying this damned Lucas Maine and when he arrived she would make her feelings so well known that he would be glad to leave.

"When will he be here, Father?" she asked as docilely as possible.

"Within a week or so I should say. It's been quite some time since I wrote to accept."

Arianne clenched her teeth against the casual way first her father and then an unwanted husband would control her life. She had not met a man yet with whom she wanted to spend more than an evening. None of the young gallants who gathered about her had created one drop of interest in the marital state.

"Then," she said as gently as her broiling anger would allow, "I had best be about some preparations."

She left her father with his brow furrowed by worry. He had learned a long time ago that one must never trust a sweet and docile Arianne, because a storm always lurked just below the surface. At that moment he felt a mild touch of pity for the man who was to wed her.

"He'd best have a strong will," Sir Reginald muttered, "or that girl will trample him like those precious horses of hers trample the dirt beneath their hooves. I pity you, sir, I truly do."

He began to think about his daughter. He had spoiled her atrociously, had given her everything she wanted, for he loved her deeply. But there were times when her strength of will actually frightened him. He had watched her ride and tame the strongest of stallions until the powerful creatures ate docilely from her outstretched hand. Yet he had seen her gentleness with the children of the servants on his estates, and knew quite well everyone on his lands nearly worshipped her.

He sighed deeply and shook his head. He loved Arianne, but he would never understand her. He wanted only to see his daughter marry well, settle down, and be happy. It never occurred to him that Arianne might want much more in a husband than substantial wealth and a good name.

"Well, anyway it's settled," he said aloud. "It's settled and when she is safely married she will change . . . she will change." He said the words, but he wasn't quite sure of them.

Arianne paced her room like a caged animal, her hands clasped before her and a look of deep concentration on her face.

Her brother Brian, to whom she had always reached out when in distress, sat in a chair nearby, his feet propped on the edge of a table.

"Ria," he said gently, "this is not going to get you anywhere."

"Brian, I can't marry a man I've never seen. I . . . I can't bear the thought."

"Why don't you at least wait until you meet him? You are judging the man too quickly. He might be the paragon for which you always seem to be looking, although I'm quite sure there is not a man alive who will ever meet the standards you have set."

"Good heavens, Brian! What kind of a man is forced to buy a wife? Oh, I can picture him. Short and fat with . . . with warts on his nose. He . . . he would probably try to beat me!"

"After which you would probably murder him." Brian laughed, and Arianne laughed with him.

"Be serious, Brian! What am I to do?"

"Remain calm and face things as you usually do—fully armed and ready for battle. You must wait until you meet him"—his eyes twinkled with mischief—"then make him be the one who decides against the marriage. Make him so upset over your obvious reluctance and your ability to make his life miserable that he will begin to think discretion is the better part of valor, and will run back to the Colonies as fast as his fat little legs can carry him."

Arianne's eyes began to glow in response, and Brian smiled, realizing he wouldn't choose to be in

Lucas Maine's shoes for a fortune, for once Arianne set her mind to a thing she usually saw it through.

"Well," Arianne said softly, "maybe you are right."

"Am I not always right?" he chuckled.

"Well, you are certainly arrogant." She smiled. "You wouldn't be laughing if the shoe was on the other foot. I should love to see Father buy you a wife you didn't want to marry."

"I know you're right, Ria, but I think I would at least give him the benefit of the doubt. Everyone deserves a chance."

"All right. I'll wait until he arrives. But I warn you—"

"I know." He chuckled. "One wart and out he goes."

They laughed together, but Arianne was still nervous about just how far her father would go to see her married. She cursed the world for its rules that allowed her, because she was a woman to be forced into a union she didn't want.

Twelve days later she stood on the dock with her father and brother and watched with trepidation as the *Mist* drew closer. She was exerting all the control she had, and was determined to give Lucas Maine every opportunity.

The *Mist* docked, the gangplank was lowered, and one of the first passengers to descend was Scott.

Arianne watched him approach. He was rather handsome, with sandy hair, a broad brow, and sea green eyes.

He walked toward the three people he felt sure he had come to meet. Scott had seen Arianne from the rail of the ship and had thought most certainly she could not be quite as beautiful as she seemed. It was the sun, it was the distance . . . but as he drew closer he became somewhat awed by the beauty of the woman who would soon be Lucas's wife. He found himself wishing he could exchange places with his friend, marry this rare creature himself. He was quite sure, even before he spoke, that one day Lucas was going to regret ignoring this woman.

Her eyes were wide, and regarded him closely, so closely that he found his hands were shaking. They were beautiful eyes, of the purest amethyst color. Her hair, kissed by the morning sun, was a burnished gold that glinted with touches of pale gold and red flame. Her mouth was wide and generous and, in his immediate impression, made to be kissed. Her complexion was like molten gold tempered by smooth cream. All in all she was, without doubt, the most beautiful woman he had ever seen. He was quite certain the figure beneath the long cloak she wore would be equally as beautiful.

"Good morning, Lucas," Sir Reginald said as he extended his hand. "It is good to see you, my boy. I hope your passage was easy."

"Ah . . . Sir Reginald," Scott began, "I am not Lucas."

"Oh?" Sir Reginald said, a puzzled look in his eyes. "Well, where is Lucas, still aboard?"

"No, sir," Scott said. He had hoped Arianne would not be with her father when they met. Now, with Arianne's eyes on him, he was uncomfortable.

"I don't understand you, sir."

"Lucas . . ." Scott cleared his throat and began again. "Lucas was unable to come at the moment. I have been sent as a proxy, sir, with a letter of explanation from Lucas. The wedding will take place as scheduled, and I am most proud to stand in

34

Lucas's place."

He had watched Arianne's eyes as he'd spoken and had seen the light of anger brighten them. At that moment, he wished fervently he were anywhere else but beneath their cold piercing gaze.

"Unable to come," Arianne said sweetly . . . too sweetly. "Is he ill by chance?"

"Uh . . . no . . . not ill . . . just . . ." He searched for a word.

"Occupied?"

Scott could have bit his tongue. He could not think rationally while she continued to look at him so. It was Sir Reginald who saved him.

"Well, come. Our carriage is waiting. We will discuss this and read the letter in the privacy of my home."

They made their way to the carriage and drove to the St. Thomas residence in absolute silence. Scott was well aware that the woman sitting opposite him and studiously avoiding any knowledge of his presence was in a rare state of absolute fury.

Upon arrival of their destination, Scott was given a room in which to refresh himself while the others retired to the study to read the letter he had brought.

Arianne had tried to control herself, but the deliberate snub and the carefully worded insults in the letter were enough to break down all the promises she'd made herself.

"He's afraid of pirates!" she cried. "And as far as worrying about me, he need not! He can go to the devil for all I care. Too delicate to travel!" she nearly shrieked. "Telling me to sit and wait and twiddle my thumbs until my very courageous husband decides to come and get me. The unmitigated nerve of this pompous ass is more than anyone could bear."

"Arianne, calm yourself. After you are together everything will change."

"Together . . ." Arianne sucked in her breath and spoke in a controlled voice through stiff lips. "Father, you may force me to marry this . . . this flea-brained excuse for a man, but if you harbor the hope that we will ever be together, then you are sadly mistaken. For when I see Mr. Lucas Maine I shall make it clear that should he put a hand on me I shall be forced to kill him!"

She turned and left the room, slamming the door quite forcefully behind her.

In her bedroom she shook with anger as salty tears burned her eyes. Self-pity overcame her. Why must she be saddled, for the best years of her young life, to a man who had no more consideration than to send a proxy to his own wedding? She solemnly vowed that she would find a way out of this if her life depended upon it.

But in the few days before the wedding was scheduled, she found no avenue of escape. Three days later she stood with an extremely nervous Scott and coldly recited the vows that made her the bride of Lucas Maine—a man she had sworn to hate the rest of her days.

After a day or two, Scott and Arianne achieved a tentative friendship. She knew quite well that he was not responsible for her dilemma, and her mind spun with plans, none as yet workable, that would give her an opportunity to escape a situation she found herself totally unable to bear.

Such an opportunity was to present itself the next

afternoon. She had taken her favorite mare out early. Riding in the morning always made her feel better. At least she was alone with her thoughts, allowed the privacy to shed tears she was too proud to indulge in before another.

Have I expected too much from life? she asked herself. To marry a man I could love and be content to live with. To have a man who understands and is sensitive to my emotions. Is it too much to want to be happy?

She thought of the elusive Lucas Maine and wished that he would in some way suffer as she was suffering. She felt like a butterfly caught in a net. No matter how she struggled she would never be free to fly again.

When she returned home she left her horse at the stable and, having ordered it to be brushed carefully, she walked up the stone path to the side door of the house.

Wide French doors stood open from the veranda. They led to the library which adjoined her father's study.

Still not wanting to expose her fragile emotions to anyone, she walked into the library. Almost immediately she heard muffled voices from Sir Reginald's study—voices she recognized . . . her father's and Brian's.

She did not mean to eavesdrop as she walked to the door. Indeed, she had intended to make her presence known until she'd heard the topic of conversation.

"I'm telling you, Father, it's the best way to catch these pirates. It is your friend's shipping line that has been struck so often, but your cargoes have been taken."

"But it is entirely too dangerous," her father replied. "If they were to suspect who you are—"

37

"They won't. How would they ever know? I would simply pretend I was one of them. Only to find out, Father. Then I would report to you and we would find a way to rid ourselves of them. I believe"—Brian laughed—"that if you were younger you would do the same."

"By George, you are right, Brian. It could be a way to discover just who they are and to identify them for the authorities."

"Then you will agree? I can outfit a ship? It would not take long and then I could sail for the Colonies."

"I will have the ship outfitted. We will catch these rascals yet."

"Good."

The conversation continued, but Arianne was no longer interested. Her brother would go on this exciting adventure while she would be forced to stay locked away, doing nothing until her husband came for her and offered her a life of again doing nothing except breeding children for him.

It took her only seconds to make a decision. She smiled to herself and left the library.

While the ship was being outfitted, Arianne watched closely, but she voiced no opinions about it.

Everyone was amazed, yet pleased, by this more docile and pleasant Arianne. Even Scott was finally put at ease. He was relieved that she seemed to have accepted the idea that the marriage was inevitable and she could do nothing about it.

Brian, the only one who would have truly recognized his sister's behavior for what it was, was engrossed in the preparation of his ship, and did not realize what was happening until it was too late.

Arianne walked the garden path with Scott, only half listening as he tried to extol Lucas's virtues. She no longer wanted to hear about Lucas Maine.

"I assure you, madam, Lucas is really a charming chap. He's been quite involved with the piracy of his father's ships. I know he would have come himself if it had been possible." Scott was trying, but something in his words didn't ring true even to him. He knew Lucas had sworn he would never consummate the marriage. He only wished Lucas had seen Arianne before making such a decision. Surely doing so would have changed his mind, for Lucas had a very experienced eye for beautiful women.

"You needn't worry so, Scott." Arianne laughed. "I assure you that will make no difference in the outcome of our relationship."

Scott wasn't too sure he understood what he felt lay beneath her words, but he was satisfied that he did not perceive threats of murder in her eyes whenever she looked at him.

At the dinner table that night Arianne was most charming. She listened to her brother speak of the ship on which he would be sailing at dawn.

"I shall have to bid you a fond farewell tonight, dear brother." Arianne smiled. "I have no intention of getting up tomorrow to see you sail away."

Brian knew quite well Arianne was an early riser, but he felt she was upset to see him go and so chose not to witness his departure. As he voiced his thoughts, Arianne laughed to herself. If Brian only knew that she would be aboard his ship when it left, he would not be so solicitous of her feelings, she thought. In fact, she was quite well aware that both her brother and her father would be apoplectic.

But it would be too late for her brother to turn back when she made her presence known.

The night came to an end with wineglasses held

high to toast the success of the coming venture. As Arianne held her glass aloft, the men's appreciative eyes were drawn to her glowing eyes and flushed cheeks.

"I wish you every success, brother. I am sure this voyage will be a revelation to us all. I expect it to be a very exciting voyage."

"Arianne," her father said pleasantly, "I must say I am very pleased at the wisdom you have acquired. You have changed, daughter. Now, was it so hard to accept what fate has offered?"

"Why no, Father. I am pleased to say that I am grateful for your solicitude and I accept very gratefully whatever fate has to offer. In fact, I am looking forward to it with a great deal of excitement."

Her father was pleased, Scott was more than elated . . . and Brian was deeply suspicious. This sweet and gentle creature was not the Arianne he knew, and he wondered what she might have up her sleeve.

The next morning Brian stood on the dock. He had been accompanied to it by Scott and his father.

"Take care, son," Sir Reginald cautioned. "I know of the reputation of these scoundrels."

"I will, Father. Don't worry so. In a few months I shall return and then we can put some of these pirates where they belong."

"I would love to sail with you," Scott said.

"Why don't you?" Brian offered. "I hadn't thought of it, but you are most welcome. I have plenty of clothes aboard and you are welcome to share them."

Scott quickly accepted the invitation, amused by the fact that he might be able to catch up with the pirates before Lucas did. Then Sir Reginald waved goodbye as the sails unfurled and the ship moved gracefully toward the sea.

Brian and Scott were fast becoming friends, and Scott finally decided that he would pray for the success of Lucas's marriage for Lucas could have found no better family to marry into.

Brian lay asleep on the sixth night out of port. He was dreaming of a very pretty girl with whom he had spent several hours before he'd sailed.

The sound of soft laughter at first seemed part of his dream and he enjoyed it . . . until it drew him up from sleep and he realized it was no longer part of a dream, but was here in his cabin.

It was dark, only frail light coming in through the small square windows of the captain's quarters, and this barely enough to show a figure seated cross-legged on the end of his bed.

"Brian, you must have been having very good dreams. I've been trying to wake you for several minutes."

He gaped open-mouthed, for there was no mistaking the voice.

"Arianne! What the hell are you doing here!"

"Sailing with you," she said calmly.

"You can't do that!" Brian fairly shouted.

"I can't?" she asked innocently. "But, Brian dear"—she laughed—"I already have. You are long past the place where you can turn back. I made very sure of that before I let you know I was here."

"You stowed away on my ship damn it."

"Very observant, brother dear. I'm looking forward to all the fun and excitement you were talking about."

41

Brian groaned and lay back on his bunk. He was sure of three things. Arianne was right about his inability to turn back, his father was going to murder them both when he found out, and he would probably spend as much time protecting his sister as he would hunting for the pirates.

Chapter 3

From the ocean only a narrow inlet led into Matanzas Bay. Their destination was not St. Augustine itself, but the island called Anastasia, which was part of the barrier off the Florida coast.

Brian had not intended to dock in St. Augustine which was overrun with British who had just "acquired" Florida from the Spanish. Redcoats manned the fort and the harbor was filled with British ships. He was aware that it would be dangerous to be asking too many questions. But, despite the danger, he had to find the man he sought. Besides, Brian was certain pirate ships would be docked near Anastasia Island. He chose to visit the city of St. Augustine, to go to the taverns, to talk and to listen.

When the shore could finally be seen Arianne was standing excitedly at the rail with him. The harbor was filled with Spanish galleons both reputable and disreputable. Brian flew no colors now, and Arianne was the first to notice that quite a few other ships did not either.

"Look, Brian." She pointed to a trim tall-masted ship that rocked gently in the harbor. "That is an

American ship, isn't it?"

"It is." Brian frowned. "Strange to see it here."

"There are so many ships, why should one more be so surprising?"

"It is not a usual harbor to find them in. The English don't get on too well with them and I'm reasonably sure the Spanish don't favor them either."

"It's a beautiful ship," Arianne said. "Can you read her name?"

"The *Black Angel*. Sounds ominous doesn't it?"

"The *Black Angel*," Arianne repeated slowly. "It's a very sinister name. Do you think he's a pirate, too?"

"Good God, Ria"—Brian laughed—"half the ships in this harbor fly the black flag when they aren't here. That ship is more likely a pirate than any of the others."

Brian turned to look at Arianne and was again dismayed by the look of intense excitement in her eyes. She was so beautiful that he was suddenly afraid.

"Ria."

"What?"

"These men"—he hesitated for a moment, then continued almost reluctantly—"they're . . . well they're bloodthirsty. They've killed and robbed . . . don't be so excited. For God's sake, Ria, this is dangerous. Don't you understand that!"

"Brian, what's wrong?"

Brian sighed. "I just wish for this one time you were not so damned pretty."

"Shall I try to be plainer?"

"You couldn't be plain if you tried the rest of your life. When they find out you're my sister I'll have to be fighting them off with both hands."

"Then don't tell them I'm your sister."

"Am I supposed to lock you in my cabin?" he

44

replied; then he smiled brightly. "Maybe that's not such a bad idea. It will keep you out of mischief."

"I will not stay locked away!" Arianne cried. "Brian, tell them I'm your woman. Tell them I belong to you. Maybe then they'll leave us alone."

Brian contemplated this. It just might be possible. He was even slightly amused. If they thought she was his woman they might admire her, but were more likely to leave them be. He might also gain a little more respect as a pirate.

"Maybe . . . just maybe," he mused.

"Come on, Brian. I don't want to miss everything."

"All right. You're my woman from now on. But"—he chuckled—"if you don't behave, I shall have to beat you in front of them, and I assure you that would give them a great deal of amusement."

"I wouldn't do that if I were you," she threatened, with a smile. "I would find some form of revenge you really wouldn't like."

"You behave," he warned.

"Brian, let's go ashore."

"All right. But first change your clothes. You must wear the dress you brought, not my rolled-up breeches and shirt. You look more like a pirate than I do."

"I'll be back in a minute. Don't go ashore without me," she warned.

"Five minutes," he called after her.

It surprised him when Arianne reappeared in less than five minutes. She had put on her dress, and with her long wayward hair bound she presented a deceivingly demure picture.

With some trepidation on his part and much excitement on hers, they walked down the gangplank. The city of St. Augustine lay before them, and slowly they began to wander its narrow, picturesque streets.

Lucas dropped his feet from his desk and stood up. He was becoming impatient and was annoyed because he had seemed to run up against a wall. He had dined and drunk with the captain of every vessel in the harbor, yet he could not put his finger on the one who was to blame for the sacking of his father's ships.

Ships' captains were usually inclined to display bravado and to bluster, so Lucas was surprised that those present were not bragging about what they had done. Then the thought came to him that the man behind the piracies was not here, and that he was strong enough to make everyone else keep their silence.

Lucas walked on deck in time to see that the attention of several of his men was fixed on an incoming ship. He went to the rail to join them.

"Beauty, ain't she, Cap'n?" said one.

"That she is, Meyers. What is she?"

"She's English. Name . . . looks like . . . the *White Swan*. Pretty name."

"Pretty," Lucas muttered. "I wonder what kind of man captains her and which side of the law he stands on."

"Hard to tell here, sir." Meyers laughed. "This place is sure brimming with a lot that wouldn't want their past looked into too close."

"Well, I guess I'll take another trip into the taverns tonight. I want to meet this captain. He just might be the one I'm looking for."

Lucas had anchored his ship in the harbor instead of tying up at the dock so that anyone who intended to board her would have to make his purpose known before he could do so. He waited until the sun began to set, then took a longboat to shore, and stepped upon the dock at the same time the sun dropped below the horizon.

The nightlife of St. Augustine was boisterous to say the least. The taverns overflowed with colorful characters from all over the world, and the town's inhabitants found it safer to stay behind closed doors when the sun set.

The breed of men walking the streets was less than savory, and Lucas was continually on the alert. Men were shanghaied easily here. Victims of a drugged drink or a heavy club, they found themselves on the high seas under the command of a relentless pirate captain.

Lucas walked toward The Boar's Head, a tavern that was a gathering place for the sailors and their captains. Once inside the semidark room he looked about.

There was a huge fireplace whose light, accompanied by that of a few lanterns, allowed him to identify those who sat about the room. Arianne, who had refused with grim determination to be forced to return to the ship, was now seated with her brother at one of the tables. She was delightedly absorbing the sights, smells, and sounds about her while Brian was nervously keeping an eye on any male who sauntered near. So far he had been lucky, he thought, but he didn't realize that despite the attraction of Arianne's singular beauty, his formidable size and dark scowl, plus the sword and knife he carried with assurance, kept the denizens of the tavern at a distance.

"What a villainous lot they are," Arianne whispered to Brian. "Which do you suppose has taken father's cargo?"

"No way to tell yet, but one of them will slip soon. They like to brag about conquests . . . any kind of conquests," he finished warningly. Arianne's soft laugh drew even more appreciative looks from the men about them.

Brian groaned softly as an intrigued captain moved in their direction. The stranger stood near their table, his eyes on Arianne, but his words directed to another seafarer who could not deny his presence.

"Evening mate," he said in a voice that openly suggested he'd like to lengthen the evening by spending it in Arianne's presence. "I aims to buy ye a drink to welcome ye to St. Augustine. Me name's Bart. Yer new here? I ain't seen the *White Swan* before."

"Could be," Brian said calmly. "She wasn't always the *White Swan*."

Arianne remained silent. Feeling the man's eyes disrobe her, she moved slightly toward Brian.

The man chuckled warmly, and there was no doubt in the minds of Brian and Arianne as to which flag this particular captain sailed under.

"I'll stand ye and yer woman to a drink, mate."

He lowered himself to the chair closest to Arianne before either she or Brian could object.

It was into this situation that Lucas and Chris walked. They knew Captain Bart Nettles for the bloodthirsty scum that he was and so both jumped to the conclusion that as water finds its own level, people of the same persuasion had found each other. They made the quick decision that the man with Nettles was cut from the same cloth, and that the beauty beside him must be a wanton who was selling her favors to the highest bidder.

From where Lucas sat, he had an excellent view of

the stunning blonde, and he had to smother the desire that overwhelmed him. He was after pirates, not a fling with someone else's whore. Still . . . he could feel his body react and was angered by his own lack of self-control.

"That must be the captain of the *Swan*," Lucas said.

"Who can look at him? The beauty next to him . . . God, she's something," Chris said admiringly.

"We're here to do a job, Chris," Lucas warned. He could not believe his own irritation at Chris's admiration. "That tavern wench is not our business."

"I've never seen one quite like her," Chris replied. "That's one lucky man."

"Chris, for God's sake!"

"All right, all right. But damn, man, you'll have to admit she's the prettiest thing we've seen anywhere. A little envy for the man is natural."

"Let's go see if we can meet him. I have a feeling we're about to contact the captain who is responsible for our problems."

"I don't need to be asked twice." Chris chuckled. "You talk to him, and I'll do my damnedest to talk to her."

"You might get him angry." Lucas grinned.

"It is worth the risk."

The girl looked up as Lucas and Chris approached her table, and Lucas found himself unable to breathe as he stared into the most beautiful amethyst eyes he'd ever seen. It was as if a wild hurricane had struck him. He seemed to have lost track of his faculties and to be unable to retrieve them. His heart thudded heavily as if coming suddenly awake. It was a strange, new, and very unwelcome emotion; and he had to struggle to control it. But struggle as he might, the closer he drew to this beauty the worse it became. He was caught in some kind of spell, and was aware only of those deep pools—her eyes—that seemed to draw him to her.

For Arianne it was as if her spirit had taken flight. She felt breathlessly expectant, as if something rare and new was touching her life. Her first thought was that an extremely handsome man was approaching. Her following thoughts were scattered like the wind. He was so large, so overpowering, so intense, so . . . Impressions tumbled through her mind and her senses until she felt her body tremble with a strange excitement . . . and the swift feeling of danger.

Brian watched the two men come, sensing it was Arianne's beauty that drew them. His mouth was a grim line, and he wondered if he could get out of this without a fight. He cursed Arianne's wide-eyed enthusiasm for the hundredth time. Her hunger for excitement and adventure might get them both in trouble. He didn't like the way she was looking at the approaching men. In fact, he didn't like the way the tall handsome one was looking at her. Everything he perceived was pregnant with danger.

Bart by now was eyeing the two men. When he scowled, Lucas was amused. What didn't amuse Lucas was the way the other man put his arm about the woman and drew her closer to him, as if he felt she suddenly needed protection. His irritation was camouflaged, however, as he spoke to Bart.

"Bart, my friend." He laughed softly. "I see you've got some new acquaintances." His attention turned to the other pirate, whose arm still encircled the amethyst-eyed beauty. "I'm Captain Gabriel Blanc. And this is Chris. You are new here aren't you?"

"That I am," Brian replied. "I'm Brian. We just

50

arrived today.''

His words again drew all eyes to Arianne. She had not spoken but had been surreptitiously studying Captain Blanc.

"This is Ria," Brian added reluctantly.

Lucas waited a moment, hoping for some additional enlightenment on Ria's relationship to Brian. None came.

"Ria," Lucas said softly. "Very pretty name ... and a very pretty lady."

Brian did not like the way he spoke her name. He moved a little closer to Ria as Chris and Lucas sat down.

"Captain Blanc," Brian said, "you're American."

"Yes," Lucas replied, leaving the answer unqualified.

"Then your ship is the beauty in the harbor—the *Black Angel?*" Ria said with interest. "Why did you give it such a sinister name?"

"But I thought the name was beautiful," Lucas replied.

"A proper name, too, I'm thinkin'," Bart laughed.

Lucas wanted to be branded a pirate, so he welcomed Bart's words, but as he watched the darkening of Ria's eyes, her controlled look of distrust annoyed him.

"The *Black Angel* is a beauty," Brian agreed. "From what port do you hail? What colors do you sail under?"

"I," Lucas said softly, knowing he was damning himself with his own words, "am master of my own ship. I sail under no one's colors but my own, and I have no port to call home."

This was an unqualified admission that he was a man who sailed under the black flag, but Ria's

51

expression made Lucas feel it provoked some deep thoughts in her. He had the strongest desire to know what she was thinking, yet with a great deal of effort he resisted asking her. She was obviously Brian's woman and he knew he had no right to ask her any questions at all. Besides, he needed to find out more about Brian's activities, not fight with him.

Ria was filled with a strange sense of dismay. This man was a pirate, perhaps the one who had been stealing from her father. It would be dangerous to get closer to him. If he found out who they were, what might he do? She couldn't trust him, but she could not deny her deep attraction to him. Why did he look at her so, his eyes full of questions and an emotion she could not read?

"It seems many of us here have no port to call home," Brian replied.

Bart chuckled. "If the Spanish had any idea of that, St. Augustine would be a hot place to anchor. Some say there's goin' to be another change around here."

"A change?" Lucas said quickly.

"Yeah, in January Governor Tonyn and the last of the British will be leavin' for Plymouth, England. That's why the town is so near empty of Britishers. The Spanish are comin' in power again here."

"And they are rather strict about"—Lucas shrugged—"homeless ships."

"Strict. They put a name to the ones on the wrong side, and they'll see ya hangin' on the square," Bart growled.

"Who's the new governor?" Brian asked.

"Vicente Manuel de Zespedes," Bart answered. "He's a tough one, too. The only reason the ships are safe is 'cause he's havin' so damn much trouble with the banditti."

"Banditti?" Chris asked. "What's that?"

"Old man Dan McGirtt. He's been havin' a happy old time around here."

"What's keeping the governor from catching him?" Lucas inquired.

"Well, ya see, the old governor ain't too fond of leavin'. He's seein' all the Britishers get gone first. So there's kinda two in power. They're playin' the old game of two cats and one mouse, and old McGirtt is makin' good use of playin' one against the other."

"Interesting situation," Lucas mused. His gaze had again returned to Ria. "Seems there's very little protection around here."

"A man is his own protection," Brian replied.

"And a woman?" Lucas questioned softly. Brian's eyes never left Lucas nor did Ria's.

"Most women," Brian said, "are protected by their own men, and it would be very very dangerous for any man to interfere; he might find himself floating face down in the bay."

It was an open threat, and Lucas was in no position to challenge it.

"Your ship is? . . ." Lucas asked.

"The *White Swan*," Brian supplied.

"I'd like to see her."

"Why don't you come aboard tomorrow?" Ria said; then, amazed at her offer, she kept her eyes away from Brian's. He was furious and had to bite his tongue to keep from shouting at her.

"I'd like that. Tomorrow morning?"

"Of course," Brian said roughly. He could have happily murdered Ria, and she had no doubt she was going to hear about this later.

"Right now, Ria and I have to get back to the ship," Brian said. He rose, grasping Ria's arm firmly and propelling her along with him.

Lucas watched them leave, startled again by his

distinct desire to follow them and rip Brian's offending hand from this woman's arm.

"Some sweet piece of female." Bart chuckled. "When he's done with her I wouldn't mind sampling a bit of it."

Lucas felt frustrated rage at Bart's words. He had no right to be angry and he knew it, but he was. He turned a hard burning gaze on Bart who chuckled, shrugged, and walked away. At this point Chris was well aware of Lucas's anger, but was not fool enough to say anything. He was quite certain of two things— no matter what or who this woman was Lucas wanted her . . . and Brian was going to have some difficulty stopping him.

Chapter 4

"What the bloody hell is wrong with you! You can see with one glance that man would like to bed you! Why did you invite him aboard?"

"Brian, I'm sorry," Ria replied, "but you must agree it's a way to find out more about him."

Brian threw himself on his bunk in exasperation. "Damn it, Ria, can't you see it's you he wants?"

"For God's sake"—Ria's anger was growing now—"does that mean what he wants is what he's going to get? I'm not a baby, and I'm not a fool. I've no intention of falling victim to him. I . . . I just thought you wanted to find out about him."

"I do," Brian said helplessly, "but this is a very dangerous man."

"More dangerous than any of the others?"

"Yes."

"How?"

"They're animals. I know you see through them. But this one . . . he's handsome and charming. I expect he's seen better days, a better life. He's a renegade, and women, for some damned reason, seem to be attracted to the mysterious I've-got-a-wicked-past type of man."

"Oh, Brian"—Ria laughed—"that's ridiculous. I know the kind of man I want. I ran away from one, I don't expect to be caught by another. He's no threat to me. I know his type. He's a womanizer. Besides, he's probably married, at least once, and he probably has six or seven children scattered about the world. No. I know what I want, and I won't settle for less . . . or for a pirate with no future."

"I wish you hadn't invited him," Brian replied defensively.

"How would you have found out about him? I believe he's the one who has been attacking Father's ships."

"I would have met him elsewhere."

"Without me? Brian, I came along because I wanted to help."

"You came along because you are running away from Lucas Maine—and marriage."

"That, too," Ria admitted.

"Ria, remember something."

"What?"

"We have a very proud name. You can't dishonor it or our parents. If you find a man you want, you'll have to annul your marriage first. Don't make any costly mistakes."

"I won't, Brian. I love my family too much. I'll be careful, and I won't entangle myself with anyone unless I'm free."

"Is that a promise?"

"It is," Ria vowed carelessly.

"Then I consider it so. You have never lied to me."

"And I don't expect to start now." She walked to Brian and threw her arms about him and kissed his cheek. "I love you, my dear worried brother. I won't ever do anything that might come between us."

"Have you thought of what Captain Blanc is

56

thinking about you?'' He chuckled.

"Why, Brian"—Arianne's eyes sparkled wickedly —"I think he thinks you are one very lucky man."

"Conceited witch. I ought to throw you to the wolves just to teach you a lesson."

"But you won't," she said with swift assurance. "We'll find out what he's up to—together. Once we get some proof and point him out to the authorities Father's problems will be gone."

"And we can go home."

Ria was silent, for in going home she faced marriage to a man she had never seen. I'll find a way between now and then to settle this, she thought. Surely when Father understands how desperate I am, he'll let me annul this farce of a marriage and choose the man I want to share the rest of my life with.

Her thoughts were read easily by Brian who put a consoling arm about her shoulder.

"We'll cross that bridge when we get to it, Ria," he said gently. "Maybe, together, we can find a way to get you out of this."

"Thank you, Brian," she responded quietly. "I think you are the only one who understands how I feel."

"I'll do the best I can to help you."

Shortly after their conversation Brian went ashore and Ria was left with her own thoughts. They might have shocked Brian as much as they shocked Ria herself. Her mind dwelt on an amber-eyed man who'd affected her in a way no other had. Why had she really invited him to the *Swan?* It was more than dangerous to do so, knowing what he must think of her . . . yet the danger was meaningless now. She had felt something so strange and new that she had to get to the source of it. She had to know what had touched her when she had looked into his eyes . . . she had to find out . . . she wasn't sure what . . . Arianne lay on the bunk and closed her eyes, hoping to eliminate the man from her thoughts. After a long while she drifted off to sleep.

Brian's mission, when he went ashore, was to find an honest merchant ship heading for England. When he did find one, he went aboard cautiously, making sure no one saw him. His conversation with the captain was short, and consisted only of a request to deliver a letter to Sir Reginald St. Thomas. The captain consented.

The letter was also short. It simply informed his father that Ria was safe with him and that he would take care to ensure her continued safety so that his parents were not to worry. Brian prayed his father would forgive him for his unwilling part in this damned mess.

If Ria was frustrated and uncertain, Lucas found himself in similar straits. He tried to sleep, but couldn't seem to do so. Instead, visions of Ria came to him, and he found it impossible to erase her face from his mind. He had cursed and cajoled himself, had struggled against them; but still she was a misty vision on the periphery of his mind for the balance of the night.

He had used logic. She was another man's mistress. She was not a woman he could take home to his family. She was more than likely wild and totally untamable. She was . . . beautiful, mysterious, and exciting.

"Damn," he grunted miserably. "She's the last thing I need. She'd befoul everything, probably be the first to turn me over to the rest of those cutthroats if she knew who I really was, and for a small price, too."

But no matter what arguments he used, he found himself dressing very carefully for their next meeting.

He wondered if she thought he was married. Would it make any difference to her? Somehow he doubted it would. *I must keep my mind on what I came here for and not on a tempting little morsel like her.* He smiled. It might be amusing to find out just how far the captain of the *Swan* would let his beautiful little mistress go before he put a restraining hand on her.

He left the *Angel* feeling much more self-assured. Surely Brian would not want to lose such a lush little piece. Now that he felt he had everything in perspective he began to enjoy the thought of seeing her again. He went ashore and walked jauntily down the dock to where the *Swan* was berthed.

Scott Fitzgerald would have been just the person to eliminate any problems attendant on the mutual attraction between Lucas and Arianne. But fate decided differently. Scott left the *Swan* just minutes before Lucas's arrival, to seek some amusement and to keep his ears open for any information that might be of help to Brian.

He now wandered the streets of St. Augustine absorbing the colorful sights around him, always on the alert for any pretty girl who might decide to cast an eye in his direction.

His final destination, when he had exhausted all

interest in the town, was a tavern called The Crow's Nest. There he found an evening meal, reasonably good liquor, and two pretty barmaids. It was late in the evening when one of the barmaids approached him, bringing the drink he had ordered. She set it down, but before she could leave he caught her about the waist and drew her down onto his lap. He found this aspect of acting the worldly sailor one of the best parts of the game they were playing. Looking for answers might be more rewarding than he had first thought. He laughed to himself.

Sophia Ruiz was a buxom dark-eyed girl whose Spanish father had sailed from St. Augustine before she had opened her eyes for the first time. Her mother, an Indian from the Florida wilderness, had carried Sophia to the village of her birth soon after. But the village could not contain Sophia's adventurous spirit, and by the time she was sixteen she had made her way to St. Augustine. There she found the excitement she wanted. She lived by her wits, and was both clever and quite able to handle herself.

When Scott had first asked questions about her, he'd met with laughter and teasing, but when he'd probed deeper he'd met a wall of silence. That made him think she might know more of pirating activities than she would admit.

"What's your name, pretty one?" He smiled, he hoped innocently.

"Sophia Ruiz," she promptly replied, "and I am too busy to be sporting with you."

"But, Sophia"—his eyes glittered—"I might be a very wealthy man. You could be missing the chance of a lifetime."

"A very wealthy man." She laughed. "I've not run across too many wealthy sailors. They're all full of pretty promises and nothing more."

"Ah," he said softly, "but maybe I am not just an ordinary sailor. In fact, I might have ways to make money that you can't even imagine."

If he was surprised when she sat still and stopped resisting, he did his very best not to show it, but his suspicions became stronger.

"So you have some plans to make a lot of money here in St. Augustine," she said derisively. "There are a lot of men with such plans—why are you someone so special?"

"Ah, because"—he now laughed—"my ship, the *White Swan*, is very special and so am I."

"Between British law and Spanish law what does it matter if you're special?"

"British law . . . Spanish law." He shrugged eloquently. "Sometimes there are those who are just a little smarter and just a little faster. The clever man doesn't really worry about which law is in power at the time."

"And you're clever?"

"I am." He grinned.

"Maybe," she said softly, "there are those who are much smarter."

"I doubt it."

"You must have some reasons for such conceit. Maybe you would like to have a drink with me . . . later, when I am not so busy."

"I've been trying to convince you to do just that."

"Good. Now let me go before these thirsty beasts get too worked up."

"You won't forget . . . later?"

"No," she said seriously. "I won't forget."

Sophia left his lap, and he watched her move among the tables depositing drinks. He knew he had intrigued her; now he had to wait and see just what results this further contact would produce.

Lucas made his way to the *Swan*, knowing he must again look into amethyst eyes and find the answers to the puzzle in his mind. No woman had ever disrupted his sleep or his thoughts the way she had, and he was irritated by his lack of self-control.

At the edge of his mind was the nagging thought that a woman who was one man's mistress could easily become another's. He wondered if he could charm her away from Brian—and just how violent Brian's opposition would be. Lucas was observant enough to know that Brian had seemed more than a little protective of her. Would he give her up easily? Lucas was certain the pirate would not, for he knew, if Ria were his, he wouldn't surrender her easily.

Just as Lucas started up the gangplank, Brian appeared at the ship's rail.

"Good morning." Brian's smile did not quite reach his eyes.

Lucas was aware of Brian's scrutiny and it aroused his curiosity. This man was not only jealous, he was prepared for some kind of battle.

"Good morning," Lucas replied. He did not want to ask where Ria was, but his gaze drifted past Brian to sweep the nearly empty deck of the *Swan*. There was no sign of her, and there was no legitimate reason for him to ask about her. "Your ship is a masterpiece," he declared. "You surround yourself with very beautiful things." It was a pointed reference to Ria, but Brian blithely ignored it.

"She is a beauty, one of the fastest made. I saw to her building myself. She's built for speed."

"As is the *Angel*. It might be interesting to race

them one day."

"It might at that," Brian agreed. "Would you like to come below and look her over?"

Lucas agreed. He needed to know as much about the ship as possible. If he were to learn the extent of Brian's guilt, he had to know as much as possible about captain and vessel.

His tour of the ship seemed to include everything but the captain's cabin. That omission provoked pictures in Lucas's mind of a warm and beautiful Ria still asleep in the captain's bed.

But this was not so. Ria was furiously dressing. She had awakened late and known immediately that Brian had deliberately let her sleep. Hastily coiling her hair atop her head, she pinned it up. Then she quickly donned her dress, refusing to take the time to put on her numerous petticoats. One is enough, she muttered to herself.

Her cheeks were flushed from an excitement she refused to admit to herself and from anger at Brian because he'd deliberately left the cabin without waking her.

Brian and Lucas had just returned to the deck, and Brian was trying to think of some way to get Lucas off the ship before Ria appeared. He was addressing Lucas when he saw his eyes focus beyond him. He watched with dismay as Lucas smiled and his eyes warmed. With a sinking heart, Brian knew that Ria was on deck.

He turned and both men were caught by the vision approaching them. Her hair, streaked by the sun from white to brilliant gold, was working its way free of hastily applied pins to frame her oval face in windblown wisps. Her complexion was clear and a soft touch of pink enhanced its creamy texture.

Ria's eyes were wide and heavily fringed by thick .

lashes a shade darker than the darkest gold of her hair. It was her eyes that held Lucas, their amethyst coloring so brilliant they glimmered with light and mysterious promise.

Her body, revealed by the breeze that pressed her dress against her, was magnificent to view, and his hungry gaze did not miss the rise of firm breasts, her slender waist, flat belly, and long slim legs.

Good god, he thought, she is the most beautiful creature I've ever seen. He could not lie to himself. He wanted her! He wanted to touch the smooth texture of her tawny skin, wanted to taste her soft moist lips and feel her respond to his kiss with a passion that could match that growing in him.

Slowly she walked toward them, and Lucas vowed to get her alone as soon as he could. If there was a way to get her from Brian he would find it. Perhaps money would cool Brian's ardor for her, or if he offered her more than Brian was supplying . . . He would pay anything, even though he knew he could not keep her for long.

Brian noted Lucas's reaction and he could have happily strangled Ria at that moment, even though he had to admit she was beautiful enough to arouse a stone.

Ria saw the two men standing together and started toward them, her heart beginning to pound as she drew closer.

The sun haloed Lucas's golden hair making it seem like a life flame. His tall, broad-shouldered frame exuded a feeling of immense power, and she could not push aside her speculation about how the strength of his arms would feel.

Her wild tumultuous thoughts were wrong. He was a pirate, a ne'er-do-well—maybe even a murderer. He had probably robbed her own family, yet she could not honestly deny that he was the most magnetic man she had ever seen. Maybe, she thought, if he were not guilty of too many horrendous crimes, she could make a change in his life. Despite what he might be, he looked as if he could move well in the best of society.

"Good morning, Brian," she said coolly. "Why did you let me sleep so late?"

Brian heard the sugar in her tone, and he groaned to himself for that usually meant she was angry and would seek revenge one way or another. But he kept his dismay hidden—he wanted to annoy Lucas.

"Why, my sweet," he said, "you were so . . . exhausted, and you looked so beautiful I hadn't the heart to awaken you."

She knew how that must have sounded to Lucas. Exhausted . . . as if they had had a wild night . . . and the caressing voice. She was mad enough to kill, but she smiled disarmingly at Brian despite the evil promise in her eyes. Then she turned to Lucas and smiled charmingly and invitingly.

"Good morning, Captain Blanc. Welcome to the *White Swan*."

"I was admiring the beauty of Brian's ship until you arrived," Lucas said warmly, his eyes so captivating Arianne could feel the seductive heat of his gaze. "Now I fully realize what beauty is. It is a pleasure to see you again, Ria."

"Thank you," she murmured, delighted to know Brian would have loved to throw her overboard.

"I was about to go down the coast for a short sail, to check out any inlets or coves. It's a lovely day, would you like to go with me?" Lucas deliberately directed the question to Ria.

"I'm afraid I'm quite busy," Brian said. "Maybe some other time." He was satisfied that at least he had kept these two apart for that day, but he had underestimated Ria's need for revenge.

She smiled at Brian. "I know you have much to do today, and I would not want to draw you from your duties knowing how important they are to you."

Brian's smile of satisfaction soon disappeared when Ria turned to Lucas.

"But I would be very pleased to go with you."

Lucas was aware that Brian stiffened and his mouth grew grim, but he wasn't about to let this opportunity slip away from him.

"Wonderful," he replied quickly. "When we return I would like you to see the *Angel*. She is quite a beauty too."

"I would like nothing better." Ria laughed.

She took Lucas's arm, and they left a fuming Brian behind.

"One for you, Ria," he muttered, "but we'll just see who has the last laugh. You and I are going to have a long talk when you get back."

As they walked to the dock both Lucas and Ria were very aware of each other, and their excitement seemed to set them apart from their surroundings. Ria wondered if she wouldn't regret her little game with Brian. She knew her brother was trying to protect her and she felt guilty, but not quite guilty enough to forego the adventure of sailing the bay with the handsome and exciting man at her side. After all, she reasoned, what harm could he do her in a sailboat? Besides, she would do her best to find out about Lucas's past and to discover whether he was responsible for her father's losses.

Lucas led her to the longboat that he kept tied to the dock to allow him to transfer from his ship to the shore. It had one mast and sail, enough for use within the bay. Already he was thinking of finding a place where he could go ashore and have a few hours alone with the enticing Ria. He wanted to know so much more about her. All her actions and words bespoke fine breeding, yet why was she traveling the seas as mistress to a pirate? She was an exciting puzzle, and he meant to solve the mystery as soon as he could.

He helped her aboard the boat, noticing how graceful and fearless she seemed. In fact, she seemed to enjoy the crisp sea breeze and the rise and fall of the boat in the water as much as he did.

The boat moved slowly out into the bay, driven by the breeze that played in Ria's sun-touched hair. Lucas found it very difficult to maneuver the craft while keeping his eyes on her. She seemed to belong to the wind and the sea. As her eyes danced with pleasure, he found himself wishing he were the source of it and not the elements.

Both avoided asking the unanswered questions in their minds, and took refuge in less complicated conversation, as if they were afraid such direct questioning would create a chasm neither would be able to cross.

"You don't anchor your boat at the dock?" Ria inquired carefully.

"No. That would create an opportunity for . . . ah . . . unwanted visitors. I find it much more convenient to have visitors make their presence known before they have a chance to board."

"I see." Arianne realized he must have something aboard he was afraid of someone discovering.

"I'd like to roam over the island a little. Sometimes it's good to be able to wander off alone, and the beach along the island can be quite pretty. If you'd like we could drag the boat up on the sand and walk for a while."

Dangerous! her mind shouted the warning, but her heart was listening to another call. She nodded her head, and with a more than pleased smile Lucas headed for Anastasia Island.

Chapter 5

The boat grated on the sandy bottom and Lucas leaped out to drag it higher up on the shore so it would not drift away. From where they stood they could look across the Matanzas River to the city of St. Augustine. They could freely count every ship that lay in the harbor. It was a beautiful sight, the tall masted ships rocking gently, and Ria enjoyed it for several minutes before Lucas's voice drew her back to where they were. He had spent those few minutes watching her. He found mastering the new and tantalizing emotions she aroused much more difficult than he could have imagined.

"It's sort of like being alone in the world," Lucas said. "The beach is long, do you want to walk a bit?"

She agreed and they started down the strand. After a few minutes she stopped. She wasn't sure how he would accept what she was about to do, but it really didn't matter what he thought now for to him she did not have much of a reputation.

She sat down and removed her shoes and stockings, and Lucas was rewarded for his silence by a good view of long slim legs. Then she rose and drew up her skirts until they were a bundle in her arms and her legs were free to feel the warm spray of water. She looked at him defiantly, as if to challenge him to criticize her. Instead, he laughed and immediately set about removing his boots and rolling up his pant legs.

Then he came to her side. His eyes were filled with laughter and she responded with enthusiasm.

She looked up at him. "Captain Gabriel Blanc," she said, amusement in her voice. "Funny but I don't feel the name suits you."

"And what would you call me, my lady?"

Again she laughed. "Shall we choose a new name for you, Captain?"

"Feel free to call me any name you choose." His virulent sense of humor overcame his judgment. "Why not call me Luke, after the saint who wandered the oceans?"

Ria laughed delightedly. "Saint?" she queried doubtfully. "I could hardly believe that, but Luke does sound better."

"You are a hoyden . . . but a damned beautiful one. I imagine life with you around would be fun."

"Thank you, kind sir." She giggled. "I can imagine what polite society would think of a lady in this situation."

"Why should you care what polite society thinks? You should enjoy this if you choose to. There's no one you have to answer to but yourself, is there?"

His question sobered her. Again she felt a twinge of irritation. She wasn't supposed to care what he thought of her, but she felt hurt because he believed that she would take her pleasure—any pleasure—wherever she chose. It made her wonder just how far he would take this idea.

He watched her smile fade and noted the thoughtful look that darkened her eyes before she turned away. Now what did I say that upset her? he wondered as he caught up to her.

"Ria?"

"What?"

"We should have brought some food along. There's a lookout inland a ways, and we could have perched up there and watched the ocean. Maybe we'll bring some next time."

"Next time?" she said quietly as he turned her head to look at him questioningly.

He grinned and reached out to take her hand.

"I hope there will be a lot of next times, Ria. In a place like this we could forget . . . the world and any ties that hold us."

"Are you held by so many ties?" she mused. "I don't know who you are or where you're from. I don't even know if I should be afraid of you."

"Afraid of me," he said gently. "I don't ever want you to be afraid of me." His eyes held hers as he reached up to touch her cheek with one finger, trace the line of her jaw, and then lift her chin. Suddenly he bent and his lips touched hers in a feather-light kiss whose effect startled him as much as it did her.

At this moment he was filled with the sudden desire to take Ria and run to the furthest end of the world, to a place where the world and responsibilities could not intrude.

Ria was overcome with sorrowful regrets. They were from different worlds, and despite how she felt about her responsibilities, she was unable to turn her back on them. She had run from a marriage she could not face to a man she did not know. But even if that marriage was not to be, she would find a husband who would bring respect and honor to her family. She could not marry a pirate with nothing but a hangman in his future.

71

Lucas again watched her face and read the conflicting emotions that warred across it . . . but he read them wrong. Is her mind on Brian? he wondered. Is she deciding to leave him? He hoped so—even part-time pleasure is better than none. She would make the most delightful mistress a man could have, and when he'd eventually had his fill of her, he'd be ready to confront the responsibilities that awaited him at home. No matter how he felt about Ria, his obligations to his family did not allow him to bring back a pirate's mistress. But he wanted her now—he wanted to love her and to protect her from the fate he knew Brian would face. He could not bear to see her hang with him or be locked away in prison. The very idea of that chilled him.

A stabbing thought pierced Ria. It would be so easy to forget everything else with this magnetic man, to surrender to the whisper of forbidden magic . . . so easy. She turned away from him to gaze across the small span of water that separated them from the world that called out to her.

Lucas moved behind her, and she drew in a harsh ragged breath as two strong arms wrapped about her, pinning her against his rock-hard frame. He buried his face in sweet-scented hair that had long since given up its struggle to be contained and now blew in fine strands against his skin.

"Ria," he whispered, "the world isn't here . . . not now."

Her every sense was filled with the need to love and be loved by this man; yet she knew beyond a doubt that if she allowed that, she would be lost, whatever grasp she had on her own pride would be gone. Her distress was heightened by the vow she had made to Brian. No. She would make no foolish mistakes. He wanted her and she knew it, but she had to fight. She moved out of his arms and turned again to face him.

"But it is," she said quietly. "We carry our world with us no matter where we go or what we do. There . . . there are responsibilities to others."

He felt she meant Brian and wondered at a mistress who was so loyal to a man who gave her very little. What hold did the pirate have over her?

The truth that kept inserting itself into his mind annoyed him: he could offer her no more than Brian and maybe even less, for at least Brian would keep her longer than Lucas could. Too soon the day would come when Lucas would have to cut her adrift. Angry at this situation he couldn't control, he selfishly pushed these thoughts away, and desire for her tore through him. He could resist it no longer. He turned her around and took her in his arms. She struggled, but with little effort, he held her close with one arm while he buried his other hand in her hair. Their eyes met and held while he slowly forced her head toward him, bringing her mouth relentlessly toward his.

Their lips met and the battle surged to white heat. She moaned softly as his assault tore at her senses. His mouth was hard and demanding. Ria had been kissed before, but never like this. Never with this hot unrelenting mastery. Her lips parted beneath his and his tongue was a seeking force that whirled her world beyond any control she had.

She lost all sense of time and place, and never knew exactly when her arms came up about his neck, or when she had molded her body so tightly to his. She could feel the hard pressure of his manhood against her belly, and the tense, firm muscles of his body were a solid pulsing force that was slowly disintegrating her resistance.

Slowly, very slowly, his mouth began to soften against hers, and what had started as a violent collision became total immersion in swiftly flowing warmth that carried both beyond anything either had expected.

Their mouths played now, each teasing and testing the other. Tongues flitted lightly at first, then joyfully, tasting a new passion that had risen like a forest fire from a burning ember.

His hands slid down her body to draw her more firmly against him, and only at this movement did Ria begin to acknowledge her own total loss of control. Reluctantly, she dragged her mouth from his and broke free of his hold to step back from him.

"Ria?" He spoke her name, his husky voice raw with desire for her. Their emotions were unmasked. Each read the other's passion clearly.

"I can't," she gasped raggedly. "I can't."

Lucas was sure she meant she could not deceive Brian. He had the answer for that and, still convinced that she wanted to be his mistress as much as he wanted her to be, spoke half in anger.

"Damn it, Ria, what can he offer you that I can't? You would be as safe as my mistress as you are with him."

That was enough to bring Ria back to cold reality. Of course he didn't love her! He wanted to use her and then set her free when he had finished with her! What could she expect of a man in his black-hearted profession? He must think her a woman who would jump from man to man like a whore. Rage replaced passion, and she reached out and struck him as hard as she could. The blow took him totally by surprise snapping his head back.

"I am no man's whore!" she cried.

"No, of course not," he snapped without thinking. "The man on whose ship you are living is agreeable to a purely Platonic relationship. Am I supposed to be naïve enough to believe that?"

"He's my . . ." She stopped before she said brother and unmasked Brian, leaving him open to betrayal and perhaps death.

"Lover," Lucas added. "And he must be very good to keep you so loyal." Before Ria could think of an answer she was jerked against an iron-hard chest and bound in two relentless arms. Lucas's mouth took hers in a frenzy of anger and a need to punish. He ravaged her lips for one fierce moment, then let his mouth play more gently across hers until he felt her tremble. His eyes were cold amber as they looked into hers.

"You can lie to yourself and to him all you want, but I can feel what you feel, I can taste the passion we could share. Be honest with him, Ria. Leave him and come with me."

"I can't do that," Ria sobbed, unable to deny his words and just as unable to tell him the truth.

"You're a fool," he said, as he set her away from him.

"Am I? Am I a fool because I don't fall at your feet begging you to make me your mistress? Because I won't love you when I know you could be gone tomorrow without caring what becomes of me?"

"Do you love him, Ria?" Lucas said quietly, his amber eyes glowing with a brilliant flame and piercing her anger.

"I . . . I care."

"I didn't ask if you cared for him," he said firmly. Her eyes dropped from his and he caught her face between his hands. "Do you love him, Ria? Is that what holds you? Could what I felt have been a lie? I don't think so. You tell me—now. Do you love him?"

Ria thought of how close she and Brian had been all their growing years. How they had shared so much and given so much to each other. She knew she was committing the deepest of deceptions, but she held his gaze firmly and spoke softly and very clearly.

"Yes . . . yes. I love him very much. It would hurt me very deeply to deceive or desert him when he needs me . . . I love him."

The words were said firmly and quietly, and he knew without a doubt she meant them. What he didn't understand was why they stung him so deeply, why he was shaken by them. Slowly he released her, and she turned away so he could no longer read her eyes.

Lucas was more than angry at himself. He wanted her and he didn't want her. He couldn't offer her any kind of life. She was a threat to him, yet releasing her was one of the most difficult things he had ever done.

"I . . . I would like to return to the *Swan*," Ria said weakly.

"Of course," he replied coolly. His words sounded hard and unforgiving to her; neither would give way to the longing that filled them.

The trip back to the *Swan* was quiet, both holding their thoughts in check. A very wary and observant Brian watched the pair board the *Swan*. He walked to join them and was surprised when Ria made a hasty mumbled excuse and fled to the sanctuary of her cabin. She closed the door behind her before she squeezed her eyes shut to control tears that burned.

Brian looked quickly at Lucas whose eyes were still fixed in the direction Ria had taken.

"Ria seems upset," he said questioningly. "There's no problem is there?"

"What problem could there be? Ria is a very puzzling young woman."

"She is that. She can keep me guessing." Brian

laughed. "To say the least her temperament is somewhat unruly. She will need a husband's firm hand one day."

Lucas frowned, irritated that Brian could so easily mention losing Ria to another man and be completely unperturbed.

"She's quite beautiful. Why don't you marry her?"

"Me?" Brian said incredulously, then he remembered his situation. He laughed. "You must believe me, my friend, I wouldn't marry Ria under any circumstances. Besides, there are too many beautiful women in the world for men like you and me to be finding. What," he added quietly, "have we to offer any of them but uncertain days and nights that can be over at any time?"

Lucas looked closely at Brian. It was the first time the man had half admitted their supposed occupations. Now Lucas was reasonably sure Brian was the pirate he sought, but if he caught him, he caught Ria as well.

"You are right," Lucas said. "It is dangerous here for Ria. Why don't you send her home . . . or wherever you found her?"

Brian was now beginning to realize that more had happened between Ria and the tall handsome pirate than either was about to admit. He had to put a stop to their relationship before she was hurt. What if she fell in love with this man and he ended up on the end of a rope?

"What I do with Ria," he declared, "is nobody's business but mine. For now, she is my woman. When the time comes to set her free, I'll do it when and where I choose."

Exerting a control so firm it caused him to grit his teeth, Lucas shrugged as if Ria were really of no interest to him anymore.

"Could I interest you in a drink at The Boar's Head?"

"You could, my friend." Brian laughed. "You most certainly could."

The two went to the tavern and ordered two rums. As he sat with Brian, Lucas was determined to find out more about the man. In the shadowy depth of his mind he was searching for a way to keep Ria from sharing the fate he knew would one day be Brian's.

In the tavern Lucas was disgusted by the way Brian flirted with the barmaids, giving each more than a little attention, although he had someone as gentle and beautiful as Ria in his cabin. Lucas suddenly felt angry at both Brian and himself. Ria wasn't his . . . could never be his . . . yet his deepest desire now was to take her away from someone as callous as Brian. At least he would be kinder to her. Could he break the hold Brian seemed to have on her? He didn't know, but he most certainly intended to try.

Brian returned to the *Swan* several hours later and went directly to the captain's cabin. He and Ria shared it to further their masquerade as captain and mistress. Brian opened the door to find his sister sitting cross-legged on the bunk, gazing thoughtfully out the porthole.

"Ria? Are you all right?"

"Of course I'm all right. Why shouldn't I be?"

He went to the bunk and sat down beside her and took one of her hands in his.

"Do you want to tell me what happened?"

"Please, Brian, I'd really rather not talk about it."

"I tried to warn you," Brian said softly. She raised her eyes to his, and he saw her uncertainty. "They are men who live by their wits or by whatever men of their type can use to prey on the unwary. In this case it's charm and a handsome face. But you must be careful of what lies within."

"You've found out something?"

"I'm reasonably sure he's the one we're after, but I need some proof. By the way, have you seen Scott since you returned?"

"No, I haven't."

"If we're lucky, maybe he's found some pieces to add to this puzzle. We'll solve it, Ria; then we'll go home where you can forget all this."

"Yes . . . maybe that would be best."

"Get some sleep. I'm going out again to see if I can find Scott."

"I will," Ria replied.

When Brian left a few minutes later, Ria again sat in silence, thinking of Luke. She had watched Luke's eyes when she'd told him she loved Brian. Had she put her brother in more danger? Could a man as handsome and strong as Luke, be so evil? Ria was torn by emotions she had never felt before. How could one love and hate a man in the same breath?

Brian was deeply troubled by Ria's obvious distress. He made a promise not to let her get any closer to their pirate friend. The man was a threat she was unprepared for. Brian again cursed the adventurous nature that had brought his sister aboard his ship.

Brian's search for Scott took most of the night. It seemed no one had seen him since early afternoon. He returned to the ship in the wee hours of the morning deeply worried. It seemed that Scott had just vanished. He wondered if his friend had stumbled upon some truth and been careless enough to make a mistake, a mistake that might have been more costly than he had bargained on.

Three people lay awake through the long hours of the night, three whose thoughts were remarkably entwined.

Lucas found it completely impossible to stop thinking of Ria. If he closed his eyes he could still feel the emotions that had soared through him when he'd held her in his arms. The bitter taste of her rejection was magnified by the look in her eyes when she'd said she loved Brian.

His annoyance at Brian's presence began to grow. It wasn't bad enough that the man was a thorough villain, but he was cold and careless toward Ria and this was the thorn that pricked Lucas, though he could not offer her much more. Yet he wanted to . . . if only there was a way. So many forces molded the decisions he must make. As the last male Maine he would have to marry well and produce heirs for the sake of the family. He was married now to a woman of suitable background. Arianne St. Thomas. Yet despite what was demanded of him he wanted Ria. Ria, the beautiful mistress of another man.

Ria's dreams were no less frustrating. She was married to a man whose family and honor were above reproach, a man who could give her a life of luxury and honor. Yet her lips could still taste the strength of another and her body would never forget its awakening to a new and frightening emotion.

She knew beyond a doubt that she could not let anything transpire between them. That Luke wanted her only to warm his bed was a blow she could not bear. Her anger was a live thing that ate at her. He had so casually asked her to leave the man he thought she loved, to become his to use and discard whenever the mood struck him. She had watched him closely when she had told him she loved Brian. She hadn't lied, yet she hadn't been truthful either. She knew it was better this way. At least he would stay away from her and give her a chance to regain her equilibrium. Her mind knew this and continued to reproach her heart, but her wayward body refused to listen and it was many hours before she finally slept.

Brian was caught in the same maelstrom. He wanted Ria safe and happy, yet he knew that would never be if she was forced to live with a man she had never seen. On the other hand, he knew he could never allow her to fall into the hands of a pirate who would have no compunctions about setting her aside when he no longer wanted her.

And what if they did fall in love? What if Blanc truly wanted to stay with Ria? How would the pirate keep himself from death at the hands of a hangman. And if he couldn't, where would Ria be? Probably with child and alone, he thought. He sighed. Tomorrow he would have to think of some way to separate them—permanently.

Chapter 6

Scott had spent a more than enlightening night in Sophia's bed. By morning he was certain she knew more of what was going on in and around St. Augustine than the two governors. He had plied her with drink, laughter, and lovemaking until she was completely engrossed in him.

Sophia was shrewd enough to know immediately that Scott was not the same breed of man that usually inhabited the docks of St. Augustine. He was a gentleman, and despite all his efforts she recognized it. He was the kind of well-mannered and gentle man Sophia had longed for. He must have fallen on hard times, she thought.

She was shocked when he remained after he had shared her bed. Most men threw a few coins on the table and left. Although Sophia was somewhat particular about her lovers, she had had to choose from the habitués of the taverns of St. Augustine. She was certain of two things: Scott was unique among her acquaintances, and she was going to hold on to him for as long as she could even if she had to involve him in some of the activities he seemed so interested in. He was almost certainly a pirate, and she was sure he would appreciate her helping him make a few very profitable contacts.

For several days Sophia and Scott circled each other tentatively, trying to find the right way to broach the ticklish subject of piracy. However, they enjoyed being together, and Scott was not averse to spending a great deal of time seeking the secrets Sophia knew. It worked to the satisfaction of both for each thought to convince the other that they should remain together.

Heavy gray leaden skies had given way to a slow steady rain. The air was breathlessly still and thick, and nearly the entire city was immobile. The ships, with the exception of the three that were making their way from the harbor, rocked gently in the breeze and their crewmen were below decks.

Scott and Sophia lay on her bed. He had propped the pillows behind him and had drawn her close as they enjoyed the aftermath of lovemaking that had been mutually satisfactory.

"Scott?"

"Uh-huh."

"You won't be leaving soon will you?"

"I don't know. Depends on my captain. He doesn't seem to have an inclination to go, but he doesn't have any reasons to stay either."

"If . . . if he had reasons—"

"Sophia." Scott laughed. "I don't think you have any idea of what I mean by reasons."

She sat up, unaware in her urgent desire to make him realize that she wanted to help him, that her lush body was having a decided effect on him.

"Do you think I'm really that foolish, Scott? I know damn well your captain flies under the black flag."

"A pirate . . . now Sophia . . ."

"Don't take me for a fool. I can help you—more than you think."

Scott's caressing hand captured one firm rose-crested breast. "You do help me a lot." He chuckled.

She pushed his hand away impatiently. "I don't mean that way! Listen to me."

"I am," he said, as he pulled her close to him again. His hands slid over her skin, stirring her senses. "I'm listening to everything you say," he murmured, as his lips traced a path across one smooth shoulder.

"Scott," she said softly, "I know where to find Dan McGirtt, and I know he'll take all the booty your ship can capture."

Scott drew back and looked at her intently.

"He also finds buyers for any slaves you can bring in or steal."

"Since there's a Spanish governor and an English one how does he keep from getting caught?"

"He has ways of playing one against the other."

"You mean he lives right under their nose?"

"Nearly. He's only a couple of days travel from here."

"And you could take me there?"

"Maybe," she said, a suggestive glow in her eyes. "If it were worth it."

Scott knew she wasn't after money, and the last thing he wanted was to make her angry or suspicious, not when he was this close to helping Brian find out who the pirates were. He had seen the *Black Angel* in the harbor and had found out only recently that her captain was American. He would send a message to Brian and then see if there was a way to find out about the man. Perhaps this was the one they sought. Scott smiled as he realized the American might even be Lucas. But there were so many American pirates—real ones—that it would pay to be careful.

He drew Sophia close and kissed her soft willing mouth until he heard her murmur in soft surrender.

"Does my lady have something special in mind?" he whispered.

"She might." Sophia laughed seductively as she moved against him. Her body was warm and willing, and the flame it ignited in him could have burnt down the city. "If you're interested."

"Interested is a very mild word for what I feel." He chuckled. "Whatever is in my power to supply, you can consider yours."

"There's only one thing I want."

"Which is?"

"That I can be your woman."

"Sophia, I—"

"I know. I know you won't be here forever, but you'll come back. One day you might have your own ship. Then we could sail together. For now . . . while you're here . . . I know you must have a woman in every port, but—"

"Hardly," Scott said quickly.

"Be mine while you're here. You won't regret it."

Scott was beginning to feel the tug of conscience. He knew he was into something that might be very difficult to get out of. Yet he was half-sure Sophia would soon lose interest in their arrangement.

"That's quite a compliment, Sophia," he replied. "You're a damned beautiful woman. You can do better than a pirate who might be hung at any time. If you want to take a chance on me, then I'm the one who's getting the best of the bargain."

"Who knows what the future might have in store?" She smiled.

"Sophia . . . when can I meet this McGirtt?"

"Tomorrow. Tomorrow we'll go."

"How long will it take?"

"A little over three days."

"I'd better send a message to my captain or I'll end up getting keelhauled for jumping ship."

She twined her arms around his neck and squirmed close enough to him to take his mind off going anywhere.

"Tomorrow . . ." she whispered.

"Yes," Scott replied as their lips blended, "tomorrow."

The next day, just after dawn, Brian and Ria stood on deck and watched a huge ship, dark of sail and very powerful looking, enter the harbor.

"He's not a merchant," Brian said positively. "In fact I'd hate to tangle with him. He seems well armed and dangerous."

"I wonder who he is?" Ria mused.

"And who it is he'll be meeting," Brian added softly.

Visions of Lucas leapt unbidden into Ria's mind. He had visited the ship twice in the past few days and on both occasions Ria had made sure their paths did not cross.

Was he meeting this huge dark ship? Was that why he was here, to contact men of the brotherhood? To find more ways to steal . . . maybe to kill?

She tried again to force the memory of his touch from her mind. But it was useless, for the feel of his lips on hers was a recurring flame that refused to be extinguished. Why? she thought in anguished denial, does he have to be the renegade he is? Why couldn't Lucas Maine, the man she had been forced to marry, be the captain of such a ship and overpower her senses instead of being a cowardly gentleman who wouldn't even come to meet her for fear of pirates. She was caught in a web from which she couldn't free herself. She was wed to one man, the obvious mistress of another, and she was filled with an unwelcome desire for a man she could not have. For the hundredth time in the past few days she cursed the captain of the *Black Angel*.

She was also annoyed because Brian, who could haunt the streets and taverns in search of clues, had ordered her to remain on his ship to ensure her safety. She chafed under this restriction and vowed it wouldn't last much longer. One way or another she was going to take part in this escapade. She watched the dark ship dock and mused that today might just be the day she could share in the excitement, for she was grimly determined she was going to meet this new arrival one way or another.

At that moment a young boy scampered up the gangplank and asked for Brian. Ria watched her brother read Scott's message. Then he handed it to her, and she read it quickly.

> Have found a way to investigate our problem. I'll be gone for several days, so don't worry. With you working from one end and me from the other we might just find an answer. I'll be in touch soon.
>
> Scott

Ria handed the paper back to Brian who tore it into small pieces and let it flutter to the water below.

"Brian, I want to go into town today to buy some clothes. I'm tired of wearing only what I've brought with me and your breeches."

"I'll go with you for a couple of hours, then bring you back. I want you safely aboard tonight before I go to see who our new arrival is."

Ria smiled but said nothing. Tonight she was going to share in the fun. Once she had followed Brian to the tavern, it would be too late to send her back and he wouldn't let her return alone anyway. He would be forced to allow her to be a part of the pirate catching.

Ashore, Brian obediently and wearily took Ria from shop to shop until she had purchased what she wanted. He was tense and quite sure he would be protecting Ria's honor somewhere along the line, and from the open lustful stares of men cast at her, he was sure Ria would have been attacked long ago if he had not been with her.

Ria seemed totally unaware of any danger and Brian wasn't sure if that was due to confidence in him or a total unawareness of her intoxicating beauty. He was more than relieved to return to the ship where he thought she would be safe for the night. He soon dressed and left again, and within minutes Ria was changing her clothes and getting ready to follow him.

The gown she had bought was the same amethyst color as her eyes. It was cut much lower than she had desired, but there was little she could do about that for all the dresses she had found had been just as daring.

She caught her hair and twisted it into a secure knot at the nape of her neck. Then she placed a hooded cloak about her shoulders before making her way on deck. She stood in the dark shadows of the companionway while Brian walked down the gangplank. Then she followed him.

Ria moved slowly, keeping far enough behind him so he would not know he was being followed. The streets were very dark now, the only light coming from a huge golden moon whose light left huge puddles of dark shadow.

Brian turned a sharp corner, and she hurried her steps to catch up. Just as she passed a doorway a huge hand reached out and grabbed her arm. As she was swung against a hard chest, another hand covered her mouth. She struggled furiously and was terrified when she smelled rum-laden breath and heard a thick chuckle.

"Where are ye goin', pretty thing? You lookin' for a good man, ol' Ben is the one. I can pleasure ye 'til ye screams for more."

Terrified, Ria suddenly seemed to find a strength she didn't know she had. She thrashed and fought, sinking her teeth into the hand that covered her mouth until she tasted blood. Her captor cursed, but didn't release her. If anything he held her tighter. His hand slid from her face to encircle her throat, and pinpoints of light sparkled before her eyes as his fingers slowly tightened. The world began to swirl about her, and darkness crowded her senses as, with an anguished moan, she lost consciousness and sagged in his arms.

"Teach ye to be nasty to ol' Ben," he grated with a harsh laugh. "Now I'll take ye where we won't be bothered and teach ye a few lessons."

"Take your filthy hands off her."

The voice was hard as steel and cold as death and Ben Tate looked up to see a large dark shadow between himself and his way of escape. Never being one overly endowed with courage he hesitated. He could smell the sweet scent of the slim girl in his arms, and the feel of her soft body incited him to exert some defense of the prey he thought he had captured.

"Outta my way," he snarled. "Go catch yer own treat. This un's mine."

If possible, the voice became colder and Tate was

shaken by the sound of a sword being drawn from its scabbard. "I am afraid if you don't let her go this instant I shall be forced to amputate both arms— somewhere around the area between your head and your shoulders."

Tate uttered a vile curse and dropped Ria unceremoniously in the mud at his feet.

"Very good." The voice chuckled. "Now, my friend, if you are not gone by the count of three I am afraid I shall be forced to spill quite a bit of your blood."

"Ya rotten bastard," Tate grated. "There's enough to share."

"One."

"She's only a woman, mate."

"Two."

The voice was entirely too self-assured for Tate to tempt fate any farther. As he slunk away into the dark, the shadowed form bent over the still, unconscious Ria. The fall had pushed her hood away, and a shaft of moonlight caught the spun gold of the hair that spilled over her shoulders.

He lifted her gently in his arms, and her head fell to his shoulder. For a moment he looked down at her still face; then, with a soft chuckle that could barely be heard on the night air, he walked into the darkness.

Brian stepped into the tavern and found a table near a shadowed corner from which he could watch the entrance. He was served a tankard of ale by a buxom wench who was irritated by his lack of attention until he dropped a coin between her ample breasts.

"Thank you, sir." She smiled invitingly.

"What's your name?"

"Belle, sir."

"Well, Belle"—he smiled warmly—"there's another coin for you if you can answer two questions for me."

"Ducky I'd be willin' to answer any kind of questions you'd like to ask."

"I want the name of the ship that just dropped anchor in the harbor today and her captain's name."

"Bless me, mate, don't you know the *Sea Rover?*"

"Can't say as I do."

"Well that's her, and her captain is Henri Duval."

"I haven't heard of him either."

Belle stared at him in total disbelief. "I didn't think there was a man walking the decks that didn't know Henri Duval."

"Has quite a reputation has he?"

"Aye, sir, that he has. Ain't many would cross him."

"Has a temper?"

"Oh no, sir. He ain't mean or nothin' like that. He's just good with a sword or a knife and his ship is bigger and faster than most. He don't take kindly to anyone interferin' in his business . . . or askin' questions about him either." She smiled to ease her last words. She was more than satisfied when Brian dropped the other coin in the valley so well displayed.

"Now, since you're so willing, maybe you'd like me to match those two with another."

Belle's warm inviting eyes raked over his tall lean form, and she licked her lips slowly in invitation.

"You're a big spender, mate," she said seductively. "You can name your pleasure."

"My pleasure later would be to find where those coins are, but for now I'd just like you to pick out Captain Duval when he comes in."

"Sure. I'll point him out."

"Good. Now be a good girl and get me another ale while we wait."

She left to bring his drink, and Brian sat wondering if he'd looked suspicious by not recognizing Henri Duval. He was sure, by Belle's reaction, that Henri Duval was well known. Brian wondered if Captain Blanc and Captain Duval were not here for some kind of rendezvous. The pieces seemed to be coming together. Now, with Scott's help, all he had to do was find one speck of proof. One tangible piece of evidence he could place before the two governors who would be more than delighted to hang pirates, banditti and all connected with them.

He sipped his drink slowly, watching the comings and goings of the clientele. He looked at Belle when each new patron came in, but she always gave a negative shake of her head.

It was long past midnight when Brian, who had just raised his tankard to drain the last of his drink, saw the man enter the tavern. He did not have to look at Belle—this was Henri Duval.

Brian's first impression was that Duval was the handsomest man he had ever seen. He was impeccably dressed in a deep wine coat with a froth of white lace at neck and cuffs. His boots shone and his breeches were snugly fit to long muscular legs. He was dark of skin, with hair as black as a raven's wing and a mustache and short square-cut beard to match. He seemed an aristocratic gentleman entering a drawing room.

Duval walked to a table and sat down, and Belle immediately approached to fill his tankard. She looked at Brian as she moved away, gave a quick smile, and nodded her head.

Brian stood, picked up his empty tankard, and

walked toward Duval's table. The impressive man was quite aware of his approach.

"Good evening, Captain Duval," Brian said.

Henri Duval sat back in his chair and looked up at Brian. His smile was white and even, but his eyes were quick and missed nothing.

"I do not believe I have had the pleasure, *monsieur*," he said. "It is the first time you are in St. Augustine?"

"Yes. I'm Captain Thomas."

"English?" Henri stated.

"Yes, English," Brian replied.

"That is not the most welcome of recommendations here in las Floridas."

Brian laughed. "No, I suppose it isn't. I have heard a great deal about you, Captain Duval."

"Oh?"

"It seems you are quite popular here in St. Augustine."

"That is important for you, *monsieur*?"

"Could be."

Henri Duval's face retained its smile as he bent forward. His eyes were like glittering glass and Brian could feel the threat in them.

"You have asked the questions about Henri Duval. That is a dangerous thing to do unless you have reasons you wish to share with me."

"I have reasons."

"Then speak quickly, *monsieur*, before I begin to lose my patience."

"I want to talk to you in private. Here even the walls have ears."

"And I am to leave this tavern with you . . . a stranger . . . and maybe find a knife in my back at the first dark alley we find."

Brian was playing a very dangerous game and he

94

knew it, but he had to take chances to find out what he needed to know. He bent forward to speak quietly. "I am here in St. Augustine to make a very great deal of money. I need some help and I don't mind sharing my gains . . . with the right person."

Henri's eyes narrowed and Brian was more than aware that this man was a force to be reckoned with. Duval was very clever and very strong, and Brian was certain there was not one ounce of fear in his entire body.

Henri spoke softly. "We will talk you and I . . . but we will go to my ship to do it."

"Agreed," Brian said quickly. On Henri's ship, he would be vulnerable, but he was sure he could find a way into Henri's confidence, given enough time.

He was grateful for one thing, that he had not listened to Ria's pleading and brought her along. He was glad she was safe in bed on the *Swan*. He had a feeling Henri Duval would be even more dangerous for Ria than for him.

They rose and left the tavern together.

Chapter 7

Ria groaned and came slowly awake. She remained still for a moment, trying to piece together not only what had happened but where she was. She was almost afraid to open her eyes as she began to remember her last moment of consciousness. She could feel softness beneath her and she almost groaned aloud as she realized two things. She was lying on a bed . . . and she had been totally undressed. As sharp fear pierced her, she cracked her eyes open slightly to see if anyone was near.

Her throat hurt and she had difficulty swallowing, but she was too frightened to move.

Slowly she tried to scan the room through the narrow slits of her eyes. It was a ship's cabin. Her fear increased. Even if she could get out of this stateroom, she would find it very difficult to get off the ship without being seen.

She remembered the gruff voice and rancid odor of the man who had accosted her, and was filled with desperation. She would die before she would allow him to touch her.

At that moment heavy footfalls sounded outside the door. Ria sat bolt upright, grasping the blanket to her as her wide eyes watched the door swing open. At first Lucas was struck by the almost ethereal beauty of her skin in the lantern's glow and the tumbled gold of her hair that caressed soft sun-kissed shoulders. Only then did he notice that she trembled violently and her eyes were wide with fear . . . and surprise. Then he laughed, for he read her well, realizing she was sure he had been part of her abduction.

"Well," he said as gently as possible, "I'm glad to see you awake. For a while you had me worried. Are you all right?"

"What . . . what am I doing here?" she rasped.

"I thought it would be a better place than a muddy street."

"What happened?"

"You don't remember?"

She caught a trembling lower lip between her teeth and shook her head negatively.

"It seems you attracted the attention of a rather violent suitor who didn't take your refusal too easily," he drawled with a chuckle.

"You find that amusing?" she snapped raggedly.

"I might, but your suitor didn't. He left without doing too much damage."

"He . . . he tried to kill me!"

"No. I don't think killing you was exactly what he had in mind." Lucas grinned.

Ria had the distinct urge to strike him, but she didn't want to lose her hold on the blanket that was doing an inadequate job of protecting her. She could feel his gaze sear her flesh, and was shaken by the sudden surge of warmth that flushed her cheeks.

Lucas was carrying a tray with a brandy decanter and two glasses on it. He came close to the bed and set the tray on a small table beside it.

When he sat on the edge of the bed, she was totally aware of everything about him from his clean scent to the breadth of his shoulders.

He had removed his jacket and wore only dark pants and a white shirt open at the throat to reveal tanned skin and a mat of golden hair. His sleeves were rolled to the elbow, and his arms were strong and muscular. His presence seemed more of a threat to her than anything else, yet she didn't know why for he had made no move to touch her.

He poured two glasses of brandy and handed her one.

"Drink this; you'll feel better."

She took the glass and sipped, feeling the heat of the brandy spread through her. As she licked the taste of it from her lips, Ria could literally feel his gaze for his eyes were caught by the soft fullness of her mouth.

She clutched the blanket even closer.

"My clothes . . ." she began.

"Sorry, they were covered with mud. I cleaned them off as best I could and they're drying."

Her cheeks grew pink as she realized she had been in a state of total helplessness while he had casually removed all of her clothing. He did not miss her confusion and almost voiced his doubts that a pirate's mistress would suddenly become so modest. Obviously she had been undressed in a man's bed before.

She was exceptionally beautiful and he would never forget the remarkable appeal of her slim body as he'd removed her clothes. He had had to control, with a great deal of effort, his urge to share the bed with her and have her in his arms when she awoke.

He had denied himself that pleasure in the hope of something better. He wanted her, but he wanted her willing surrender. Their coming together would mean nothing to either of them any other way.

He took her free hand in his and bent toward her. "Ria, what the hell were you doing wandering the streets alone?"

"I was following Brian." She saw his eyes darken with an emotion she could not read.

"Didn't you sense the danger you were in? Can't you see? . . ."

"See what?"

"Ria," he said intensely, as he drew her to him taking her shoulders in both hands. "I don't want you to go back to him. I want you to stay here . . . with me."

"I can't do that. You don't understand."

"What is there to understand?" he said angrily. "The man's either stupid or blind. He's using you, can't you see that! You're too beautiful to be left to trail after a man like a . . ."

Her face grew pale. "A whore?"

"I didn't say that."

"But you meant it."

"No, Ria, I didn't." He drew her even closer. "I'm not sure what I meant. Maybe I'm just a little jealous. Maybe I can't believe any man in his right mind would leave you like that when he could have . . ." His words died to a whisper as he bent to touch her mouth with his. "Heaven," he murmured as their mouths blended in the gentlest of kisses.

Both were taken completely by surprise, for totally different reasons, however. Lucas was aware of a tentative fear in Ria, almost as if this were her first brush with desire. Ria was shaken by the wild flame of need that blossomed in her against her will.

"Please . . . I must leave here," she moaned softly.

"To go back to him," he grated roughly. "Why do you lie to yourself? You want to stay with me. You want me as much as I want you."

"No," she sobbed. "No . . . you don't understand. I—"

"I do understand. Now I will show you."

Her ineffectual struggles were less than useless, for all she succeeded in doing was to eliminate the fragile barrier of the blanket that stood between him and what he desired most. A wave of excitement made him quiver in expectation.

He captured her hands and drew them over her head, holding them firmly with one hand. Then his lips scorched her flesh as he devoured the soft, scented skin of her shoulders. Her body arched in resistance, but his hand stroked gently. Cupping one of her breasts, he teased the nipple erect with his thumb in a slow swirling motion. She wanted to scream at the jolt that shot through her as he caught the hardened nipple in his mouth, loving it slowly, seductively. Then he began to suck, first harshly, then gently.

A wild tempest was growing within her, and she moaned out a need she did not understand.

With agonizing slowness, his hand stroked the smooth texture of her skin. Down the length of her body, across the flat plane of her belly, until his fingers lightly caressed the source of her agonizing pleasure, which throbbed with an aching need for his touch.

She was on fire with a blaze whose source and whose method of extinction were lost to her.

Lucas was growing more and more aware that Ria was a novice at the art of love, and if his body had not been shrieking with desire he might have paid more attention to this fact. But he was caught in a consuming passion he had known with no other. Her skin felt like satin, and the scent of her was a heady perfume that entangled his senses.

Lucas stood only for a moment, to rid himself of the unwanted barrier of his clothing. In profound admiration, he gazed at the golden beauty that glimmered against the dark blankets.

Ria was just as spellbound by the sleek muscular grace of his body. Her eyes only widened when the removal of his pants gave her the first look at the proud force of his manhood which had grown to proportions that amazed her.

She gave a half-cry and began to rise. But again he was beside her drawing her close, his mouth capturing hers. His tongue traced the outline of her parted lips, then thrust deeply, tasting the honeyed wine of the depths of her mouth, before his lips slipped down the arched curve of her throat to the pulse that throbbed with passion, then went further. To catch a hardened nipple and moisten and arouse the peak. His hands again trailed lightly up and down her thighs until she quivered beneath his touch.

Gently his fingers found the pulsing bud beneath the soft mound of gold curls. He caressed it gently until her moan of utter abandon told him she was lost to any other need than one.

Her eyes were closed as he rose above her and, in one swift movement, he pressed himself deep within her. Her cry of pain brought him to an astounding realization. Her eyes had flown open in shock, but she was only a little more shocked than he when the undeniable truth of her virginity struck him. But they were beyond retrieving the damage already done, and beyond the point of return.

For a moment she fought the intrusion, and he held her helpless while he slowly began to move. He watched the fire build again and felt her renewed response.

When their bodies had joined, Ria had been plummeted from the heights of complete sensual ecstasy to the depths of sudden pain. She had no time to deal with either emotion, for again her senses were being lifted and all pain was forgotten. There was a magic that wove the threads of her desire with his until the fire of his possession stole every ounce of will she had and molded it to blend with his. She was lost in a world of sensual pleasure as he filled her and touched the core of a need that raged like a forest fire.

She wanted to be part of him, and her arms and legs enclosed his body as she moved to match the rhythm of each thrust.

Lucas had possessed many women but none like this. Her passion matched his in every way. Her giving was complete, and he felt a unique possessive oneness, as if she had suddenly filled a void that had been dark and hollow all his life.

They soared, caught in the grip of a volcanic explosion swirling them to the heights, then both tumbled, together, into the blinding oblivion of completion.

For long moments he held her trembling, sweat-sheened body close to him while the truth of their situation finally began to bring reason to his mind.

He looked down into eyes awash with the combined tears of completion and fear. With a low groan he moved to be beside her. He held her with one arm, keeping her body close to his. With the other hand he captured her chin and tipped her face so he could read her eyes.

"Ria," he whispered, "why the hell didn't you tell me?"

"You never gave me a chance to tell you anything," she said, and the rough catch in her voice told him she was still shaken by their encounter. He rose on one elbow.

"I don't understand this. I thought—"

"Yes, I know what you thought," she replied bitterly. "What is one more tumble in bed for a woman of my kind."

He could hear the hurt in her voice. He was beginning to have a lot of questions about this mysterious lady, but he knew one thing: he was not about to let her go easily and he was definitely not going to let her return to Brian. He had heard of pirates who sold young virgins in far-off countries. He was sure Brian had somehow enticed her aboard his ship, and was planning to make a large profit when she was sold. He knew Ria could not possibly be aware of this.

He brushed strands of her hair from her sweat-moist cheeks. Gently he bent to kiss her quivering lips.

"Ria, I'm sorry. I wanted you, but I never wanted to hurt you. Loving is not like that. It's something very special. If I had known . . ." Her wide eyes lifted to his. "Tell me why you're here with him? What do you know of his motives? Surely you wonder why he has never touched you."

"He . . . he wouldn't. He couldn't . . . he's . . ." She could not reveal Brian's identity no matter what he was thinking. Doing so would put Brian in too much danger. "He's not . . ."

"Like me?" he finished with a half-smile. "Ria, no man in his right mind would be able to remain celibate with you around. He has other motives, and I'm damn well not going to let you go back to him. You are staying here."

"I can't," she cried.

"Are you afraid of me?"

"No . . . but . . ."

"Then why? You said you loved him, yet it's clear that he's never made love to you. Don't you question that?"

Ria thought frantically. She was lost in a maze of lies and couldn't find her way out. Finally half-truths seemed better than nothing.

"He's promised not to touch me until I'm free."

"Free?"

"I . . . I'm married."

The puzzle was only deepening for Lucas. But the word *married* had dark thoughts for him too, for no matter how he felt about Ria, he was not free to offer her anything either.

"Married . . . and he talked you into running away from your husband on your wedding night?"

"No . . . not really. I ran away myself. Brian was only a way to escape a marriage my parents had forced me into. To an ugly old man I had never seen in my life before. I couldn't! I just couldn't honor a marriage to a man I detested. I ran, and stowed away on Brian's ship. He agreed to help me until I decided what to do."

"I'll wager," Lucas said grimly, still sure Brian had darker motives that included some profit.

Ria's eyes flashed angrily. "Brian has helped me. He's kind and—"

"What do you know about him?"

"All I need to know. He has been good to me." She tried to move from his arms, but he held her with a strength she could never hope to master. "Let me go. I must go back before Brian returns and misses me."

"I'm afraid he's going to do more than miss you. I'm not letting you go."

"You must!" she cried in alarm.

"Must I?" He smiled. "I think if you stay here tonight he might get the idea I don't intend to let you go back."

"You can't do that! He'll come for me."

"I'm sure I can convince him, if he is stupid enough to come for you, that I have no intention of letting you go."

Ria envisioned scenes of blood and death. "I want to go," she said as firmly as possible. "I don't want to stay with you."

"Don't you?" he said gently, as his arms began to tighten about her. Awareness leapt into her eyes.

"No," she gasped.

"Ria, it's too late to turn back the time. I know what you felt was new and difficult, but I promise you it's better than that. You've never tasted love before," Lucas murmured as his lips brushed her cheek. "Let me show you what it can be."

She was mesmerized by the intense hold of his passionate gaze as he slowly bent his head and his parted lips met hers. Leisurely his mouth savored hers, and she felt as if she were drowning in a sea of fire. She ran her hands along the rigid muscles of his shoulders, at first in resistance, then tremblingly as she became more aware of his warm male flesh.

His arm curled more tightly about her shoulders, and he let one hand caress her spine before pressing her hips close to his. As his mouth played gently on hers, tasting the softness of her lips, her mouth warmed to his and she brought forth a wordless moan. The fragrance of her filled his brain, just as her slim warm body filled his arms.

She felt as if she were suddenly boneless, melting against him, flowing about him until they blended into a single heartbeat, a single breath.

Gently, almost against her own volition, her hands began to explore his back, drawing him closer, as her body began to respond to the gentle touch of his

106

hands. Without words her flesh seemed to know and to desire his, despite the recent taking of her innocence. Every sense she had was bombarded by raging desire.

But it was too soon. He didn't want to take her to the pinnacle so soon. His mouth trailed over her shoulders and down to encircle a hardened nipple. He nipped it hard enough to make her moan in ecstatic pain, then traced a path to her navel where his tongue gently probed, making her twist in his arms. He slid his hands down over the curve of her hips, and gently ran them up inside her thighs to separate her trembling legs.

She was nearly irrational now, her hands tangled in his thick hair; and she cried out her surging ecstasy as he found the center of her. His tongue was moist and hot, and pierced her like a sword. He taunted and teased her quivering bud of desire until he knew she was on the brink. She wept with the agony of her pleasure, cried out for completion. She wanted him . . . and he knew the call of her body echoed his.

He rose as her body arched to meet his; then, in one thrust, he was pulsing within her. His whole being soared, as they meshed savagely, and he increased his force, expertly lifting them both higher and higher until their senses spilled about them like sparkling stars, bathing them in a glow of satiated passion and leaving them clinging to each other, reluctant to move, to talk, or to do anything that would break the magic spell that had welded them together.

He turned slightly so his weight would not rest on her, but he did not release her. Her head rested against his chest and he could feel the heat of tears, but this time he knew her tears were not from pain. He stroked her hair gently.

Ria was torn with a new sorrow. This was all she

had ever wanted from the man she would love, all she had expected from marriage. Yet the light of truth tore the shield from her heart. This was the one man in the world she could never have.

He was a man who stood against all that society and family demanded she have. He had no future except to run and hide, to pillage and steal; and one day . . . one day he would be caught. She closed her eyes as she remembered that his capture was exactly what she and Brian were here for.

Lucas's thoughts were not far from hers, only he was searching for a way to keep her from being hurt when he brought Brian justice.

His first step was to make sure she did not return to Brian's ship, and he'd do it no matter what means he had to use.

He tipped her chin up to look into her eyes. They were warm amethyst pools, and he could easily have spent the rest of his life swimming in their depths. His plans were simple. He would keep her with him. Somehow he would get around the barriers of his unwanted marriage and Ria's background. Those plans could be made later, for now there was Ria . . . just Ria.

"You see why I can't let you go," he said gently. "I can't take the chance that his sense of honor will last much longer."

"Why can't you believe me? He won't do anything to hurt me. Please," she whispered, "I must go back before he comes for me. I don't want anyone hurt."

"Are you afraid for me or for him?"

"For both of you."

Lucas was torn by a jealousy he had never felt before. *Did Ria truly love Brian in an idealistic kind of way? Was he, to her, a knight in shining armor, the honorable one who protected her purity?*

108

He wondered if he himself was only a force she could not withstand? Could she forget the magic they had shared? He could not.

"Whatever you fear you are not leaving here. I'm not taking any chances. If he comes for you, he'll have to pass me first."

Ria was frantic. She knew what Brian would think and do as soon as he returned. She wanted desperately to tell Lucas who they were and why they were here, but she was not sure that he would not turn on them both. Her trust in him was still tentative. She had to find a way out. She could think of only one . . . his anger.

"You take a lot upon yourself," she said coldly. "I have not asked for your protection. Has it occurred to you that I would prefer to stay where I am?"

His eyes regarded her intently. With more determination than she felt, she held his gaze, hoping he would believe her.

"You're trying to tell me this meant nothing to you, that you still prefer to be with a man whose motives might be as black as the night?"

"It . . . it was an interesting interlude," she replied flippantly. "You are a very able teacher. Obviously this is a common occurrence for you, Captain. You will understand if I don't believe it was more than that. Really, when one lives the free life, it is exciting to learn to take what one wants with no regrets. As I said you are an excellent teacher." She shrugged. "One has to learn sometime, and I feel I've been fortunate that it wasn't the vermin on the docks who instructed me."

She wanted to cry out a denial of her words, to reach for him and hold him close. But she could not, and the anger that leapt like a live flame in his eyes caused her more pain than he would ever know.

109

That he was nothing more to her than an "interesting interlude" cut Lucas deeply. She was what he had thought at the beginning, a whore in angel's guise, ready to deliver her body and her love to the man who promised more. He could play her game too.

"Why go?" he asked angrily. "I'm sure no matter what he has offered you I can give you more. What's your price?"

His barb struck home, and she forced back tears. This was what she had wanted. She had succeeded, but it had cost almost more than she could bear.

"Take me back," she whispered.

"As madam wishes." He laughed. "But you will call on me if my . . . services are ever needed again? The . . . interlude was, as you say, very enlightening."

Ria could not speak for fear of loosening the dam that held back her tears, and she remained silent while they dressed. She needed to memorize every plane and curve of his body. Memories would be all she would have to sustain her.

He took her back to the *Swan,* and once she was inside her own cabin, Ria threw herself on her bunk and cried.

Chapter 8

In his cabin on the *Sea Rover*, Henri Duval sat across the table from Brian. The men had glasses of excellent wine before them. Brian had been surprised at many things when he'd boarded the *Sea Rover*. One was the cleanliness of the ship and of the cabin in which they sat. Brian's ideas on pirates would have to be changed if Henri was to be his example.

"So," Henri said pleasantly, belying the shrewd glow of his eyes, "you have come to Henri to bargain, *non?*"

Brian felt attack was the best form of defense. He smiled and raised his glass in a silent toast; then he spoke quietly but with assurance.

"Shall we put our cards on the table, my friend. I know what you are, and you know what I am. I need your help . . . and I can make it profitable for you."

Henri threw back his head and laughed heartily. When he finished, he drained his glass and refilled it.

"You are an arrogant one. Why would Henri Duval need you?"

"To double your profits."

"Oh, and how do you expect to do that?"

"You have the contacts I need . . . and I have a ship

that can outrun any merchant that sets sail. You get all the profit from what you bring in and a quarter of mine. Seems like you have a lot to gain."

"Ah, my friend, you are right on one point and very wrong on another."

"How so?"

"I do have a lot to gain . . . and what I have to gain is half your profits."

"Half! That's robbery."

"Good comparison." Henri roared with laughter. "You . . . ah . . . confiscate profitable cargo for the betterment of . . . wayward sailors and you call it robbery if I take my share. It is so, *monsieur?* Half— or we have no deal at all." Henri's voice was low but very firm and very cold. Brian knew he had no option but to agree. This was the only key he had to unlock information on the pirates and their contacts.

"You strike a very hard bargain."

Henri shrugged eloquently. "But I am a pirate, *monsieur.*" He smiled. "As you knew when you tried to bargain with me. We are agreed then?"

"Agreed."

"Good. Now . . . tomorrow I would see your ship."

"My ship?"

"*Monsieur*, I trust no man until I see what kind of ship he captains and how he treats her. A ship is like a woman. Treat her well and she performs. I shall come tomorrow."

Brian's thoughts were on Ria, but there was no choice. He consented and Henri walked with him to the rail, then waved as he left.

Henri stood at the rail for some time before another man came to stand beside him. It was Louie Savon, his first mate and one of the few men he trusted.

"So, *mon Capitaine.* We have made a friend?"

112

"I am not too sure, *mon ami*. We will see, we will see."

When Brian returned to the cabin he shared with Ria, he was satisfied to find her curled on the bunk, her back to him and, he thought, asleep.

He made ready to find his own bunk and some much-needed sleep. He had to find a way to keep Ria and Henri from coming into contact. He would think about it . . . he would find a way . . . only . . . Again he wished Ria were safely at home even if she did have to face an unwanted marriage. That would certainly be much better than this.

Ria had turned her face to the wall as soon as she heard Brian coming. Her reddened eyes and tear-stained face would be wordless proof that something had happened. She and her brother had been entirely too close for her to be able to fool him now.

After some time she heard Brian's slow regular breathing, and she knew he slept. For the first time Ria honestly faced the fact that she truly wished she had not come on this journey. She had thought it would be a grand adventure, but this adventure had been much more than she had bargained for. She could not even expect to return and pick up the pieces. What man would want a wife who had run away, given her body freely to another. Why, she thought miserably, she might even be—"Oh, God," she groaned—with child.

She closed her eyes as she mentally cursed herself, and lay very still. But subtler and much sweeter memories refused to be denied.

She wrapped her arms about herself, remembering all too well the strength of other arms. Her lips still tingled from the touch of his lips, her body trembled with a new emotion she could not control—desire. She bit her lip to keep the tears from falling. She should hate him, she should be angry; but she wasn't. Instead she was frightened of this new and stronger force. It urged her to return to him and feel the security and warmth he had given. The first gray light of early dawn streaked the horizon before her eyes closed in exhausted sleep.

If Ria had a bad night, it was comparable to Lucas's for he could not sleep either. He was torn between two opposite forces: his desire to possess Ria again and his knowledge that even if he did he would have to relinquish her before he went home.

His anger and disappointment had receded before the fact that he could not wipe the memory of her touch from his body. Even with his eyes determinedly closed he could still feel the soft texture of her skin, smell the scented perfume of her hair.

To make matters worse he could picture her with Brian. Now that she had surrendered to passion once, it might be easier to surrender again, this time with another man.

He groaned in frustrated anger. She had thrown his own intentions back into his face with her taunting reminder that he had no ties on her. He had only been the teacher and now she was free to give her passion to another if she chose. He damned her in one breath and longed for her with the next. Then his emotions began slowly to gel into a grim determination to take her from Brian any way he could. If she wanted to play the wanton, then he would make sure the play was on his stage and no other.

Any future problems he pushed to the back of his mind. He would handle them later. For now he wanted Ria . . . and he meant to have her.

Chris shared a silent breakfast with Lucas, well aware that something drastic had happened since the preceding afternoon when he had left the ship to go into St. Augustine. He had worked apart from Lucas in the hope that he might make contact with someone connected to the elusive pirate. So far he had been less than successful.

He had not returned to the ship until well past two in the morning and he'd gone to bed without going to Lucas's cabin. He'd been sure Lucas was asleep, and he hadn't wanted to disturb him when there was no news to report.

Now he sat across the table from an obviously deeply troubled captain.

"Lucas—"

"You have to get out of the habit of calling me by that name, Chris."

"I know. I'll try to call you captain. It's easier than trying to tie the name Gabriel to you. It just doesn't fit."

The reference to his ill-suited name brought a reluctant tug at his memory, the tug of a bright-eyed woman who couldn't accept him as what he was.

Did she have an intuitive knowledge that he was not what he pretended to be?

"Nothing about this whole affair seems to fit," Lucas said disgustedly.

"What's the matter, Lu— Captain?"

"I can't seem to find a lead. With the exception of the new ship in the harbor, which I'm going to look into today, I seem to have run up against a stone wall."

Chris was reasonably sure, knowing Lucas as he

did, that there was much more wrong than that. Lucas was one to handle problems without showing any signs that they existed. Now he seemed caught up in something he didn't want to talk about. They had been friends a long time, yet Chris suddenly felt this was no time to press the issue.

"I've heard the new arrival's name is Captain Henri Duval."

"Find out anything else about him?"

"Yes, a few things. Everybody is pretty close-mouthed about him, but I'd say Captain Duval is involved in a rather shady pastime."

"Then I think I'll pay the captain a call today."

"And I guess I'd better do some more nosing around."

"Don't be conspicuous." Lucas grinned.

"Don't worry about me. I'll be careful. You just watch yourself with Duval. I have a feeling, from what I've heard, that he's nobody's fool."

"No, I suppose not. But I've got to beard the lion in his den anyhow."

"Let's get started."

They rose and walked on deck. It was late morning and the sun was already simmering. Both men stood by the rail for a few minutes, looking over the bay and the city of St. Augustine which lay before them.

Turning to say something to Lucas, Chris noted that his attention was riveted on the *Swan*. He followed his gaze.

"Seems like there's traffic between the *Swan* and our new friend Duval," Chris said.

"Yes, doesn't there?" Lucas said. "Maybe we've found our contacts. It's about time my birds were all in one nest."

"You're going over there?"

"I certainly am. I couldn't hope for a better time."

They took the small boat to shore, where they parted and Lucas walked toward the *Swan*.

Ria was exceptionally quiet, and Brian might have paid more attention to this if he had not been nervous about Duval's arrival.

She had dressed in a rose-colored gown that had a very demure scoop neck and short puffed sleeves. The slenderness of her waist accentuated her high curved breasts. She looked half-woman, half-child—a gentle creature on the verge of becoming an exciting one. If Brian was aware of it he knew for certain Henri would be.

He was just about to present the problem to Ria and ask her to stay as far away from Henri as she could. But he never had the opportunity. There was a sharp rap on the cabin door, and Brian opened it to find one of his sailors, red-faced and obviously annoyed by the fact that Henri Duval stood right behind him.

"Sorry, Cap'n. This gent says you was expectin' him."

"I was," Brian replied with a smile that eased the bristles of the aggravated sailor. "Come in, Captain Duval."

Henri entered and was about to speak when his gaze fell on Ria. For a moment he stood quite still, absorbing the fact that this exceptional beauty was truly here. Ria watched his face, and was annoyed by the fact that he thought the same of her as Lucas—that she would freely distribute her favors.

She rose and went to Brian's side, then laid a gentle, yet possessive, hand on his arm. To Henri it was the affectionate touch of a lover, and he knew Ria was making an obvious point. However, her move

117

titillated his imagination and made her even more desirable. Henri was always one who liked a challenge.

"Brian," Ria said softly as she gazed up at him in what she hoped would look like an adoring gaze. "I shall leave you to talk."

"*Non, non,* my sweet." Henri chuckled. "Nothing stimulates a man's conversation more than the presence of a pretty woman, and you are one of the loveliest I have seen. Please stay."

"Ria, this is Captain Henri Duval. Henri, this is Ria."

"Ria?"

"Just Ria," Brian stated firmly.

"I am pleased to meet you, Captain," Ria said.

Henri came to her side and took her hand. He raised it to his lips and kissed it while his eyes held hers. "The pleasure is mine," he said softly.

Ria felt a quiver of real fear. This was no man to be played with. He was dangerous, to Brian . . . and to her.

"Would you like some wine?" Brian was quick to ask, intending to draw Henri's attention from Ria.

"Yes, thank you."

Ria moved away from Henri to sit on a high bench near the window, but Henri's eyes followed her, enjoying the vision.

"So, Henri"—Brian smiled—"you've come to a decision."

"*Oui,* I can see," Duval said smoothly, "that you take great care of all of your . . . possessions. Your ship, all I see, is in excellent condition and quite beautiful. I think"—he smiled broadly—"that you and I can negotiate many beneficial bargains."

Brian and Ria were both aware of the double entendre, yet they kept complete control over the emotions that gripped them.

"Then you will take me soon to meet the people you deal with?"

"*Non, monsieur,* we cannot be too hasty. First I . . . and they . . . must see that you can provide your part of the bargain. Take a prize, and I will give you a safe harbor to bring it to. Then you will meet the people who are willing to pay for what you can provide."

"Take a prize," Brian repeated. He had seen Ria's eyes widen. This was one thing they had not counted on. Brian must prove he was pirate in fact as well as in name.

"Of course, *mon ami,*" Henri laughed. "We cannot expect to answer too many of your questions before we know you can accomplish what you promise. There is no difficulty with this?" he queried quickly.

"No . . . no of course not."

"Of course." Henri's smile glistened. "It would be difficult to take so lovely a lady into a battle. It would be no problem if you"—he looked at Ria—"would accept my hospitality for the short time your . . . ah . . . captain is gone."

Ria's face flushed, and she clenched her hands in her lap.

"You needn't worry about Ria's care," Brian said in a deadly quiet voice. "I will take care of her."

Henri shrugged, but before he could answer another knock echoed throughout the cabin. Its three occupants were surprised.

Again Brian went to the door and opened it.

If Brian's second mate had been annoyed by the arrogance of Henri's arrival he was more so now, for behind him stood a casually smiling Lucas.

"Cap'n . . ." Briggs began lamely. But Lucas

stepped past him. He folded his arms across his chest and leaned against the frame of the door. His smile was broad, and his eyes glowed with a humor unrecognized by the three.

"Good morning, Captains. It's a fine day for a meeting—a meeting I'm very anxious to be part of. I think, if I'm not mistaken, you are about to discuss some plans that could be profitable for all of us."

Henri looked at Brian's cold face and was certain there was not too much affection between these two. He was quick to realize a confrontation might be beneficial for him, but first he had to find out what lay between them.

"You are friends?" he asked Brian.

"Hardly friends," Brian replied.

"Now, Captain Thomas"—Lucas chuckled—"we are brothers of the sea are we not? Or am I wrong in my suspicions? We both—or we three—sail under the flag of our respective countries."

Henri chuckled. "You accused us of being pirates, *mon ami?*"

Ria had drawn in her breath at Lucas's appearance. Now she was absorbing everything about him. He overpowered the room and every one in it with the breadth of his shoulders and his height.

He seemed amused by the situation, but Ria sensed more than saw that he was totally aware of every glance and every move. He also was well aware of the currents within the small room.

Lucas felt he had stumbled on just the situation he was looking for. These two worked together. Both were guilty of robbing ships and possibly worse.

Despite his smile and his seeming unawareness of her presence, Lucas was more than aware of Ria. The sunlight behind her turned her hair into a golden

120

halo and gave her skin a tawny glow, and he felt again that he could drown in her amethyst eyes. God, he wanted her, and maybe, if he played his hand well, he just might have her. For one quick moment he wondered if he were given the choice of catching these two or of having Ria, which would he take. He also wondered what it would take to get Ria to change loyalties.

"Let us not joke with each other, my friend," Lucas said softly. "You and I both know what we are after and how to get it. We would be damned fools if we spent time fighting each other instead of combining our forces. I was always taught three are more profitable than one . . . or two."

Ria's breathing became constricted. He had admitted what he was! He was as guilty as Henri Duval. It made her furious when she had to fight the denial she felt. Why should she care what happened to a pirate, a man who had a black and bloody past. He had taken her virginity and offered her the life of mistress in return for it.

"So, *mon ami*,"—Henri smiled a calculating smile—"maybe we might sit down over this so excellent wine my companion has offered, and talk of many things."

Brian felt he was being outnumbered. "What makes you think you can trust him?" He snarled.

Henri chuckled. "My dear friend, Henri Duval trusts no one—no one who does not prove who and what he is."

Lucas now chuckled, which stirred Brian's anger even more. Ria was afraid fury might cause Brian to say something he shouldn't. She rose from her stool and walked to Henri, then smiled as she took the half-empty glass from his hand.

121

"I'll refill your glass for you, Captain. Please, sit down," she said in a satin-coated voice. "When I bring your wine, you can discuss this as gentlemen should." Her free hand rested momentarily on his arm, and her eyes were warm with a promise that did not exist in her heart. Her gesture struck Lucas, but he retained his casual smile while he struggled to control the urge to beat her and then make violent, passionate love to her.

Henri took Ria's hand in his. This time he kissed her palm. "Of course, *mademoiselle*," he said gently. "We too shall talk soon . . . about many things."

She smiled, and moved from Henri's side entirely too slowly to suit Lucas who, though he retained his casually interested look, had already promised himself to make certain, one way or the other, that Henri Duval would never touch Ria while he was alive.

Ria had deliberately taken Henri's attention from her brother's anger to allow Brian to regain his hold on it. He was grateful, but more aware than ever that Henri Duval wanted Ria. The pirate was powerful and deadly, and he would do anything to get her.

Ria moved to the furthest side of the room and sat in silence while the three men talked and planned—planned the ravaging of ships.

Lucas, though his attention seemed to be on Brian and Henri, missed nothing about Ria. Her presence was an almost physical stimulation to his senses. His blood warmed, filling him with renewed desire as he remembered the past night when she had been warm and willing in his arms, filled with a passion he had never tasted in a woman before.

Such a surging desire to hold her flooded through him that he could barely control it. She seemed to

122

glow in the sunlight, and with every glance, his eyes caressed her. It would have consoled him to know that Ria felt the same tantalizing need, but her eyes fled from his, denying any contact lest she be caught in something she couldn't control.

Ria had no idea that in this case Lucas's thoughts paralleled hers. Both were wondering how they were going to manage this situation without exposing their feelings.

It was finally agreed that Brian and Lucas must each capture a prize ship and bring it to an appointed harbor whose location Henri would give them when they departed from St. Augustine.

Brian and Ria were both exhausted, tense, and frightened by the time Henri and Lucas had left. They would have been much more frightened if they could have followed the devious Henri Duval back to his ship.

As Duval started below he motioned his first mate to follow him. They entered his cabin and he closed the door and then poured them both a drink.

"There's something you want, Capitaine?" Louie asked.

"*Oui*, my friend. There is something I want. There is a little process of elimination I want you to perform for me."

"Aye, Capitaine." The mate grinned. "And who is it you want eliminated?"

"Actually two men."

"Two?"

Henri grinned. "Both are captains, and both stand in the way of something I want."

"And who might they be, Capitaine?"

"Captain Brian Thomas of the *Swan* and the mysterious Captain Gabriel Blanc of the *Black Angel.*"

"You may consider them dead." Louie laughed harshly as he tossed down the drink.

"Good . . . good," Henri said softly. Now, he thought, my lovely purple-eyed wench. We will see to whom you belong. He tossed down his own drink in satisfied anticipation.

Chapter 9

Two days passed while Henri kept Brian waiting. Henri did it to force Brian to concentrate on what they were about to do so he wouldn't realize he was being followed every time he left the ship.

Lucas was also tense, but the afternoon after the meeting on the *Swan* he became aware that someone haunted him at every step he took. He was reasonably sure of the reason, but not certain whether Henri or Brian was having him followed. He suspected his shadow intended to trap him in a dark alley, so he made it a point never to frequent any.

The third day found the early evening sky filled with gray rain-laden clouds. By the time the sun set, thick jagged bolts of lightning touched the sky to reveal, in bright flashes, the steady pouring rain. Another two hours found the storm at its height.

Brian and Ria sat together as they had for the past two nights, waiting for some word from Henri. They were hopeful that word had come when there was a light tap on the door. Brian opened it to find one of his own crew in the passageway.

"Someone brought this message for you, sir," the seaman said.

Brian unfolded the piece of paper he'd been handed and read rapidly.

"What is it, a message from Duval?" Ria asked.

"No," Brian replied, a puzzled frown on his face. "It's from our other pirate friend Captain Blanc."

Ria moved quickly to his side and read over his shoulder.

I have interesting news about our mutual friend. Meet me at The Boar's Head and we'll talk. I think you will find the information valuable.

G. Blanc

"What do you think, Brian?"

"I don't know. I'm curious as hell though. Duval is a pirate, but I wonder what else he knows about him."

"It's a trap," Ria said fearfully. "Don't go. Ignore it."

"I can't do that. What if these two rats are turning on each other? I have to go and see what this is about."

"I want to go with you!"

"No! For God's sake if this is a trap at least I can fight. You don't stand a chance."

"Brian, please . . ."

"No, Ria. That's final. I'll be back soon."

He grabbed his cloak and hat from a hook by the door and left without another word.

Ria stood for a minute and watched the door. Then she made her decision. She took her hooded cloak from another hook, put it about her shoulders, and left the cabin.

Lucas found himself in much the same situation.

He couldn't keep his mind off Ria. For two nights he had tossed and turned in a sleepless bed, and tonight promised to be no different.

His mind told him one thing; his senses another. He could still inhale her scent in his bed.

He stood up for the hundredth time and stretched his tightened muscles. He looked unseeingly through the rain-splattered porthole and wondered again what was happening aboard the *Swan*.

He was tempted more than once to go to that ship, but he knew he might scare Brian away from the project if he did so and he wanted Brian and Henri caught. He had decided long ago that he would do whatever he could to protect Ria when that happened.

He sighed impatiently, walked back to his desk, and picked up the glass from which he had been steadily drinking from all evening. He was about to take a sip when he heard the approaching footsteps.

Lucas went to the door and opened it before the sailor outside could knock.

"What is it?" he demanded quickly.

"Message came for you, sir," the young sailor said, as he handed the note to Lucas.

"Thank you, Jack. Good night."

"Night, sir." The young man left while Lucas unfolded the message and read it.

I have some important new information about our friend Duval. I think it's something you should know. Meet me at The Boar's Head. I think you will find this information valuable and we might make a profit.

Captain Thomas

Every alert sense in his entire body registered the fact that this was most likely some kind of trap. He

127

knew Duval and Thomas were treacherous and he wondered if they had somehow conspired to kill him. He also wondered if he had slipped somehow and they knew who he was.

He mentally shrugged; it did no good to wonder. He must go and find out. He buckled on his scabbard and slid his sword out to test its condition. Satisfied, he slid it back into the scabbard. Then he slid a knife in the sash about his waist, took his hat and cloak from a small cupboard, and left the cabin.

He took the longboat and rowed, alone, through the steadily falling rain toward shore.

The night was often brightened by the flashes of lightning that lit up the sky with an eerie white light. Brian walked slowly, unaware that Ria was some distance behind him. He was watchful for any sign of ambush as he slowly drew closer and closer to the tavern.

Ria knew he was headed for The Boar's Head, so to keep from being discovered she let Brian disappear from sight. She moved cautiously, remembering well her last encounter with the characters that inhabited the waterfront streets at night.

Not far away, Lucas, too, slowly and carefully approached The Boar's Head, prepared to defend himself at any moment should the need arise . . . but when it did he was taken completely by surprise.

Brian, moving slowly, was semiprepared for attack, and it came. When two men leapt from the shadows, he drew his sword as they struck. He was shaken and hard put to defend himself against the expert assault of these two predators, and one of them found an opening in his defense at the same moment Lucas entered the alleyway. As the knife pierced a vulnerable spot, Brian's sword fell to the cobblestones and he clutched his side. Hot blood squirted from between his fingers, and he barely had time to utter a curse before blackness enclosed him.

The two men would have finished the job then, but Lucas's cry startled them and they ran. Lucas ran toward Brian just as he slumped forward, and he fell into Lucas's arms. Lucas could feel blood on his hands as he eased Brian to the ground. He bent over him, trying to see if the wound had been fatal, and was encouraged by the rapid beating of Brian's heart.

This was the scene that met Ria's eyes as she rounded the corner. A brilliant flash of light illuminated Lucas as he bent over Brian's inert form. Giving no thought to her own safety, she screamed Brian's name and ran toward them. She fell to her knees beside Brian and cradled his head close to her.

"Brian . . . oh God, Brian. Don't die . . . please," she sobbed. "Don't die."

"Ria," Lucas said. But he was stopped by the intense hatred that glowed in her eyes as she looked up at him.

"Murderer!" she cried. "You've killed him! Damn you, you've killed him!"

Lucas was struck to the core by the look in her eyes and by the knowledge that she really did love Brian.

He knelt beside her. "He's not dead, and we have to get him out of here before we're all killed. Come on. I'll help you get him to safety."

"Safety!" she shrieked. "You mean somewhere where you can finish the job."

Lucas knew she was very nearly hysterical and now was no time to try to convince her of his innocence. He had to get the three of them out of the alley before the men who had been sent to kill him as well as Thomas ran across them.

He reached down, grabbed Ria's wrist, and pulled her to her feet. She fought, but he grabbed her shoulders and shook her violently until she was gripping his shirt front and weeping in bitter anger.

"Ria, damn it, get yourself together. No matter what you think it will take both of us to get Brian where we can care for him. You've got to come with us; you're in danger too."

"Where . . . where can we take him?"

"My ship. It's the only safe place I know."

"No! No!" she cried.

"Ria, we have to. If we go back to the *Swan* whoever did this will know he's not dead. They'll come again."

Ria was torn, but Lucas was not about to wait until she thought the situation out. He knelt and lifted Brian in his arms.

"Come on," he ordered as he headed for his ship. He was relieved when, in a moment Ria followed.

Aboard the *Black Angel,* Lucas placed Brian on his bunk and began to examine the wound. As Ria knelt beside the wounded man, Lucas could see that tears streaked her face. The resulting pain tore something deep within Lucas, and he had to push it aside for the moment. He wanted Brian to live, for he did not want Ria longing for a memory. He would fight Brian's hold on her, take her from him any other way; but he knew if Brian died Ria would forever blame him.

He opened the door and called out for help, and soon the young cabin boy came running. Lucas snapped out orders, and several minutes later Brian was being cared for by Jemmy McGinnis, an ablebodied man about whom Lucas knew little except that he was excellent at treating wounds and could be trusted.

Lucas went to Ria whose wide eyes and stark face

told of her emotional attachment for the man who lay so quietly on the bunk. He had to get her out of the cabin before McGinnis started to work on Brian. If Brian died, he didn't want Ria there to see it.

"Ria," he said gently. Her eyes moved slowly from Brian, and he could feel the pain within her. "Come with me. You need something to drink."

"No . . . no," she murmured raggedly. "I'll stay with him." Her eyes returned to Brian as if they were willing him to live. Lucas could tell by her trembling body and her defenseless gaze that she was very near hysteria. Without another word he scooped her up into his arms and carried her to a much smaller cabin, Chris's quarters.

She twisted in his arms, but he held her with little effort. By the time he stood her on her feet, she was wild with anger. He kept himself between her and the door, and he was prepared for the bitter fury he saw in her eyes. Even that would help keep her mind from the plight of the man she so obviously loved.

"Let me out of here! Let me go to him. He needs me!"

"Have a glass of brandy and let them bind his wounds. Then you'll be free to go to him."

"I don't want your damned brandy! Why didn't you finish the job in the alley? Why didn't you kill us both so you would have no witnesses to your treachery?"

"Because no matter what you think at the moment I don't want to see either of you dead."

"Am I supposed to be stupid enough to believe that?"

"I can't help what you believe," he replied angrily. "Right now it's your safety I'm worried about." As he reached out and took hold of her wrist, she swung with her other hand, but it was caught in midair. The

131

force of her gesture brought her against his body. Both were angry, both were breathing heavily, and both, against their wills, felt that same magnetic current draw them together.

As he had said his main interest at the moment was her safety . . . not Brian's. Yet he couldn't see him die. He knew Ria would never know the truth if Brian died.

"Do you want to remain on my ship to look after your . . . lover's interests, or do you want to be taken ashore now . . . without him?" he said coldly.

"You wouldn't—"

"Yes, I would. Make your decision. Do you want to calm down and wait here with me, or do I throw you to the wolves now?"

"Damn you," she snarled. "You truly are a cold-hearted beast."

"Whatever you think I am, you have five minutes to make your choice."

She glared at him murderously, and he knew for certain if she held a knife at the moment she would happily bury it in his heart.

"Well?" he forced himself to say.

"I'll stay," she said frigidly.

"Good. Now you'll have that brandy."

"I don't want—"

"Ria," he declared, "at the moment I don't give a damn what you want. Drink the brandy or get off my ship and leave your lover's fate in my hands."

She stepped back from him, a cold murderous glow in her eyes, but whatever her mental state, he had never seen anyone quite as beautiful. Her cheeks were pink from the enforced control of her anger, and her lips trembled with the harsh words she wanted to say. He would have given anything he owned to have been able to take her in his arms and comfort her, to tell her the truth and hold her.

"I will drink your brandy, Luke, but if Brian dies I will find some way to kill you. That I swear." On the last words her voice died to a ragged whisper.

He did not doubt for one minute that she meant what she said. He walked to a small table where a bottle of brandy stood beside two glasses, poured her a liberal amount, and took it to her.

She took it from his hand, and for one swift moment their fingers touched. It was a small thing, but it sent through Lucas an unexpected quiver of excitement as brilliant as the jagged lightning that touched the night sky.

Her eyes held his defiantly as she took a small sip.

"Drink it down," he commanded. He could see she yearned to throw the glass at him. Her hand shook, but she refused to give him any reason to separate her from Brian.

She tipped the glass and gulped down the amber liquid. It was fiery, and she nearly choked as it burned her throat, then a spreading warmth flowed through her limbs. Lucas took the glass from her still-trembling hand. Going back to the table, he filled it, then went to her.

"This one you can sip slowly."

He could see a visible change in both her color and her posture. She was not used to the drink, and it had begun to affect her. That was the reason Lucas had forced her to drink it so quickly.

"Now, I'll take off that wet cloak, and then you can sit down."

He went to her and removed her heavy wet wrap. His fingers brushed her skin lightly as he did so, and his touch combined with the warming brandy played havoc with Ria's nerves. She moved away from him as quickly as she could.

133

It irritated Lucas to see the wary distrust in her eyes.

"Sit down, Ria. We should hear something soon one way or the other."

Her eyes widened as she blinked to hold back tears of fright. "He won't die . . . he can't die . . . he can't," she said in a little girl's whisper.

Lucas could no longer keep himself from going to her. He drew her into his arms and held her for one fleeting moment; then, with a sob, she pushed him away.

"Leave me alone," she raged bitterly. "Am I expected to fall into your arms while Brian might be bleeding his life away. Have you no heart or conscience at all!"

Lucas had no answer she would accept. He poured himself a rather large glass of the brandy and drank it swiftly; then he poured another. Brandy in hand, he turned back to Ria.

"I had nothing to do with it," he said.

"Don't lie. I saw the message you sent Brian. You are the reason he was where he was . . . and you are the reason he is where he is now."

"You're wrong, Ria. When he comes out of this, he will tell you so. What have I to gain by his death?"

"What does any pirate have in mind?" she cried. "Profit of course."

"Damn it! Be sensible. This means a loss of profit for me. Besides," he retorted, "I received the same note . . . from Brian . . . to meet him at The Boar's Head. Maybe he intended to get rid of me."

"That's a lie. Brian would never . . . He wouldn't commit murder."

"You're so sure? He has as much to gain from doing so as I do, and he is a pirate too, with profit on his mind."

"I don't believe you. Where is the note?"

After Lucas had read the note, he had crumpled it in his hand. But he had been so absorbed in thought that he could not remember what he had done with it.

"Right now I don't know," he began, "but—"

"Of course." Ria sneered. "The note has just conveniently disappeared."

"There was a note."

"Of course," she replied in a cold disbelieving voice.

Lucas shrugged. There was no way to convince her until he found the note.

They were silent for several minutes. Lucas knew Ria's mind was in his cabin with Brian, but despite the fact that he wanted Brian to live as badly as she did, he was unable to cope with the idea that she loved him so deeply.

He watched her hands clench and he read the deep worry in her eyes.

"He'll live, Ria," he said gently. "He's young and strong, and the wound didn't look fatal to me. He's in good hands with Jemmy. Why don't you try to rest a little?"

Ria wanted desperately to believe this. She was torn between her need for comfort and her belief that Luke was responsible.

"I don't understand you," she said. "You are like a shadow. Always changing shape. I cannot afford to believe you anymore. Doing so almost cost Brian's life. The note was from you, I read it."

Lucas moved close to her, and she stiffened but refused to back away.

"I didn't send it," he repeated.

"The word of a pirate is hardly to be believed."

This time Lucas struck back. "And what are you and your . . ." He shrugged. "He is of the same

135

brotherhood." Lucas momentarily lost his control. "Tell me, Ria, have you told him that you have been with me? Have you told him you are no longer the sweet little virgin he enticed aboard his ship. Has he shared your nights now, Ria. Has he?" Lucas gripped her shoulders and shook her as he spoke.

"No! I have not told him, and he has not touched me. He never will."

Lucas was surprised at the relief that flooded through him. Again, it took a concerted effort not to hold her gently and lovingly.

"He is a man like any other," Lucas snapped. "One day he will sell you to the highest bidder. His heart is as black as that of any man who sails under the black flag. Why do you trust so completely a man who admits to what he is while you call me black? Tell me, Ria, how do I carry more guilt than he?"

She wanted to scream the truth at him, to shout the fatal words that Brian was no pirate, but an honorable man. She wanted to cry out that he was her brother and that she loved him. But she couldn't. Brian was too helpless, too vulnerable now. He was at the mercy of the man she faced. Ria could not betray him when doing so could cost him his life.

She started to speak, but the door swung open and Jemmy stood framed in the doorway. Ria and Lucas were silent as they gazed at Jemmy's expressionless face.

"Jemmy?" Lucas questioned quietly.

"He's lost a lot of blood, but we've patched him up pretty good. If you want my opinion, Cap'n, I'd say he stands a good chance of makin' it."

Ria's knees suddenly weakened and she sagged forward, clutching Lucas in relief. Lucas held her close, savoring this one short moment of pleasure.

"Is he awake, Jemmy?"

"No, sir. I'd be safe in sayin' the lad won't be wakin' up for a long time. I'm hopin' fever doesn't set in. If it don't I'd say he'll come around in a couple of days."

"Thanks, Jemmy. Go back and keep a close watch over him. I want him watched day and night. As soon as he wakes up, I want to know."

"Yes, sir," Jemmy replied. He stepped back and drew the door closed.

Ria regained her composure though her face was still pale from shock and tension, and Lucas reluctantly let go of her as she moved away from him.

She turned to face him again.

"Ria," Lucas said gently, "you haven't answered my question. If we want to talk about truth, suppose we start with you and your . . . benefactor."

"I don't have to explain anything to you," she retorted. "I owe you nothing. Brian's past life and mine are none of your business."

Lucas crossed the room and stood close enough to touch her. But he didn't. Instead his words were like a sharp-bladed knife, and she felt real and terrible fear when she heard them.

"We will see, Ria. We will see if the secret of your beloved pirate, and of you, cannot be solved. He will be cared for carefully until he is well, and you will remain here, with me. We will have a great deal of time to talk . . . of puzzles to be solved."

Chapter 10

"I can't stay here with—"

"With me? Why not? I thought you would be afraid to leave him. What if someone decides to finish the job while he's helpless?"

Ria was immediately certain he'd been suggesting he had the power to do.

"I must go back to the *Swan*," she protested. Yet she knew her resistance was feeble.

"You will stay here," Lucas said firmly. "Don't you realize whoever did this might be waiting for you to come back so they can do the same to you."

He could see her resistance growing, and he knew there was only one way to put a stop to any thoughts she had of going back to Brian's ship.

He shrugged nonchalantly. "All right, if you insist. I'll have one of my men get him out of bed."

Ria's eyes widened in total disbelief. "You . . . you aren't inhumane enough to do that! It would kill him!"

"That is your responsibility. You are the one who has insisted on leaving."

"But he can't move."

"We could move him I suppose," Lucas said with a

coolness that camouflaged his worry that she might not fall for his ploy and would really decide to leave.

"He needs care," Ria cried.

"Well, if he survives the trip back to your ship you can give him all the care he needs."

"Oh, I hate you, you arrogant animal!"

"Now, Ria," he said with aggravating calmness, "that is no way to talk to the man who saved your . . . friend's life."

"And now you would let him die!"

"Not me—you."

"I don't believe you would do that," she said, trying to sound confident.

"No?" he asked softly. "Ria, if you do not stay here, in this cabin, as long as it takes to nurse him back to health, I shall order him tied up like a beached whale and have him dumped into your lap dead or alive. It will not take the wolves long to know he is out of commission . . . and you may be seized."

Ria's face had grown whiter and whiter as his words had washed over her. When he finished they stood for a moment in a silence filled with soundless battle. Then she seemed to shudder and regain her composure.

"I will stay. But I will stay in Brian's cabin and care for him."

Lucas was so relieved that for a moment he was speechless. He was about to tell her he would do all he could to help her when she spoke again.

"But you stay away from me. Don't come near that cabin, or no matter what happens I will leave. I want no more help from you, nor do I want to look at you again until Brian is well enough to leave. We will leave together and after that I hope never to see you again as long as I live."

Her breast heaved in passionate fury, and again he

was struck by her exceptional beauty, for even as she was breathing fire he could not control the urge to touch her.

Lucas moved to her side so quickly, Ria had little chance to move. He caught her up in his arms, in a binding grip that left her breathless.

Her arms were pinned between them and his eyes, burning with deep flames of anger and controlled passion, caused her to gasp with a new fear. His voice was deceptively soft.

"Let me make one thing very clear to you, my sweet," he said gently. "This is my ship. I am captain here, and it is only by my kind heart that I allow your wounded friend to stay. You will stay; you will care for him if you choose. But you don't have the power to order me from my own cabin. I will come and go as I choose. If I wanted you in my bed, do you think I could not take you? If I wanted to resort to force, do you think you could stop me? Let me prove something to you, Ria—a little beneficial lesson you should remember."

She turned her head to keep his lips from hers, but he held her with one arm and gripped her hair with the other to hold her head immobile.

Her eyes grew wide and she whispered "no" softly as his mouth parted and twisted to slant against hers. His tongue forced her softer lips apart and thrust into the moist sweetness within.

Her world suddenly seemed to skitter to an abrupt stop as his mouth, insistent and relentless, snatched her breath and all thought away.

She struggled to regain some form of control over wayward senses that paid no attention to her struggle.

Finally, his mouth released hers only to seek the soft column of her throat. He brushed heated kisses

141

down it, then down to the soft curve of her breasts.

Her lips were dry, and her body trembled as, against her will, it arched to mold more boldly against his. Her hands were free now, but she could not seem to control their flight upward to draw him closer to her.

She felt every nerve scream at the shattering emotions he was drawing from her. Suddenly realizing how he was commanding her senses, she struggled weakly against the hot raw pleasure that possessed her. The touch of his lips on hers again became sweeter . . . gentler . . . softer.

Then, as swiftly as he had taken her, he let her go and she stumbled backward a step or two.

A new fear began to build deep within her. Not a fear of him, but a fear of herself—of the wild and untamable passion he could unleash in her.

"Go to him," Lucas grated through clenched teeth. "But remember well what I said. There are many men, Ria. No two alike. Don't be so free to judge unless you know. And don't be so sure your own emotions are lying to you."

He left her trembling in the center of the room. It took her some time to regain her composure.

Finally Ria brushed away the tears on her cheeks and determinedly left the room and returned to Luke's cabin, where she found him bending over Brian, examining the bandages. He stood up, satisfaction on his face.

"His heart is beating soundly. In time I expect he'll be fine. Jemmy's a good doctor."

"Luke . . . I . . ."

He turned to look at her again. This time he smiled. Her face was filled with uncertainty.

"It's all right, Ria. Believe me, he's fine."

Lucas walked to the door. When he turned, his

smile died. Ria had knelt beside Brian and was holding one of his hands gently while she caressed his brow. Her gaze was loving and warm, as he wanted it to be when she looked at him.

The talons of the green monster of jealousy bit deeply. Something twisted sharply and painfully within him. He wanted to go to her, lift her in his arms gently, tell her how alive she made him feel. Tell her . . . He turned away and left the cabin, closing the door softly behind him.

For two days Brian remained unconscious and Ria refused to leave his side. She cared for him quietly but effectively. Lucas came and went, trying not to disturb them. Each time he came, Ria seemed quieter and more tired. And every time he left the room, he left part of himself with her until at last he couldn't separate his thoughts from her.

Very late on the second night after Brian had been struck down, Lucas entered his cabin. He looked at the scene before him. Brian lay still, and Ria sat on the floor, one of his hands in hers, her head resting against the bunk. She was asleep, driven to it by exhaustion. He had prepared for this. He went to her side and squatted down beside her.

Her hair fell in a tangled mass about her, and he reached to lift a thick strand of it to feel the texture between his fingers. When he bent and lifted her in his arms, she stirred awake. Her eyes came open and for a moment she was disoriented. Then her body stiffened in his arms and wariness leapt into her eyes. Before she could protest he spoke.

"Don't be afraid, Ria. I'm not going to touch you. You're exhausted. You need some rest."

"But Brian . . ."

"Is resting and healing. You must do the same."

"Where are you taking me?"

"Shhh. Just relax." He smiled.

He pushed open the door of Chris's cabin. In the center of the floor sat a wooden tub of steaming water.

"Ohhh." She sighed as Lucas stood her beside it.

"Into the tub. There's one of my shirts on the bunk. Bathe and then get into it and climb into that bunk and get some sleep."

Ria started to protest again, but the hot water was too inviting and her whole body was exhausted. Lucas answered her protest before she could put it into words.

"I'll keep an eye on him for you," he said quietly. In a few minutes he was gone.

Quickly Ria undressed and slid, with a deep sigh of contentment, into the bath. She did not leave the tub until the water was cooling. She toweled herself dry and then slipped into Lucas's shirt. She was asleep almost as soon as her head touched the pillow.

Lucas had gone back to his own cabin, where he stood and looked down at Brian.

How easy it would be, he thought, to eliminate this barrier. As soon as the thought formed, he angrily pushed it aside. Ria loved Brian, and the only way to get her would be to change what she felt.

"Watch out, my friend," he said softly. "When you get up from that bed, you are going to have one hell of a fight on your hands. Ria belongs to me . . . and I'm going to take her."

Lucas left the cabin and walked on deck for a while. Then he returned to Chris's cabin to see if Ria was comfortable.

He opened the cabin door quietly. The tub was empty, so he looked across the room. Pale moonlight bathed her in its light. She had kicked away the covers, and the shirt had tangled about her, revealing more than it concealed.

He didn't plan to stay, but he was drawn across the room to her.

Ria dreamt. Due to her exhaustion and worry, her dream was of Brian. She stirred and mumbled softly.

"Brian . . . Brian . . . don't die."

Her words left a bitter taste in Lucas's mouth, but his resolve was iron firm. One day Ria would forget she ever loved Brian. He turned and slowly left the room.

Firm gentle hands kneaded the tension from her as they slowly worked over the taut muscles of her back. Ria murmured in pleasure, and began to drift up from sleep.

She lay on her stomach and was so completely relaxed that she didn't immediately understand what was happening. The hands seemed to ease her tight muscles and send a tingle of warmth through her. They were thorough and moved down the muscles of her back expertly to her waist, then up to curve over her shoulders. She sighed in utter contentment and began to drift into lethargic comfort when she suddenly realized to whom the hands belonged. Her eyes snapped open, and she twisted her head about to see Luke sitting on the side of the bunk.

She gave a groan of half-anger, but half-dismay for she didn't want to admit that she didn't want him to stop.

Lucas grinned and sat back as she turned to glare up at him.

"Good morning. Sleep well?" he questioned innocently.

Ria then became aware that she was as close to naked as she could be. She quickly pulled the blanket over her and was annoyed by his soft chuckle of amusement.

"How long have you been here?" she demanded.

"All night," he answered casually.

"All night . . . here!"

He knew she meant the bunk, and he again laughed. "No. I slept over there." He pointed to a long benchlike affair beneath the porthole. A pile of tangled blankets attested to the truth of his words.

She looked at his makeshift bed and realized that for his large frame it must have been very uncomfortable. She felt guilty.

"I'm sorry . . . I'll . . . I'll sleep there tonight and you can have your bed back."

"No. You stay where you are." He grinned evilly. "Of course, if you'd like to share the bed, I'd be very grateful."

"You may have your bed to yourself, Captain," she responded quickly. "I wouldn't want to put you out."

"I certainly wouldn't consider it a problem." He chuckled. "You can share my bed anytime you choose."

He saw the flame of anger leap into her eyes at his teasing, so he rose and walked to a small table on which a covered tray rested. Ria became aware then of the scent of food, and discovered she was extremely hungry.

Lucas uncovered the tray. "Come and share breakfast with me, my lady," he said. "I imagine you must be hungry."

"I'm starved," she admitted.

146

"Well, come and eat," he said pleasantly.

Ria rose from the bed. Her slender body seemed lost in his shirt, but she drew his undivided attention.

Her hair fell about her in wild abandon, and her eyes were still heavy with sleep. She looked warm and flushed and very inviting. He had to crush the desire that stirred in him. He wanted to carry her back to the bed and spend the day making love to her, slowly and perfectly.

He had awakened very early and had gone to the bunk to sit by Ria as she slept. He hadn't been able to resist touching her, and as she had lain on her stomach, he had reached out to run his hands gently up her back. She had sighed deeply as if his touch pleased her, so he had continued to massage her, letting his hands roam a little more each time. He had taken as much pleasure in the massage as she had, and he'd desired nothing more than to extend the touch until her body responded to him. It was only when she fully awakened that he had reluctantly ceased. But his desire was now alive and vibrant.

Ria felt his eyes rake heatedly over her, and was annoyed by the swift touch of illicit excitement that coursed through her. She had never felt so vulnerable. She sat down at the table opposite him, and without asking, he took her plate and began to fill it.

"That's too much," she protested.

"You need to eat. I know you haven't had a bite since breakfast yesterday, and then you didn't eat much. I don't want to have to be nursing you."

"Don't worry about me." She laughed. "I've always been healthy."

"Eat anyhow, just to make me happy."

Lucas began to enjoy himself. He felt as though they were lovers or maybe just married and spending the days learning about each other. He wished fervently that they were on the high seas together . . . and that she truly did belong to him. Sailing the ocean with a wife like her would be . . . The thought brought the truth home to him with a jolt. He was already married and could promise her nothing, and if her words were true, she had run away because she'd been forced into marriage too. Their situation was disastrous, yet one fact held true. He wanted Ria . . . at any cost. And he meant to have her.

Ria seemed to relax as they ate, then began to talk and to laugh together. These were magical moments that ended too soon.

The rap on the door made Lucas want to curse, but he rose and opened it.

"The captain of the *Sea Rover* is on deck," said the seaman with obvious distaste. "He says he wants to talk with you . . . it's important."

The young sailor's eyes could not help seeking out Ria. He was awed by a beauty such as he had never seen before. Lucas's stern eyes and dark scowl, however, quickly drew his attention back to the master of the ship.

"Tell Captain Duval I'll be on deck in a few minutes."

"Aye, sir." The crewman stole one last look at Ria then left.

Lucas's mind was moving swiftly. He was more than certain, despite what Ria might think, that Henri was responsible for Brian's condition, so he did not want him to know that Brian was still alive. He turned to Ria.

"Ria, you must get dressed quickly."

"I don't want to see that man again. I'll just go stay with Brian."

"You can't."

"Why?"

"Because we have to convince Duval that Brian is

148

dead. The best way to do that would be for you to let him think—''

''That I now belong to you,'' she put in, her voice stiff with distrust.

''It's only temporary,'' he explained. ''I don't want him to know Brian is still alive.''

''Why?''

''Because I'm certain he's responsible for the attack on Brian, and if he thinks he has succeeded, he just might become careless.''

''What could he have to gain from disposing of Brian?''

''Your ship,'' Lucas said firmly, ''and you.''

''Me!''

''Ria,'' he said patiently, ''I'll wager my life Henri Duval wants to take over the *Swan*.'' She looked at him questioningly. ''If he does . . . then he expects to have you along with it.''

''I would kill myself before I would let that beast touch me,'' she said angrily.

''Then dress and come on deck, because he won't hesitate to come below. If he does there might just be a battle none of us is prepared for now.''

''I'll dress.''

''Good,'' he said. He walked to the door, then turned to look at her. ''Don't be afraid. You can be certain of one thing. I will kill him where he stands before I let him touch you.'' He left before Ria could answer.

She looked at the closed door for a long time, realizing that she couldn't quite believe that she felt relieved or that she trusted in his last words.

Ria dressed quickly, and after she had looked in on Brian she went up on the deck of the *Angel*.

Henri stood at the rail and watched Lucas appear

and approach him.

"*Bon jour, Capitaine.*" He smiled as if the day were like any other and they were the best of friends.

"Good morning." Lucas's smile matched Henri's, as did his cold unrelenting gaze. "What brings you aboard so early?"

"Business, *mon ami*, business. I have just gotten word of two fat merchant ships leaving London for the Carolina coast. If we time it well, I can take one and you can take the other." Duval smiled again. "It should be a rich conquest."

"We should both do well," Lucas agreed. "But where do we go with the ships once we have them?"

"We could, or we should, sink them on the spot."

"That is not very original thinking."

"But the better way, *mon ami, non?* It leaves no . . . uncomfortable evidence."

"I don't like the idea of putting a good ship on the bottom," Lucas said. Much less killing the people aboard her, he wanted to add. "If we were smart we would put a prize crew on her, sail her to a more comfortable port and sell her. There's a double profit to be had."

"You are a very clever man," Henri declared as he eyed Lucas shrewdly. "I think you and I will make good partners, *non?*"

"Speaking of partners," Lucas said nonchalantly, "have you heard of the . . . problem with our other partner?"

"Problem . . . Ah, yes. There have been rumors that he has . . . ah . . . disappeared."

"He's dead," Lucas said bluntly. "He was stabbed in an alley."

"Dead," Henri repeated. "As I said before our occupation is quite dangerous. It is a lesson to be learned . . . to be very careful. It would be quite easy to end up like your compatriot."

Lucas remained silent, but the urge to throttle Henri and toss him overboard was hard to suppress.

"Too bad." Henri shrugged. "But even though the young *capitaine* has met with an . . . ah . . . accident, there is still his ship. When I heard the sad news, I took it upon myself to put a crew of my own men aboard her. For all purposes"—his eyes were hard—"the *Swan* now belongs to me."

"I see."

"You disagree?"

"No. The *Swan* is yours."

"Now I must ask you"—Henri's voice became velvety soft and dangerous—"where is the lady from the *Swan?*"

"The lady from the *Swan?*" Lucas replied innocently. "Why, Henri"—he smiled—"to the victor go the spoils. I'm afraid the ship may be yours . . . but the lady is mine."

Henri was enraged, but his expression did not betray the fact. Lucas, he was sure, would soon be taken care of.

"So the lady came to you?"

"No. Like you, Henri"—Lucas chuckled—"I believe in taking what I want."

Henri's fury was a force Lucas could almost taste. At that moment Ria appeared. Lucas had to admire the way she controlled her aversion to Henri. She played her part very well as she came to Lucas's side and tucked her arm in his and smiled radiantly up at him.

"Good morning," she said seductively; then she turned her wide gaze on Henri. If Lucas was devastated by the warmth of it Duval was intoxicated.

"Henri, how nice to see you again," she declared smoothly.

151

"And you are as beautiful as I remembered, *chérie.*" Henri smiled, but with effort. "It is sad to hear of the . . . sudden demise of your friend."

"Yes," Ria murmured. Lucas could feel her grip on his arm tighten. "A tragedy. He was waylaid by . . . by vermin. I hope whoever is responsible rots in hell," she added in a soft voice.

"I shouldn't worry too much about that, Ria," Lucas said softly as his eyes turned to Henri. "I have a feeling he will. One day justice will find him."

Henri, whose hatred of Lucas was second only to his desire for Ria, found it expedient to change the subject.

He was already planning the fates of the elusive Captain Blanc and his beautiful new mistress.

Chapter 11

"It would not take too much time to mark your maps," Henri said. "If you will allow me to accompany you to your cabin, we will discuss our next move."

Lucas most certainly did not want Henri in his cabin, and he could feel the quiver of alarm in Ria. Though her face was well masked, he knew she feared Henri and him. Yet he was half-certain he was the lesser of two evils in Ria's mind.

"Ria," he said, exerting firm pressure on her arm. "Go down to my cabin and get my map. It's unfolded on the center of my desk."

Lucas had no intention of leaving Ria alone with Henri. The man might try to intimidate her or question her forcefully, and he didn't know how well Ria could keep the secret that Brian still lived. If angered, she might slip and fling it in Henri's face.

He was pretty certain that though Ria didn't trust him, she trusted Henri even less. He also sensed, from Ria's tenseness, that she was frightened of Henri, even though, he thought with amusement, she would most certainly be the last to admit it.

Ria welcomed the chance to get away from Henri,

and she was aware that this was a means to keep him from finding Brian. She could feel the eyes of both men follow her as she moved toward the companionway.

"So," Henri said softly, "our pretty bird has lost her nest."

"Only temporarily." Lucas grinned.

"Why did she run to you? Why did she not stay aboard her lover's ship?"

"A ship that now belongs to you, Henri old friend." Lucas laughed. "Maybe the lady likes to make her own choices."

"And she chose to run to you." Henri chuckled. "I wonder if there is not more to it than that?"

"The lady simply cannot fight my irresistible charm," Lucas said with malicious humor.

"Very amusing. I would think you would be more careful than that."

"Why, Henri," Lucas responded quietly, "is that a threat?"

"*Non! Non!*" Henri smiled coldly. "Would I threaten a friend with whom I am about to enter into a business arrangement. I only . . . advise a friend not to make a costly mistake."

"A mistake?"

"*Oui.* This is a dangerous profession we are in. One can lose one's life so easily . . . especially if one interferes with people more powerful and more easily upset by the interference."

"Oh, I promise you, Henri, I shall walk very carefully. I shall protect my back, and I shall most certainly not trust . . . anyone. But," Lucas concluded firmly, "I would like to be able to warn such powerful people that no one takes from me what I want. I am quite willing, and quite capable, of defending what is mine—and Ria is mine."

Henri's eyes narrowed as he tried to decide whether Lucas was bluffing or not. Lucas's eyes held his, coldly and without a flicker of movement. After a few minutes, Henri smiled again.

"We will make good partners, you and I. We both know what we want, and are not afraid to reach out and take it . . . no matter what the opposition."

Lucas knew the gauntlet had been thrown down. Henri was still a forceful threat. The pirate wanted Ria and he intended to have her. He decided that he must be prepared for any kind of treachery in the future.

Ria entered Lucas's cabin, her mind half on her mission and half on the confrontation taking place on deck. She had been frightened of very few people in her life, but Henri Duval was one of them. It was beyond her understanding, however, that though she didn't trust Lucas, knew him for what he was, she was not afraid of him.

She went to Lucas's desk and found the map beneath some scattered papers. She began to fold it, still a little reluctant to rejoin the two captains on deck.

She was so caught up in her confused thoughts about Henri and Lucas that when Brian spoke it startled her.

"Ria." His voice was hoarse and ragged, but he was lucid. Her eyes flew to him, and her relief was so violent it brought tears to her eyes. She ran to the bunk and knelt beside it.

"Oh, Brian, Brian, you're all right," she whispered through her happy tears.

"God," he croaked, "I feel like hell. I'm so thirsty."

Ria ran immediately to the table where Lucas

155

always kept the brandy decanter. She quickly poured some out, slopping it over the side of the glass in her haste; then she ran back to Brian and lifted his head to help him drink.

Brian took a deep gulp, gasped, and choked as the hot brandy flowed through him.

"Ria, are you trying to finish the job?" He laughed, but he caught her trembling hand and held it while he took a mere sip.

Then he laid his head back on the pillow as if he were totally exhausted. But his eyes, which had regained their alert look, took in Ria's tear-stained face.

"Are you all right?" he asked.

"I'm fine now that I know you are going to recover."

Brian looked about him, aware for the first time that he was most certainly not in his own cabin. In another moment, the assault began to come back to him.

"Where am I, Ria? How did you get me here?"

"You're in Luke's cabin on the *Black Angel*."

"Luke?"

"Oh . . . Captain Blanc."

"How did I get here?"

"Don't you remember what happened?"

"Bits and pieces of it. I was on my way to The Boar's Head to meet Captain Blanc when I got ambushed."

"Did you see who it was, Brian?"

"Two scurvy thugs. Dock rats I'd say. Anyway I made a mistake and one got to me. How did you find me?"

Ria went on to explain that she had followed him, and she described what she had found when she had entered the alley.

"Well, I don't know if he was behind it, but I sure know he wasn't one of them. I'll never forget those two."

Ria told Brian that Lucas had carried him back to the *Angel* and had had him cared for.

"Why would a man want to see me dead, then help nurse me back to health? Ria"—he took one of her hands in his—"if he really wanted us out of the way he could have taken care of both of us in that alley. You certainly couldn't have stopped him. I have a feeling there's much more to this Captain Blanc than meets the eye."

"Brian, Henri Duval has taken over the *Swan*. He believes you are dead."

"There's nothing I can do to stop him right now," Brian said grimly, "but when I can get up from this bed, we'll see who the *Swan* belongs to."

Ria informed Brian that Lucas and Henri were on deck at that moment discussing future plans.

"And Captain Blanc has not told him I am alive and in his cabin?"

"No. In fact he is making sure Henri knows nothing about it."

"Again he's protecting me," Brian declared, in disbelief. "I don't understand this at all. If he's what we think he is, it would be to his advantage to let Henri have me. One competitor out of the way."

"We have to play along until you get your strength back. I'll take this map up. Henri is about to tell Luke where they are going to take these two prizes."

"Good. Get a look at the maps once they're marked. I'd like to know just where they're taking the merchants."

"I'll try," Ria replied as she rose to her feet.

"Ria?"

"What?"

"You be careful with both of them."

"I will."

She left, and Brian gazed at the closed door for a long time, wondering if there were things Ria hadn't told him. He sensed it, yet Ria had never been dishonest with him before. She had made a promise, and he chose to believe her.

Ria returned with the map and handed it to Lucas who, in turn, handed it to Henri. Henri unfolded the map and braced it against the rail. With a finger he traced the courses the ships would take, stopping where they would cross the paths of the merchant ships.

"It should be easy. They will be heavy with cargo and nearly defenseless."

Lucas nodded. He had watched the map intently and was unaware that Ria, who stood near his shoulder, had watched just as intently.

"Now all we have to be told is where we dispose of the cargo and with whom," Lucas stated.

"I am afraid not," Henri said matter-of-factly.

"I don't understand."

"You will meet me here." He pointed to another location on the map. "I will be the judge of your abilities. I will decide where we go from there."

"Why, Henri"—Lucas chuckled—"it sounds as though you don't trust me."

"Trust is something I lost at my mother's knee. When profit is to be made, one cannot trust too far or one will lose too much, sometimes more than he can afford . . . including his life."

"You're right," Lucas replied. "I'll remember

that and not spread my trust too far."

"We leave in two days. Since we are in port until then, I invite you and Ria to dinner in my cabin tomorrow night. It will be a celebration of what I hope will be a very profitable relationship."

"Dinner tomorrow on your ship." Lucas was not enthused about putting Ria or himself in such a vulnerable situation. He smiled. "I'm afraid," he said suggestively, "that Ria and I have a private celebration already planned. We really haven't had much time alone. We could meet you at the tavern the following evening, however, and share a drink or two." Lucas drew Ria against him, and despite the fact that she shook with what he knew was slowly growing anger, he bent his head to kiss her lightly.

Henri's eyes sparked with desire for Ria and virulent hatred for Lucas. "Ah well," he replied, "too bad. But . . . maybe soon"—he smiled as he took Ria's hand and kissed it—"we will have more time to spend together."

"Maybe," Lucas said as again he drew Ria close to him.

They stood together and watched Henri leave the ship. Then Ria moved quickly from Lucas's embrace, causing him to raise a questioning brow.

"Would you really like to step into the spider's web?"

"Hardly."

"I thought not." Lucas chuckled. "I doubt very much if either of us would survive his hospitality, although my fate would come more quickly than yours."

Ria quivered at the thought. But at least one occurrence had given her new confidence.

"Brian is awake," she stated quickly, watching

Lucas's reaction closely.

"What has he said? Does he know who attacked him?"

"No. He doesn't know who they were."

"They?"

"There were two of them."

"Well," Lucas said quietly, "at least he made it clear that it was not me."

"He doesn't even remember seeing you there," Ria admitted.

Lucas knew she still harbored sincere doubts that he had not ordered the killing done and then come at the last moment to make sure the attempt had succeeded.

"Shall we go below and explain to him what we are involved in?"

She nodded, and he motioned her to precede him as they made their way to his cabin.

Brian heard the approaching footsteps. He knew the lighter ones were Ria's, and he was fairly certain the others were Blanc's. He had never felt quite so insecure and vulnerable in his entire life. Questions for which he had no answers filled his mind. Why had Captain Blanc saved him? Why was he now hiding him on his ship and why was he protecting him and Ria? What was the man's purpose? He hated to think of the answer to that question.

Ria opened the door, and Lucas followed her into the room to stand by Brian's bed.

"So you've finally decided to wake up."

"Just how long have I been like this?"

"A couple of days."

"I've got to get back to my ship," Brian said, as

160

he tried to struggle to a sitting position. Lucas sat down beside him, and with little effort pushed him back against the pillow.

"You have all the strength of a two-day-old puppy. Besides, Henri has taken over your ship. He is quite sure you are dead. Temporarily it's best we let him continue to believe that."

"Why?" Brian demanded. "Take me back to my own ship."

"And you'll defend yourself?" Lucas's voice became hard. "And Ria? Will you defend her too?" he said as he rose and walked across the room.

Brian didn't answer. Ria knew his misery was due to the loss of his ship and to Lucas's statement that he was helpless. She went to her brother and sat beside him.

"Don't, Brian," she said softly. "You're alive, and you'll be well soon. Then we'll take our ship back. We'll be all right."

Lucas watched them, and at that moment he hated Brian so deeply it shocked him. He found himself struggling against the thought that if he had been smart and let this man die, his rival would be out of the way.

As he watched Ria's solicitous attention, feelings grew within him, feelings he had never experienced before. The combined monsters of lust and jealousy nearly overpowered him.

It was good that Brian and Ria were concentrating on each other, for if they had looked into Lucas's eyes at that moment, they would have been shaken. When Ria had calmed Brian, she turned to speak to Lucas. She and Brian were both surprised to find him gone.

Ria returned her attention to Brian, but a voice deep within her sent a ripple of warning. Dismissing it, she concentrated on her brother.

"Ria, where have you been sleeping?" Brian asked.

"His second mate Chris is off the ship, so I'm using his cabin. Don't worry about me." She smiled. "I'm fine, really."

"When I get out of this bed, we're going home. Pirates or no, this is too dangerous. It may have seemed like fun at the start, but—"

"No, Brian. We can't. We're all right, and you'll be better soon. We won't make the same mistake twice."

"I am worried about you."

"Don't be. I'm going to get you some food. Eat and rest, and in a few days you'll have recovered."

"At least you can move back in here." He chuckled. "I need care day and night."

"Of course you do," she replied tartly. "You were always the spoiled one."

"Nasty wench."

"You're getting better," Ria chided. "I'll go and get your food."

She made her way to the galley, where she convinced the cook to make something for Brian. Then she carried the tray back to him and sat beside him while he ate.

Trying to be cheerful for Brian's sake, she teased him and coaxed him into eating all the food she had brought. Deep within, however, something alarming was beginning to make itself felt, and she began to wonder just where Lucas had gone so quickly—and why. Had he left the ship to share another rendezvous with Henri? Was he making plans she didn't know about?

When Ria had changed Brian's bandages and

had made him comfortable, he drifted again into sleep. Then Ria quietly left the cabin.

Hesitantly she went to Chris's quarters, but she found that cabin empty. On deck, no one seemed to know where Luke was until she finally spoke to an old man.

"The cap'n, ma'am?" The old sailor scratched his head. "Well, Mr. Chris came aboard for a spell, and the cap'n said they was goin' ashore for a bit, but that he'd be back soon."

"Would you ready a small boat for me? I'd like to go and find him."

"I'm sorry, miss, but I can't."

"Why not?"

"Cap'n's orders, miss. You ain't to leave the ship."

"What?"

"Cap'n says we ain't to let you leave 'til he gets back."

"He can't keep me here if I choose to go!"

"Sorry, miss. We follow the cap'n's orders. If he says we's to keep you here, then I expects we'll keep you here."

"I want a boat—this minute!"

"No, miss. I can't do that," the old seaman replied miserably. He was finding it quite difficult to follow his captain's orders in the face of the anger that sparked in the eyes of this pretty young lady.

Ria spun away from him and then asked one man after another to ready a boat. It was soon obvious that she could not leave the ship without Luke's permission. She didn't want to awaken Brian, so she returned to Chris's cabin where she sat on the edge of the bunk and wondered just what Luke's next move would be.

Lucas had left his cabin because he could not stand to see Ria and Brian together. Now vivid memories of the night he had shared with her only made his bitterness and jealousy worse. He was glad to see Chris come aboard.

"Where have you been the past two days?" he asked.

"Busy on your behalf," Chris replied. "I've run across a couple of men who may have a lot of answers we want. Anyway, I came to tell you I'm going to be gone for three or four days. I"—he grinned—"think I'm about to get a chance to meet the famous Dan McGirtt."

"How did you manage that?"

"Fell into a rather sordid group the other night." Chris chuckled. "We drank each other under the table, and one of them, while he was in his cups, talked a lot about a friend of his—old Dan. That man seems to be able to provide a lot of money to a lot of people."

"Sounds like our man."

"Now I have to find a way to meet him, so I've decided to join forces with my drinking companions. I told them we had a fight and you threw me off the ship. I think they feel a little sorry for me."

"Chris, I leave here in two days." Lucas explained his arrangement with Henri. "I'll be gone at least two weeks."

"That will give me enough time to find out all I need to know, but how are you going to take that ship? Seizing it might cost lives."

"I've still got to figure that out." Lucas shrugged.

"It's not going to be simple."

"What is?" Lucas replied.

"Lucas," Chris said gently, "we could always forget about all this, and just go home."

Lucas remained silent for a while as if he were seriously contemplating Chris's words.

"Of course," Chris added, "if we don't come home with our pirate, you go back to a marriage you don't want and a very angry father."

Lucas joined Chris in laughter over his friend's vision of the future, but thinking of the marriage in which he was entangled brought a vision of Ria.

"Well, I'm going back to my doubtful friends," Chris declared. "You said you'd be gone about two weeks?"

"About."

"Then I'll meet you here at the end of that time, and we may be able to put an end to all of this."

"Good luck . . . and Chris?"

"What?"

"Don't get caught," Lucas said softly.

"I won't. You be careful too." Chris turned away and left the ship.

Lucas thought of all the twists and turns his life had taken lately. He had to drive Ria from his mind, so he decided to have a drink or two before he again faced her and Brian. Leaving orders for her protection, he went to the closest tavern where he sat at a shadowed corner table and ordered a drink.

The sun was a red rim on the horizon, and dark

165

shadows were filling the corners of the cabin Ria paced in worried silence. She rose and lit the lamp that hung from the heavy beams above her. Its glow filled the room with pale yellow light. She sighed as she resumed her slow pacing of the small cabin.

Brian was asleep. After sharing a late supper with him, Ria had decided to return to Chris's quarters so that Brian's rest wouldn't be disturbed. She had eaten a very small amount of supper and had drunk a glass or two of the wine provided. Now she was supposed to sleep . . . but she couldn't.

Knowing now that Henri must have been responsible for Brian's near brush with death, Ria was fighting the visions of Luke lying in an alley bleeding his life away. As a result her nerves were taut, and she could have wept in frustration.

When the door handle turned, she gazed at it in surprise. Then it swung open, and Lucas stood framed in the doorway.

"Luke," she breathed out in relief. But her smile faded as he stepped inside, closed the door, and slid the lock in place to prevent any intrusion.

Chapter 12

They looked at each other across a cabin that seemed as wide as the ocean. Ria could read nothing of his feelings on his face. She was unaware of the seething need that had eaten at his vitals all evening, until he could think only of his frustrated anger at the position she had him in. He had raged at his own inability to change his situation and at the knowledge that he could have her for only a little while . . . if he could have her at all.

Slowly Lucas's anger simmered, finally solidifying into grim determination. He would spar with her no more. He knew she had responded to him, that physically, at least, she wanted him as much as he wanted her, and he was not going to let Brian, who seemed to have no serious regard for her, keep her as a beautiful plaything. Brian was helpless now, and Lucas's conscience was overcome by his burning need for Ria.

He was not drunk, but he had had enough to blunt his annoying qualms. He gazed at her now, barely containing the desire that raged through him. Why did she look so defenseless—so damned beautiful?

His face told her nothing, hers was very revealing.

Her cheeks were unusually flushed, and her eyes were wide, a defiant, almost self-protective look in them.

Ria had to force her gaze to meet his as a tumultuous new emotion cut at her already frayed nerves.

"I . . . I'm glad you're back," she said softly. "I was worried about you. I thought you might be hurt or . . ." She let her words die beneath his intense gaze.

"Would that really make a difference to you, Ria?" His voice was cold and brittle. "I should think getting me out of the way would make things easier for you and your lover."

She gasped at his bitter gibe. Why was he so angry at her, she was not responsible for the position they were in?

"That's not fair. I don't want to see you dead."

"No?" He laughed shortly. Then he began to move toward her with a light catlike tread that made a feeling of panic rise in her throat. She backed from him until she came into contact with the bunk. She could retreat no farther.

"Tell me," he said softly, "just what do you want? You say you love him, but when you look at me with those lovely eyes, they reveal so much. You love him, but you want me. Why can't you admit that you want me as much as I want you?"

He was within inches of her now, his eyes bright and pitiless as he reached out and took her wrist in a bruising grip. The world seemed narrowed down to just the two of them as slowly, and despite her resistance, he drew her toward him.

"Why do you continue to play games with me? The sweet innocent virgin first and now this untouchable wanton. You can't play games if you're not willing to pay the price."

168

"Games," she hissed furiously. "I've never played games with you! Damn you, I didn't come to your bed. I didn't ask you to take my virginity!"

"Are you saying I took you against your will?" He laughed harshly. "Your memory is shorter than mine. I remember your cries of pleasure. Are you crying rape now?"

"Oooh!" she cried. "I hate you. I don't want you to touch me."

"No?" he taunted. "I think you lie to yourself, Ria. I think you truly believe you can have everything your way. Well, it's time you made some choices, and I think it's time I convinced you of what your choices should be."

She knew a moment of sheer and utter panic as his arm encircled her waist to bring her body close to his. She could see the sudden opacity of his eyes, could read his intent, and she knew she had shattered his control. Mentally she reached for some weapon to fight with—for the defense Brian had always provided.

"What kind of a man waits until another cannot fight back before he tries to steal from him?" she snarled.

Her words grated against Lucas's guilt, but his desire brought anger to his defense.

"Steal, am I stealing from him or do you just need to hide somewhere? Are you afraid to admit the truth to yourself?" He smiled. "You tempt me to find out how much you really hate me . . . and how much you care for him."

"Brian will kill you!" she cried.

"I don't think so. Considering the attention he's given you, he just might not care whose bed you find comfort in."

"I belong to Brian!" she nearly shrieked as he

tightened his arm about her and she could feel the heat of his body, pressed so close to hers there was scarcely a heartbeat between them.

"Do you?" he said softly. "You're fooling only yourself, Ria. Why deny what you want? Why not let yourself surrender to it? You don't belong to him. You belong to me."

"No," she groaned, as he caught her hair in his fingers and forced her to meet his gaze. She saw gold flecks of flame leap to life in his amber eyes, and their heat seared her soul.

"I will never belong to you. You cannot just take what you want."

"Are you so sure," he said softly, "that I will have to take? Are you so sure you won't be more than willing?"

"You are a . . . a dirty filthy lecher!" she shrieked. "Let me take Brian and go! Let us leave your ship!"

Lucas chuckled. "I've no intention of letting you go. Now about Brian—"

"Beast! Animal!"

"You're filled with nasty words, my sweet. You need a little lesson in manners, along with a few other things, and I am interested in teaching you."

She nearly choked on her rage, but a brilliant heat was coiled like a snake within her. Her gasp was filled with outrage, yet the arm that held her to him was relentless and his hand remained tangled in her hair so she could not look away.

"I'm sure you've known from the very beginning, from the first time we touched, that I went on wanting you. You've been a poison in my blood though I've tried to stay away from you. This whole thing is mad, because whether you will admit it or not, this is what you want."

Before Ria could fling an angry retort at him his

mouth came down to cover hers in a kiss filled with tumultuous emotions. It was angry, yet passionate, and it took her breath away. There was no gentleness, no tenderness. He was savage and thorough. His tongue ravaged her mouth, seeking her will with its destruction as an end. Then his lips blazed a heated trail from hers to the hollow at the base of her throat, where a pulse beat frantically.

She heard her name whispered . . . almost a groan. "Ria . . . Ria."

She struggled, but she was firmly imprisoned against him, her arms pinned between them.

The spreading heat in her loins made her incapable of anything but feeling and needing.

Only then did his mouth soften against hers, when he had provoked the response he sought. Ria voiced her need in an inarticulate whimper, and his mouth moved slowly and lingeringly over hers, while his hands gently explored her body.

"No . . . no," she moaned. "I won't give in to you. I won't."

"Don't make vows you can't keep," he whispered against her cheek. Again his hand tangled in her hair, and he drew her head back and began to kiss her mouth, forcing her lips apart, then letting his tongue seek the sweet deep taste of her.

She could feel his other hand caress her breast, taunting a nipple to hardness even with the soft material of the gown between them.

When their eyes locked again, he knew this was a battle she could never win, for he could feel the trembling of her body against his. He gripped her hands, forced them behind her back, and held them with one of his. Then, his eyes still holding hers, he determinedly began to remove her dress.

She groaned and writhed in his arms, but it was

useless to resist. Her dress slipped away, and his hands moved over her body touching, invading, probing until she felt he was strumming every nerve she possessed. His mouth, when it touched her body, was like a hot iron. Suddenly he released her hands and pulled her down onto the bunk with him. She was pinned beneath the leg he placed across the lower part of her body, and he continued the torment that was tearing her resistance down.

She wanted to cry out against him, to fight him; but all strength was drained from her as his hands played on her senses.

Oh God, what was he doing to her control? His lips had caressed her breasts, moved over the smooth flesh of her belly, and were now working a melting magic on the sensitive flesh of her thighs.

She wanted to scream in outrage as his hands gently pushed her legs apart and his lips sought the core of her, turning her body to liquid flame. She heard her own wild sobbing moans of ecstatic desire as his tongue dove deeply into her softness.

"Ohh," she moaned. She wanted to push him away, but her hands caught his head pulling him to her.

His mouth seared into her like a live flame, branding her as his.

She lost all control, reached the limit of endurance, as spasms of pleasure shuddered through her, leaving her half-fainting and totally helpless.

Only then did he enter her and begin to move with mind-draining slowness.

No matter how she hated him, she could not control his power over her body. In spite of everything, he was lifting her again, slowly and steadily, and her treacherous body was surrendering again.

"Put your legs around me, Ria," he whispered. Immediately her legs complied, and she wept hopeless tears as he made her body sing with passion. When they reached a fiery pinnacle together, she clung to him.

One elbow braced on each side of her, Lucas looked down into Ria's eyes. His were wary yet triumphant, and though she felt a shiver go through her, she forced herself to keep her eyes locked with his.

"You make it so easy to hate you," she said in as cold and controlled a voice as she could muster.

"Still the self-deception?" he queried with a half-smile. "Do you know that you look so beautiful I'd still like to make love to you?"

Her eyes blinked then grew wider. She would have struck him, but he saw the signal in her eyes and grabbed her hands, raising them over her head and holding them.

"Haven't you played with me enough! Aren't you satisfied? You've taken what you wanted. You've humiliated me. Isn't that enough for you?"

She felt helpless, and her frustration grew as he continued to keep her immobile.

"Ria, you damned fool," he said coldly. "Did you really believe I would leave you now? For us this is just the beginning."

"Begin— You can't mean that!" But she saw the intent in his eyes. "You can't," she cried. "Let me go!"

"The night is young yet," he whispered as he casually bent his head to kiss her throat. "And besides . . . you haven't seemed to have gotten the idea yet."

"What idea is that?" she demanded.

"That you are no longer mistress to Brian

173

Thomas . . . you will be mine. It's a simple exchange, Ria—his life for you. All you need to do is tell him you will no longer be his mistress . . . that you have exchanged loyalties."

She gazed at him in a kind of desperate, mindless fury. "I will never tell him that. Damn you! Damn you!" She felt utterly frustrated.

His lips curled in a slightly mocking smile. "Your mind should tell your body that." His voice was teasing. "It doesn't seem to understand . . . but it understands this." One hand held hers in an iron grip while he gently skimmed the other down her body, caressing her smooth skin. Seeking the soft fullness of her breasts, he cupped one and swirled his thumb across the nipple to torment her. Her body quivered in response and she glared at him.

"Is this what you want—all you want! A whore to warm your bed. Doesn't it matter to you that I don't want you to touch me. Haven't you done enough?" Bitter tears stung her eyes, but she bit her lip, refusing to let tears betray her as her wayward body had done. "If you think being some man's mistress is all that is left for me, if you think that I willingly choose to be a whore, then at least I can choose the man I would be mistress to—and it isn't you! It will never be you!"

His face was grim and his eyes danced with the flame of open challenge. "And do you think I'm going to believe words when I know what exists between us. Must I show you again that you have no choices left?"

"I will always have a choice," she snapped.

"So . . . that is how you want it?" The question was filled with so much intent that she became still.

"Then you'll let me go?"

"No. We'll fight our battle here. This battle ground is much more fun."

174

"Just how long do you think you can keep me here before Brian asks where I am, or comes for me? If he doesn't kill you, I will."

"Ah, Ria." He smiled the half-smile of the devil, and her alarm rose. "You have an unfortunate knack for making me forget any good intentions I might have."

She saw the sudden flare of renewed passion in his eyes. "I . . ."

"Are you going to tell me you hate me? Don't. It's a waste of energy you're going to need for other things."

"Don't you realize the consequences you face!"

He grinned evilly. "I surely do."

She knew he had deliberately twisted the meaning of her words.

"You may do what you want tonight," she said furiously, "but morning will come. Brian and I will leave your ship."

"Ria"—his voice was firm now—"you have a habit of jumping to conclusions that aren't valid. Come morning, you will be as much mine as you are tonight . . . and for a long time."

"A long time. Until you tire of me and give me to someone else to share a long time with. You are a heartless monster, and I will never willingly stay with you."

"We shall see," he murmured, and before she could answer he bent his head and covered her parted lips with his. His arms gathered her close and to her distress her body again fell prey to his ruthless ministrations, as if it had a will of its own.

Lucas was now completely unscrupulous—and totally intoxicating. His mouth, though hard and demanding, was no longer brutal, yet it slowly destroyed the barriers she had had very little time to raise.

"You are a hypocrite, my sweet. You and I both know that no matter what enemies we might be or how much we fight each other, there is still this . . . and there will always be this."

What good is it to protest? she thought. All he had to do to set fire to her was stroke her flesh, kiss her, and the core of defiance in her body would melt and flow through her, leaving her powerless to prevent him from doing as he pleased. It was bitter to realize that not only was there nothing she could do to stop him, but her body responded to his will.

"Stop fighting me," he whispered, as his hand slid down her belly to rest between her thighs. "Open your legs, Ria . . . stop fighting me."

His voice, a soft insidious whisper, was followed by hot blinding kisses. He took his time caressing, teasing and subtly exciting and stimulating, until she knew complete and utter defeat again and all her resistance was drained away. Her body, vital and young was responding to his seeking a renewal of the joy it remembered.

She heard him laugh softly as his hands and mouth aroused her until she began to twist beneath him and moan softly against his mouth. She wanted him and arched to meet him. With agonizing pleasure, she felt him push her legs apart. Then he was within her, hard and male, and he drove deeply with an unending demanding force, drove them both to mindless ecstatic wonder . . . up and up until they took flight as one. Then they were falling together, gently, from wild possession to fulfillment.

Only after he lay beside her, holding her close, did feelings of distress and shame return. She knew that to him she was merely a prize to be taken by the stronger man, a mistress to use and discard. Worse, she knew he exerted a power over her that she must find some way to fight.

Lucas listened to her efforts to control her tears. He tightened his arms about her in silence, and held her until she grew quiet and slept.

Finally, when he turned and looked down at her exhausted tear-stained face, he felt the first heavy weight of guilt. Also, at the back of his mind was a nagging thought that he did his best to ignore: one day he would have to let her go. He wondered if he really would tire of the excitement she held for him, and he wondered if he would be able to part from her.

"At least I don't have to think of that now, Ria my love, for you're sailing with me. I have you for now and I intend to enjoy you as long as we can."

He curled his body about her and smiled in satisfaction as she turned to him and nestled closer. Then his eyes closed, and he slept beside her.

Ria was caught somewhere between sleep and waking. She felt warm and very comfortable. She enjoyed several moments of this relaxing state before reality intruded and she suddenly realized that she lay curled against a hard, but warm, body.

One of his arms rested about her waist, and one of his legs was thrown possessively over her legs. She didn't want to open her eyes. She tried to move, but found she was trapped in more than one way. His arm held her, and her hair was caught beneath his shoulder.

Gently she tried to ease from his embrace, but the slight movement awakened him and he tightened his arms about her, drawing her closer into his embrace.

"I'll have to teach you another thing, I see"—he

chuckled warmly—"that staying in bed in the morning can be more entertaining than watching the sun come up. Are you always an early riser, my love?"

She stiffened as he brushed a light kiss across the base of her neck and his hands slid up her body to caress her lightly.

"Damn you, stop it!" she groaned. "Can't you let me go!"

"Truthfully, no." He laughed softly. "I'm having a difficult time of it."

She tried to wriggle from his arms, but it was useless.

"Stop struggling, Ria. You know it's not going to do you any good."

That was true. She knew he had the strength to take what he wanted, but this knowledge only increased her futile rage. His hands were moving very slowly now, but she had reached the end of her endurance. She lay quiet, and in a few moments Lucas got the idea that she was no longer going to fight. He rolled her over so she faced him.

"Well, at least you've come to your senses. You're a smart girl. It's time you realize how enjoyable this situation is going to be."

"You insufferable, arrogant, deceitful bastard," she grated out. "How are you going to explain what you've done? Someday you must let me go, and I shall have revenge for this."

"Ria, such talk." Lucas laughed. "My mother, a truly honorable lady, would be highly insulted. Besides, I don't intend to explain anything to anyone."

"You think Brian won't be asking for me. You think he will allow you to live after what you have done."

"You give the man a great deal of credit he doesn't deserve. What makes you think he'll give the loss of his mistress a second thought. He'll find another as he's been doing all along. Besides, I plan to take care of that."

Lucas rose from the bunk, and Ria, unused to waking with a naked man in her bedroom, blushed and turned away while he dressed. He was amused by this and teased her gently.

"You'd better get used to it. We'll be sharing a lot in the future."

"Please . . . just let me go."

"I'm afraid not, love." He laughed again, and she looked up just in time to see him stride to the door. When he opened it and turned to her, she realized that he carried her clothes with him. She flew from the bed just as he closed the door, in time to hear the lock click. When she tried the door, she found it firmly locked.

In frustration and rage she pounded on it. Then the empty cabin was the receptacle for her opinions on Luke.

Chapter 13

Lucas went immediately to his own cabin where Brian was sitting up, pillows at his back, eating food from a tray on his lap.

Brian smiled warily.

"Good morning," Lucas said. "Did you sleep well?"

"Yes." Brian watched Lucas approach, feeling a vague sense of unrest. "Did you?"

"I spent the night in the tavern in town so Ria could have the small cabin. She needed her rest too."

Lucas dragged a small bench near the bed and sat down. "Brian, we have a problem."

"A problem?"

"I thought it was going to be a simple thing to protect you two. I have you safe, but there've been two attempts to abduct Ria already."

Brian was shaken. "Ria! Is she all right?"

"She is now. She's up on the hill overlooking the town in a small Spanish convent. The sisters have been more than gracious. I took her there and asked for their protection."

"She went alone . . . without asking for me?" Brian said suspiciously.

"No, not exactly." Lucas laughed. "But after the last attempt I forced her to see reason. I had my men take her there under cover of night. She was angry, and the only way I could pacify her was to tell her I'd bring you to her as soon as you woke up. I'm afraid if you don't appear rather quickly she'll come storming back, most likely right into Henri's waiting arms."

"This is not like Ria at all." Brian's eyes narrowed. "She would have come to me."

"She came in and checked on you last night, but you were sleeping comfortably. She knew you needed all the rest you could get. She did this against her will, but it was either the convent or Henri, so she really didn't have much choice. If you feel up to it, my men will take you to her."

"I'm up to it," Brian said quickly. "You're sure Ria is all right?"

"She's fine—upset, worried, and waiting for you, but fine. She's been quite concerned about you. In fact last evening she mentioned your name quite often," Lucas added glibly. "She's very intelligent, and after the second attempt to kidnap her from my ship she agreed to go. I'll arrange for a boat, and get you to the convent as soon as possible. We must do it quickly so we don't arouse Henri's suspicions."

"Well, if Ria agrees I guess I do. I just wish I were well enough to sail with you. If you take the ship you're after it will bring a great profit."

"Half of which, now that Henri thinks you're dead, goes to him."

Brian needed evidence of Luke's and Henri's guilt. Some tangible booty from the ship they were to take would be just the thing.

"By the time you return I expect to be strong enough to let Henri know I'm still very much alive."

"I suppose you will."

"I want a share of the loot," Brian said firmly.

"You will have it. I intend to see that you get exactly what you deserve. Now I must go and make the arrangements."

"I wish I could get up from this confounded bed," Brian exclaimed angrily. "I want to see Ria."

"You needn't worry. Ria is well and is going to be taken good care of. If you want to get well, you had best be patient. Good care at the convent will see you on your feet soon. By the time you're well, we'll be back. Then we'll share what needs sharing."

Brian watched Luke leave, feeling there was more to his words than he'd understood.

On deck Lucas snapped orders and sailors moved. One went to the convent and soon returned to tell his captain that sanctuary for a seriously wounded man would be happily given.

Lucas smiled. The first step in his plan to permanently separate Brian and Ria was underway.

Now he had himself rowed to Henri's ship, where a recently awakened Henri welcomed him aboard.

"You are up early, my friend."

"Yes. Henri, I'm going to leave a day earlier than we planned. I want to make sure I arrive at the rendezvous with the merchant on time."

"You are leaving today?"

"Within a few hours if you have no objections," Lucas replied.

Henri shrugged. When the merchants were taken he planned to dispose of Lucas, thereby securing himself a third ship . . . and Ria.

Lucas had a reasonably good idea of the treacherous thoughts stirring in Henri's mind, but for now he merely wanted to keep Henri's suspicions under control until he had Brian safely tucked away and he and Ria were under sail.

Lucas went over the maps he already knew by heart, appearing casual about his departure and meeting to come.

He was satisfied when he left Henri's ship and returned to his. Once aboard, he returned to Brian's cabin.

"Several of my men are prepared to take you up to the convent. We must be very careful and keep you hidden. If Henri is watching we wouldn't want him to see you."

"You're sure he doesn't know Ria is there?" Brian asked suspiciously. "It would be easy for him to pick us both off."

"He has no idea. I just left him. Both Henri and I are leaving today. By this afternoon neither you or Ria will have to worry about Henri. Both of you will be where you should be safe."

Brian had very little time to think about Luke's answer. Two sailors appeared at the door with a makeshift litter, and they gently lifted Brian and placed him on it. Then Lucas covered him well.

The convent was several miles up the coast from where they lay at anchor, so the seamen took the longboat. Lucas stood at the rail, a wide smile on his face as he watched Brian being taken—he hoped—out of Ria's life.

When the two sailors returned they told Lucas they had safely deposited Brian who, they said, was arguing with one of the sisters because she was calmly insisting that no one named Ria was in the convent. Lucas threw back his head and roared with laughter. Then he ordered all sails up. Within a half-hour they were leaving the bay and heading for the open sea. Only then did Lucas go below to face an angry Ria who, he knew, was going to be a great deal angrier when he returned her to the captain's cabin, where she would spend the next two weeks.

Brian was placed in a comfortable bed, and as the two sailors walked to the door a young dark-eyed sister entered the room. She went quickly to Brian's side.

"You are comfortable, *señor?*"

"Yes, sister, I am," Brian replied. "The wound is already healing."

"Very good, *señor*. If you should need anything, you need only call."

"Well, there is one other thing. The young lady who came here earlier. Would you go and tell her I'm here and that I'd like to talk to her."

"Young lady, *señor?*" she replied blankly.

"Yes . . . the girl who came here before me."

"I am sorry, *señor*, but there are no other women here except the sisters. Maybe she has remained in the town and will arrive later."

Suspicions were already forming in Brian's mind. He struggled to get to the edge of the bed, and the young sister ran to his side.

"*Señor*, you must not try to get up. You will harm yourself."

But Brian was already pushing himself to his feet. With supreme effort he made his way to the window that looked out over the bay, only to see the longboat slowly making its way to the *Black Angel*. Less than fifteen minutes later he saw that ship's sails unfurl and watched her slowly leave the bay. There was no doubt in his mind that he had been expertly tricked. His anger grew to black rage. He knew Ria must still be aboard, only now she had no one to stand between her and the merciless pirate that captained the *Angel*. He gritted his teeth and guilt overwhelmed him. When she needed him most, he would not be there for her.

"Damn your black-hearted soul," he muttered. "I shall be free of this place soon, and I shall hunt you down like the beast you are. If she comes to any harm at your hands I swear I shall find the most horrible and painful way for you to die. Damn you . . . damn you!"

There were tears in his eyes as he wondered what Ria would think when she found she had nothing but her own courage to put between her and the heartless man who now had her at his mercy. Brian watched until the *Black Angel*'s sails could be seen no longer. Only then did he stagger back to the bed and to the dark visions that danced before his eyes.

Ria paced the cabin, at first naked, then wrapped in a sheet she'd taken from the bunk.

"How long does he think he can hold me here?" she muttered. "Brian will ask questions. He will want to see me."

Even if Luke told Brian lies, Ria knew Brian would soon be well enough to seek her out. Then where would the revolting pirate captain be?

Interminable minutes dragged on, and still there was no sign of anyone. She was desperate for some word, some sign that someone remembered she was aboard. She was hungry and furious. She sat on the bunk, only to rise again and pace the cabin like a caged tiger. Indeed she felt like one. Her claws were sheathed now, but when she again saw Luke's arrogant laughing face, she intended to claw it until he could laugh no more.

She heard heavy feet running about on the deck above her, confusion, and wondered what was happening. Then she uttered a mournful cry as she felt the ship lift and move beneath her. They were sailing! Real fear struck her. Then she heard footsteps stop at her door, heard the lock click. She lifted her chin and turned cold unwavering eyes toward it and toward the man she knew would enter.

Lucas opened the door and, stepping inside, closed it after him. Under his arm he carried a bundle of clothing. Ria knew it was for her, but she wondered what she would have to do to get it.

She felt trapped and mute despair filled her as he set the clothing aside and walked toward the bunk on which she sat coiled.

"If I must be a prisoner," she snapped out bitterly, "at least allow me the pleasure of doing without your disgusting company."

He frowned, a muscle twitching in his cheek. "You're not in a position to make demands."

"No," she said miserably. "I am only a woman you have decided to honor temporarily with your lust. Should I be grateful and fall at your feet, begging for more."

Lucas laughed harshly and then sat down beside her. Deliberately she turned her face from him; then she yelped in surprise and pain as he yanked her hair to twist her head toward him. His eyes sparkled with a promise of what would happen if she continued to resist him, but Ria was angry and frightened enough to ignore the obvious signal.

Brutally he forced her to hold her head still, his fingers digging into her flesh.

"Ria, you'll have no problems here if you just learn to relax and accept the inevitable."

"Inevitable! Are your desires always inevitable?

What about what I want!"

"You won't honestly admit what you want," he said with a casual grin. "Once you do, all our battles will be over."

"Oh, you conceited ape! How long do you intend to keep me locked up here?"

"The door won't be locked again. You have the freedom of the ship."

"I want to go to Brian. I want to see him now!"

Lucas's eyes darkened, but he still smiled deceptively. "I'm afraid that's impossible unless you're a very good swimmer."

She narrowed her eyes and tried to remain calm. "Why are you moving the ship?"

"I'm not exactly doing that."

"We're not ... Nooo," she groaned. "You miserable wretch, let me go ashore. Let me take Brian and go ashore."

"I can't do that. Brian is already ashore. He's being taken care of there while you and I settle our differences on this two-week journey."

"Taken care of!" Ria's eyes grew wide. "You've killed him! Damn you! You've killed him!" She attacked him with both fists, and Lucas received several hard blows before he could capture her arms and pin her against him.

Her eyes were swimming with tears, and her lips quivered despite her useless attempt to control them. He saw deep pain momentarily replace anger, and he hated Brian even more. How could a man have the love of a woman such as Ria and not want to treasure it, nurture it.

For a moment Ria lost control as the idea of Brian's death penetrated her mind. She shivered and a heart-breaking sob tore from her lips. Then, in defeat, she bent her head against his chest and wept.

For Lucas her reaction was shattering. Did she really love Brian that much? If so, why had she surrendered to a passion so wild that he was lost in it. He wanted to comfort her, and stroked her hair gently.

"Ria, he's not dead I swear. He's in good hands. I had no need to hurt him. I saved him once, remember? If I wanted him dead, he would be dead already. I don't want you loving a memory. I want you to forget him. He has probably already forgotten you," he finished cruelly, hoping the reality of his words would help her exorcise Brian from her heart.

"You think you're so very clever, but you don't know Brian as I do. He would never desert me. When he's strong enough, he'll come after me. He'll kill you for this."

"We'll see what time brings," Lucas said with finality. He stood up. "Would you like some water for a bath?"

"I want nothing from you! Nothing!"

"I'll send some water. There's plenty of time. When you're finished come on deck."

"I'll stay here and rot first!"

"Ria, I'm giving this cabin to my new first mate for this journey. If you want to share it with him be my guest. If you choose not to, you'd best meet me on deck."

He walked to the door and turned to look into the angriest, most frightened eyes he had ever seen. She was a puzzle, a mystery he could not understand.

Lucas assumed that when she'd come aboard Brian's ship, she had been a wild girl seeking adventure. That he had possessed her first was an accident of fate, but he was sure she intended to become the mistress of some lucky captain . . . and he intended to be that captain. He knew the physical attraction that existed between them could not be denied. It was enough for now. His life was too complicated for further difficulties. This would be a nice interlude. Then, once he had proof of Henri's activities, he'd go home and settle the entanglement of his forced marriage. That done, he would be free. Ria would also be free to follow the life she chose.

"Hurry up, the weather's beautiful," he said to her.

"You can go to hell," she responded through clenched teeth. "You may have me trapped here, but I'll be damned if I'll follow your orders. Where do you think I'm going to sleep, in the captain's bed?" she sneered. "Well you'll rot in hell before I do. I'll sleep on deck first."

Lucas knew very well no man aboard his ship would dare put a hand on Ria, but he counted on her not knowing it. He grinned. "Go ahead. My men haven't been home for a long time. They are at the very least hungry for feminine attention. I'm sure they'd be grateful for your invitation."

Anger flushed her cheeks and lit her amethyst eyes with a gold flame that threatened to burn him to a cinder.

Before she could give voice to the words that choked her, Lucas was gone. Combined tears of self-pity and anger touched her cheeks, and she brushed them aside. She would not let him make her cry.

Ria began to think of her position. She was totally at his mercy. Slowly she began to organize her thoughts. She had to find a way to thwart Luke.

It was more than obvious that he considered her just a casual mistress, a soft body on which to take his pleasure for a time. Then he would walk out of her life just as casually as he'd walked in. Well, she would be damned if he'd let him use her and discard her as if she were unimportant.

Slowly a plan began to form in her mind. What if she turned the tables on him? What if he began to really care for her? What if he made the mistake of falling in love with her? She began to smile. He would not be the first man she had dangled on a string.

She envisioned his passion growing into love, saw herself deny him and walking out of his life as easily as he meant to walk out of hers. She could hear him beg her to stay, imagine his profession of love, see herself laughing.

"Maybe," she whispered to herself, "you are not quite as clever as you think . . . maybe you will regret this. You need to be taught a little lesson: every woman is not your plaything. Outside of rape, my dear Captain, you will never get what you want— never—but the game might just be enlightening."

She laughed softly as determination began to build in her. She could play the game as well as he.

A knock on the door caused her to start. She rose and wrapped the sheet about her as she went to answer it.

The men who brought the water did their best to keep from gazing at her, but her beauty was not something they saw often. Both seamen were amazed when Ria smiled and thanked them graciously.

"It was kind of you to bring my bath. I'm very grateful."

"It's all right, ma'am," the younger one stammered, his eyes wide with disbelieving pleasure at the gentle attitude of the lady his captain had locked in the first mate's quarters. He was not quite sure of what was going on, but he began to feel a touch of sympathy for this beautiful fragile woman who was obviously being forced to remain with his captain. This was the first step in Ria's plan, and she smiled to

191

herself in satisfaction as she saw it begin to work. If she had charmed one of his men so easily, she mused, her wiles just might work on Luke.

Ria bathed slowly, thinking of what strategy would be best, playing the wild wanton, the demure lady, or . . . Her lips curved in a half-smile.

She rose from the tub, toweled herself dry, and dressed in the clothing Luke had brought: a forest green dress and several petticoats. The gown had a scooped neckline that enhanced her soft curves and golden skin. Its sleeves were puffed and the skirt, once it settled over the petticoats, whispered as she walked.

She brushed her hair, with what she surmised was Luke's brush, until it shone and fell about her in gleaming profusion. About the waist of the dress was a thin ribbon. Since the waist fit her snugly she saw no use for it as a belt, so she tied the ribbon about her head to hold her thick tresses back from her face and still let them hang free, knowing her hair was one of the things he liked about her. She remembered how he had tangled his hands in it and inhaled its fragrance. Now, she thought, it will annoy him that I let it hang loose and free to draw the attention of other men.

Satisfied that she was in control of herself, she left the cabin, and walked up the steps and out the companionway door.

Lucas stood at the wheel, his attention had been on the full white sails and on the wheel as the ship dipped and rose before a soft breeze. Gradually he became aware of a stillness on deck and a sudden lack of activity. He dropped his gaze from the sails, and his eyes met Ria's across the length of the ship. She approached him with a seductive walk meant to entice, and it was having just the effect she wanted.

He stood for several minutes in captivated amazement, quite sure he had never seen any woman as majestically beautiful as the one who slowly made her way toward him. This was the last thing in the world he had expected. He had imagined that he would have to go for her and that he would eventually have to seduce her into complying. He had envisioned long days and nights of subtle persuasion, not a soft smile and a subdued attitude. Something within him jangled a warning, but his senses were already caught.

As she neared him he returned her smile, and Ria was pleased that the first step in her plan was a success.

Chapter 14

When Ria stood beside Lucas, she was more than satisfied by the look of suspicion mixed with desire in his eyes. He was unsure, and that was the way she wanted him.

Lucas may have been uncertain of what she was about, but he was prepared for whatever might happen. The stern cold look he cast about him set his men back to the work of running the ship. Then he turned to Ria with a smile, a look of deep appreciation in his eyes.

"I'm glad you've come to your senses and decided to accept things as they are."

"Discretion is the better part of valor I'm told," she responded.

"Does it take such valor to spend some time with me?"

"Maybe less valor than endurance."

"Whatever you were looking for when you boarded Brian's ship, I'm sure you'll find here . . . maybe even more of it than you were looking for."

"You are right. When I boarded Brian's ship, I had no idea of what the future would bring. But there is no way out of this . . . and I can only hope that you, too, will find more than you were looking for."

Despite the silken sound of her voice, Lucas wasn't sure what she was saying wasn't meant as some kind of threat. Did she plan on trying to do him in in some way? He would have to remember to keep one eye on her all the time. It was a distinctly uncomfortable feeling.

His discomfort was to increase as the day lengthened and he watched Ria make herself completely at home on his ship. It seemed she belonged there, had roamed its deck often.

She stopped to talk and laugh with each man, and invariably the crewmen first cast surreptitious looks at their captain's dark face before surrendering to the pleasant situation.

Lucas was taken unprepared by Ria's seemingly quick adaptation to her surroundings; it made him nervous. She was too docile, too relaxed and easy, as if she had been a part of this environment all her life.

He'd been certain it would have been much more difficult to get her to comply with his wishes, so he reserved judgment until he found out just how far her compliance extended.

What started out to be a pleasant interlude became totally annoying when she seemed to be inclined to laugh and share her time with everyone but him. She became elusive, keeping out of his reach, yet she did so with such a seeming lack of deliberateness that he wasn't sure of what she was doing.

He hoped she had just accepted a situation she could not change, that she had decided being the mistress of one man was no less profitable than being mistress to another.

Brian was helpless, but catlike, she had landed on her feet. What Brian couldn't provide he could.

In midafternoon the sea became rough when they

sailed into a storm, and for some time Lucas was forced to attend to the safety of the ship. He had crisply ordered Ria below, and had smiled in the face of her irritation.

I'll be damned, he thought. She seems to be enjoying the challenge of the sea. He would have been less than surprised had she tried to take control and guide the ship safely through.

When the storm abated it was near sunset, and Lucas made his way to his cabin. He was exhausted, but he felt he had best be prepared for some kind of battle with Ria.

The scene that met his eyes was definitely the last thing he expected. He stood just within the room, one hand still on the door handle.

The same tub he had secured for Ria sat in the middle of the floor, filled with steaming water. Nearby, on a table, was a tray of food, covered so he could enjoy his bath, and Ria stood near the porthole in the sunset's amber glow.

Lucas gazed at her serene, smiling face with narrowed eyes filled with suspicion.

"Come in, Captain. I hope everything is the way you like it. Your bath and your food are both hot. I have laid out clean clothes since yours are salty and wet. If there is anything else you would like, you have but to tell me and I'll see to its doing."

"No," he said cautiously. "I hardly expected all this."

"Oh?" she questioned in wide-eyed innocence. "But I thought that was what you wanted from me . . . to see to your comfort."

"You're not a servant, Ria."

"Perhaps I choose that position instead of the one you would allot me." Her eyes had become shuttered. "You are in command here, and I have tried to provide what you wish. Now I must go and speak to the cook about your breakfast. What time do you rise and what will you eat?"

He was suddenly aware of what she was doing— acting submissive, placing herself in the position of one unable to help her circumstances. Pretending to be unaware of his real motives, she was forcing him to accept her this way or to force her into another situation. She had placed him in a position he had not expected.

Ria smiled slightly and started for the door, but Lucas had no intention of letting her get away with her little plan. He reached out and gripped her arm as she tried to pass him.

"So, you would choose the position of hand-maiden, would you?" he questioned almost casually.

"Better that than harlot," she snapped, fear arousing her anger.

"Very good." He chuckled. "I accept. You can begin," he said smugly, as he reached beyond her and pushed the door closed, "by washing my back."

He slid the bolt home and stood before her, hands on hips and a challenging laugh in his eyes.

"You can damned well bathe yourself."

"Now, now," he cautioned. "You chose your place. Either do your duty or," he finished hopefully, "choose another position."

She glared at him. "I am not a maid, you damned pirate!"

"Maid or mistress . . . take your choice."

She spun from him, walked to the window, and stood gazing out to sea. Her stiff back and uplifted chin bespoke her disdain more eloquently than any words.

Lucas went to her and turned her to face him. "I said maid or mistress—take your choice."

198

Ria had no way of knowing that the idea of forcing her to his bed was as repugnant to him as it was to her. Since his eyes gave no sign of his thoughts, she was certain he meant to do just that.

"You are an unmitigated scoundrel . . . a beast . . . a—"

"Your name calling is becoming repetitious and annoying. I'm waiting for your choice."

"Maid!" she said furiously.

"Good." He grinned. "I'm tired enough to appreciate one. Now, let's see about that bath."

Ria was miserable. The last thing in the world she wanted was to minister to him, but her pride refused to let her back down. She had only one other choice and that frightened her even more.

She gave forth a muffled moan of dismay as he leisurely began to undress. Her eyes fled in every direction except toward him, and at the sound of his sigh of pleasure, she finally looked over and saw him easing himself down into the tub.

His grin was decidedly evil as he held out the bar of soap. "As a maid you're sadly lacking in your attention. Would you have me believe you've changed your mind? If so, I'll be out of this tub soon."

Ria gritted her teeth and contained her urge to shove his head beneath the water and hold it there until he drowned.

She walked to him and snatched the soap from his hand. Kneeling behind the tub, she dipped her hands into the water, then lathered the soap between them. After she laid the soap aside she began to rub her hands over the broad expanse of his heavily muscled back.

She could feel his strength and against her will her mind pictured another time when her hands had caressed . . . No! she refused to admit the tingling sensations in her fingers. Her hands became gentle as her mind drifted, and her fingers began to trace lines and figures.

His sigh of pleasure returned her to the present, and she looked at his back. Her finger had traced *I Lo* . . . Her mind refused to allow her to complete this thought, and she brushed her hand across his back.

Lucas turned slightly and caught her wrist, drawing her close to the tub.

"It is not just my back that needs washing," he said softly. He drew her hand against his chest.

Their eyes held, and a tremor shook her resolve. Slowly he forced her hand to caress the breadth of his chest. She wanted many things at the same time. To strike him, yet to caress him. To scream her denial, yet to press her lips against his hard demanding mouth.

Desire swirled through her like a tenuous mist. It took every bit of her control to master it.

She jerked her hand from his grasp and stood up. "Anymore washing you can do for yourself."

He laughed softly, but continued with his bath.

Ria walked again to the porthole. There was a narrow ledge beneath it, and she braced one hip upon that and gazed out over the now calm sea.

Lucas looked up at that moment, a laughing remark dying on his lips as he gazed at her. He wondered if she had any idea of how breathtakingly beautiful she was.

Her face was set in profile, and its contours were highlighted and shadowed as if by the touch of a master painter's brush. The last touch of the dying sun haloed her hair so that it looked like a golden flame tumbling about her.

The rise and fall of her breasts beneath the soft material of her gown made his breath catch as he remembered how those warm firm globes had felt to his touch. She was slim waisted, and the flare of her gown hid from his view the tempting softness he knew was beneath. He felt a stab of desire so strong it took the breath from him.

He wondered what she was thinking, for it was obvious she had retreated to a place where he could not follow.

It did not occur to him that he desired much more than what a mistress could offer. Without understanding his elusive need, he searched for the oneness, the complete sharing that a wife could give a husband.

Surely if he made love to her, held her in his arms, shared this short time they would have together, that would be enough to assuage the heat of passion. He knew her body would respond to his, and the wisp of thought, that he would not be satisfied with the possession of her body, again eluded him.

He rose from the tub, but Ria didn't notice. She was caught in her own web. She had drawn the lines of battle between them, yet deep within her she mourned the fact that possession of her body was all he wanted.

The total impossibility of their relationship tore at her. She did not want to be any man's mistress, yet the husband chosen for her was unacceptable. She raged against a fate that wed her to one man and gave another the command of her body.

She vowed silently that she would never surrender to him again, never let her body answer the call of his. It reduced her pride to ashes to know that what her mind demanded and her body desired were so far apart.

She was startled from her reverie by Luke's voice. He had dried himself and had put on his pants . . . but nothing else.

"Ria?"

She turned to him when he spoke her name softly. He stood too close . . . his masculine scent was disturbing to her already vulnerable senses. His eyes were solicitous and warm. She wanted to order him to leave her alone, but he had not made any move to touch her.

He saw the startled self-protective look in her eyes, and it irritated him to think she was almost afraid of him.

"Come and eat with me. The food looks delicious, and I hate to eat alone."

She was hungry. She had not eaten all day. Her brow furrowed in a deep frown.

"Put your shirt on."

"Why? It's more comfortable this way, and besides I'll just be taking it off again anyway."

"Don't suggest that I—"

"Ria," he interrupted innocently, "I mean to go to bed. I don't sleep with my clothes on, do you?"

She flushed, knowing he was teasing her, but well aware of the unwanted vision that leapt into her mind.

As she moved to the table, he pulled out a chair for her, then walked around to the other and sat down.

Again she was struck by the fact that his manners were polished. She gazed at him, realizing he would be at home in any circumstances. He was a chameleon. He would adapt well. She pushed the thought aside. The idea of returning home, married to one man and bringing a pirate with her, was out of the question. She would play the maid, she would serve him—but she would not let him break down her guard again.

She ate little, for despite her hunger his presence grated on her nerves. Finally she pushed her plate aside and sipped from the glass of wine he had poured her.

"I know so little about you," he said. "I don't even know if Ria is your real name. Do you have a family name? Where are you from?"

"As your servant, my lord, you have the right of my services. You do not have the right to know my past or my thoughts." She rose quickly. "I'll see to these dishes."

Lucas had reached the end of his endurance. Ria had just reached for his glass of wine to remove it when he rose abruptly. Her hand bumped the glass and it tipped. She tried to catch it, but the wine spilled across her fingers just as Lucas gripped her wrist.

Their eyes met, hers wide with surprise and his burning with a combination of anger and desire. When he drew her to him, she seemed suddenly unable to control her body's will. They stood almost close enough to touch.

Slowly he drew her wine-damp fingers to his lips, and while his eyes held hers he pressed his lips to her fingers. Hardly able to bear the erotic sensation that tore through her, she gave a sudden gasp of pure shock as his tongue licked at the wine. He turned her hand in his and pressed his lips to the palm, licking gently at the moist wine. Her breath seemed to stop, and her heart pounded so hard she was sure he could hear it.

Ria jerked her hand from his grasp because another instant of his subtle torment would have shattered her will. Only now his desire was beyond his control. He reached out, gripped her waist, and pulled her against him. Her hands pressed ineffectually against a broad expanse of fur-matted chest.

"Why do you fight yourself?" he questioned, as his arms brought the length of her body tighter and tighter against his.

Her defenses were crumbling; her will was bending like a willow before a rising gale.

"Because," she whispered, "being your mistress is not my choice. I don't want you commanding my life! I belong to myself and I will never belong to you—never!"

"I don't ask you to belong to me. I don't own you, and you don't own me. One day we will go our separate ways, but for now there's this. . . ." His voice was velvet-soft, but the words were steel. He drew her to him, molding their bodies one to the other, and his open mouth caught hers as swiftly and responsively as a falcon snatches its prey in full flight.

Ria felt as though she'd been tossed into a current she could not fight. She was sure of nothing now, except that her body raged with a fire she was unable to extinguish.

He was too vital, too overpowering; she could not think clearly while his mouth played havoc with hers. Her body, at first stiff and unyielding, seemed suddenly to disintegrate beneath the onslaught of his raw and fiery passion.

Some evil voice deep within her whispered, "It doesn't matter. You want him . . . you want him."

His arms held her pinned against the length of his body, and he kissed her savagely, demandingly, until she could feel the fevered pounding of her blood and her legs grew so weak she had to cling to him for support.

He seemed to sense the moment her body surrendered, but the battle continued as his hands caressed her and he kissed her over and over. Mentally, she struggled to regain her body's defenses, but after a while a soft whimpering sound told of her failure. All protest was slipping away, and being replaced by a wild and explosive warmth that seemed to uncoil within her.

Lucas could only think of the miracle that seemed to occur when he held her. He knew her body was yielding . . . but would she ever yield completely? Would Ria, the sweet essence of her, his maddeningly unpredictable mistress, ever truly yield.

When she was in his arms like this, her mouth opening under his, her body arching to press closer to him, she drove every rational thought from his mind.

It was easy to lose sight of their battle and its causes when she filled his senses.

Now he could do nothing more than take her and lift them both to the magical plain of forgetfulness where they did not have differences, where the brilliance of their blending was the only truth.

His hot mouth found the rapid pulse at the base of her throat and she groaned, almost a sound of agony, as he tasted her flesh.

His hands moved on her body, releasing her clothes and seeking soft warmth. His fingers teased and aroused her senses until she trembled in his arms, desiring release from this fiery furnace. She whimpered against his mouth, craving more and more of this delicious and tumultuous desire.

He lifted her in one swift movement and carried her to the bed. His body was hard and hot against hers, and his weight held her immobile.

Slowly he began to caress her, taking his time, playing with her, teasing her with hands and mouth until she was twisting and turning beneath him, her world filled now with nothing but him and a virulent pulsing need.

His lips skimmed down her body nipping, then caressing her flesh with his tongue until she wanted to scream out in ecstatic torment.

Everything, every thought, every breath was completely mixed up. Gently he caressed her thighs, separating her legs. His lips, gentle and seeking, stroked her flesh, until he found the pulsing center of her sensual being. He was fierce and possessive, and hands that had wanted to push him away drew him closer. When she felt she could stand no more, when she stood on the edge of oblivion, the torment ceased . . . but only for a moment.

Then he was deep within her, his hard maleness driving into her again and again—endlessly, demandingly lifting her higher and higher.

From a great distance, she could hear her own voice sobbing and begging. He whispered incoherent words of love and desire into her ear as they both dove beyond the boundaries of reason.

It was a nearly violent, explosive release that tumbled them from the brink of fulfillment to the world of reality.

Ria's reality was a cold agony as feelings of shame and revulsion engulfed her. She wept in uncontrolled misery. She had been exactly what he had wanted her to be. The touch of his hand and the power of his kiss had reduced her will to ashes. She wept, knowing he thought of her as a convenient mistress, a passing pleasure.

In a moment she had gone from remarkable pleasure to doubt and insecurity.

Lucas held her close to him. For a strange reason he wanted to comfort her, but he didn't know why.

He knew she had felt the same pleasure as he. She had been woman to his man, Eve to his Adam . . . she had been completely his.

Their lovemaking had been unique, and he wanted to think of nothing but the present. With enough time, he would prove to her that she belonged with him, not Brian.

He would teach her that they could share a blissful time despite the fact that their separation was inevitable.

He could not keep her, he knew that. But for now he could not let her go. Why think of anything but the present? The time to let her go was still a long way off.

Why does there always have to be an afterwards? Ria wondered. That moment when, tossed from Olympia's highest plateau of shared passion and fulfillment, she hit the jagged rocks of absolute despair. If only there was a future to their passion . . . if only he would be . . . But he couldn't be what she wanted or needed. He was what he was, a man with no name and no future.

"It's not wrong, Ria, to enjoy the pleasure we find in each other. Neither of us can look forward to anything permanent. Brian could not offer you any more than that. Why not just accept me?"

The words, like cold water, were spilling over her. How casually he spoke of her, as if she were a commodity he and Brian could share. She sat up abruptly, her amethyst eyes spitting fire.

"How easily you decide whose bed I will share. How convenient it is for you. And I suppose when you're tired of me, you will just return me to Brian with a polite thank you for the temporary use of his whore."

"To tell the truth, love"—he smiled—"I can't seem to put any serious thought into letting you go at all, although I expect one day you will choose to leave me."

She felt a murderous rage. Without telling him who she was, for doing so might cost Brian his life, she could never convince him she was any more than what he thought, but she swore her moment of weakness had passed. With every ounce of strength she had, she would fight him and never let him possess her again.

She turned from her futile anger and lay down, her stiff back to him.

"Ria?"

"Leave me alone," she said through the heat of tears she didn't want to share with his cold possessiveness.

He heard the sob in her voice and forced her to turn and look at him. He saw defiance mingled with anger he didn't know the cause of. One thing was certain, however, his desire for her was as vibrantly alive now as it had been the first time he had ever touched her.

"Forget it," he declared. "You can want him all you please, but I'm here and I hold you now."

She only had time to groan one word of protest before he gathered her to him and his lips sought to renew their passion.

Chapter 15

Meeting William Cunningham would be the first step in reaching Dan McGirtt, leader of the banditti. It seemed that Sophia and William were more than friends, but Scott couldn't be sure. Sophia had many friends in many places as he had discovered.

At least Scott knew he was on the right trail. Sophia, relaxed and secure with him now, had told him a great deal about the McGirtt group.

The banditti reaped benefits from the dual control of St. Augustine. For months they had been left undisturbed; yet from what Sophia had said, the banditti were very active, attacking persons and properties along the lower reaches of the St. Johns River. Even with the help of William, Sophia assured Scott that he could only meet Dan once he had made the acquaintance of John Linder, Jr., Dan's close compatriot.

Sophia opened the door of the room she and Scott had been sharing for the past week. Though Scott had tried every ploy he knew, Sophia had still not arranged the contact he wanted.

Now she smiled at Scott and went to him to be warmly welcomed.

"You've been gone all day," he complained with a smile. "I've missed you."

"And I've missed you," Sophia purred contentedly as Scott put his arms about her and kissed her most thoroughly.

"Where have you been?"

"Well . . . you have said there is someone you want very badly to meet."

"Dan McGirtt!" Scott said excitedly.

"Shhh, we don't say his name aloud. There are many who would like to know where he is. He knows about you, but first I will take you to meet William."

"William Cunningham?"

"Yes. He is a friend of mine. He is also Dan's very good friend."

"I see."

"He will decide if you are to meet Dan or not."

Again Scott responded with a very thoughtful, "I see." Then he turned his full attention to Sophia before she noticed his disappointment and gave more thought to why he was so anxious to meet Dan McGirtt.

"When do I meet this Cunningham?"

"In a couple of days. I've already sent word. When he wants to meet you, he'll let you know."

Scott had to be satisfied with this; he couldn't press too hard, for Sophia, although he knew she was growing fonder of him every day, was no fool. One misstep and he might find himself very dead.

He caught her in his arms and was immediately rewarded as her arms encircled his neck and she pressed her lush curves close to him. He had to admit he was becoming fond of her, but he certainly didn't intend this involvement to be more than a way to meet the banditti and help Brian and Ria.

"As I said," he declared softly, "I've missed you."

His mouth savored her willing lips until he felt her press even closer.

Sophia was a woman well versed in the art of love, but she had found more pleasure in Scott's arms than she had ever known before. Although she had been the mistress of many men since the age of fifteen, in no one's arms had she found a gentleness or consideration to match Scott's.

But Sophia was wise enough to know there was no invitation to marriage forthcoming. She would enjoy Scott for as long as she could have him; then she would let him go.

They tumbled to the bed together in mutual pleasure. With laughter and heated kisses, they undressed each other. Still awed by her tawny beauty, Scott took elaborate care to seduce her each time they touched, and to give her as much pleasure as she gave him.

She felt his tongue in her mouth, seeking, felt his hand on her belly, sliding downward until it rested on the soft inner flesh of her thighs. Then his hands were drifting, touching, probing, invading until her body arched in response as she sought more of this titillating pleasure.

Her hands too, familiar now with his body, stroked and caressed knowingly. She ran her fingers lightly over taut muscles, and down the lean length of him until she caressed with knowing fingers the pulsing shaft of his manhood. Scott groaned as hot streaks of pleasure rippled through him.

Sophia caught her breath sharply, and her body shook momentarily as quivers of sheer bliss raced along the sensitive nerves he was stroking. Her every sense seemed to be aware of each minute thing about him, from the glaze of growing passion in his eyes to the male scent of his body.

The stimulating sensations were overpowering, and her body knew a piercing demand for the fulfillment his passion promised. When that came, it left her shaken and completely helpless.

They lay together, content to remain silent for a short while in order to regain their equilibrium. Scott held her, but allowed his mind to drift. He was wondering what Ria and Brian had found out. He knew he was getting close to the desired meeting with the famed Dan McGirtt, but he wondered if he ought to contact Brian again just to make sure everything was all right.

He made up his mind quickly. There was time before he went to the meeting with Cunningham. He would go after dark, make his way back to the *Swan,* and tell them of his progress. Brian would be pleased, for soon they would have evidence of Henri's guilt to lay before the authorities—evidence that would eliminate threats of piracy against the Maine line and in the long run against St. Thomas shipping.

Sister Maria Esperanza stood by in utter fascination as Brian struggled to exercise his arms. The sweat of exertion filmed his face as she watched him grit his teeth against the pain the movements cost him.

She had never seen such a determined man. From the day he had arrived, the day he had stood at the window and shocked several of the sisters with the wild and threatening curses he had directed at the man he felt responsible for his condition, he had forced his strong young body into obedience. He was driven by an anger such as she had never seen before.

"*Señor,*" she protested gently, "surely you push yourself too hard. You will undo all the nursing my

212

sisters have done."

"Sister, I'm grateful for your concern, but I'm afraid I can't delay. It's too important for me to get out of here."

"You do not enjoy our company, *señor*." She smiled.

Brian chuckled, his eyes warm and kind. "I have never been treated better in my life than I have here, even by my own mother. But"—his eyes darkened— "there are lives at stake now, and a debt needs to be paid. I must be able to leave here as soon as possible."

"*Señor*," the sister said softly, "it is not our place to seek vengeance. Everything is in God's hands."

Brian went to her. His smile was gentle, but his eyes refused concession. "You've been more than kind, more than generous; and maybe you are right and I am wrong. But this is something I have to do. A man has stolen my sister and my ship. He will abuse both. Despite my gratitude, sister, I will see him dead. I know that goes against your beliefs, so I am leaving here tonight."

Her eyes widened in surprise and disbelief. "But you cannot do that! Reverend Mother will be furious."

"Does that frighten you?" Brian grinned.

Sister Esperanza laughed with him. "Truthfully yes, *señor*. Reverend Mother is a formidable woman, and it is unheard of to go against her wishes."

"Well, you are not going against her wishes, I am. So if she is angry she can be angry with me. But no matter what, I leave here tonight."

Sister Esperanza sighed deeply, gave a negative shake of her head, and left the room. Brian was almost certain he would be receiving a visit from the Reverend Mother before long. He was right. Just before the sun set, just before he was ready to leave, she appeared in the doorway.

She was very tall and extremely thin, and Brian could not begin to estimate her age. She had the most profoundly piercing eyes he had ever seen. He could see why she was spoken of with some awe and a great deal of respect.

"So, my young friend"—she smiled—"Sister Esperanza tells me you are determined to leave us. Are you sure you are well enough?"

Her voice was gentle, but for some unfathomable reason he had the feeling if she truly wanted him to stay she would find a way to make him do so. He also felt an unreasonable urge to make her understand why he had to go.

"Come in, Mother," he said. "Please . . . I would like to talk to you. I would like you to understand."

She nodded, walked into the room, and sat on a chair next to the bed. She seemed to be waiting patiently for his words. He went to the bed and sat on the edge. Then, in a subdued voice, he began to tell her of the deep and abiding love he felt for his sister. He told her of the anguish of his guilt at not defending Ria when she needed him most.

"And so you see why I must go? I must find her. I must know what has happened to her, and, God forbid, if she is lost to me . . . then I must avenge her."

"Will it ease your guilt my son," she said softly, "if you commit murder?"

"Is it murder to pay a man in the same coin for what he has done?" Brian demanded.

"It is murder if you take a life—under any circumstances. Justice is for God to dispense. It would be better if you were to stay a little longer; maybe you would change your thoughts."

Brian stood, and after a moment he spoke. "No, I

214

cannot stay. I will find him, and if he has harmed Ria in any way, I will kill him."

He said the words softly, and with the same quiet deliberation, he gathered up the sword and knife he had had with him when he'd arrived and then left the room.

Brian walked down the stone floor of the convent halls, his boots clicking sharply at each decisive step. Behind him, he left a woman whose eyes were saddened by her knowledge of men. Deep inside she prayed that Brian would not be able to find the man he cursed so bitterly.

The first thing Brian found out was that Henri Duval had acquired another ship—the *Swan*. Rumor also said that the young captain of the *Swan* was dead and his beautiful mistress had just vanished . . . but of course the *Black Angel* with its handsome captain had sailed and the lady in question could have been aboard.

How like a woman to choose the man fortune favored and leave the weaker one. She was a very clever lady, because it was also known that Henri Duval wanted her. It would be interesting to see which of these strong men eventually claimed her.

Brian's black fury grew into an obsession. He knew Duval and Blanc were up to something, and he was reasonably sure if he kept a close eye on Duval's comings and goings, eventually he would again cross the path of Captain Blanc.

He found a quiet room in an inn and kept to himself, going out only at night to haunt the docks and to keep a close eye on the *Swan*. Because of this habit, he found himself in the shadows late one night when he noticed a lone shadowy form that seemed to have the same intention as he, to keep an eye on the *Swan*.

He watched the figure for some time before it took on a touch of familiarity. Did he know this man? He crept closer and closer and was nearly upon him when he finally recognized Scott Fitzgerald.

He worked his way close behind Scott and would have kept silent until he was in a safer place to talk, except that he quickly realized his presence had been sensed. He whispered a quick warning, and Scott remained motionless until he had satisfied himself that the men near the *Swan* had no idea he was there. Then Scott backed into the deeper shadows, where Brian was only a darker form, but he had recognized his voice.

"Brian?" he whispered.

"We've got to get out of here," Brian replied. "Go someplace where we can talk."

"There's someone in my room. We can't talk there."

"Then follow me. We'll go to mine. Right now it's the only safe place I know."

The two moved through the dark streets quickly and quietly, and only when Brian had closed the door of his room behind them did they breathe a sigh of relief.

"Now," Brian said, "suppose you tell me just what's going on? Where is Ria, and where's that devil Blanc?"

"Brian, the truth is you seem to know just about as much as I do, which at this moment seems to be nothing." Scott went on to relate what he was involved in. "I came back to the ship tonight to talk to you and Ria, and this is what I found. Where have you been? Why don't you know what has happened

216

to them?"

Brian's face was pale with the rage he had tried to contain for so long. In a dull, even voice he explained all that had transpired since the last time he had seen Scott.

Scott reacted with an anger that matched Brian's.

"The rotten bastard! What kind of a man would pull a trick like that?"

"What worries me is his treatment of her. He is unscrupulous, and until now he thought of Ria as my mistress. He might be harsh with her. He might expect her to be"—he shrugged helplessly—"just what he thought she was. You don't know Ria; she'll fight like a tigress." Brian gritted his teeth. "If he hurts her I swear—"

"You won't be alone," Scott said grimly. "But first we have to track him down. There is no way to find a ship on the ocean, but I think I know a way we can meet up with this thieving devil and give him what is due him."

"How?"

"Well, we were thinking the banditti and the pirates are in this together. I've found out that's right. When these two scum come back here, there will be a meeting . . . and we can be with the banditti when that meeting comes about."

"All I want is the chance to have my sword in my hand when I cross his path again. I want to hear him beg when I slice him into the smallest pieces."

"You'll get your chance. For now, despite how we feel, we must wait until Sophia helps me make contact. We have to find out where the banditti are."

"Damn!" Brian exclaimed. "When I think of Ria—helpless—and all I can do is wait."

"I know how very hard it is, but we have very little choice."

"I will have to remain in this room," Brian said disgustedly. "If I'm seen by too many people, it won't be long before Henri knows I'm still alive."

"I heard men talking. Henri leaves tomorrow."

"Good, at least then I'll have some freedom." Brian thought for a while. "You know, Scott, what is most puzzling about this whole thing is why Blanc didn't just let me die in that alley. It would have saved him time; he wouldn't have had to lie. He could have taken Ria then. Instead, he had me nursed back to health. What he did is not logical at all."

"We'll learn the answer when we find him. If he doesn't want to give it we'll ... convince him otherwise."

Scott walked to the door, then turned to look at Brian again.

"I have to get back before Sophia wakes up and finds me gone. You stay put. I'll see that you have plenty to eat and drink, but I think it's safer for you if you stay off the streets."

"Scott," Brian asked quickly, "what chance do I stand of getting my ship back?"

"Two of us?" Scott looked skeptical.

"If you found a way to get word to some of my men ..."

"I'll try, but I won't jeopardize our chances of finding the banditti, Sophia is a very quick young lady. One drop of suspicion in her mind and any chance I have of getting to McGirtt will vanish. We'll just have to pray that Ria will be all right until we have a chance to get to Blanc. Right now Sophia's our only hope."

Scott could see how worried Brian was. "I know it's not going to be easy for you. I'll do the best I can. Try to remain calm, and I'll come or I'll find some way to send word to you when Sophia decides to take me to them."

"Sophia decides?"

"Well, not really. Someone named William Cunningham does the deciding."

"When he does, I want to go with you."

"I'll find a way. Give me a day or two to figure all this out."

"Thanks, Scott. At least it's good to know one of us is doing something."

"I'll be back."

"Be careful."

"I will."

Brian watched the door close behind Scott. He had never felt so miserable in his life.

He rose, walked to the window, and looked down into the deserted streets. Alone and afraid, he wondered, what must Ria be feeling.

Slowly he fed and nourished his murderous hatred of Gabriel Blanc until it was fanned into a bright flame. One way or another, Blanc would pay for what he had done.

Chapter 16

The banditti had come into the province from the Carolinas and Georgia, where some of them had served in the American revolutionary forces, but for one reason or another they had abandoned their former allegiance and had sought safety in the south. Here they had fallen into the evil practice of attacking the persons and properties of the residents, especially along the lower reaches of the St. Johns River.

Governor Tonyn, wanting to leave his administration on a note of leniency, and Governor Zespedes, wanting to start his on the same note, left the banditti free to maneuver. The leader of this band, Dan McGirtt, and his chief lieutenant, John Linder, Jr., had one liaison man, William Cunningham. These three were known to be murderers and thieves.

The banditti were now gathered on the San Sebastian River for the supposed objective of robbing the plantations, but Dan McGirtt had a much different motive than the one the watchful authorities suspected.

McGirtt's men began to swell his camp by twos and threes, coming slowly so the actual ranks of his camp could not be known. It was in the company of three such men that Chris found his way into the camp. These three were renegades, and Chris was very careful around them for he was sure they would have sold their own mothers for the right price. The four men had left St. Augustine together, Chris having been the only one who hadn't known their final destination. Now he squatted before a campfire and stirred it to brighter life. He would have given anything at the moment to know where the main camp was located.

He looked across the fire at the men who were wolfing down the remains of their evening meal. No matter how they bragged about feats he felt were imaginary, they would not give him any real information about "Dan'l," the location of the camp, or even how far they had to travel. It was obvious McGirtt was enough of a threat to keep them silent.

"Do we travel any more tonight?" Chris asked as nonchalantly as he could.

"Ya don't have to worry, we'll be there soon enough," one man offered.

"That doesn't tell me much," Chris replied. "Do we make camp and sleep here or not?" He motioned about him.

The night was thick and heavy, and he could sense the swamp that surrounded them. The shrill calls of crickets were answered energetically by bullfrogs, and the soft swishing sound of flowing water was punctuated by the creaking of trees bending in the night breeze.

Night creatures surrounded them, their scuttering noises accompanied by squeaks and screeches. To Chris the swamp seemed alive and very awake. It is not, he thought, the most comfortable place to be.

Long streamers of moss hung from gnarled misshapen trees, giving a ghostlike aura to the area. Chris was sure the trees had been there since the beginning of time.

"Don't be too anxious, mate." The big man grinned. "Ya gets a good night's sleep and we'll see Dan'l come tomorrow noon."

"Tomorrow noon," Chris repeated. The main camp could not be too far away.

He took his blanket and found himself as comfortable a place as he could. Then he lay down, clasped his hands behind his head, and looked up through the trees at the millions of stars that sparkled in the black night sky.

If this were not such a dangerous situation he might have laughed. A few weeks ago he had been a man enjoying the comfort and peace of a wealthy family and good friends. Who would believe, he thought, that Chris Martin would be sleeping on the ground in a swamp, and in the company of three of the most obnoxious characters he had ever met?

"Lucas, my friend"—he chuckled to himself—"I hope you appreciate the extent of what I've done in the name of friendship. I sure hope this is worth it."

Thoughts of Lucas brought Chris's mind to Ria. It was a sad situation when a man was in love with one woman and married to another. He wondered if Lucas realized he was in love with Ria. Then he hoped this was the one time the Maine luck would hold.

They might find the pirate. They might pull this whole thing off, but then . . . would Ria understand the situation? How would they work it out?

Despite what Lucas thought, the St. Thomas family might not be amused by his attempt to toss his wife aside. It just might not be something they

223

would allow.

Chris sighed and turned on his side, trying to put his nagging worries aside and sleep. He had to be alert tomorrow. He was going to close the link between Henri Duval and Dan McGirtt.

Despite his determination, it took him a long time to get to sleep.

Chris was awakened rather abruptly when one of his fellow travelers nudged him a little roughly with his foot.

"Wake up. Want to sleep in this place all day? Maybe a big fat snake will curl up with you if you lay still long enough."

Chris rose and packed what gear he had. Within a half-hour after sunrise they were on their way again.

Chris could feel the sweat beading on his forehead and between his shoulder blades, and he realized the day's heat had not even begun. They walked without speaking, a situation Chris favored, for he had very little to say to his companions anyway.

As the sun rose higher and became hotter, Chris's breath got ragged and his clothes became wet with perspiration. "Lucas, old friend," he muttered to himself, "you are going to owe me a lot for this."

Chris was shocked when they suddenly stepped from the heavily forested swamp into a wide clearing that looked almost like a small town. He followed the others toward the center of this group of huts, to a hut somewhat larger than the rest. In front of it stood a large bear of a black man whose white smile flashed in a wicked grin as they approached.

"Hello, Matt," the first man said. "The boss here?"

"Been here fo' some time. He be 'spectin ya."

Chris could almost hear the acceleration of his

heart. Without speaking a word he entered the hut behind his three guides. The small village was not Chris's only surprise. The two men who stood near the center of the room were the last thing he expected.

"Zeb?" a soft and almost cultured voice said. "You've brought a guest with you. How many times must I tell you to let us know of any contacts you make before you bring them here. Do you want the authorities to locate us?"

"Ah, he's all right, boss. He's down on his luck. Got thrown off his ship and didn't have any other place to go. Ya said ya allus needed more men."

The voice was controlled, but Chris could sense the undercurrent of exasperation in it. "Yes I did, Zeb. But I'd like to know about them and talk to them before you bring them here."

Zeb nodded, but Chris realized the man who had spoken was still annoyed at him. He seemed to know Zeb did not have the ability to retain an idea for any length of time. He turned to look at Chris, and Chris suddenly felt as though he were being turned inside out for a thorough examination by the most piercing eyes he'd ever seen.

The man was not tall, standing just over five foot nine, nor was his build large. Yet Chris sensed something charismatic about him. His face was angular, its flesh drawn taut over fine bones. His mouth was broad, the lower lip fuller than the upper; and his nose was long, straight . . . almost aristocratic. His eyes, set wide apart, were crystal blue and piercing.

"Who are you?"

"My name is Chris Martin, and as Zeb says I had a run-in with my skipper and he tossed me off the ship. I have need of some way to make a coin or two so I can afford passage home."

225

"What ship are you from and who was your skipper?"

"Who are you?" Chris countered. For a moment there was absolute silence; then the man's smile broadened and he spoke even more softly.

"I'm Dan McGirtt. This is my friend John Linder. Now suppose you finish answering my questions."

"I'm off the *Black Angel,* under Captain Gabriel Blanc. He's the devil's right hand I'll tell you that."

Chris took perverse pleasure in libeling Lucas. He thought he deserved some little revenge for the chances he was taking. But he was again surprised when Linder smiled and gave a slight nod to Dan.

"He's a newcomer, but he's getting close with Henri. I wouldn't be a bit surprised to find them two of a kind." It was obvious John Linder kept close contact with what was going on in St. Augustine and the harbor.

The mention of Henri's name made Chris's pulse leap. He'd found the connection. Now if he could just find the proof. He had to maneuver himself deeper into this gang, to find out just where and when McGirtt and Duval came together. It was clear that McGirtt and Linder knew a great deal about what was happening in Mantanzas harbor.

"Well, make yourself comfortable," McGirtt said. "We'll see if we can find something for you to do." Again the words were spoken in a tone that suggested slight amusement.

"Thank you," Chris replied. He started for the door.

"Mr. Martin." McGirtt's voice was firm and cold— and very final. "Don't try to leave the camp. You might meet with an accident in that unfriendly swamp out there. We wouldn't want anything to happen to you before you found . . . whatever it is you're looking for. You said money for passage home, didn't you?"

Chris nodded, unprepared to acknowledge or to respond to the open threat.

"Then I think we might find you something. Until then . . . you're our guest."

Chris knew quite well if he took one step beyond the camp he might just disappear into the swamp and never be found. He would have to plan very carefully if he wanted to escape the situation in which he had put himself.

Henri was prepared to leave Matanzas Bay. It was just two days since Lucas had sailed, but once he had made provisions for the security of Brian's ship, he'd felt he had all his loose ends thoroughly tied.

Most of his men were needed aboard his ship, so he had placed a skeleton crew aboard the *Swan* and had forced most of Brian's men below decks. The hatches were locked, making the ship a very effective prison.

Satisfied that his plans were safely in motion he left to fulfill his own part in them. He looked forward to taking another vessel. A new prize would reward his crew and add to his own considerable profits.

His ship was beyond doubt a fine one—strong, well manned, and carrying enough cannon power to blow the largest vessel from the water if necessary. He had a smooth sea and enough breeze to carry him to his destination at almost the exact moment he had planned.

He was in his cabin when word was brought that the ship he sought was on the horizon.

"We've sighted her, Captain."

"Has she spotted us yet?" Henri asked quickly.

"I don't think so, sir, but she's sure runnin' heavy.

She don't stand a chance of gettin' away. We're comin' in at her out of the sun. I expect she'll see us in a few minutes."

"Good." Henri laughed as he stood up and began to buckle on his scabbard. Sliding his sword into it, he tucked a pistol into the wide sash he wore about his waist. "Run up the flag. As soon as you're close enough fire across her bow. If she doesn't submit at once, make her understand who is master of the sea here."

"Aye, sir."

Both men went on deck immediately, Henri going to the quarter deck where he watched with interest the slow approach of his victim.

On board the merchant ship, word was being brought to the captain that a vessel was coming toward them from out of the sun, and because of the glare they could not as yet see what flag she flew.

Captain Horatio Bimms had been enjoying a comfortable breakfast with two passengers. It was unusual for a ship of this kind to carry passengers, but an emergency had made it imperative that Thomas Herald return to his Carolina plantation at once. With Thomas was his daughter Louisa, whose presence made both the captain and Thomas nervous. They knew travel on the high seas was dangerous, but Thomas had had no choice.

Since his wife's death several years before Thomas had kept his only child close to him. She was the joy of his life, and had taken quickly to the responsibility of being her father's hostess when he entertained.

She was an intriguing young woman. She looked extraordinarily delicate and, with her porcelain beauty, somewhat fragile. But she was not. Dedicated to her father, she handled his affairs with a crisp efficiency that both astounded and pleased him.

Louisa was quick to laugh, and her blue eyes were observant. Her pale blond hair was a thick shining crown of curls that framed her heart-shaped face. She was boyishly slender and somewhat tall for the fashion of the time, yet she had a beauty that drew envious whispers from women and looks of deep admiration from men whenever she entered a room.

Horatio Bimms apologized, reluctant to leave such company.

"I am truly sorry, but I must be on deck. One can never tell in these waters whether an approaching ship is friend or foe."

"Oh, Captain," Louisa said excitedly, "I should love to come on deck with you."

"No, no, Miss Herald. I'm afraid I shall have to ask you to remain here. We are not prepared for battle, but if this ship is unfriendly we might be forced to defend ourselves."

Thomas's face paled. He looked into Louisa's excited eyes, and began to regret that he'd given in to her to accompany him.

"Daughter, I want you to promise to stay below decks. It is going to be difficult enough if we have to face some bandits—"

"Pirates," Captain Bimms put in reluctantly.

"But I want you safe below decks," her father continued.

"Father, I'll be no safer here than on deck if we are overcome. At least there I will have time to find a way to defend myself."

"No! I want you to stay here. Is that understood?"

Louisa realized her father was truly upset, and she was suddenly very afraid. "All right, Father. If it makes you feel better I'll stay here."

The two men left the cabin and quickly went on deck. They watched the ship that was still a dark blot on the horizon slowly come closer and closer.

The captain raised the telescope to his eye and stood motionless for some time.

"She flies no flag yet," he muttered. "I've a feeling we had best be prepared." He snapped quick orders that set his crew moving. They readied the few guns they had; then each man armed himself so he could help repel a boarding party.

The *Sea Rover* drew closer and closer while Henri stood in watchful silence. Then, when his ship was so close the merchant had lost any chance of evading him, he gave two orders.

"Run up the flag." He laughed. "And send a shot across her bow. I want it as close as you can bring it, so her captain will understand we mean business."

The black flag with the skull and crossbones fluttered in the wind, and the first shot splashed within two feet of the bow of the merchant vessel.

Captain Bimms gave a groan of despair. He was much too heavily laden and underarmed to present any form of defense. At any other time he would not have cared. He would have fought his best, even given up his cargo if necessary. But in the present situation his hands were tied. He could think only of the young woman in his cabin.

If he surrendered, they might just take his cargo and not think, since he was on deck, to look in his quarters. He spoke quickly to Thomas, who agreed; the man wanted his daughter protected at all costs. Then, his brow furrowed with worry, Captain Bimms ordered the white flag of surrender raised and the British flag lowered.

Henri was more than pleased, but he was slightly puzzled too. It was rare that any prize he took did not put up more of a fight. He began to wonder if the captain of this vessel had something of exceptional value to protect.

The *Sea Rover* came alongside the merchant, and in a short time grappling hooks were tossed out and the two ships were drawn together.

Captain Bimms stood with Thomas, his teeth gritted in anguish, as he prepared to sacrifice his cargo with no struggle at all. The two men watched Henri come aboard and swagger arrogantly toward them.

"Bon jour, mon Capitaine," Henri chuckled. "It is a lovely day no?"

"Thieving bastard, don't play with me. Take what you have come for and leave."

"Now, Capitaine," Henri chided, "you test my temper. Do not forget I can easily sink you here and now."

Henri watched both men pale, and intuition told him he was right. Aboard this ship, there was something of more value than the cargo she carried.

"Do not worry, *mes amis,*" Henri laughed. "I do not need an invitation to take your cargo; I take what pleases me. But"—he watched the two men astutely—"I have the feeling you are much too anxious for me to be gone. I think we must discuss the matter of whatever it is you are trying to hide."

"What can I hide? Your men are already taking what cargo I carry. I only want you to be gone."

"Again, *monsieur,* I think you are lying."

"The captain is trying to protect me," Thomas said. "I am a wealthy man and he didn't want me involved in his difficulties."

"Hmmm." Henri eyed Thomas. "A wealthy man, and who are you?"

"My name is Thomas Herald."

231

"And you thought I sought prisoners for ransom. *Non,* I am not interested in you, Mr. Herald. I have no time for prisoners." He watched relief touch both men's faces, but some inner signal still shrieked an alarm. Henri Duval did not like to be bested. He would not have these two men laughing at him once he was gone. He raised his sword until the point was only inches from Thomas's throat.

"I think, *monsieur,*" he said softly, "that there is more here than meets the eye. You have something you wish to tell me?"

"I've no idea what you are talking about. I booked passage on this ship like any other traveler. I have nothing to do with the cargo in any way."

"And you have brought nothing valuable aboard with you?" he questioned softly.

Henri was quick to see the fleeting fear in Thomas's eyes. His sense of satisfaction grew.

He quickly called out an order, and several of his men rushed to his side. "Go below. Go to every cabin, every nook, everyplace where anything can be hidden. Bring me whatever you find. I want a thorough search."

Thomas's face had gone gray, and he shook from the first real fear he had ever known as the men rushed away to follow orders.

"No! No!" he groaned. He would have rushed to his daughter, but the point of Henri's sword did not waver.

"Be still, *mon ami,*" Henri said quietly, "or you will spill much of your blood on the deck of this ship."

In less than ten minutes the men returned, dragging a struggling Louisa between them. When they stopped near Henri his smile was wide and his eyes held a wicked gleam of pleasure.

"So." He grinned. "You have brought nothing of value aboard. Well, if this lovely creature is not yours, you will not be too alarmed if I take her with me. She is, after all, part of the ship's cargo."

"No!" Thomas replied. He was prepared to beg. "She is my daughter, my only child. Take me, she will see that any ransom you want paid. You cannot be monster enough to do this!"

"Monster? I, *monsieur*? But no. I intend to show the young lady what a gentleman I can be." He snapped to his men, "Take her to my cabin."

Louisa screamed and fought bravely, but it was useless. Thomas surged forward in her defense, but one of the pirates struck him with a heavy club and he crumpled to the deck in a heap. Henri turned to Captain Bimms.

"Tell your friend, when he awakens, that I will send him a message to tell him what her ransom will be. Until then"—he laughed softly—"she will be my guest."

Captain Bimms watched Henri leave the ship. In his heart he doubted if Thomas would ever see his daughter again.

Chapter 17

Lucas tasted defeat, a new kind of defeat, one he could not battle or understand. It had been over a week since he had left Matanzas Bay, a week whose nights were filled with unparalleled ecstasy and whose days were filled with a subtly waged war.

He was at the wheel now, watching Ria indulging in laughing conversation with one of the many crewmen she had charmed.

Every man aboard knew she was the captain's woman, but most of them, although they were flattered and enjoyed her company, were aware of the icy strain that existed between her and their captain.

Lucas knew every move she made, each person she spoke to, and even what they spoke about. Every day ended with the same battle and the same result. He could tame her body, but he could not seem to capture or even hold for a moment the gentle loving Ria. Always he possessed her only when he forced her to surrender. And each night ended the same way: Ria wept bitter defeated tears and Lucas lay awake long after she slept an exhausted sleep, wondering if she would ever truly surrender to him without self-recrimination.

He chastised himself, knowing it was better that they felt no love for each other. But doing so could not erase the fact that he wanted some subtle thing from Ria, something she had vowed never to give.

He watched her now, and even from this distance he could feel the soft texture of her skin, taste the mouth that laughed in obvious pleasure at something the seaman said. That she had been adopted totally in some capacity—sister, daughter, or wife— by every member of the crew did not escape Lucas.

She had twisted her hair into one long thick braid, and had acquired a pair of the cabin boy's breeches and one of his shirts. The breeches were rolled up to her knees. Her feet were bare. Because of its length, the shirt was tied at her waist, and the sleeves were rolled to her elbows. Her hair had been streaked lighter in the sun, and her skin had acquired a golden tan.

Although he wanted her every time he looked at her, he cursed her ability to shatter his tenuous peace of mind. As he watched she turned her head to look at him and her amethyst eyes reflected the defiance that was always under the surface.

Again he felt the frustration that plagued him when she was near. What was the key to Ria? What word or action would bring a light to her eyes? Surely he offered her as much as Brian had. Surely she knew her physical response to him was not a lie. Yet he knew without doubt there was a Ria she had locked away from him.

Lucas was surprised that he cared. He possessed her body. She was as much his as he had wanted her to be. What more could either of them ask for?

He knew she deliberately spoke of Brian with loving affection. That was a thorn in his side—the only weapon she had and she used it with skill,

236

wielding it like a spiked club to leave his spirit bloody each time they came in contact.

Ria watched as Lucas turned the command of the ship over to one of his men and then walked in her direction. Her brow furrowed in a deep frown as she realized, with annoyance, that he drew on her senses with a magnetic pull. She hated the power he seemed to have over her, yet she watched his approach with a tingle of what she refused to recognize as excitement.

The sailor she had been talking to swiftly removed himself from her presence as soon as he noticed his captain's approach. This annoyed Ria, for she hated knowing that every man saw her as the captain's possession.

With calm deliberation she turned her back to Lucas and leaned on the rail, studiously watching the pale blue sky and the fluffy piles of white clouds that hung on the horizon.

Lucas stopped beside her, and without looking at him she could envision his arrogant stance as he leaned against the rail and crossed his arms over his chest.

He reached out a hand, brushing it against her hair. How beautiful she is, he thought. Another open sign of his passion, she thought, as she backed away a little from his touch.

"Don't do that," she snapped, a slight trace of panic in her voice.

"Easy, love," Lucas said softly. "Pull in your claws, I only want to talk to you."

"I do not see that we have anything to discuss. The situation is as you chose it to be." She sneered. "What do I have to say about it?"

She started to walk away from him, but she was taken totally by surprise when he seized her arm and dragged her to him. One arm bound her against his chest which seemed suddenly to fill the entire scope of her vision.

She gazed up at him in shock, then began a useless struggle that left her exhausted. Finally she stood still in his arms.

"That's better," he said. He loosened his grip only enough to let her breathe. "I think it's time we talk about what choices we both have."

"I don't understand you."

"You've never tried. You've only forced me into the position we're in," he replied in a tone laced with enough humor to prick her anger.

"I!" she gasped. "I forced this situation! You unmitigated scoundrel!"

She writhed in his grasp, but his grip only tightened a little and she again realized the futility of struggling. Her amethyst eyes glinted with anger.

"That's better." He chuckled. "You simply insist on not facing what you know to be the truth."

"Truth! You wouldn't know or understand truth if it were a snake and bit you!"

"Ah, Ria," he said gently, his amber eyes dark with a glow she fully understood. "I accept the truth as it is. I don't lie to myself about what I feel when I hold you. You are the one who deceives herself into believing there is nothing between us." He let his voice lower to a soft whisper. "Shall I remind you of last night? Were your sighs and moans of ecstasy a lie? Did I imagine the soft touch of your arms about me, the full response of the woman who gave herself to me completely as her passion would allow? Ria, I'm not the one who lies."

Her cheeks warmed at his casual reminder of the past night's encounter. She remembered it well . . . all too well. Though she had tried to resist, he had again subdued her body and had coaxed it to respond to him completely.

He raised an eyebrow and considered her flushed cheeks, her soft trembling mouth. Then his gaze moved lower to survey the soft curves beneath the loose shirt.

She could feel the heat of it, and began to wonder whether he could see through the cotton material. She found it difficult to control her rapid breathing.

One of his hands moved up her back in a slow casual caress that made her squirm against him, and his smile broadened to a grin. "Are you woman enough to admit that we have found something delightfully fulfilling for both of us?"

Now she became still in his arms. He could feel the rapid pace of her heart as he pressed her to him.

"That is how you judge my womanhood, by what pleasure you can get from my body? Is there nothing more? Is there no other scale by which to measure value?"

"What scale do we need to measure passion? We share it. Isn't that enough? Has it not always been enough for you in the past?"

She was stung by his words, and unwanted tears sprang to her eyes. She bit her lip to hold them in check. It was no use to speak to him of her pride and her honor. A man of his kind did not possess these attributes, and did not understand them in another.

But Lucas was well aware of the pain that had leapt into her eyes. He saw her tears and felt the trembling of her body. He regretted his stinging words and would gladly have recalled them if he could.

He wanted to hold her gently, to comfort her somehow. Yet he didn't have the words to dispel the anguish he saw in her eyes.

With grim realization he knew that in any other

situation, he would have asked her to share the balance of his life with him, as his wife. But fate had molded their lives. Taking her home as his wife was a total impossibility. Society would never accept Ria, a pirate's mistress. Her life would be a hell, and he could not make her suffer through that. The reality of his emotions shook him. He cared enough not to want to hurt her anymore, yet he hungered for her with a depth of passion he could no longer control.

He knew, somehow, some way, he had to make her surrender and accept their situation. He wouldn't—couldn't—let her go.

"Passion," Ria said softly. "Is there honor in passion? Is there a future in just passion?"

"We live dangerous lives, in doubtful situations. There is no way to plan any kind of future when our paths may sever at any time."

Ria forced back tears. She knew that as well as he, knew she would one day have to return to her old life. But could she cut off the new one? If not, could she give up her past life and remain with the man who awakened her senses to wild passion? No. That was not enough for her. She had to have a life with a future. She wanted more than he offered. If she had children, she did not want them to be nameless . . . homeless.

"Ria, you told me you were married and you ran away from your husband. Would you believe one more truth? I'm in the same situation."

"You . . . you're? . . ."

"I'm married. To a woman I have never seen and never choose to see. You see our lives are alike. Why can we not just make the best of the situation . . . until we are forced to end it. At least we could part as friends."

"Friends," she whispered through stiff lips. "No,

240

Luke. We can never be friends." Ria suddenly pushed herself away from him and ran. She had to reach the seclusion of the cabin before she gave way to the tears and the pain whose cause she still didn't understand.

It would be better for her if he did let her go, if, at the end of this crazy voyage, they parted friends. Yet she could not face the two thoughts at the back of her mind, thoughts she had refused to acknowledge: she did not want to leave him, and she could not reduce what she felt for him to friendship.

Only minutes after she closed the door, it was opened and Lucas came into the cabin.

He had watched her run from him, and had felt a deeper misery than he had ever known. It was beyond his ability to offer her more, beyond his ability to let her go. He had to find a way to make her face what they shared and what their future would have to be. He followed her.

Ria spun about to face him, choked back the words she might have said, and swiftly turned away from him.

Without a word Lucas came up behind her. With a quick movement his arms encircled her, pinning her arms and holding her tight. She struggled briefly.

He pressed his cheek against her hair. "Be still, Ria," he said softly. "I only want to hold you . . . talk to you."

"Let me go, Luke. It's no use for us."

His low laugh had an edge to it that said more than any words could have.

"When you hold me like this I can't think," she protested, "and you can't listen. There is only one thing on your mind."

"And the same one in yours." He turned her to face him. "But I am the only one to admit it. No matter how many times I hold you, make love to you, you

241

turn away from me without admitting you have wanted me as much as I have wanted you. I want to hear you say it," he said with calm determination. "For once I want to hear you say it. I want you, Ria, and you will admit you need me too."

She saw the glint of fire in his deep amber eyes, felt the power of his hard body as he drew her closer and closer.

Her hands pressed ineffectually against his chest in an effort to keep some little distance between them.

"You will never force me to say anything. I will never become what you want me to be."

"What is it you think I would make of you? A woman who is no longer afraid to love?"

"Love! You call what you do love. Lust is a more appropriate word. Lust! Like two animals in heat!"

Now he was stung to anger. He wanted to hear her say she loved him, and subliminally he realized he had often been on the verge of telling her he loved her.

"Far from it, Ria. There is a world of difference between what we share and lust. I think it's about time you put another name to it."

She could not stand the heat of his flaming amber gaze, yet she could not tear her eyes from his.

Slowly he drew her closer and closer, until their lips were only inches from each other. She was a fire in his blood and he could not seem to find the means to quench it. At first his lips touched hers gently, as if this were their first taste of her. "This is not lust," he breathed softly. "This is so much more. Let your mind free your body, Ria. Come to me once without battle. Come to me and see if this is not all you seek."

His mouth was gentle again as it took hers, playing softly, drinking deeply from the sweet wine of remembrance.

Ria could feel his nearness with every fiber of her being. The manly odors of sweat, leather, and tangy salt invaded her senses. Her pulse began to race, drumming against her chest to match the increase in his; and her heart seemed to take flight.

She wanted to do something—anything—that would release her from this powerful invasion of her senses, but she had lost her equilibrium and the foundation of her resolve was beginning to crumble.

Her head tipped backward under the branding force of his kiss, and her body arched against his. The way of love often ranges from violence to passion. Her hands, instead of forcing him away, now slowly crept up to encircle his neck. Her lips slanted to more fully accept his, and suddenly they were locked in a frantic embrace.

The fragile dam that contained their passions by day shattered, and the force of the flood carried them along in a wild current.

Her eyes closed, she felt him deftly release the buttons of the shirt, and beneath searching hands and lips it fell away. Strong hands caressed the length of her body until they curved around her slim buttocks. His mouth found a passion-sensitive breast, encircled it, and tormented it with tongue and lips until she moaned softly. The tension in her body began to mount with each kiss and caress until she could only cling to him as glorious sensations surged through her creating a demand for more . . . and more.

But there was a need within Lucas that Ria did not yet understand. He released her for a moment, and they stood facing each other, breathing raggedly from the need to be together.

With both hands, Lucas slid the breeches down over her slim hips. Then he drew her to him. "Help me," he whispered.

Trembling fingers slowly assisted him in removing his clothes; then, almost against her volition, they began to stray across his taut bronzed flesh.

Despite a feeble nagging need to resist him, her hands and her body wanted to know him, as completely as he knew her. She moved close enough so that the tips of her breasts caressed his chest, but he made no move to touch her. Gently she touched her lips to his throat, letting her tongue gently flick against his flesh.

Meanwhile she allowed her hands to roam over warm hardened muscles. He held his breath and strove for control as her mouth moved across his skin. She teased his hardened nipples and then descended to his taut belly as she slowly knelt before him. She meant to conquer his wayward passion by taking her fill of it so she could once and for all drive him from her life. Once her cup was full, she thought, then she would no longer be plagued by desire.

Her hands caressed him as her fiery teasing tongue played across his belly and hips, bringing forth a softly muttered groan as he tried desperately to keep his hands from drawing her to him.

Her hands continued their assault on muscles and nerves as they caressed his hips and thighs, then gently found his pulsing heated shaft. Slowly she caressed him until he was forced to grit his teeth as a flame of intense brilliance shot through him.

He had thought this pleasure-agony was all he could bear until her moist lips and soft gentle fingers encircled him and drew from him all his strength of purpose.

Her tongue sent streaks of flame through him, as slowly she fueled the fire within him until he gasped at the pure white heat of ecstasy.

Urgent hands lifted her, and she closed her eyes as he placed her on the bunk. Now he sought to return the longing and pleasure with which she had filled him.

She quivered with sensual delight as his lips moved over her, heightening tantalizing sensations until she felt she could no longer breathe. For a moment she felt she might faint as his tongue worked a miracle of exotic sensations. She wanted to feel the hard thrust of him deep within her. Only their forging together would release tension built to the highest peak.

Her amethyst eyes opened wide and met his glowing amber gaze. He braced himself, an elbow on each side of her, and held his body so that his impassioned manhood pulsed at the entrance to her melting hot core.

Their eyes fused and she moved to arch against him, seeking release for her demanding body. But he held himself in check, which took all the iron control he had.

"Tell me, Ria," he whispered. "Tell me you need me. Tell me you want me."

"Luke," she gasped, "please."

"No," he grated. "For once in all our time together I won't take you. I won't force you. You must tell me that you want me to make love to you. You must tell me you want me."

Her eyes filled with frustrated tears. Always he had taken, always he had forced her into submission, and always she had had this shield to hide behind when rationality returned.

Now he was destroying her shield. She had to admit that the magical power of their bodies' demands was as strong for her as it was for him.

To tease her even more he pressed himself within

her just a fraction, just enough so that her body's response was undeniable.

"Tell me, Ria, or I swear if it kills me I'll leave you now."

"Luke . . . please . . ."

"Say it. Admit the truth for once. Say it."

"I want you," she groaned.

"Not enough," he demanded brutally.

"Luke—"

"Not enough, Ria," he declared.

"Love me, Luke. Make love to me . . . I need you . . . I want you . . . damn you . . . Damn you!"

His heart pounded exultantly as his mouth smothered her last words. He drove to the depths of her in one hard stroke, then began to move, to lift her higher and higher.

Ria arched upward, taking his entire length. She matched him in every way—in need, in demand, and in fulfillment. They became part of each other, one in rhythm and passion.

Their bodies quivered and grew slick with sweat; still they climbed the volcano's peak.

Both were lost now in a cataclysmic explosion that ripped their senses and then left them drifting in a star-studded blackness, clinging to each other, the only solid forms in the void.

There would be time for words . . . later. There would be time to solve problems . . . later. Now there was only the brilliant consuming fire of mutual surrender.

Chapter 18

Ria was lost, totally lost. There was no retreat this time. She had no resources on which she could call. He had totally destroyed her defenses.

Yet she held within her the one thing he could never have. He could possess her body, but never her heart. She would submit, but when she found a way she would return home and try to forget him.

Lucas held her close; then he tipped up her chin to look into her eyes. Submission was there, some kind of defeat was there. He should be pleased, for he had won . . . but he wasn't. There was something else he he had wanted to see in her eyes. It was lacking. There was no pleasure, no love, no warmth in them.

She turned her head from him, and he felt the heat of her tears as they slipped unheeded down her cheeks.

"You are right, Luke," she said softly. "I suppose you have shown me the truth. I am what you say I am. If you want me so, I will be your mistress."

"Ria," he said, "it is not a death warrant for God's sake. Our days together can be wonderful. I've been thinking about it. I'll take you somewhere"—he was thinking of home—"and I'll find a place we can share. We can spend time together."

"That's what we'd have to do for the rest of our lives, isn't it?" she said softly. "I would be the woman in the shadows of your life while she . . . she shares the light. No, Luke. I will be here, on your ship, until we return to St. Augustine. Then you must set me free."

"And where will you go, back to Brian?" he groaned angrily. The sharp bite of jealousy took command. He had tamed her body and her spirit, but still she held from him that strange intangible thing he wanted but could not name.

"If you think you're going back to him, you had best think again," he growled.

"Why, Luke? You've had your way. You've proved your power. Why do you care who I go to? I'm not your wife. You have no claim on anything but my body." She was beginning to fight back again.

Lucas sat up abruptly and jerked her to a sitting position beside him. He took hold of her shoulders and shook her roughly. "You're not going back to him. You belong to me."

Again a decisive barrier was between them, and both were silent. Lucas was about to speak when a knock on the door startled them both.

"What is it?" he called out angrily.

"Sail off the port bow, sir. We've sighted our target."

"Damn," Lucas muttered. "I'll be right there," he called out.

"You're really going to take that ship?" Ria cried out.

"I don't have much choice," Lucas replied as he rose from the bed.

"No choice!" Ria exclaimed. "To be a pirate is your choice. To rob and to kill that's your choice."

"And you and Brian," he roared in exasperation, "what are you? Damned bloody pirates too. How can you criticize my choice when you've made the same one?"

Ria could not deny his words, much as she wanted to, for she had no way of knowing whether he had lied to her or not, whether Brian was safe or not.

Dressed now, Lucas started for the door. His face was dark with anger, and inside he seethed with jealousy. Always her thoughts were on Brian. Could he never erase that man from her mind. Would Brian always be a ghost that stood between them? Lucas turned as he reached the door.

"Stay here, below decks. I want you safe in this cabin in case we're forced into action."

"Forced into action," she responded bitterly. "You mean in case that innocent merchant decides to defend herself."

He pointed a finger at her to punctuate his words. "You stay put here. If I see your face on deck, I swear I'll throw you in the hold until this is over."

Ria wanted to scream out an angry response, but he was gone and the door was slamming behind him while the words were forming on her lips.

Lucas made his way to the quarter deck and took the telescope from the startled first mate's hand. He soon found the oncoming ship and measured in his mind the speed of her approach. The last thing he wanted was to kill anyone or to damage a ship. But he had to take her. Slowly a plan formed in his mind.

"Jacob," he said to the first mate who stood close by awaiting orders.

"Aye, sir."

"Jacob, we are going to test how good your gunners are."

"They're the best, sir."

"We'll be in range soon. There will be a reward for the gunners who bring down her masts."

"We'll do that, sir." The first mate grinned. "It should stop them dead."

"Jacob, I don't want anyone hurt." Lucas chuckled. "I just want them scared to death."

"Aye, sir." He laughed. "Keep 'em in sight, sir. You'll soon have 'em with no sails and waitin' for you to board."

As the two ships drew closer to each other, the gunners aimed their cannons. At Lucas's signal there was a thunderous roar.

The merchant ship rolled sharply under the attack, and the captain cursed the fleet ship that bore down on him. Masts splintered and sails tumbled to the decks, causing confusion as men tried to dodge the spars and sails.

It did not take the captain long to realize he was outclassed and helpless before the pirate ship. Within half an hour the ships were locked together and Lucas was boarding the merchant.

"Take what ye've come for," Captain Marks snapped at Lucas, "and get yer bloody pirates off my ship."

"Captain," Lucas said mildly, "if you will invite me to your cabin we might be able to discuss how you can save your cargo . . . and have help repairing your ship."

Captain Marks blinked in surprise. This was the last thing he expected.

"I don't understand."

"If you've a mind to offer me some brandy I will enlighten you." Lucas grinned.

Captain Marks was shaken and suspicious, but he led the way to his cabin and Lucas followed.

A half-hour later a totally amazed captain looked

at Lucas. "So you're Lucas Maine. I've known your father a number of years, I can see the resemblance now. This is a strange thing you're involved in."

"You have nothing to lose," Lucas said firmly. "Take this letter to my father and he will replace your losses. The second sealed letter is personal, and I trust you will see he gets it."

"Aye, I'll see he gets it." Captain Marks chuckled. "I do hope you are not ever going to take up pirating. The seas will not be safe."

"Don't worry." Lucas laughed. "This is the last cargo I ever expect to . . . ah . . . borrow."

"Well, let us go on deck and see to the borrowing."

When they returned to the deck, crisp orders were given and soon everything of value was transferred to the *Black Angel*. Lucas also took the log and papers from the captain as proof to offer Henri along with the cargo.

"I assure you, sir, this temporary loss will eventually rid the sea of a conscienceless blackguard."

"If you were anyone but Charles Maine's son, I would not be party to this."

"Thank you, Captain. I am grateful for your trust. Now I must go. This cargo will lead me to the proof I need to hang a genuine pirate. It will also make the sea a little safer for you, and for my father's ships." Lucas held out his hand to Captain Marks who took it in a firm grip. "I hope we meet again, Captain Marks. And if we do I owe you a drink."

"I'll hold you to that, lad, I surely will."

Lucas and his men returned to his ship, and soon the merchant vessel was a receding dot on the horizon.

Lucas had accomplished the first step in the capture of Henri . . . and of Brian. It gave him a

251

sudden sense of satisfaction to know that before long Brian would be imprisoned or hung. One way or the other he would be out of Ria's life.

Thinking of Ria, he saw to the cargo's safety with dispatch and then set his course for the rendezvous with Henri. He started toward his cabin, prepared for a confrontation with Ria that would put an end to any thoughts she might have of leaving him.

His thoughts were a tangled mess. He was saddled with a wife he didn't want and physically caught in the quicksilver web of an enchanting mistress he wanted to hold for as long as he could. He didn't have an answer to his dilemma yet, but he was grimly determined to find one.

Ria dressed slowly, knowing the increasing motion of the ship meant it was closing in on its prey. She heard the roar of cannons and felt the ship quiver. Then feet running across the decks and loud shouts told her of the bloody battle that must be taking place.

She sat down on her bunk slowly, trying to erase the pictures that formed in her mind. Luke with a bloody sword in his hand. Killing, maiming, and all for profit. She wanted to hate him, but could not understand the bittersweet taste of her emotions. Why did he have to be what he was? Why could he not be a man of honor, a man she could love?

Again the thought of Brian's fate crossed her mind. She had to survive. She had to be what Luke wanted until she knew her brother was alive and well as he had said. Only then could they throw the truth at Luke. With proof in their hands, they would be able to leave the misery and pain behind them and go home. Home, she thought with renewed anguish.

Home to a man who had married her and who would expect all a wife could give.

She could offer him nothing now. He would never accept her as she was, a woman who had been used by a ruthless pirate. She wondered what recourse he would take. Surely he would give her her freedom. It was all she wanted now anyway. The freedom to be alone . . . and to forget Luke and the magic he wove over her senses.

Suddenly she realized it was nearly silent again. The battle was over. Had he sunk the ship, killed those who manned it? That was a terrible thought. She closed her eyes and saw visions of blood and death about her. Then another thought struck her. Maybe Luke was injured . . . dead . . . and she was left to the mercy of the crew.

"Oh, God," she groaned. She wasn't sure which caused her more pain, fear for herself or for him.

She was startled to awareness when she heard approaching footsteps. Were they Luke's or another's?

Lucas opened the door and stepped inside. He noted the sudden look of relief that crossed her face before her eyes turned cold and they were again foes, caught in a battle neither had wanted but in which neither would surrender.

"So," she said, "it's done."

"The cargo is mine," Lucas admitted.

"And the ship and its crew?"

Lucas shrugged, hoping she would form her own conclusions before he had to tell any more lies.

Her eyes seemed to dominate her pale face as she whispered, "You've sunk it . . . you've killed them . . . all of them."

"I dealt with them the best I could. It certainly wouldn't have been very profitable to drag the ship back and let Henri and your . . . friend deal with them. Would they have been any more merciful than I? I doubt it." Lucas sighed deeply. "I suppose I will never understand you, Ria. You love a man who is as guilty of piracy as I, yet you condemn me and absolve him. You lie to me and to yourself about what exists between us, and your love for him is a wall between us."

"Then let me go," she whispered.

Lucas's brow furrowed in a frown of disbelief. He had never tasted the bitterness of unrequited love. He found it hard to handle. With any other woman, he would have laughed and walked away without a second thought. But this was different somehow, and he couldn't believe his own actions.

"I wish I could do that," he said bitterly, "but you're addictive. I can't seem to let you go."

"You don't understand me, Luke," she said sorrowfully, "and I understand you even less. I ask what you want from me, and you expect me to enjoy the fact that you, in your arrogance, only want the temporary use of my body. Do you truly expect me to fall joyously into your arms. Well, I want— I need— more than that."

"Then why do you insist on going to a man who can offer you even less?"

"Brian," she said meditatively.

"Your precious Brian," he grated out. "Bloody-handed, careless of you, a man destined to be hanged for piracy." He watched her eyes darken and his voice eased. "Do you really love him that much, Ria? Do you really want to return to a man who seems to care so little for you?"

"You . . . you just don't understand. Brian and I . . . It's different," she ended lamely. If she told him the truth and Brian was not dead yet, he soon would

254

be, and her careless words would be to blame.

But she longed to speak out, to tell him that Brian was not what he thought him to be . . . and that she was not what he thought her to be. She never questioned why her heart so desperately wanted him to know the truth, why she wanted him to know her as something more than a pirate's mistress. Why couldn't he? . . . She aborted the thought quickly. There was no future for them. There was only now. Now was all they would ever have.

Lucas was watching her, a puzzled expression on his face. Clouded thoughts stirred his mind. Why couldn't he just let her go? Why did he continually think of her in a permanent way when he knew the reality of his position. Why! Why did thoughts of her and Brian stir wild angry emotions in him. There were no answers and the questions only left him unsettled and searching for something vague and just out of reach.

Lucas wanted to hear no more about Brian and the "difference" Ria had referred to. He had seen Brian's open seduction of other women, and was more than exasperated at Ria's obvious blindness to the man's flaws.

"We have several days of travel before we reach the rendezvous with Henri."

"Yes . . . I know."

His gaze never left hers, and his eyes blazed with an intense amber fire. "It seems we can only agree by necessity," he continued, "so I will bargain with you, Ria."

"Bargain?"

"I want you," he said gently. "We must put aside everything else and consider our circumstances. You want to . . . to go back to him. I'll release you." Her eyes brightened, and he felt another surge of black anger. "Only on my terms."

"Your terms?"

"I don't want to talk of any tomorrows. I don't want to talk of future plans. We'll share the rest of this voyage. Then, if you still want to go, you'll be free to do so."

"Free," she whispered, wondering if she would ever be free of the mastery of his touch. She would carry these memories forever. She knew she had to leave him but . . . An insidious inner voice urged her to take this short time of pleasure, for when she returned home it would be to a life of loneliness or to the arms of a man she did not want.

She held his gaze, but could read nothing in his eyes. She made her decision. If she were to be damned and deserted by a husband she had never wanted because of this interlude, then why should she not take from it all the pleasure and excitement she could. There would be no chains to hold them together. In time both would go their separate ways.

"Well?" he asked, his voice tense and expectant.

"I agree," she said so softly he wasn't sure he had heard her right. He went to her and tipped up her head so he could study her face.

"You said—"

"I said I agree. We will have this time together. When the voyage is over, before you meet Henri, you will let me go and we will both be free."

They were momentarily silent as the word *free* struck them. Would either of them ever be free again?

"Agreed," he said softly.

He cupped his hands about her face and bent to lightly touch her lips with his. Then he looked into her eyes again.

Suddenly Ria felt shaken and insecure. "It . . . it is

so difficult to . . . to begin," Ria stammered.

"We need time," Lucas said gently. "Relax, Ria." He smiled to gentle his words. "I've no intention of throwing you on my bed and ravaging you now. Suppose we start with something much easier. Suppose we begin at the very beginning?"

He was totally beyond her understanding—one minute the bloodthirsty pirate, the next a man who forced her to his will, and now a gentle lover. Would she ever know which man was the real Luke.

He, too, was just as bemused by the thoughts he could not control. He had not won her by taking, could he convince her before they sighted land to make the choice to stay with him. She was an effervescent wisp of moonlight that continued to evade his capture, yet she taunted him to reach for her again and again.

"The beginning?"

"Let's leave this cabin and walk on deck in the sunlight. Let's put what is past in the past where it belongs. Let's . . . let's at least talk to each other."

He watched her expression change from wary distrust to puzzlement, and he felt the tension in her slowly ease. At least, he thought with amusement, she isn't afraid I am going to rape her. One step accomplished . . . but God only knew how many steps there were before she would come to his bed willingly.

She nodded her head and noted his quick smile. Then they left the cabin.

It took the crew a short time to realize the tension between the pair had dissipated. Their captain smiled at the beautiful woman beside him and she smiled in return. The whole ship seemed to move at an accelerated and happier pace, and the men raised their voices in happy song as they handled the ship's canvas and rope.

Lucas was determined that he would not ask Ria any questions about her past, so they said little as they began a tentative relaxation of barriers.

As Lucas stood at the wheel, he watched Ria reestablish herself on her own ground. There would be no more possessiveness from him, even if he had to grit his teeth and grip the wheel until his knuckles were white.

He could not push her again. This time she had to come to him. If he did not capture the elusive Ria now, maybe he never would.

Ria watched the sun slowly drop to the horizon. The pressure of keeping her bargain was making her nerves taut. She turned her head to watch Luke. He was in conversation with his first mate who would have control of the ship during the nighttime hours. The sunlight caught in his hair like a flame and it heated his bronze skin until her fingertips could almost feel it tingle. She could not deny the truth of her thoughts. Luke was almost unbearably handsome.

He stood tall and straight, and even from a distance she could sense the iron strength of him. His white smile flashed against his dark skin as he laughed at some spoken word.

The fire he had the power to ignite stirred deep within her. For the first time in the days and nights they had spent together she had to admit, if only to herself, that she wanted him, that he had touched a place within her no one else had.

It is only a passing thing, she thought. One day he will walk out of my life as casually as he walked in. She knew that was best, for she had to let him go.

A few minutes later Lucas turned to find her gone. His heart thudded painfully as he walked toward his cabin. Which Ria would he find? The tigress or the frightened girl . . . or the woman?

Chapter 19

In the wee hours of the morning, Scott sat quietly at the table in the tavern where Sophia was working. It was nearing the time when her work hours would be over, but that was not what kept a very tense Scott from moving about and sampling the companionship of the last patrons.

He waited, more impatient than he had ever been and much more nervous, waited for his long-sought meeting with one William Cunningham.

Sophia came to his table finally and slid onto the bench across from him.

"Well"—she sighed—"that's all for tonight. It was terrible. I'm glad it's over."

"Sophia . . . where is he?"

"William?"

"Of course William. Who did you think I meant, King George?"

"Don't get touchy, love." Sophia laughed. "William won't be showing his face until the last of these blokes gets out of here."

Scott looked about. There were only two men finishing their drinks. One sat at a table very close to them, the other across the room. The closest man

261

seemed obviously the worse for drink.

"Damn it!" Scott said. "It might take the rest of the night to get these two out of here. Maybe I ought to toss them out myself."

"No. I don't think you should do that. I'm sure William will be here soon and these two will be gone. Why don't I get you one last drink?"

Scott nodded. If he had to wait he might as well enjoy it.

When Sophia returned she set two drinks on the table and again sat down opposite him. "You're really anxious to meet William, aren't you?"

"I am. Sophia, this may be a big chance for me. I've heard he has . . . well, contacts. I need to meet the right people. I can't just laze around here day after day and night after night, not if I want to get somewhere."

"Somewhere . . . where? Where's somewhere?"

"Come on. We both know what I am. We also know my captain has gotten himself killed and my ship has been taken over by another unscrupulous man."

"Why don't you just join him?"

"When I was first mate I had a lot to say on the ship, and I had a bigger share of all the prizes we took. Under this captain I'd get a whole lot less. I'm not a man to sit around and let myself get robbed. I'll find the head man and make my own way. Why so many questions?"

"Because," a firm hard voice at his elbow declared, "Sophia is getting my answers for me."

It was the man from the table next to them, the one Scott had thought was drunk. He was very sober, and his steel gray eyes were watching Scott closely. He was tall and solidly built, and he looked as though he had weathered many of life's storms. He had the chiseled, rugged face of the adventurer.

"William Cunningham I presume," Scott said with a casual smile. "Sit down Mr. Cunningham and let me buy you a drink. I've been wanting to meet you for a long time."

William stood immobile for some minutes, and Scott could barely breathe as the tension grew. If he wasn't accepted he had no other way to make contact with the pirate.

Suddenly William smiled and sat down next to Sophia, who silently slid over to give him room. "They call me Will . . . and I'll take that drink, thank you."

"Sophia," Scott said softly as he still held Will's eyes, "suppose you get . . . Will a drink. Then we can talk."

Sophia did as Scott told her, returning with a drink for Will.

"You are a determined man, Mr.? . . ."

"The name is Scott . . . Scott Fitzgerald."

"We've been watching you for some time."

"Why?"

"To make sure."

"And now you're sure."

"Reasonably. We know what your captain was. We know he was dealing with our old friend Henri, and we know he's dead."

"Then you know I'm not lying."

"We only know what you're not lying about. We don't know if you're . . . just omitting things you don't want known."

"What do you want from me?"

"Me? Nothing."

"Then why bother with all this."

"Because a friend of mine wants to talk to you."

"A friend. I suppose he has a name."

263

"Of course, a rather popular one."

"Dan McGirtt."

"Don't use his name."

"There's no one here but us."

"Carelessness becomes a habit. It could be a habit we can't afford."

"All right. I won't use it again. You said your friend wants to talk to me."

"Yes."

"When . . . where?"

"When I'm ready, and where I choose."

"I see."

"What do you see?"

"That you still have some deciding to do. You're not completely satisfied yet."

"You're very clever."

"Thanks, but that doesn't tell me anything."

"The day after tomorrow. Be here. We'll talk some more."

"I don't have all the time in the world to play games."

Will chuckled softly. "Take the time," he said quietly. Then he turned and left the tavern.

Scott sighed, and Sophia came around the table to sit beside him.

"Well," he said disgustedly, "that seems to have settled that. I don't think I have a chance at what I want."

"Don't jump to conclusions."

"What are you saying?"

"Will liked you."

"Of course," Scott said wryly. "You could tell from his enthusiasm. He was just overjoyed to see me."

"Scott, I know Will very well. If he hadn't wanted to talk to you he would have just gone and you would never had known. He's been watching you all evening. Besides he wouldn't have set a time and place if he hadn't thought it would be all right."

"You're sure?"

"I'm so sure I'll tell you a secret. Dan's camp is up on the San Sebastian River, and I'll bet when Will comes again and you meet, he's going to take you there."

"Great." Scott smiled. "Now all we have to do is wait."

"Well," Sophia said softly, "I know a place much more private and much more comfortable for us to wait in."

"Lead on, my lady. Right now I could use some . . . comfort."

Sophia laughed, and they rose and left the tavern together.

They made love with a wild new abandon that bordered on ferocity. Then, when the night was deep and Sophia slept soundly, Scott rose from the bed, dressed, and quietly left the room.

He moved through the dark streets with easy familiarity, and soon he was rapping softly on Brian's door. It was opened so quickly that Scott knew Brian had not been asleep.

"It's about time," Brian declared. "For God's sake, man, I've been cooped up in this room for two days waiting for word from you."

"Well, I have word all right. Tonight I had my first meeting with Will Cunningham, and in two or three days I'm going to meet the elusive Dan McGirtt."

"Wonderful! What about me?"

"I've been thinking of a new plan."

"What do you have in mind?"

"We have two days before I meet McGirtt."

"Yes?"

"I have no legitimate excuse for your presence."

"I'm not just staying here," Brian protested.

"No . . . you're not."

"Just what am I going to be doing?"

"Tomorrow night we are going to get your ship back."

"Are we? Just how are we going to do that."

"I'm working on a plan. After we get it back you will sail up the San Sebastian River, and at the first sign of your ship I'll signal where the camp is located and we'll meet."

"Sounds risky."

"It is, but it's our only chance."

"I want the *Swan* back."

"Well, we're going to get it. Be ready tomorrow night at the same time. I'll be back and we'll see what we can accomplish."

Sophia murmured in her sleep, but did not waken when Scott slipped back into bed. He was grateful, for it would have been difficult to try to explain where he had been, especially since he had just met Will. He did not doubt that both Sophia and Will would believe he was betraying them to the authorities.

The next day Scott made his way to the docks. He came as near the *Swan* as he dared and watched her closely.

It was not long before he realized the decks of the *Swan* were nearly devoid of life. He surmised where her original crew might be.

On the decks, according to his count, were only six of Henri's men. He wasn't sure there weren't some below so he waited throughout the entire day. If they

266

were changing shifts he couldn't see it. By early evening he came to the final conclusion that the original count of six was accurate. Only when he was sure of that and had worked out a tentative plan, did he return to the tavern. Then he had to pass the hours until Sophia slept before he could go to Brian and divulge his plan.

Scott was less than amused by the fact that when he had nothing to do but enjoy Sophia the time slipped rapidly by, but now that he had a goal the time almost seemed to stand still.

If Sophia was aware of his attempt to keep his impatience under control she gave no hint of it. She seemed quite happy that Scott and Will had finally met, and she remained under the impression that the drawing together of these two men would keep Scott with her for as long as she could hold him.

Sophia had never tasted love with any of the men she had known, and Scott's gentleness and consideration soothed her into believing in him. If Scott didn't love her it was all right, but she was beginning to build a mystique about him that would have surprised even Scott.

They returned to Sophia's room very late and before long found themselves deep in the sensual pleasure both enjoyed to the fullest. Afterward, the time really seemed to crawl by, and Scott's nerves were taut before Sophia was sleeping deeply enough for him to slip away.

It was a cloudless night with a full bright moon that brought a curse to Scott's lips. If he'd ever needed moonless darkness, he needed it now.

Well—he shrugged—there was nothing else to do. They would have to go through with it, for the next night he was to meet Will and he wanted both Brian and the *Swan* to be gone by then.

267

He wished they could have had more help, for two against six was rather unbalanced odds. But there was no one he could trust. He made his way to Brian's room, where he found a very impatient Brian who had been pacing the floor for hours.

"Where the hell have you been?"

"Sorry. I just couldn't get here any sooner."

"Have you seen that damned moon?"

"Bright as gold. It's going to make things a little harder, but we have to do it tonight. After tonight I don't think we will have much more contact."

"If this works, I'll see you upriver somewhere. If it doesn't, we'll be dead."

"Let's get going."

"You said you had a plan?" Brian questioned his friend as they left the room.

"Well"—Scott grinned—"it's a little too uncertain to actually call it a plan." He began to explain it as they made their way through the dark streets. Finally even Brian had to laugh.

"You call that a plan?"

"Can you think of something better?" Scott challenged.

"No. I guess not, but it's going to be chancy and dangerous."

"Better than sitting here and waiting for Henri to come back. For certain the *Swan* would be permanently gone then. We might, too."

"All right," Brian said as they drew closer to the nearly deserted docks. "Let's get to it."

"How good a swimmer are you?" Scott asked.

"It would sure take the edge off your plan if I couldn't swim, wouldn't it?"

"To tell you the truth that was one thing I never thought of," Scott admitted.

They stood some distance from the *Swan*, and in

the dark shadows they removed their clothing until both wore only breeches.

"You can get some clothing from your crew if this works, and I can come back for mine," Scott whispered.

"If this doesn't work, clothes will be the last of our worries."

"Put one knife between your teeth and slide the other into the waistband of your pants. We're going to need them."

"I wish there was a way to carry my sword. I'm handier with it," Brian replied.

"Well, there is no way, so we just have to make do with what we have. Ready?"

"Let's go."

They slipped into the dark water as silently as they could; then, knives clasped firmly between their teeth, they began to swim as silently as possible toward the *Swan*.

It did not occur to the six men on the *Swan* that someone would actually try to take her, or that danger might come from the bay side of the deck.

Four of the men were curled on blankets asleep. The other two were keeping a rather negligent guard. They sat together, casually involved in a game of dice, only occasionally casting an eye on the moon-brightened docks.

Scott and Brian moved very carefully now as they approached the ship that rocked gently with the current. When they finally touched her side, they worked their way to the anchor rope and, in utter silence, climbed until they could peer over the rail of the ship to spot the men who guarded it.

Both were grateful that the two men awake had their backs to them. They looked at each other; then Scott nodded. Now was the test. If they could reach these two men without drawing their attention, they could dispose of them without arousing the others.

They moved slowly—very slowly—until their feet touched the deck. To both of them it seemed as if even their breathing had stopped in their efforts to remain silent.

One step . . . two . . . three. Hearts pounded heavily, and nerves were drawn to the breaking point. Another step . . . another. Now they were within two feet of the guards, who had drunk quite a bit, and were unaware of the danger so close behind them.

Within seconds swift and silent death assured that they would remain unaware for eternity.

It had gone well so far, almost too well was Scott's feeling as they began to make their way past the sleeping forms and to the bolted door of the companionway.

They moved in a breathless silence until they came to the door. Then Brian and Scott exchanged frustrated glances.

"You should have come equipped with a key," Scott whispered humorously.

Brian laughed softly. "I have one."

"Where?" Scott said quickly.

"In my desk in the captain's cabin."

"Great. What will we do?"

"Break it in," Brian said.

"They'll be wide awake at the first sound." Scott gazed at the door. "It's a small door. I can defend it against an army for a short while. At least until you go down and free your men."

"The hell you will. It's my ship. You go below and I'll defend it."

"Brian, if we don't do something fast, we'll both be defending nothing," Scott said. Before Brian could protest again, he stuck his knife through the bolt and sprung it loose with a sharp crack. As he swung the door open, the four sleepers stirred awake. Scott gave Brian a push.

"Get below," he said as he placed his back to the door. "Get help!"

Brian protested no further; there was no time. He dashed below leaving behind the sounds of battle and, to his surprise, of Scott's joyful laugh.

The battle was vicious, but short, for it took Brian only minutes to release his men. He called to them to follow him and dashed back to the deck where a force of their number quickly did away with the remaining four guards. Their bodies were unceremoniously dumped overboard.

Brian turned to Scott. Both men were sweating and panting raggedly, but their smiles were broad.

"You'd best get this ship out of this harbor as quickly as you can," Scott said. "I don't have the slightest idea where the camp along the San Sebastian is, but I do know that Henri will go there eventually. I think the best thing you could do would be to get upriver, find a secluded place, and watch for Henri."

"Good idea. When you get to the camp, you be damned careful. I owe you a debt and I don't want you to get yourself killed before I get a chance to repay it." The words were spoken in jest, but Scott knew Brian meant them.

"Brian, you be careful too, and remember, I want to be with you when you catch up with this Captain Blanc."

"I'll be glad to take you with me, but I want to be the one who gives him what he so justly deserves. I have to know where Ria is."

"If she is anything like your description of her, I'd

271

say she can take care of herself. We just have to hope he's been smart enough not to harm her. No matter what, Brian, you can count on my support . . . and any help you might need."

The two men clasped hands firmly. Then Brian watched Scott make his way down the gangplank and disappear into the shadows of the docks before he turned to his men.

"Get her sails up," he ordered. "Get us out of this harbor before all hell breaks loose."

Men scattered, climbing the rigging to unfurl the sails so they would snap into place and fill with the breeze that lifted the ship and eased her from the dock.

Brian felt exultant as the deck shifted beneath his feet. He held the wheel, feeling life shudder through the ship as she moved before the breeze, headed for the channel to the open sea.

When the *Swan* was safe on the open sea and Brian knew no one had followed her, he turned the wheel over to one of his men and went below to find some fresh clothes.

He opened the sea chest he had brought aboard, then paused as swift painful memories flooded over him. A small amount of Ria's clothing lay folded in one corner. Among those items was the turquoise dress he had once given her as a birthday present.

For a moment tears stung his eyes. Where was she now? Was she hurt, lonely, helpless? Did she need him?

He felt poignant guilt and stung himself with harsh recriminations. He had not been there when she had so desperately needed him.

His jaw clenched in anger and he bent over the chest, picking up his sword in one hand and Ria's dress in the other.

"I'll find him, Ria. I swear to you I'll find him. And when I do I shall make him pay in blood and pain for every single moment you spent with him."

Brian dressed swiftly and went on deck. He carried his map with him to set the course. He knew it was not far to the mouth of the San Sebastian.

Ria was a constant presence on the periphery of his mind, as was the man who had stolen her from him, and his need for vengeance grew until it was a huge dark cloud that controlled most of his thoughts.

Scott was having some difficulty locating the clothes he had discarded. It took him longer than he'd thought it would to find them.

Quickly he dried himself on his shirt, then donned the rest of his clothing. The moon was already descending when he half-ran half-walked back to Sophia's room.

Scott eased into the room, his eyes intent on the sleeping form in the large bed. He tried to muffle the sounds but the door gave a sharp click when he closed it that cut the room's silence and made him freeze as Sophia stirred.

When she slipped back into sleep and remained motionless, Scott breathed a deep sigh of relief.

He moved to the bed, and removed his clothes, and slid in beside Sophia, drawing her warm soft curves close to him and smiling as she twined her arms about his neck and wriggled even closer. After a few minutes his still jangled nerves relaxed, and Scott drifted off into pleasant dreams.

They might not have been so pleasant if he had known that Sophia was not asleep. She had wakened when the door had clicked and had known immediately that the bed was empty. When Scott had slipped into bed and drawn her to him, she had put her arms about his neck and had been shaken when her fingers had come into contact with his hair and found it wet.

Even after she had heard his deep and regular breathing she had lain awake while tears assailed her. Where had he been, with another woman? Why was his hair wet . . . and worse, should she tell Will of his night excursions . . . was he a spy, a traitor? All these questions were held in check by another more urgent one: did she want to lose Scott? For the first time in Sophia's life she began to think of someone other than herself, and she found it the most painful thing she had ever done.

Chapter 20

Dan McGirtt's camp, for all its seemingly randomly placed huts and campfires, was really a well-run, well-disciplined organization. Chris had quietly waited and watched through the hot lazy days. He knew the entire camp waited for something, and he was sure it would be the arrival of Henri and Lucas. Once that happened, he and Lucas would find a way to talk together. Then they would be able to combine what proofs they had of piracy and go to the authorities.

He had learned a very great deal while he had been here. Although most of the men gathered about McGirtt were unsavory types who were there for profit only, some of McGirtt's followers told stories of the persecutions that had driven them here. He also saw a side of Dan's character that negated all the stories he had heard. He saw a justice in McGirtt's leadership that would have been rare in civilized society and was even more rare under these circumstances.

He looked at Dan from a totally new perspective now, and saw him as a man whose confidence he would like to have and one he would like to confide in. This shocked him for he'd been well prepared not to trust Dan, but now judging by the trust of the men under Dan's command and Dan's own charisma, he instinctively knew he could tell him everything, though he had no idea how soon he would be doing just that.

Chris had learned that Dan had tried to live in peace, but Zespedes's efforts to finally rid Florida of the banditti had led to vicious attacks on his home. Dan himself had been captured once and imprisoned in the fort at St. Augustine, and it was only after this more than brutal confinement that Dan McGirtt "disappeared" into the Florida wilderness.

Dan also had a private affair now to settle. He had once been, some said, court-martialed in South Carolina and, whipped to action by that injustice, had sought vengeance by harassing the inhabitants of South Carolina and Georgia for several years. Hunted, he'd fled to the woods and swamp. After peace followed the Revolutionary War, he had begun to come forth.

It was quite a bit of time after Chris's arrival before John or Dan would talk freely to him, but he knew that there was no move he made they did not see, nor was there a conversation he had that was not repeated to them. No one limited his movements, but he knew damned well they were restricted.

The camp was quiet when Chris rose. He walked out of the hut he shared with two other men and headed over to the main hut where food could be found. He'd been clever enough to make friends with the rotund wife of one of the bandits, and she made sure there was plenty for him to eat. Once he'd finished eating, the day lay ahead of him—another day of doing nothing.

It was nerve-racking not to know what to expect

next, but what happened was the last thing he'd expected. He walked out of the hut and was met by Dan McGirtt himself. Chris knew immediately that Dan was there on purpose.

"Good morning, Chris." McGirtt's voice was casual and warm.

"Morning," Chris responded.

"Come; take a walk with me."

Chris fell in beside him and they crossed the large open area of the camp in silence. Then they walked into the cover of the moss-shrouded trees.

They followed a path Dan seemed to know well, so Chris said nothing. When they reached a small clearing, Dan stopped. In the center of the open space was a tree stump, and Dan sat comfortably upon it.

"So, Chris. You have been with us nearly two weeks."

"Two weeks of doing nothing."

"Well"—Dan laughed softly—"in a short time we will have something that will keep you busy."

"I came here to make some money."

Again Dan laughed. "Let me tell you why you came here, Chris. Much as you would like us to believe you are a renegade, I have found it very difficult."

"Just what do you think I am?" Chris replied as casually as he could, considering he was shaken.

"A gentleman gone wild. Looking for excitement maybe. Tell me. Why did you take up with a pirate like your Captain Blanc, and why do you want us to believe you parted company . . . unhappily? We know he is dealing with Henri, and we know they are both on their way here with some prime cargo we will take off their hands. What is going on between the three of you?"

"Nothing, I—"

"Chris, don't lie to me."

"What do you want to know?"

"The truth."

"What do you think the truth is?"

"For the sake of conversation let us say that you and your captain did not really have a fight. Let us speculate also that you were not thrown off his ship, but that the two of you are still working together."

"For what purpose?"

"That is what I want you to tell me."

Chris looked into Dan's eyes, and knew that more lies were only going to breed more suspicion. Eventually it would grow and there would be a very slim chance that he would be alive for Lucas to find. He had to build a new story, and he had to do it quickly.

"All right. I admit Captain Blanc really didn't throw me off the ship."

"So. Maybe you are working with the authorities who want to capture McGirtt and his . . . family."

"No!" Chris said with finality. "We don't want you. We never started out to get you."

"Just what have you started out to accomplish? Who do you intend to get?"

The question was quiet, firm, and Dan's eyes held Chris's. Now was the time for truth.

"We want Henri Duval," Chris said, mentally crossing his fingers in the hope that he wasn't decreeing his death.

"Why?" came the quick response.

"Henri has done Captain Blanc some harm. My captain is not a forgiving man. He wants Henri's hide nailed to the door."

"Henri is really not a sound man to deal with."

"You've dealt with him long?"

"No, he did me a favor once, and I owe him one. He

has asked me to move some cargoes for him, and I have agreed. Chris, this camp is only a temporary stop for me." Dan's voice lowered. "I wouldn't want it to be . . . disrupted, wouldn't want any of my people caught, or hurt." He laughed softly. "In fact, I don't want to be caught either. I have an aversion to dying."

Chris didn't know why he believed Dan, he only knew that he did.

He was in an extremely dangerous situation. He needed Dan on his side, because if he couldn't have Dan as a friend, the man was going to be an enemy— a deadly one.

Chris squatted down before Dan. His eyes were level with McGirtt's and matched them in intensity. "I'm going to come clean with you. I know just what you're going to say and you're right: I have to. But, I just have a feeling I can trust you damn it! I have to trust you."

"You're right." Dan smiled. "I'm the only one you've got between you and a nice quiet death in the swamp."

"Dan, we want Henri Duval and only Henri. We have to get him off the sea. We have to put an end to his piracy. You can't cause us any problems, but Henri can and has."

Chris went on to explain the whole situation from beginning to end. He told of his past and of why he and Lucas were there. He knew he was putting his life and Lucas's on the line but he had no choice.

"And what about me and my friends?" Dan said.

"I told you. We don't want you."

"I'm to believe that?"

"I swear it on all I hold sacred. We want Duval."

"You know he will be here soon?"

"Yes . . . but so will Lucas."

"Lucas?"

"Captain Blanc is Lucas Maine."

"And we must wait for him?"

"I can't do a thing without him." Chris grinned. "How else am I going to get out of here? I have a feeling when we get Duval you're going to vanish, and none of us would be averse to turning our heads the other way when you do. Anyway, I wouldn't want to get back to St. Augustine alone. I wouldn't even try to do it."

"You have said one very wise thing. You are alone and even when your captain comes, with Henri and his men you are outnumbered. You could all die out here."

"I don't think you'll let that happen."

"And why not?"

"I've been here two weeks as you say. I've listened and I've seen. Henri may be a bloody cutthroat—I'll even admit some of the men around you aren't so palatable—but you're not of the same breed."

"You're sure of that?"

"Yes," Chris said softly. "I'm sure of that."

"Just what do you think you know about me?"

"That you're a man who's been painted a lot blacker than you are, a man who's been pressured and pushed. That you've not seen your wife and sons in a very long time."

"You have been observant," Dan mused softly. But his eyes took on a deeper respect. "You are right about many things. I will think about what you have said." He rose. "Let's get back."

Chris stood too. "What are you planning to do?"

"Just think," Dan said bluntly. He started back to the village, and Chris had no choice but to follow.

Chris spent the balance of the day with tightly drawn nerves. He was quick to observe that Dan had called John to him and they had spoken for a long time, but nothing had seemed to come of it. He went to sleep that night wondering if he had made the largest mistake in his life . . . and had put Lucas's life on the line as well as his.

Brian paced back and forth on the quarter deck. He was only a few miles from the mouth of the San Sebastian, but he wasn't sure of the river. Obviously Henri knew the way up it, knew the reefs and shallows and sand bars, but he didn't. He would have to feel his way.

He entered the mouth of the river carefully, furling almost all the sails to slow the ship. When the *Swan*'s speed made him nervous, he slowed her again until he was barely moving.

He had so many things on his mind that he hadn't slept: thoughts of Ria, anger at Lucas, and worry about the river. And he was frustrated. To add to his worries he didn't know whether Henri was ahead of him or behind him. If Duval was ahead, Brian didn't want to overtake him, and he was even more certain that if the pirate was behind him he didn't want to be overtaken.

The majority of the men, with the exception of Jake Cade, his first mate, stayed as far away from him as possible while he was in such a black mood. Two men stood at the bow, taking continual measurements, and Brian kept one eye on them as slowly, laboriously, the *Swan* made her way further and further up the river.

It was twilight when he realized he must soon rest at anchor for he could not see the river much longer. He kept a close watch for a wide area near the bank, where he could slip out of the main flow and lie at anchor without anyone going up or down the river seeing him. From such a position he could easily spot any other ships going up or down the river.

He gave orders that all lights were to be extinguished and voices were to be kept to soft whispers. He knew well that over water voices carry a great distance.

Now there was nothing he could do but sit and wait.

Chris couldn't believe he'd had to wait for another whole day before knowing his fate. At supper, he noticed that John was gone. His questions about this provoked blank stares, shrugged shoulders, smiles of complacency, and once a muttered "I have no idea, señor. He comes and goes as the boss chooses."

Chris was more than sure John had been sent back to St. Augustine to get information, but what information? Was he searching for answers about him and Lucas . . . or was he meeting Henri to urge him to come quickly and help dispose of a problem. The last alternative actually made Chris sweat, and he did his best to push it from his mind.

He had given up his futile attempts to question the banditti. There was nothing he could do but wait and face whatever Dan had in store for him. He had never felt so utterly helpless.

He gave a great deal of thought to the conversation between himself and Dan, and he felt, despite his present circumstances, that he had done the right thing in confiding the truth to Dan.

He tried to console himself with the thought that with Lucas gone there was no one in St. Augustine who knew about him, so there was actually no way that Dan could find any clues to Chris's authenticity.

But one thought always recurred to him: John had not gone until he had spoken to Dan, so they must feel there was a connection between him and someone else. But who?

Scott had awakened the next morning to find Sophia gone. This was not unusual, but the events of the past night had made him jumpy and suspicious.

He knew Sophia was fond of him, but was she fond enough not to turn him over to the banditti if she suspected he was not what he'd said he was? At one moment he wanted to leave the room and search for her; in the next he chose to be more careful and remain in the room as if nothing exceptional had happened. It was nearly midday when she returned, and he almost sighed with relief at finding her alone. If she knew about him and intended to betray him, she would have been accompanied by enough men to do the job.

Sophia had slept little in the hours after Scott had returned. She had been torn by emotions that were new to her. Till that time, she had always taken her men where and when she chose, leaving nothing of herself behind.

Scott was the first man who had touched a place within her that had always been empty. Now she had to decide which course to take. Would she tell William, or would she hope that Scott cared enough for her not to betray her trust?

She had walked the early morning streets, her mind in confusion. She had even gone so far as to go to the tavern in which William had a room, but she couldn't go through with it. She finally had to admit to herself that Scott had begun to mean more to her than the people to whom she had given loyalty for so many years.

She had returned to their room, hoping that the path she had chosen would prove right.

"Sophia, where have you been?" Scott said as soon as the door closed behind her. He went to her and took her in his arms. With a soft laugh, Sophia put her arms about him and smiled.

"Did you miss me?"

"You're damned right I did." He chuckled as he nuzzled the softness of her throat.

"Maybe you should show me how much you would miss me if I were gone," she said softly.

Scott held her a little away from him and studied her face, but he could read only seductive invitation in her eyes. Certain now that all his suspicions were unfounded he relaxed and began to devote serious attention to making love to Sophia. His hands caressed her gently as he expertly removed the barrier of her clothing. Sophia responded with a soft throaty laugh, and her hands began a similar endeavor, ridding them of all that stood between them.

Scott's hands and mouth bathed her in a cauldron of seething desire. With the tip of his tongue he delicately outlined her mouth; then he gently nibbled her lips coaxing and teasing until he could feel her search for him, her mouth hungry.

At last, his mouth left hers, to trail kisses down her throat and to tease her nipples with unnerving delicacy until she quivered with the impulses that raced along her nerves.

It seemed to Sophia that their lovemaking never followed the same pattern, and that she was always expectant. Scott brought her to the brink of ecstasy, then held her back until the control of both was shattered. Her quick gasps of heated passion became groans of mounting pleasure.

Then he felt the tremor that built within her and knew he could wait no longer. He allowed the flame to engulf them both, and they were propelled into an explosion of ecstasy that consumed them both.

They lay together, entwined bodies warm and throbbing . . . yet minds and hearts drifting slowly further and further apart.

"Scott?"

"Yes?"

"We go to meet William tomorrow night."

"I know. Sophia, you know William better than I. What do you think he will do?"

"I think William trusts you."

It was said so softly and directly that for a moment Scott was silenced.

It had been said for just that purpose. She wanted Scott to receive the subtle reminder that more than one person trusted him, and that trust creates a debt of sorts.

Scott's conscience received the message, and he was momentarily prepared to abdicate his plans—but only momentarily.

He thought of Ria and Brian, who had been hurt by the pirates. He thought of Lucas, who had lost a very beautiful wife, because of that pirate Blanc. He held to his resolve. They must find the pirates, prove their guilt, and rid the seas of them.

Still, the last person in the world he wanted to see hurt was Sophia. He had grown quite fond of her, although he knew his feelings were nothing more than that. Being fond of someone was a far cry from being in love and planning a life together.

"Trust," he murmured softly.

She turned in his arms so her eyes would meet his. "Isn't that what you wanted?"

"Yes of course."

"Then, what's bothering you?"

"Sophia, if William takes me to Dan will you be coming with us?"

"Do you want me to?"

"Is it safe for you?"

"Dan's camp?" She laughed softly. "I have spent many many hours there. Of course it's safe for me."

"Sophia, I know it's none of my business but . . ."

Sophia laughed again and slid her arms tighter about him. "You are asking if William has ever been my lover. Are you jealous, Scott?"

Scott didn't want to tell her that she had misunderstood his planned question. He had wanted to learn her position in the McGirtt camp, but now he must lie again or provoke anger that could turn to betrayal.

"I don't want to be taking you back to someone who might revive old memories and take you away from me while we're still getting to know each other."

"Getting to know each other," Sophia whispered seductively as she slowly drew his head to hers to put an end to a conversation that was slowly building barriers between them. Sophia did not want to face barriers . . . not that day.

They spent the remaining daylight hours and the night evading questions and answers in each other's arms, wandering the streets of St. Augustine, and delighting in simple pleasures. He bought her flowers from a street vendor, and they laughed together over nonsensical things. For a very short time both Sophia and Scott put aside the realities of their lives and lived only for the moment. Then the sun began to set, bringing the night Scott was to meet William again.

Sophia had gone to the tavern ahead of him. She had to work as a barmaid, and he had been entirely too nervous to sit out the entire evening there.

Now he walked slowly toward the tavern, still unsure of himself, yet very sure of the reasons behind what he was doing.

He entered the tavern very late, as he had planned. Most of the patrons were already gone. He recognized William immediately and walked to his table.

"Good evening, Scott. Sit down. You have time for one drink."

"One drink?"

"One. Then we will leave."

"But I have to go back to my room. My things—"

"Are already being packed for you . . . at least the small amount you need to bring along."

"I see, and just where are we going."

"Why to see Dan," Will answered mildly. "I thought meeting Dan was your main reason for coming here."

Before Scott could answer, a man who had been silently watching walked to the table and sat down beside William.

"Is this to be a matter of choice for me?" Scott said.

"Oh, this is a very dear friend of mine, and of Dan's. Meet John Linder."

"John Linder, I've heard of you."

John smiled. "Have you, Mr. Fitzgerald? I suppose the reports haven't always been good."

"My name is Scott."

"Scott . . . yes. This is a matter of choice for you. Are you not the one who wanted to meet Dan? I have merely come to escort you"—he waved a hand to include Sophia and William—"all of you, to the camp. Dan is most anxious to see all three of you."

"I don't understand," Scott said. "How would he

know about me?''

"I think that is something you are going to have to find out for yourself. If you decide to go, we have to leave within the hour.''

Scott suspected there was something of great importance he should know and didn't. But he realized he would have to go with Linder to find out the answers.

"I'm ready when you are," he said as casually as he could.

True to John's word the group left St. Augustine in the early dawn. Their travel was rapid, as rapid as the group could manage considering Scott was a novice. He tried his best to keep up, helping Sophia when he could, which came as a complete surprise to the others.

They arrived at the camp at a preplanned time.

"Everyone is asleep except the sentries. I suggest we all get a good night's rest, and we'll take you to see Dan in the morning," John said: "Sophia, go and join the other women. I'm afraid Scott will have to share a hut with a couple of other men. You don't mind do you?" He turned to Fitzgerald.

"Makes no difference. I'm tired enough to sleep anywhere," Scott replied.

"Good." John pointed to the left. "The hut's over there."

Scott picked up his gear while the others watched and then walked to the appointed hut. When he went inside he stood just inside the door and gazed in absolute shock at the man across the room, a man who was as surprised as he. It was Chris Martin—the last man in the world he'd expected to see.

Chapter 21

In a state of tension, Ria had entered Lucas's cabin. She knew he would come soon, and knew as well that she wanted to be with him. Any barriers she'd erected against his ability to make her body sing with heated passion had long been destroyed, but now her conscience was drumming reality into her heart. They would be together only as long as it would take to get to St. Augustine, or wherever Henri and Luke had decided to meet. Then anything that existed between her and Luke would end and she would have to return to her life.

It seemed unbelievable that she would be forced to share her life with a man she had yet to meet. Could she lie in the arms of another and not long for Luke and the magic he could weave about her? She laughed miserably to herself. She was seeking the pleasure she wanted—needed—from a man whose name she didn't even know, a man who already had a wife. She found, to her dismay, the thought brought pain.

She wondered if Luke would be able to forget her as easily as he expected her to forget him. He had made her position clear. She was his mistress, and that was all she could ever be. Her brother's words rang in her ears. "We have an honorable name, Ria, and we must not dishonor it. If you choose this man, you must annul your marriage first."

Bitterness held her for a moment as she remembered her vow and the fact that Luke had never asked her to think of annulling her marriage. It was more than clear that he didn't want this relationship to be more than it was.

Her bitterness was aimed as much at herself as at Luke, for she knew, despite the fact that they would part soon, she wanted him with a fierce passion that, under the circumstances, created more pain than pleasure.

As Lucas approached his cabin he, too, was preoccupied by thoughts of his relationship with Ria. For a man who was only going to share the night with a mistress, Lucas was strangely moved. He was excited about being with her, about sharing hours without battle; yet he found his mind had drifted to the day when she would want to be set free.

He wanted her for longer than a day, but he couldn't offer her more than the shadows of his life . . . unless . . . but the thought was pushed aside. Obviously she did not love him, nor did she want to be tied to him for any longer than necessary. But what if he said to hell with the world and the judgments of society? What if he divorced the woman he knew he could never love and took Ria as his wife? Again he was caught in the same circle; it ended with Brian . . . and Ria's obvious love for him.

By the time Lucas reached his cabin he firmly believed just one thing. For now Ria was his. Even if he didn't have her affection, he could rule her senses.

He would take his bridges one at a time.

Lucas opened the door of his cabin and stepped inside. As he pushed the door closed behind him, his eyes met Ria's. As always he was stunned by her extraordinary beauty. He had made love to her until he was mindless, yet she drew him to her over and over again, always with the haunting feeling he'd left something untouched, untasted.

Ria trembled slightly under his regard. In spite of herself she couldn't help wondering what it would be like to be married to him. Even though she knew he was a pirate with only a hangman in his future, even though she couldn't trust him an inch . . . it would be exciting.

Through his narrowed eyes Lucas was seeing her in many ways: in a turquoise gown, all innocence and reserve; in rolled-up breeches, her eyes sparkling and her laughter sounding in the warm breeze; in his arms, a passionate woman. Would he ever know her? Would he ever be able to hold this mercurial woman any length of time?

Sensing Ria's tension, Lucas crossed the room and knelt before a small cabinet. From it, he removed two bottles of wine. Then he rose and turned to her.

"I told cook to bring some food, and I've a couple of bottles of wine to warm up our dinner."

Ria had changed into the only dress she had. She didn't want to face him again in the worn breeches and shirt. She felt more womanly in the soft violet dress, and in the lantern's glow her eyes seemed to match its color. Her skin, which was flushed and looked warm to the touch, stirred something deep inside Lucas that he couldn't name.

Unbeknownst to him, Ria was trying her best to set her inhibitions aside for the sake of her peace of mind. Before she could speak, Luke was responding to a knock and helping place the tray of food on the table.

When the door was again closed, he concentrated on pouring the wine. Then he set both bottles on the table, took a wineglass in each hand and walked to where Ria stood near the porthole. He handed her one glass, leaned a broad shoulder against the wall, and contemplated her. When he lifted his glass to her, she raised hers to lightly touch his.

"Shall we drink to the present?" he said softly.

Her eyes were wide, and deep and mysterious as forest pools.

"Today is what you live by, isn't it?" she asked softly. "For you there are no tomorrows, no yesterdays."

"For people in our position, tomorrow just might not come to be."

Her eyes, which a moment ago had appeared soft and cloudy violet seemed to darken like a storm-touched sea. The sudden deep sensitivity that seemed to be growing between them was startling because of the harshness of every battle that had gone before.

"Oh, Luke . . . I want . . ."

"What, Ria?" he urged gently. "What do you want? What do you expect? Life is not so simple that we can just grab at what makes us happy and run and hide. We have—"

"I know," she whispered. "We have other obligations."

There was a suspicion of tears in her eyes, and hurting her now had not been his intention. He reached out and laid his hand against her cheek, then slowly shifted it so his fingers tangled in her hair.

"Do you know you have a beautiful, exciting mouth that begs to be kissed?" he murmured.

He drew her head to his and touched her lips softly,

gently, leaving her slightly breathless.

"You're a woman, Ria. Don't be afraid to feel like a woman."

Before she could answer he was kissing her again, yet he had not taken her in his arms. In a moment he stood back, knowing she was trying to justify emotions he could sense.

"Come on." He smiled. "Let's eat. I know you haven't had much today; you must be starved."

She sat opposite him and found, to her surprise, that she was hungry. He began to talk about anything he could think of, except himself, and was pleased when he saw her relax. Of course she wasn't paying attention to the fact that he continually refilled her glass until she had consumed nearly a bottle of wine.

Ria felt Luke was right. People who lived the life he had chosen could not think of tomorrow; she couldn't afford to either, she knew where those thoughts led. She made a silent vow. She would ask no more of him. What they were to share would begin and end in this cabin.

So their silent vows were made. They would take, they would enjoy, and they would both be able to forget each other and walk away with no regrets.

When the meal was finished, Lucas walked to the porthole and gazed out over a tranquil scene. The sea was an undulating dark green, lit by bright stars and an even brighter moon.

"Ria, come over here."

When she rose and went to stand beside him, he turned her so her back was to him and she was facing the window.

"Look," he said softly. "The stars are so very beautiful. Nights like this are a sailor's delight."

"Why?"

"We travel by stars, moving from one to another, not from one land to another."

Ria turned to look up into amber eyes lit by moonlight, and Lucas braced one hand on each side of her, trapping her against the frame of the window. Before she could speak, before she could resist, he was kissing her again, his arms going about her to gather her closely against him.

She closed her eyes, feeling any desire to struggle or protest slip away to be replaced by something stronger, something fierce and all consuming, something that grew and grew within her until, like a brilliant sheet of lightning, it exploded into raw desire.

She was aware of everything about him: the sudden gentleness of his touch, the pressure of his long hard-muscled legs against hers, the feel of his thick hair which she ran her fingers through.

So this is what true passion is like, she thought. She felt as if she hung suspended in space and in time. There was no denying, even to herself, the strange, almost unnatural physical desire she had for him. She could not resist the power his lovemaking exerted on her. Knowing that, a challenging new thought came to her.

Could she wield the same power over him? Could she, for once in his life, make him taste the helplessness of complete and total surrender? She had to find out for herself; it was the only way she could free herself from his memory when the time came for them to part.

Ria stepped back just a little from Lucas. Her eyes held his, and their warm glow tingled through him and aroused something close to suspicion. A Ria he'd never known now faced him. He knew what to expect from the others, but not this warm inviting Ria.

She reached up and put her hands on each side of his face; then she rose on tiptoe and very softly caressed his mouth with her moist parted lips. Lightly, she teased with her tongue until his hands circled her waist and his mouth began to seek hers with heated passion.

But Ria couldn't allow that. This was the one time he would remember for the rest of his life. If she could neither have him nor forget him, then she wanted him to be unable to forget her.

She pressed her hands against his chest, and he raised a questioning brow and looked at her. Did she tease? Did she invite and reject in the same moment?

"Don't," she whispered softly. "Let me." She slowly unbuttoned his shirt while her eyes read the surprise in his.

Lucas was quick to understand and just as quick to surrender to the pleasure he knew awaited him.

Her hands undressed him slowly and the sensations their touch created were almost overpowering as her fingers trailed delicately over his skin. His body began to respond instinctively. His senses—bombarded by the sweet taste of her, the scent of her hair, and the warmth of her body—were beginning to swirl about the mystery of Ria.

As much as she wanted him, Ria held herself in check. She worked slowly, carefully, and he remained as still as he could. But she could hear his sharp intake of breath, feel the rapid pounding of his heart beneath her fingers.

With tantalizing slowness, she explored his body, marveling again at his lean hard frame, lost in the wonder of his masculinity. She slid her hands down the breadth of his chest to the curve of his waist. His stomach was taut and flat, and she let her hands seek total knowledge of him. His legs were long and supple and sleek, and there was no excess fat on his entire frame. His flesh was sun-kissed bronze, firm and warm to her touch.

Lucas had begun to perspire lightly while he strove for control of these new and erotic sensations. He had always been the one to dominate, and the newness of this invigorating experience stunned him.

When Ria stepped back and, with a few motions, let her gown slide to a heap at her feet, every nerve and fiber of Lucas's being was concentrated on the extraordinary woman who faced him, and on the subtle and fiery response she was drawing from him with the torments of sight, smell, and touch. It took all his effort to remain still.

Ria was almost breathless as she slowly began to focus on the shaft of his desire, which now throbbed with a life of its own. She could only marvel at the size and power of it. She well knew the strength with which he could drive her body to passionate response, but she was not going to let that stop her now. She trailed her hands across his flat belly, and felt his muscles quiver in response.

Now he could no longer control his need to touch her. She was a live flame beckoning him closer and closer, and even if he was burnt, he had to touch that flame. He reached up to lightly cup her breasts in both hands, letting his thumbs circle their hardened nipples until he saw her half-closed eyes glow with anticipation. She moved closer so their bodies touched, and he slid his hands around so they rested on her back, then gently ran them down to her soft rounded buttocks.

Her lips traced a path that felt like a fiery hot sword as she tasted and teased his flesh. From his hard mouth to his shoulder, to the pulse that beat raggedly at his throat. Across his chest to nip and lick at each nipple.

His eyes were half-closed now as he was caught in a maelstrom of sensual pleasure that he could no longer control.

Her hands slid down over his hips and she let her tongue tease across his stomach; then slowly she knelt before him.

He could not help but gasp, almost in agony, as her lips traced patterns on his belly and thighs until he thought he would go entirely mad. Eyes closed, he shook with a tempest that tore every nerve as her lips found his pulsing shaft. He groaned softly as she kissed, caressed, and captured. He was gasping now, hanging perilously on the edge of oblivion. He could bear no more.

She seemed to sense this, and she rose and lifted her hands to draw his head to hers. Only then did she resign herself to him and to a blazing passion she had whipped to near frenzy.

He laughed huskily as he swept her up into his arms. He could feel the silk of her hair as it swirled against his shoulder and arm. It seemed his every sense was heightened, her every touch was a prick of flame. Impatiently, he laid her on the bunk, and he began to devour her flesh hungrily with mouth and teeth, nibbling and kissing until she moaned in ecstatic agony.

She shimmered in his arms, and he could only see the gleam of her gold body through a haze of passion so intense he thought his heart might stop. His hands parted her thighs gently. His lips and tongue tormented and probed until she cried out in choked moans of ecstasy.

Now neither knew any reality but the need to surrender totally. He drove into her with a powerful thrust spiraling down into her depths until he felt her close about him, holding him in her fluid heat.

Over and over they joined, becoming one, driving each other up and up and up until they rode the wings of rapturous passion and enchantment enfolded them in a world devoid of anything but each other and the bond that drove them wild. They knew completion in one flaming explosion as they melded into each other and became one single pulsing entity, each knowing this surpassed all earthly boundaries. They both knew that a bond was formed no other would be able to match.

They held each other in gasping mindless pleasure, their sweat-slicked bodies pulsing entwined as they plummeted from the heights to finally lie together, eyes closed and clinging to each other until their ragged breathing and pounding hearts returned to normal.

For a long time neither could put words to the experience they had just shared, but both were certain of one thing, each had left an indelible mark on the other. No matter what the future held, neither would be able to forget this one star-studded night of unparalleled passion.

Lucas turned and rose to brace himself on one elbow. He looked down into eyes still heavy with completed passion. They glowed like amethyst jewels, and he wondered if they would always dance between him and any other woman he might touch.

If his conflict had torn at him before, it was worse now. Ria had imprinted herself on him in a way he would find difficult to forget, yet forget he must.

He wanted to probe deeper into the mystery of Ria. Could she still love Brian and give herself to him as she just had? He had no answer to that, and it tormented him that, if he couldn't hold her, when they reached St. Augustine she would leave him and go to Brian.

"What a mysterious creature you are," he said in a remotely puzzled voice.

"I? I am no more mysterious than the elusive Captain Blanc—Luke—or whatever your name is. Don't speak of mysteries when you cannot even put a name to yourself."

"In the long run"—he sighed—"I guess a name is not really what matters."

"What does matter, Luke?" she asked softly.

Lucas could not supply the answers she sought. He wanted to say to her, forget who and what you are, Ria. Be my mistress even though I am bound by rules I cannot change.

Ria, too, was caught in the same stream of thought, its current pulling her to remember that she must go home to live the life expected of her—a life that could never include Luke.

Never once, she thought bitterly, has he said he loves me. He wants to be free to go when the passion dies.

He saw the elusive need in her eyes. It came and was quickly gone as she steadied herself. He lost it too quickly to be able to read what the need was. What did she want from him, just passion then freedom? The thought of seeing her walk away from him drew him to the brink of words he dare not say.

"I'm not sure anymore, Ria. When I first came to St. Augustine, I had my own answers. I knew who I was, what I wanted, and where I was going. Now I have run across a violet-eyed witch who has disturbed all my plans."

"As you have disturbed mine. Do you think you

were the only one with plans for your life?"

Again the specter of Brian leapt between them, but Ria could not understand the sudden tensing of his muscles or the cold spark of gold flame in his eyes.

"You still persist in your plans?" he said.

"I have no reason to change them," she challenged, hoping he would say one word of love to alter her position.

"Ria . . ." He began to say the words that would change her path from Brian to him.

"Yes, Luke?" she urged softly.

But he knew it was useless. They had no path on which to meet. He resorted to the old battleground.

"I told you once you weren't going back to him. I meant it."

"You said you would let me go!" she cried, alarm rising in her. "Now are you refusing? Is it because Brian is dead, is it!"

He hated the intonation in her voice. It told him clearly her love for Brian had not changed. Again the black seed of hatred for the man grew in him. He almost wished that he had let Brian die. At least then he could be sure she would never lie in Brian's arms as she just had in his.

"Damn you, tell me. Is he alive? Is he?"

She was desperate, but he was determined. Before they reached port, he would kill her love for Brian. He never thought to offer her love to replace it. He never knew the key to Ria's complete surrender was just within his grasp.

Chapter 22

"He's alive," Lucas ground out from between clenched teeth. "He's very much alive." He lay back on his pillow and clasped his hands behind his head, staring up at the wooden planks above him and trying to control the murderous jealousy he knew he had no right to feel.

"Then why did you say I couldn't go to him? You made a bargain—"

Lucas sat up abruptly and gripped her shoulders, jerking her up beside him. Her eyes were wide with shock at his sudden reaction.

"I don't understand what you want!" she cried. "You don't want me; then you do. You bargain with me; then you deny your own vow. You would discard me like a whore, but you are angry when I want to go to Brian. Damn you, Luke! What is it you expect of me? When you are gone do you expect me to cry and long for you! Why, Luke, why! Why can't you just let me go when you're finished with me, or is it just that you want to make me beg again? If that's your goal, I'll do it now."

Ria would have given her life to hear him say he loved her and that was why he couldn't let her go. At that moment she was prepared to sacrifice everything to become the mistress of a pirate . . . if he would just say he loved her.

Lucas looked down into anguished questioning eyes. *If she doesn't understand me she would be pleased,* he thought, *to know that I don't understand myself.*

He knew all she said was true, but if, just once, she had said she loved him and wanted to stay with him, he would have tossed away everything and kept her. If she would only say the words that he needed to hear . . . But he knew those words were reserved for Brian, and he would have to settle for the last hours he could hold her.

"I'm sorry, Ria. No, I don't want you to beg. I made a bargain and I will keep my end of it. When we get back to the bay, I'll send word to the convent, or to his ship. He has probably fully recovered and retaken his ship by now."

She was shaken and totally unprepared for the swift change in him. She never knew the effort it took. She knew only her own confusion and a strange unnameable pain that caught at her heart.

"I must see him," she whispered. "I must know he is well."

Lucas sighed and reached out to brush her tangled hair. "Yes, I suppose you must." Even though her love was something he would never have, he was grateful that the bay was still a day or two away. Maybe . . . just maybe . . .

"Ria," he said, as his arms drew her close again. "We were to forget tomorrow, remember?"

Ria wished fervently that she could tell him Brian was her brother, but as long as she was uncertain about Brian's fate, and as long as she was unsure of

Luke, she would not jeopardize any chance of seeing Brian.

"Yes . . . no tomorrow."

He bent to kiss her again, and slowly the night began to blossom into renewed passion.

The next two days and nights were full of magical hours for Ria and Lucas, yet despite their mutual need to express their emotions the void between them grew. Their bodies touched and tasted passion, but their hearts remained guarded against the pain they both knew was coming.

If Lucas had thought Ria had many aspects to her before, he was now introduced to a Ria who had as many facets as an expertly cut diamond.

He often took pleasure in just watching her. One minute she was like a playful child, the next she was quiet and contemplative. During these latter moments, he would have given his soul to share the thoughts in her head. He saw her with the wind in her hair, the sun turning her skin a deeper gold. He saw her when white moonlight turned her amethyst eyes to glittering jewels. Every mood, every moment was carefully stored in his mind against the time when he would have to let her go.

The day finally dawned when he knew land was not far over the horizon. Ria stood at the rail, and Lucas came up to stand beside her. He had been at the wheel, watching her, wondering if her mind was on Brian. He had finally decided that parting on gentle terms was going to be more than he could handle. If they had to go their separate ways, anger would be better.

He knew now that he could never tell her how he

felt. He found it impossible to speak of his passion when she was lost in desire for another man.

Both had hoped that their interlude would sate their passions, but it had not. It had enhanced them so that they had grown beyond desire, beyond passion, beyond a feeling they could name.

"We'll reach land soon," he said.

"How do you know?" She turned her head to look at him.

"Look," he replied, as he pointed to the sky where several birds were dark specks ahead of them. "Land birds. They don't fly too far from shore, only a few miles."

"I see," she said softly as she returned her gaze to the cloud-filled sky. She found it impossible to put her regret into words; regret was the last thing she had expected to feel.

"You should be happy, Ria." Lucas laughed harshly. "You'll be welcomed with open arms I'm sure. Your lover should be glad you're being returned . . . no worse for wear. In fact, he might enjoy being the recipient of . . . shall we say your new expertise?"

His words stung with the cold whip of bitterness. Again Ria was taken totally by surprise by his mercurial change. Her eyes snapped up to meet his. Would she ever be able to understand this man? One moment he was a lover, gentle and sensitive; and the next he struck at her with a viciousness that stunned her. She wanted to leave this strange situation with as much self-control as she could manage, but it seemed he wasn't going to let her go that easily. He needed to hurt her for some unexplainable reason.

His harsh, implacable tone, the ominous drawing together of his brows, sparked her temper. She bit her lip suddenly, her eyes shooting daggers of warning—

a warning he paid no heed to.

"I do hope he appreciates his good fortune. But then"—Lucas taunted—"when he takes you to bed, I'm sure you'll be efficient in showing it to him."

At the sight of her face, completely drained of color but defiant for all that, Lucas began to regret the words he couldn't recall. Why, he thought, does she always make me lose self-control?

She was staring at him through wide amethyst eyes; deep pools, he remembered thinking once. Her eyes could change so quickly when they were making love. He didn't want to remember the soft sounds she made deep in her throat, or the way she tossed her head, spilling her hair about him, or how her body writhed beneath him—all this would be for Brian. Brian the unappreciative, the callous, the uncaring. Why did such thoughts still have the power to make him ragingly jealous?

"What do you want me to do to please you?" she snarled in self-defense. "You are finished with me, yet you don't want me to be content with anyone else. You don't want me to be happy, do you? You want only to hurt me. If you're squeamish, I could just throw myself overboard. That should make it a little easier for you."

Lucas reached for her, gripping her wrist in a hold that brought a small cry of pain from her. She moved closer to the rail as if she meant to put action to her words, and Lucas grabbed her in his arms. It was purely an instinctive action, something he could not help, but once he held her, it was impossible to let her go. She was shaking. Holding her, he could smell the fragrance of her hair, feel the well-remembered softness of her body as she pressed against him.

In Ria, anger blended with frustration. "I don't understand you," she groaned.

305

"I think you do," he replied, his voice harsh and hateful. "Your kind of woman always does. You always know when a man wants you. Damn your wanton soul. I want you."

"You want me! No," she snarled. "You want to ease your own damned lust without caring who you hurt. You think I'm a slut you can just bed when you choose. Well, I haven't been able to fight you, and that damns me, but I'll learn, Luke. I'll learn. I'll remember your hate and your selfish lust, and some way, somehow, I'll learn to hate you no matter how long it takes."

"Why waste all that passion and hate, Ria. I'll make you a proposition—the final one. Be my mistress, Ria. Don't leave this ship and go to Brian. Be my mistress."

He knew the words crushed her spirit. He could see unwanted tears fill her eyes. He watched her determinedly strive for control, and he felt her body tremble in his arms.

She could only see the coldness in his eyes, only feel the brutal way he held her, molding his lean body to hers.

He knew now that she was on the brink. He meant to push her over. Only with her hatred and rage could he protect himself. He held her with one arm and, deliberately hurting her, gripped the thick mass of her hair and drew her head back until she cried out softly. Then his mouth descended to hers, savaging it, grinding its softness until he heard her moan softly. He could taste salty tears and blood. As abruptly as he had grasped her, he pushed her from him and she landed with her back against the rail, her eyes wide with hurt and anger.

Without thinking she swung her hand outward and up, only realizing how hard she had slapped him when she saw the print of her hand against his cheek and felt the stinging of her hand.

"You are a brute and a coward," she said through clenched teeth, "and I would surely fling myself overboard for the sharks to feed on before I would be mistress to you. Yes! Yes! I'll go to Brian. He is twice the man you will ever be. He knows what kindness and gentleness are. Things you will never know. Damn you to hell! I hope I never see you again!"

She spun away from him and ran to the cabin, and Lucas watched her go, hating himself as much as she did. He wanted to go after her, gather her in his arms, and comfort her. Damn! he thought angrily. Amidst all this hatred he wanted to make love to her until she cried out to him in complete surrender.

Ria closed the cabin door and leaned against it, tears blinding her. She shook violently. She prayed weakly that the ship would soon dock and she would be freed.

Brian had lain in wait on the river entirely too long. There had been no sight of anyone, and he found he could bear his impatience and inactivity no longer.

He called his first mate to him and spoke the words that made his decision final.

"Get us downriver, Jake."

"Sir?"

"You heard me. I can't stand this inactivity. I want to find out what's going on in the harbor. So get us downriver as fast as you can. I have a feeling it's important we get there as soon as possible."

"Aye, sir. We can probably make it down faster than we came up what with ridin' with the current instead of against it."

"Good. Get about it."

Jake was puzzled, but Brian's scowl and the dark mood his captain had been in for the past few days kept him from questioning the order.

Brian stood, in a dark well of meditative silence, while the ship eased its way from the cove and started downriver.

When night came, it was black and moonless, so black that the two ships drifted past each other on the wide inky river, with neither captain aware of the presence of another vessel.

By morning, Brian was nearing the mouth of the river. He moved into the bay cautiously, keeping his eyes alert for the ships anchored there. From what he could see neither Henri nor his mortal enemy Captain Blanc were in the harbor. Thinking of either of these men made his hands twitch with the desire to commit murder.

Painful thoughts of Ria, and of what she might be going through, clung to the edge of his mind. Yet he refused to acknowledge their presence, for to dwell too long on them would drive him to a murderous rage. He wished he knew where Scott was and what he might have found out. He was reasonably certain his friend might be upset by his return to the bay, but Ria was still uppermost in his mind. He had to try to find her; he hoped Scott would understand.

As soon as he found out the news on Captain Blanc he would go back upriver and seek out Scott. He was more than certain Scott could handle anything that might come up. Certainly the banditti had no idea of who he was, and if he kept his identity a secret, they would have no way of knowing.

Brian anchored the *Swan* near Anastasia Island, so a returning ship would be well into the bay before anyone aboard would know of his presence.

Once another vessel did enter, it would be no great feat for Brian to quickly place his ship between it and the channel that led from the bay to the ocean. At the moment he would have given anything to see the sails of the *Black Angel* at the harbor entrance.

He was worried because even if Captain Blanc returned to join his pirate friend Henri, Ria might not be with him. Visions of the multitude of things Blanc might have done to her set Brian's teeth on edge.

Henri's absence gave Brian a freedom of movement he had not had in a long time, and he made use of it. He visited every tavern in the town, subtly searching for word of an American named Scott; but it was as if his friend had never existed. He could only hope word of his search would get to Scott somehow.

On the dawn of his third day in port, unable to sleep, Brian had taken the early morning watch. He stood on the quarter deck gazing at the star-blazoned sky and listening to the soft lapping of water against the side of the ship.

Lost in thought of Ria, he hardly noticed the speck of sail approaching the harbor inlet. Awareness struck him only when the sails drew nearer and the ship, having reached the entrance of the inlet, started into the harbor.

A sudden thrill of excitement coursed through him. The one man he most wanted, the one ship he craved to see—these were quietly sailing right into his waiting arms.

His sails were furled, and he lay at anchor so far from the docks that he was sure he was not recognizable.

His smile little more a grimace, through narrowed eyes, he watched the ship approach the dock. It was anchored and tied down before he quietly gave the order for a longboat to be gotten ready. He was about to find the answers—and the revenge—he wanted.

Ria had cried until there were no tears left. Now she sat, with dry, burning eyes, on the edge of the bunk.

So many conflicting emotions filled her that she felt as if she were being smothered by a dark heavy blanket of despair.

She cursed herself. She had been ready to toss aside her pride, her family, her sense of honor—everything she had held dear all her life—for a man who could only think of her as a common slut, a woman to bed and forget when the time came.

Luke can be so cruel, she thought. She could still see the taunting glow in his amber-gold eyes, could still feel the whiplash of his words as they had struck her.

"Be my mistress, Ria," he had said, sure that passion was all that would ever satisfy her. No words of kindess, of warmth. No sign of love.

"He is a cold-hearted brute," she whispered gratingly, "and I could never be part of his life on his terms."

Then why, she asked herself bitterly, did it hurt so badly? Why did she ache deep within from wanting something she knew she could never have.

She felt the ship slow, sensed the current change beneath her, and knew they had entered Matanzas Bay.

Soon she would be free of him, free of his touch and of his tempestuous presence which assaulted her senses. She hoped she would not see him again until she left the ship, but that hope was quickly destroyed.

She turned with a startled jump when the door

opened and Luke stepped into the cabin.

He stood just inside, leaning against the door frame, his arms folded across his chest and a wry twist to his mouth. Her anger flared. Was he laughing at her! At first Ria was torn between a desire to give vent to hysterical laughter and a need to scream furiously at him.

Lucas was aware of her pale face and wide eyes, but he intended to use every weapon he had to keep the distance between them.

"So, despite your little fit of temper, have you decided what you'll do? I'm wealthy enough to support you in any style you'd like to specify."

Ria's face grew paler. He could see crystal tears lingering on her lashes, but he watched with satisfaction as her shoulders straightened and her chin firmed. She rose slowly.

"I would die before I would ever consent to your . . . suggestion. You are a vile depraved monster, and I hate you."

The words ripped at Lucas who firmly held himself immobile.

"We will be docking soon. Since your choice is made, why don't you come on deck?"

"Yes. I want to be ready to leave this ship as soon as possible," she said frigidly.

He nodded, then stood for a moment, to imprint what he felt would be his final look at her on his memory. Then he turned and left the cabin, leaving the door open behind him.

Slowly, Ria walked through the door and then climbed the companionway stairs. She stepped on deck the moment the ship bumped lightly against the dock and the gangplank was lowered.

Lucas stood on the quarter deck and watched her. She walked to the rail and turned to look up at him.

Their eyes met and held, and the tempest that swirled between them was so potent that not a person aboard didn't sense it.

Ria was nearly overcome by an urge to run to his arms, but her pride held her; and Lucas gripped the rail until his knuckles were white to control the urgent call of his senses, telling him to keep her even if he had to do it by force.

Their fixation on each other was interrupted by a voice calling Ria's name. Both looked toward the dock on which Brian was approaching.

Lucas watched, grim-faced, as Ria cried out Brian's name, then flew down the gangplank and threw herself into his waiting arms.

Chapter 23

Nothing could have startled Scott or Chris more than coming face to face with each other in a hut in the center of Dan McGirtt's camp. The last time they had been together was when Scott had sailed away as proxy for Lucas's wedding. Neither had dreamed their paths would cross here.

Knowing the third man in the hut was probably quite loyal to Dan, they could not freely acknowledge that they were not strangers. It was difficult. Both men had hundreds of questions to ask—questions that would have to be answered at a more opportune time.

"Evening, gentlemen." Scott smiled. "I guess I'm to share this hut with you two."

"Evenin'." The third man spoke softly, but his eyes were alert and Scott knew he would not be easy to fool. He and Chris would have to be very careful.

"Evening," Chris said in an impersonal and uninterested voice. "You can toss your things in that corner over there. The bunk, for what it's worth, is yours."

"My name's Scott Fitzgerald. I just arrived with William Cunningham."

313

"You came with Will?" the third man asked.

"Yes. We just got here."

The man held out his hand. "My name's Marco Santee."

Scott shook his hand, then turned and held out his own to Chris who took it quickly, as if suddenly reminded they were supposed to be meeting for the first time.

"I'm Chris Martin."

"You're American too?"

"Yes." Chris smiled. "It's surprising to run across another American here."

"Oh?" Scott grinned in return. "It might surprise you to know there are a lot of Americans near."

"Ain't likely too many Americans will be findin' this camp though." Marco chuckled. "Most people in St. Augustine are afraid of them tryin' to steal the land. The boss, he don't usually take to Americans. He's had his troubles with them whilst he was up in Carolina."

"Really?" Scott was interested, but Santee realized he was talking too much to men neither he nor his boss knew enough about.

"Yeah," he said shortly. Then he turned to his equipment and studiously ignored the other two men.

Soon after Santee lay down on a cornhusk mattress atop a rough-cut board bunk. Although he seemed to go to sleep, neither Chris nor Scott felt safe enough to talk or to try to slip away. Their questions would have to wait for a more secure moment. They found their way to bunks that matched Santee's in discomfort.

Sleep evaded them, and both men lay awake for a long time.

*   *   *

They were not the only ones who were awake. Dan sat with Will and John, listening intently to all that Sophia knew about Scott.

"He seems to be all you say he is, Sophia," he declared, "just as Chris seems to be an unusually honest young man, but doesn't it seem strange to you that two Americans are looking for me? That's hard to accept. I'm tempted to believe there's a connection between these two."

"What are we going to do about it?" William asked.

"Listen," Dan said as he leaned toward them. "We're expecting Henri soon. Along with the cargo he's stolen, he's bringing me some things I need. Once he comes, we'll take what we need and we'll slip away from this camp. I think someone is sniffing us out, and we have to find a way to keep these two from getting too much information before we're ready to leave."

"Scott is what he says he is," Sophia protested. "Will and I were very careful."

"I'm sure you were, Sophia," Dan replied. "I'm not accusing him of anything . . . yet. I'm just saying we have to be careful."

Will turned to McGirtt. "What's making you so leery of Scott?"

"I know a lot more about Chris now than I did before."

"What?"

Dan proceeded to relate what Chris had told him.

"And you believe him? You believe he's only after Henri? Then maybe you're right about a connection between Chris and Scott."

"The best thing to do right now," Dan said finally, "is to be cautious. We'll watch both men very carefully . . . and wait for Henri. When he arrives, I'm certain we'll know what these men are really after."

"What are you going to do if they're lying?" Will said.

Dan sat thinking for a moment; then he spoke in a quiet voice that all of them recognized as his final word.

"If they're lying"—he sighed—"we'll turn them over to Henri. Then we'll disappear from here and let him clear up the problem."

"He'll kill them," Sophia said in a dry whisper.

"Yes . . . most likely he will. He is not exactly a man to look to for mercy, but at least he'll rid us of an unwanted problem."

Sophia was silent, but she was just as determined as Dan that Scott was not going to die—not if she could help it.

It was dawn, pale streaks of first light masking everything in black and gray shadows. The sentry moved swiftly and silently to Dan's hut. He whispered words to the man who guarded it, and that man promptly went inside to kneel beside Dan's bed and shake him gently.

Dan, from habit, slept like a cat. He came instantly awake at the first touch.

"What is it?" he inquired in a whisper that did not carry across the room to where Will and John slept.

"Sentry signal downriver," came the soft reply. "Says Henri's ship's been sighted. He should be here come full day."

"Good. Thanks."

The man rose and left as silently as he had come. For a few minutes Dan lay in contemplative silence, then he rose from the bunk and walked across the room to wake Will and John.

Their swift questions quietly answered, both men rose and dressed.

Chris and Scott became aware, an hour or so later, of a sudden increase in the activity of the camp. They also realized that Marco was awake and dressing.

"What's going on?" Chris inquired.

"Ships comin'," Marco answered shortly.

Scott feigned disinterest in Henri's arrival, for as far as Dan and those in the camp were concerned he was not involved with Henri.

"Ship on the river? What is it, a supply ship?"

"Not exactly supplies." Marco laughed.

"What do you mean not exactly?" Scott countered.

"If you want to ask questions, why don't you go and ask Dan?" Marco said gruffly.

"Sorry . . . didn't mean to get nosy. I just couldn't figure out what a ship would be doing up the river this far if they weren't bringing supplies."

"They could sure use a little change in the food supply here. There's nothing creative about the meals." Chris chuckled, but his attempt at humor was lost on Marco who gazed at him too sharply.

"You ain't happy here, you can always move along. Sounds to me like you're too much the fancy gentleman to be stickin' yourself here . . . unless you're lookin for something."

"Everybody's looking for something, Marco," Chris said softly. "Me, you, and Dan. I'm not prying into what doesn't concern me, and I don't like insinuations about my past."

"I don't trust you." Marco retorted. "Maybe Dan ain't lookin' close . . . maybe he ain't keepin' an eye on you like he should." His voice became hard and cold. "But I sure as hell am, and I ain't the only one who thinks you're not what you say you are."

Chris and Scott were both alarmed at the idea that

more than one person was suspicious of their motives, but they hid their feelings well. Scott was about to break the tension when the three heard running footsteps approach.

A man stuck his head in the door.

"Marco, Chris, and you"—he nodded his head toward Scott—"Dan says come down to the river. We got a lot of unloading to do."

The three men summoned rapidly finished dressing; then they left the palm-thatched hut and half ran toward the river.

The ship rocked gently against a roughly made dock that extended just far enough into the water to provide the depth a seagoing vessel needed to keep from going aground.

The gangplank was just being lowered as Chris, Scott, and Marco arrived. Most of the men from the camp stood around Dan, waiting for the gangplank to be in place.

McGirtt acknowledged the new arrivals with a quick nod, and Scott went to him.

"Shall we go aboard and start unloading?"

"No. Wait until Henri comes ashore, then see Will for instructions on where everything is to go."

Scott and Chris stood close to the end of the gangplank. They wanted to be the first aboard to make sure they knew what was in every crate and parcel that was taken off the ship. They were prepared for the arrival of Henri, but not for the slim beauty he dragged with him. Even disheveled, her clothes torn and dirty, Louisa was a vision that took every man there by surprise.

Her hands were bound together before her, and Henri had a painful grip on her wrist as he dragged her to the top of the gangplank. He laughed exultantly at the amazement on the faces before him;

then he continued to drag Louisa relentlessly behind him. She stumbled once, and her soft anguished sob could be heard by the men who watched as Henri jerked her upright.

When Henri reached Chris, he thrust Louisa roughly toward him.

"Here's more cargo to store. Lock her up somewhere . . . somewhere close in case I decide I want her." Henri laughed boisterously and most of the men joined him, thinking of the beauty they, too, might share.

Chris was far from amused as he caught Louisa. He felt her body tremble violently against his, and heard her muffled sobs. He did not want to drag her about and amuse the ruffians any further, so he lifted her gently in his arms and started back toward the camp through jeering men who called out suggestions that made Louisa grow cold and rigid in his arms.

He tried to keep the outrage he felt from showing on his face, and only Scott, who knew him well and shared his anger, knew what he was feeling.

Once inside the hut, Chris walked to his own bunk and placed Louisa gently upon it.

With sensitive fingers he brushed her tangled hair from her dirty tear-stained face, and he was stunned by the look of pain and abject terror in her eyes.

When Chris's hands moved to touch her torn dirty dress, she groaned in helpless fear.

"Don't," she gasped. "Please . . . don't."

"I'm not going to hurt you," Chris soothed.

But Louisa was beyond believing this. "Hurt me," she choked out. "Your kind takes pleasure in hurting people. Oh, how can you be such animals. Please, I can bear no more. Don't touch me."

"Don't judge all men by Henri's example. I have

319

no intention of hurting you. I'm going for a little water. We'll wash some of the dirt off and see what we can do about a dress. That one is nearly torn off of you."

Her eyes flashed with the brilliance of remembered pain.

"It has been torn off. Henri has . . . This is the best I could do to repair it. He . . . he told me . . . oh"—she sobbed—"he told me to leave it off because it only got in his way when he wanted to . . . God damn his soul to hell."

"He most likely will," Chris muttered, "and I'd like to be the one to send him there."

His last words were not heard by Louisa as Chris had already turned away to get a pail of water. On his way back from the river he stopped at the hut in which Sophia slept.

"Sophia!" he called out.

She appeared, questions in her eyes.

"Do you have an extra dress I could have?"

"A dress?" She frowned, wondering what he would be wanting with a dress.

As quickly as possible, Chris explained Louisa's presence. He merely referred to her clothes as "damaged." He did not have to explain any further. Sophia knew Henri's nature well, and she could accurately guess why Louisa's clothes needed replacing.

She ran to fetch a flowered skirt and a white blouse, one of the few changes of clothing she owned. She handed the garments to Chris and watched him purposefully stride into his hut.

Sophia intuitively sensed that Chris did not belong here any more than Scott did. She watched him through knowledgeable eyes and wondered about his

320

real reason for seeking out Dan McGirtt. Was it in some way connected to Scott?

Louisa lay with her eyes closed. Her hands, still bound, were clenched into tight fists. She could cry no more, nor could she muster any defense. She felt as lifeless as a rag doll. Desperate, she wanted to cease to exist, to drift into the black world that surrounded her and let it extinguish the misery she dwelt in now.

She could not bring herself to respond when she heard returning footsteps. Why could he not leave her be? She felt the bunk sag as he sat beside her and heard the sounds of water splashing. When he gently began to wash the tear-streaked dirt from her face, she summoned the strength of will to open her eyes.

Louisa saw him through a hazy mist, her eyes still blurred by the tears she'd shed earlier. She could not move, but she watched him as he cleaned the dirt from her face and hands.

He had unbound her, and had pressed a cold wet cloth to the rope burns that circled her wrists.

"Why are you doing this?" she whispered.

"Because," he said gently, "it needs to be done. How do you feel now?"

She turned her head from him and fresh silent tears slipped from beneath closed lids.

"It no longer matters how I feel. My life is ruined. Oh God, I wish I were dead."

"But it does matter. You're young and very beautiful. Your life is just beginning. I'm sure there are those who would grieve if you were to die."

Again her eyes swung to meet his, only this time he was aware of the bitterness in them.

"You would not understand," she said. "How

321

could you? You are one of them."

It was impossible to refute this statement without telling her the truth about himself, and he was reasonably sure she would not believe him if he was honest with her.

"If you want . . . if you feel able, I'll step outside and you can change into this."

He picked up the clothes and handed them to her, pleased to see the small gleam of surprise in her eyes, even though it was almost hidden behind suspicion. She reached a trembling hand toward the clothes, almost as if she expected him to withdraw them at the last moment.

"Can you stand?"

"I'll . . . I'll try."

She exerted the maximum effort. Chris could see her entire body tremble and sweat bead on her forehead. Again he mentally cursed Henri and his breed. He also, despite his own surprise at this reaction, vowed no other man would put his hand on this fragile woman again, not even Henri.

He saw her safely to her feet, then stepped outside the hut. He waited for what seemed to him an interminable amount of time.

Unable to contain himself any longer he went back inside. She was seated on the bunk, her hands clenched in her lap. Chris had never seen anyone who looked so vulnerable and delicate.

Instinctively, he wanted to go to her, cradle her gently in his arms, and protect her from anymore pain.

He knew one thing for certain. Such a move might be all it took to push her over the edge into a void she might not have the strength to return from.

"Are you hungry?"

"No . . . no. I don't want anything."

322

"What's your name?"

"Louisa . . . Louisa Herald."

Chris thought if he could get her to talk he might break the tension that pulled her nerves so tight.

"Louisa . . . look at me," he said gently.

Slowly she turned and raised her eyes to his. "What do you want from me?" she said brokenly. "Please . . . can't you just let me go? Haven't you done enough!"

"Louisa, I've done nothing. I'd like to help you."

"You'll forgive me if I find that hard to believe," she replied.

"Well"—he grinned amiably in the face of her cold response—"can you name one thing I've done to hurt you since you were deposited in my arms?"

"N-no . . . but—"

"But I'm here, right?"

"I . . ."

"And I've really been harsh to you," he continued. "No . . ."

"And," he went on, "it's logical to believe that because one man is an ignorant beast all men are." He watched as her cheeks flushed and she gripped her hands tightly together. "Louisa"—his voice gentled and he reached to take both her hands in his—"you've got more strength and courage than you know. Don't let him rob you of those things. Remember, what is taken by force is no fault of yours, but"—he tipped her chin to hold her eyes with his—"all that you are is still untouched."

He watched emotions cross her face—disbelief, wonder, relief. He saw her eyes well with tears and knew she had reached her breaking point. She began to sob; then he gathered her into his arms as she cried in ragged heaving gasps while her spirit began to wash itself clean of the agony she had borne so long alone.

He simply held her, allowing her the outlet she needed. Then, when her tears had begun to dry and he felt she had regained some fragile hold on her control, he laughed softly.

"Do you know the one and only clean shirt I've got is soaked?"

She sniffed and lifted her head from his chest. "I . . . I'm sorry. I just—"

"Louisa, I was only wanting to see you smile," he protested. "You'll be all right," he said firmly. "This is the hut I sleep in with two others. I'll keep you here, and I promise you," he said softly, "he'll never touch you again."

"I don't understand you." She spoke in a whisper. "Why are you doing this?"

"Maybe"—he brushed the last glistening tear from her cheek—"I'm a knight in shining armor coming to a lady's rescue." Chris became more serious. "And maybe it's because I have a mother and a sister whom I love very dearly. I hope they will never be in this situation, but if they are, I want someone to be there to help pick up the pieces. Does that make any sense to you?"

Louisa grasped one of his hands in both of hers, and she pressed her lips to it, taking Chris totally by surprise.

"I'm grateful . . . I'm so grateful."

"I imagine you have not slept much. Suppose you lie down and try to sleep. I'll be back with some food later. Right now I have to get back before my absence is noted."

"Thank you . . . I'll try."

Chris helped her lie down on the bunk; then, reluctantly, he left her and went to face whatever situation he might find, for he truly had no intention of letting Henri, or any other man, near Louisa again.

Scott had noted Chris's rage, had almost felt it, but he knew it wouldn't be wise to follow him. In fact, as far as Chris was concerned, too many eyes followed Chris already. He turned to face Henri whose narrowed eyes were on the retreating forms of Chris and the girl he carried.

"Shall we start to unload?" Scott asked.

Henri's attention was drawn from Chris to Scott. He glared at him for a few minutes, then the glint of recognition came to his eyes.

"I know you," he stated. "Another American. You, I think, were on the *Swan*."

"You have a good memory," Scott retorted with a grin. "I was aboard the *Swan* at one time, but I thought it wise to . . . ah . . . exchange loyalties while the opportunity still existed. I am one to follow fortune, but only good fortune."

"So"—Henri chuckled—"you want to join those who make the profit."

"I thought I already had," Scott said mildly.

Henri looked at Dan, who smiled in a benign way that told Henri not to interfere with those he chose to employ or in what he did. Henri chose to comply . . . for the moment. He turned from Scott and began to issue orders. But Scott was certain he was still on Henri's mind.

The unloading went smoothly but some of the cargo was taken ashore by a few men hand-picked by Dan. Scott could only see the hut to which it was taken, not what the crates contained.

Chris returned by the time the cargo was half-unloaded, but Scott refrained from asking him any questions because Chris's grim face told him that one push would make Chris explode into violence neither of them could afford.

When the cargo was safely dispatched, most of the men, including the crew of the *Sea Rover,* set about opening kegs of rum. Scott and Chris were both happy about this. With most of the men drunk, it might be easier to find a safe place to talk.

In the communal hut, the evening meal was boisterous. Chris was pleased to find that one of the girls who stayed in the village had caught Henri's eye. At least, Chris thought, for this night Louisa would be safe . . . and so would he, for he meant to stop anything Henri tried. He knew that would mean more trouble than he had ever met before.

Late at night, Chris took a bowl of food and walked toward his hut.

Chapter 24

The hut was completely dark, and Chris opened the door almost silently. A shaft of white moonlight made a path from the door to his bunk, on which Louisa lay, still asleep.

He left the door standing open, walked to the bunk, and sat down on the edge. He placed the bowl of food on the floor beside him.

For a few minutes he just sat, immobile, and looked at her. In the whitewash of moonlight she seemed almost unreal, like a vision from a dream.

Her pale blond hair spilled about her in tangled profusion, and he noticed the dark shade of the lashes that fanned out against her cheek. Her skin looked so soft and pale in the moonlight that he had to stifle the urge to touch it.

She sighed in her sleep, and a frown drew her brows together. Then she cried out softly and murmured, "Don't . . . don't hurt me . . . please." It was a poignant cry and it touched him deeply. He reached out to comfort her, but at that moment her eyes opened.

All Louisa could see, with the moonlight behind him, was a dark broad-shouldered form. Past terrors

327

surged through her and she struck out violently.

Her first blow caught Chris totally by surprise, and he was forced, in self-defense, to grab her hands. She battled fiercely, and Chris was again surprised. Considering what she had been through, she had rebounded with more strength than he had expected.

"Louisa . . . Louisa, it's me. Don't be frightened. No one's going to hurt you. Calm down. You're safe."

Relief flooded through her, and she sagged weakly in his arms. He held her until her trembling ceased and he could feel her regain some control. He was shaken by the fact that he was most thoroughly enjoying holding her.

"I'm sorry," she whispered. "I was dreaming."

"I thought you were." He smiled at her. "But you do have a good right hand there." He rubbed his chin and heard, with pleasure, her soft embarrassed laugh.

"Did I hurt you?"

Now Chris had to laugh. "You're a little small to cause much harm. I'll have to say I've been hit harder, but not quite as unexpectedly." He bent to retrieve the bowl of food. "Here, I've brought you some of what they laughingly call stew around here. It's just edible. But you need to regain your strength."

"I'm grateful again," she said softly as she accepted the bowl from him. She ate a few bites while he watched in satisfaction. Then she smiled at him for the first time since she had arrived.

"My knight in shining armor," she said. "I don't even know your name."

"It's Chris . . . Chris Martin."

"You're a paradox, Mr. Martin."

"Chris," he urged. Then he added gently, "I'd like to hear you say my name."

"Chris," she responded quietly.

"What kind of paradox?" he inquired with an engaging grin.

"You're here with . . . with a band of monsters, yet you're kind and considerate, not like any of them. You're here . . . but you don't belong here."

"And where do you think I belong?"

She gazed at him meditatively for a few moments.

"At court . . . on the quarter deck of a grand ship . . . in a drawing room . . . on horseback commanding troops or workers . . . someplace where you are in control of everything about you."

"Thanks, my lady." Chris chuckled. "I consider that quite a compliment." He contained his urge to tell her the truth. He didn't want her thinking he was a part of the rabble in which she found him, but he knew one slip could cost him his life. At least she seemed to trust him, and that would have to be enough for now.

"Finish that food." He laughed. "Show a little appreciation for the cook."

He enjoyed her responsive laughter. "It does leave just a bit to be desired."

"Anyway, it's filling. You need your strength."

Her eyes became shadowed as she misinterpreted his meaning.

"What . . . what will happen to me now?" She reached out to touch him, and renewed fear filled her eyes. "You . . . you won't let him take me back? I would rather die first."

"Don't worry. You're not going back to him. I'll try to negotiate with Henri. One way or the other, you're free of him. So relax."

"Negotiate. There's only one way to negotiate with an animal like him!" Her eyes glowed with anger and fear. "I don't want anything to happen to you because of me."

"Nothing is going to happen to me. I have the devil's luck."

Louisa returned the half-empty bowl to Chris who set it on the floor.

"It's really a beautiful night. Would you like to take a short walk?"

"I ... we won't go ... I mean ..."

"Near the so-called festivities? No."

He rose and extended his hand, and was grateful for the confidence with which she put her hand in his.

They left the confines of the hut and walked the path to the river, enjoying the soft breeze. They might not have enjoyed the night so well had they known what Henri was doing.

Duval had a buxom, laughing woman on his lap and a bottle of rum in one hand. Near him sat Louie Savon, the man who had served as first mate under Henri for many years. Henri was never privy to Louie's thoughts at any time and now was no exception.

Louie was a tall man, nearing thirty-five. His body was already giving way to dissipation from over-indulgence in drink and debauchery. His lust had been ignited by Louisa. He wanted her, and had begun to feel Henri was tired of her and drunk enough to surrender her to him.

"The wench ya had on the ship should be on your lap." He laughed.

"Bah! She's spineless and no good in bed. She has no fire, just lies there like a lump and cries."

"Maybe ya should have been easier on her."

"Easier!" Henri laughed. "It takes a good woman to handle a man like me; and she's nothing."

"Then," Louie prodded, "ya wouldn't mind someone else samplin' a piece of her."

Henri was drunk, and the woman in his arms was warm and willing. He laughed loudly and shouted, and Louie was grateful that everyone heard what he said for the next day Henri might be in a less magnanimous mood.

"Take the wench!" Henri shouted. "Take her and bed her and see if you can shove a little fire between her skinny thighs."

Louie was satisfied, but he did not want to appear too anxious lest Henri see his enthusiasm and change his mind. After a while he rose and started to leave amid the jeers and suggestions offered by Henri and the members of his crew.

Louie walked casually toward the door and left.

As Chris and Louisa had walked and talked, he had made every effort to make her forget the circumstances in which she found herself. He had found out much about her and her life, and he was slowly becoming enmeshed in a new emotion he didn't quite know how to handle. He knew Louisa was in too delicate a frame of mind to be able to accept any kind of physical touch without retreating into a self-defensive shell; he didn't want to lose the tenuous rapport they now shared.

They returned to the hut and Louisa stopped by the door.

"I know you don't think you're tired, Louisa, but you've been through a lot. I want you to go in and get back in my bunk and try to sleep. It's the best medicine for you right now."

Louisa laid a gentle hand on his arm and then smiled. "You are the medicine I need. Without you, I would surely have killed myself at the first opportunity. At least now I am not so afraid."

"Good."

"Chris . . . where will you be? Where will you sleep?"

"Don't worry about me. I can find a place just about anywhere. Now, go to bed."

Louisa watched him for a moment; then she rose on tiptoe and kissed him softly on the mouth. "Good night Chris . . . and thank you."

She was gone before Chris could voice his surprise, and she left him trying to control a new and fragile emotion he had never felt before.

Chris walked back to the large hut where the raucous celebration was at its height. The best way to protect Louisa, he thought, is to keep his eye on the man who is her greatest threat. At the moment he thought this was Henri . . . but he was mistaken.

Louisa stepped inside the dark hut. She let the door stand open so the moonlight would permit her to find the bunk.

She started toward her bunk but just before she reached it, a soft self-satisfied chuckle spun her about, her heart pounding heavily.

He stood like an ominous shadow between her and the door. His features could not be seen, but she could feel the threat hanging in the air.

"Who . . . who are you? What do you want?"

She wanted to sound firm, but fear turned her words to water.

Again the soft laugh made her pulses pound.

"Now don't ya recognize me," he taunted. "I came to sample a little more of the treat I had aboard ship . . . and I came to teach ya a little lesson on how to love a man."

"You!" Louisa cried. She remembered well Louie's one lustful possession of her and the agony and pain he had caused her.

"Ah, I see ya do remember." His voice turned cold and brutally hard. "Now get them clothes off. I'm anxious ta mount ya and let ya feel what a good man's for. I'd hate to have to tear 'em off . . . again."

Louisa felt as if she were strangling on her fear. She backed away a step or two, and Louie advanced as many. They stood no more than two feet apart.

His patience at an end, he reached out and gripped her by one arm, dragging her to him. She fought, but he was much too strong.

All the torment she had felt, all the fear, welled up in a piercing scream. Before his hand could close over her mouth, she screamed again and again.

Relentlessly he dragged her to the bunk and threw her down upon it. Then he stood over her and began to unbutton his shirt.

Louisa was nearly paralyzed by fright, but her fear changed to shattering relief when she heard a familiar voice from the open door.

"Get your filthy hands off of her," Chris snarled, "or so help me God you'll be lying in a pool of your own blood."

Louie spun about, shock on his face. Interference was the last thing he had expected.

"What the hell are you doin' here? Get out. Henri gave her to me, and I intends to enjoy her. Find another place to sleep."

"Sorry chum," came Chris's less than amused response. "Henri tossed her into my arms, and I don't share with anybody."

Louie eyed the sword Chris had in the scabbard at his side, and wondered if he could best Chris.

"Don't even think it, my friend," Chris cautioned.

"Ya got nothin' to say around here," Louie snarled. "Henri says who gets her." He reached down and dragged Louisa to her feet beside him. Then he slipped a thin-bladed knife from the sash at his waist and held it to Louisa's throat. "Stand aside and we'll see just who gets her tonight."

It was impossible for Chris to move without endangering Louisa. He needed time. He stood aside, and Louie dragged Louisa toward the door. As they passed close by him, Chris tried to give Louisa a look that told her to have confidence in him. He followed at enough distance to keep Louie from getting nervous and doing Louisa harm.

Henri threw back his head in a roar of laughter when Louie dragged Louisa to him. He had never enjoyed such an occasion.

"So my two young cocks want to bed the same wench do they? Well, why not just take turns and share her. A female is just a well that never goes dry."

"I don't share any woman I choose with scum like him," Chris said calmly. "I'm afraid his filth will rub off."

Louie almost gurgled with rage, which was just what Chris wanted.

"Chris . . ." Louisa choked on her desperate fear.

"What's the matter, girl?" Henri shouted. "Two of 'em ain't too much for ya."

A deadly silence filled the room as each man held his breath in expectation of what was to come.

"You," Chris said in a deceptively soft voice, as he gazed at Louie with the glow of death in his hazel eyes, "learn very slowly, my friend."

"Ya think yer man enough to take her?" Henri challenged Chris.

Louie was not too sure he liked the way events were

going, but he could do nothing to stop them now.

"More man than he." Chris grinned with an irritating humor directed at Louie. "He has to use force. I could have the lady eating from my hand, and when I chose she would be more than willing."

He saw Louisa stiffen at these words and her eyes grew wide, but he had no choice. He just hoped he'd be alive to explain to her later. "The wench is mine!" he thundered.

"She's mine," Louie countered.

"Then a fight it is," Henri said with satisfaction.

Chris watched as Louisa was dragged aside to stand by Henri. Then he stood and drew his sword to face a deadly challenger. Louisa would be the prize. He knew he had to fight well. He couldn't afford to lose.

"You have your blade in your hand, bastard!" Louie snarled. "Do you know how to use it?"

Chris nodded slowly and raised the point of his sword. He smiled at Louisa who wanted only one word of assurance from him, a word he could not yet say.

"To the death then," Louie rasped as he drew his sword and advanced slowly until their blades touched.

Suddenly Louie lunged at Chris. His attack was vicious and intense, and it might have killed Chris if he had not stepped lightly aside. Chris whipped his sword to strike Louie on the seat of his pants as he went by, which drew a loud laugh from the onlookers and a snort of wild rage from Louie, who spun about to face his tormenter again.

Now Louie's attack was more cautious, and Chris felt the sudden thrill of real challenge. He cut and thrust, and began to swing his blade into the attack in earnest. Feeling his opponent out slowly, he soon realized Louie was no novice with the sword, though he depended on brute force and had no real finesse with the blade.

Chris attacked him repeatedly until a slice appeared in Louie's shirt sleeve. The few drops of blood Louie lost increased his bull-like rage, and soon Chris saw an opening and another bloodstain appeared on Louie's other arm. The room grew silent as Louie finally realized he was facing a man who had no fear, an expert with the sword.

Chris backed away, prepared to give quarter, but Louie's rage was too great to allow him to take it. He leapt to the challenge, swinging his glistening silver sword through the air.

Chris caught Louie's sword on his and for a heart-straining moment the two stood face to face, swords crossed above their heads and every muscle straining.

Louie quickly retreated, and Chris jumped back to escape a wicked slash at his belly. It would have split him in two had it landed successfully. He riposted and Louie recovered barely in time.

The battle was depleting the strength of both men. Their swords met repeatedly in heavy-handed blows. Louie thrust and Chris parried. Chris had wanted to let Louie live. The death of the man had never been his goal. But now he could clearly read the faces of the crowd—the battle was to the death.

He understood the rules, and wanted to bring it to an end as quickly as possible. His attack was relentless. He could have smashed through Louie's light defense, but that would have left him open, perhaps unable to meet a speedy recovery. His sword was silver fire, continually finding a mark until Louie bled from hundreds of pricks and panted raggedly. The Frenchman was probably tasting the first real fear he had ever known.

Chris gave Louie no room to recover, but continually forced his defense. He pressed and pressed again. A thrust caught Louie's leg, and blood stained his pants. Then for one heart-stopping moment, Louie's guard fell and Chris found a fatal spot. When he withdrew his sword Louie gazed at him in openmouthed surprise. Then his sword tumbled from his lifeless fingers and he fell to the floor.

Chris's face was dark as he gazed around to meet the astonished stares of both pirates and banditti. Scott, who had had complete confidence in Chris, gazed at him in open admiration. No one challenged him any further, and after a moment, he bent and wiped the blood from his sword on Louie's shirt, then returned the blade to his scabbard. He turned and faced Henri again.

"I take it the rules still hold," Chris said arrogantly. "I fought for the girl and she belongs to me."

"So she does, lad. What do you say men? He's earned her!" Henri laughed. He pushed Louisa roughly toward Chris. "Take her and enjoy her for as long as ya like."

Chris gripped Louisa's arm and drew her close to him. He was well aware of her resistance, and he read the look of angry betrayal in her eyes. She was certain the only reason Chris had been kind to her was to make a fool of her and to have her, as he had said, "eating from his hand and coming to his bed willingly." Now she refused to accept his kindness or the fact that he had fought to the death for her.

A rousing cheer went up, and much ribald laughter followed. New tankards of ale were brought, and toasts were shouted to his victory while, to Louisa's burning shame, Chris seemed to gloat over his conquest and to look almost as leeringly suggestive as the worst of the lot.

Chris was putting on an act for the crowd. With a fiendish, wild laugh, he crushed her against his chest and forced a savage kiss on her lips. When he boldly stroked her buttocks, Louisa squirmed in mute protest.

He held her close, feeling a relief she knew nothing of. Despite her struggles and the slow-burning fury that was growing in Louisa, he dragged her from the hut and across the clearing.

Before she could protest more violently, and knowing that many had followed them to watch their progress, Chris spun Louisa about and amid more cheers, with both hands on her buttocks, he pushed her into the hut, then followed her, closing the door quickly behind them. For a moment he leaned against it, breathing a sigh of relief.

Then he turned to face Louisa. "Now don't be stupid enough to believe the show I put on to please those vermin. I had to do something, and quickly, or you would have been sharing your favors with all of them this night."

"Oh, God." Louisa was torn with doubt. "Would you have me believe you do not intend to take me?"

Chris's face grew stern. "Louisa," he said, his voice brittle with disappointment and fatigue, "go to bed and sleep. No one will trouble you since they think you're . . . busy for tonight. I'm just too damned tired to argue with you. It seems to me, since I've saved your life and tried to make you as safe as possible, you might have the gratitude to trust me a little."

Louisa bit her lip, trying to find an answer for the elusive Chris whom she distrusted at one moment, and trusted completely the next.

"I'm sorry, Chris. I'm truly sorry." She buried her

face in her hands and wept. "What am I to believe? You bragged about what you plan to do, you challenged them and treated me like . . . like a whore. What am I to think?"

He went to her and put a consoling arm about her. She had, he was forced to admit, been through enough to have broken any other woman.

"It's all right, Louisa. Get some sleep. Tomorrow we'll talk. Maybe we can find a way out of this."

"Do you think? . . ." she began hopefully.

"I don't know . . . but we'll try. Now, go to bed."

She obediently lay down. Chris saw her safely tucked in; then he left the hut. He had to think, to form some kind of plan. He walked down the dark forest path, and had been doing so for some time before he realized he was being followed.

He stepped into the shadows beneath a low-hanging tree and waited. Soon a dark form moved through the shadows. He reached out and grasped the man as he passed by, and only a hissed call of his name made him recognize Scott.

"What are you doing?"

"Following you," Scott replied. "Let's go into the forest. I think it's the time we've waited for. We have to talk."

Chapter 25

Brian crushed Ria to him, nearly overcome by the joy of knowing she was alive, well, and here. For a time he could do nothing more than hold her as relief flooded his being. Then he held her from him and his eyes missed nothing in their close examination. She had always been breathlessly lovely, but now, to him, she seemed even more so. Everything about her seemed to have blossomed. Her skin was peach tan; her eyes were the deepest pools of amethyst he had ever seen.

He searched her face, looking for a sign of fear or suffering and found none.

"Ria, dear sister, you're well . . . you're all right?"

"Yes, Brian," she sobbed. "Now that I know you are safe and well. I'm fine."

His eyes sought out Luke who stood at the rail, watching intently. Then he scowled, and he muttered an almost unintelligible curse as he released Ria and started for the gangplank.

Ria caught her breath, wondering at the sudden feeling of weakness that made her want to scream—not at Brian, but at Luke—demanding he go anywhere except where he stood now lounging

341

against the rail, awaiting Brian.

The two men in the world for whom Ria would have given her soul meant to fight—to kill each other.

Brian was halfway up the gangplank before Ria's senses forced her to action. "No, Brian. No!" she cried, as she ran after him. But before she could reach him Brian and Luke stood face to face.

"You damned thieving bastard!" Brian grated through clenched teeth. "You are the lowest form of man. No, not man, for that attributes to you a sense of decency you don't possess."

Luke laughed, and the sound of his laughter sent chills up Ria's spine. She knew with complete certainty that he would never back away from Brian.

"Damn you both. You can't do this! Not over me." She turned to glare bitterly at Luke, but it was no use. Even as she spoke, flinging her words at him as if they were knives, she knew her effort was futile.

Too well she recognized Luke's temper, the high-strung recklessness that made him choose his path then hold to it despite anything. She saw the grooves deepen on either side of his mouth, noted his broad sarcastic smile.

Luke seemed to be quite at ease, but Ria had seen immediately that his lips were drawn taut with suppressed anger. Now the slight drawing together of his brows was giving him a frowning look.

How calm he looks, she thought, but she knew he was raging inside, his anger barely controlled. She had seen him like this before, and she knew too well what it meant when a gold flame glowed in the amber depths of his eyes and his nostrils flared—he was furious.

"Who are you to challenge what I've done?" Lucas demanded. "Have you offered the . . . lady more than

I have? I would say to the fleet belongs the prize." His sardonic laugh cut through Ria like a sword.

His eyes held Ria's for a moment, and she felt a strange sensation of timelessness as she found in his look the same unrelenting barrier she had seen so often before. That sensation deepened until the world contained only the glow of his mesmerizing gaze—the amber fire she had loved and hated. If he died here he would be out of her life forever and she would be free. Yet that thought tore her to shreds, and the horrible realization that Brian might kill him was even worse.

She parted her lips to say no, but only a whisper emerged.

Lucas could interpret her distress in only one way: she was terrified that her beloved Brian was going to be killed. But, with a strange weight in his heart, he realized he could not kill Brian even if he wanted to. He would never be able to bear the look he would see in her eyes, or the condemnation he would always sense.

"I'm going to kill you," Brian said evenly, "and I don't intend to do it easily, quickly, or pleasantly. I will treasure the memory of doing it for a long time."

Ria pressed her knuckles against her mouth to keep from screaming. As Brian moved toward Lucas, she thrust herself between the two men, her back to Lucas and her hands pressed against Brian's chest.

"No, Brian. Please. You must not. I don't want his blood on your hands. For me, Brian! Please, for my sake don't do this."

But it was as if Brian had not heard her.

"You've been running from me," he said furiously. "Where will you run to now? Will you hide behind her skirts like the coward you are? Will you leap into the ocean to escape the punishment you so richly deserve?''

All the men aboard Lucas's ship were stunned that their captain had not silenced the man who challenged him. Lucas was well aware of their murmurs of surprise. He could not afford to be pushed much further.

"I'm going to skewer you to that rail behind you. With my sword through your belly, I'll listen to your screams of anguish!"

Ria screamed silently. She bit her lip until she tasted blood to keep from fainting. Lucas was now pushed beyond the point of return.

Hard, familiar hands gripped her shoulders, and she was being relentlessly moved aside.

"This," Lucas said with a satanical half-smile, "will be cold-blooded slaughter, if you think to go through with it."

"Are you afraid for yourself?" Brian sneered.

Lucas did not break into a sweat, nor did his tongue moisten dry lips. Instead he laughed softly, and Ria would remember for a long time the ugly sound of his laughter.

"I'm afraid I did not have my slaughter in mind, but your own. For Ria's sake, if you leave my ship now I will let you go with your life, but if you persist then I've no alternative but to rid myself of your obnoxious presence as rapidly as I can."

Brian growled, a wild furious sound, and reached for his sword, but again Ria leapt to grasp his arm. Despite his efforts to push her aside, she clung tenaciously to him. She could not allow them to kill each other.

"Please," she begged Luke, "don't do this. I plead with you. Don't do it."

"I seem to have no choice," Lucas answered coldly.

"Ria let go!" Brian roared, but she clung to him

in desperation.

"Will you listen to me!" Ria cried, flinging her words at Lucas. Her eyes were abnormally large, and she was shaking.

Only her condition shook Lucas's anger and made him look deeper into her eyes.

What he saw crushed his rage and tore at his vitals. He saw the desperate agony of her pleading. Finally he heard her beg.

He stood near the rail where the belaying pins rested in their sockets. His hand closed about one, and swiftly as a striking cobra, he whipped it forward and struck Brian on the side of the head. Brian was unconscious before he hit the deck.

Ria screamed and fell to her knees beside her brother. Then she raised a tear-stained face to Lucas. Although his expression was inscrutable he winced under the look of cold hatred she cast at him.

"I'll have two of my men help you. Get him aboard his ship—get him out of here, Ria," he said coldly.

"You are a monster," she declared in a half-whisper. "So cold and unfeeling. How could you do this?"

"It was either that," he said brutally, "or kill him. Why can't you make up your mind or"—he challenged wickedly—"are you perhaps thinking if you play your cards right you could be mistress to two men at the same time?"

She gasped at this unfeeling attack, but before she could regain control of her thoughts, he thrust again.

"Get him the hell off my ship before I change my mind. If he wakes up here, I guarantee you I won't be so lenient the next time. Warn him not to come here again, and if you're smart, Ria, you'll take your lover and get out of these waters."

He knelt and caught her face in one hand. "And

you—I don't ever want to see your lovely whore's face again. If I do, I might not be so gentle. Now get out of here."

He stood and motioned to two seamen who came running.

"Help the lady. Take him back to his ship," he ordered.

Ria watched as Lucas strode away from her, knowing the strongest feeling of loss, as if some vital part of her life was being drained away. She wanted to cry out to him, to follow him and throw herself into his arms. But she couldn't. The two sailors were lifting Brian, and she slowly rose and left the *Black Angel* with him.

Back in his cabin Lucas was overcome by rage. He was unreasonable, and he knew it. He was aflame with a wild jealousy that knew no bounds. Ria . . . Damn her violet eyes and her lovely yielding body. She was the only woman capable of making him fly into a jealous rage that blinded him to everything, even caution and reason. He should have done what he had threatened to do. He should have rid himself, once and for all, of her lover and taken her for as long as he chose to keep her.

A deep insidious voice inquired evilly if he would have been able to let her go.

"Damn her wanton soul to hell," he gritted out as he lifted the third glass of brandy to his mouth.

He glared at the bottle in his hand; then in a fit of tremendous anger, he flung it across the cabin and watched it splatter against the wall. Amber liquid ran down to make puddles on the deck. He spent the rest of the day and all of the night trying, with brandy, to wash Ria's memory from his mind and his body.

Ria had the still-unconscious Brian placed on the bunk in his cabin. Then she sent for water and gently bathed his head with a cool wet cloth until he moaned and began to regain consciousness.

His eyes finally focused on a pale-faced Ria.

"Brian," she said softly, "are you all right?"

"Where am I . . . what happened?" He grunted. Then memory flooded back and he sat up abruptly, wincing as pain shot through his head.

"The cowardly bastard hit me," he said angrily. "Ria, am I aboard—"

"No, Brian. This is the *Swan*. Please lie still for a while."

He fell back on the pillow as the cabin began to spin dizzily about him.

"I will kill him," he muttered.

"No," Ria said, a tinge of anger in her voice. "It's over, Brian. This terrible, terrible mistake we made— it's over."

"But, Ria, we came here for a reason."

"And we found what we came for. We know that Henri Duval and that nameless captain of the *Black Angel* are pirates. We have just failed to find the proof necessary to stop them. We must go home and find another way to defeat them."

She rose before Brian could protest again. "Rest. On tomorrow's tide we can go home." She walked to the door and left the cabin.

Brian looked at the closed door for a long time, realizing that Ria had changed drastically. His head ached, and he was bombarded by confusion. He

347

closed his eyes to try to erase the pain, and after a while he slept.

Ria tried to avoid thinking of Lucas, yet he had seeped through her every pore. She wanted to cry out in anguish.

She lay on her bunk and felt the breeze coming through the porthole from the bay. She could not sleep. Over and over she told herself of the futility of thinking of him. Yet her body betrayed her mind.

No matter how much she hated him, she was still tortured by the need of her flesh for his, by the feel of his hands on her body, of his lips crushing her half-hearted protests into silence, of the now-familiar weight of his body claiming hers. He could make her forget everything but the need for fulfillment.

Ria sprang from the bed, unable to stand the direction her thoughts were taking. She twisted her hand in a gesture of self-contempt. I am no better than he, she thought, ruled by passion. She hated her own weakness, and she proclaimed her hatred of Lucas over and over.

Yet her body knew the truth. She found it difficult to fight its call.

"I hate him!" she groaned aloud. But her words were silenced by the honesty of her heart. When he kissed her or touched her, her senses ruled . . . and she was aware that he knew it.

He had laughed at her constant denial, because he had known the truth, that his touch brought forth a slumbering languorous sensuality in her. It was a thing designed by nature, and just as uncontrollable as nature's severest tempest.

* * *

It was near midnight before Brian could fight off the sickening dizziness and stand. He washed in cold water and dressed. Then he made his way to Ria's cabin.

He knocked, and her quick answer told him she could not sleep either.

The wick of the lantern in Ria's cabin had been turned low, so the light was softened to a mellow glow. She was standing by the porthole, looking out, when Brian entered.

Brian walked to her side and stood quietly looking out at the bay. Besides being brother and sister, they had been friends too long to allow anything to hover between them without talking it out.

"Ria?"

"Yes, Brian?"

"Look at me."

She turned her eyes to his, and he was shaken by the unnamable sadness he saw in them. Again he felt a cold desire to kill Luke.

"Tell me the truth, Ria. Did he hurt you?"

"Not the way you think."

"How then?"

"I don't know," she said softly. "It's almost as if . . . as if he has taken some part of me and I can't seem to retrieve it."

"And yet you didn't want him dead."

"No . . . no, I didn't."

"Why?"

"I don't know the answer to that either. I couldn't let you fight him, and I couldn't let him fight you. I have no logical reason. I have been asking myself why for hours."

She reached out to touch him. "Brian, I don't understand, and until I understand myself how can I make sense of all that has happened. I want to go home."

"I would leave on tomorrow's tide, Ria, but—"

"But?"

"Ria, in all honor I cannot just desert a friend who needs help."

"A friend . . . help . . . what?"

"Scott. I am supposed to be upriver to get him if he needs me. I only came back to the bay because of you."

Brian went on to explain where Scott had gone and why. He told her all that had happened since he had seen her. He was quick to notice that Ria offered no explanation. Whatever had happened, she intended to keep it to herself.

"I suppose you are right, Brian. We cannot desert him. He will need us. On the tide we can go back upriver and wait for him."

"It can't take too long. Maybe he will meet with success, and we will accomplish what we came for. Then we'll leave."

Ria agreed.

"Can you forget, Ria?" he asked gently.

"I will forget," she said determinedly. "I have obligations at home that will help me forget. Soon, if he will still have me, I will be the wife of Lucas Maine."

"Unless he has warts." Brian chuckled, hoping her past words would still amuse her. She smiled.

"Even with warts. I will no longer run from my obligations like a romantic child. I will honor my marriage"—her voice died to a whisper—"and I will forget . . . I will forget."

"Ria—"

She interrupted him. "I really am exhausted and if we are leaving before dawn I must get some sleep."

"All right. We'll talk tomorrow."

"Yes." She agreed only to get him to leave. She had to be alone to face her struggle and to sort out her thoughts.

Brian kissed her lightly on the cheek, then his arm tightened about her shoulders in a quick hug. Within moments, she heard the door click closed behind him.

She stood for a long time watching the moon rise and a million stars sparkle brilliantly in the night sky.

"A sailor's delight," she whispered to herself.

We sail from star to star not land to land, he had said.

Slow tears formed and ran unheeded down her cheeks. Then she turned from the window and lay across her bunk, letting tears help wash away her pain.

Dawn was only a pale streak across the horizon when the *Swan* unfurled her sails and left the bay, but gradually the first rays of sun heralded in a new day.

A sharp rap or two awakened Lucas who had, just an hour or so before, found exhausted sleep. He rose, washed and dressed, and walked out of his cabin to go on deck, determined not to look in the direction of the *Swan*. The first mate came to stand beside him, quietly awaiting the day's orders.

Lucas still had to keep a rendezvous with Henri. After he had the proof he needed, he would sail for home and try to let the future wash away the past.

"See to her sails, Mr. Jacob," Lucas snapped. "Put her before the wind and get speed up. There is a map in my desk with our rendezvous point marked. While you're there bring my glass."

"Aye, sir."

The first mate called out the orders, and men scattered to their duties. Then he went below to fetch the map and the retractable telescope. He quickly returned and handed the glass to his captain who tucked it under one arm.

Lucas watched the sails unfurl, felt the ship lift beneath him as his trim craft answered the command of sail and breeze. They headed out of the bay.

No, by God, he thought, I will not look. Lucas had been grimly holding himself in check, but a call much stronger than his will to resist made him turn, take the glass from beneath his arm, and put it to his eye.

At first he thought he had just forgotten where the *Swan* lay, but when he looked for the second time, he realized the truth: the *Swan* and the lovely creature who was carrying his soul with her were gone.

He gazed for a long time in utter disbelief, realizing that Ria was truly no longer a part of his life. He knew it was best for both of them, yet bittersweet memories would not release him. They clutched his heart in an iron grip until he could not bear the pain.

Would he forever envision her as he did at that moment. As if she stood beside him, he could smell the intoxicating scent of her, could still hear the softness of her laughter in the breeze.

Despite all the facets of Ria he had seen, he knew the one he had truly wanted to know was the one he had never touched.

Chapter 26

Chris and Scott moved deeper into the thick black shadows of the forest to make very sure they would not be overheard.

"Scott, for God's sake. The last person I ever expected to see here was you."

"You were no more surprised than I was."

"How was the wedding?" Chris's smile flashed white in the pale streaks of moonlight that penetrated the trees.

"To say the least it was cold," Scott admitted with a laugh. "But as I said before, Lucas was a fool not to go and meet her before he made his decision. She's one of the loveliest creatures I've ever seen."

"I guess Lucas was too angry at having his marriage arranged for him, and too caught up in the exciting idea of hunting down pirates."

"Right now," Scott said disgustedly, "that's lost a little of its charm and excitement."

"But that certainly doesn't explain what you're doing here."

"Same thing as you are, I guess. Hunting pirates. Chris, has Lucas had any luck? What brought you here, and how did you and Lucas get separated?"

"We didn't get separated."

"I don't understand this at all."

"Maybe it would be best," Chris said thoughtfully, "to start from the beginning."

"Good idea. You go first and I'll fill you in on my story later."

Chris agreed and began to explain. "When Lucas and I started, we had only a remote idea of where to start looking. So we just decided to make the right impression on the citizens of St. Augustine and let the pirate element find us.

"While Lucas waited I started to sniff around and see if I could get news about the banditti. We needed a link to the pirates, so we sort of branched off independently. I ran across a couple of McGirtt's men and made friends. Eventually they brought me here. I knew for certain Dan was waiting for someone. I felt I only had to wait for the links to come together." Chris chuckled softly.

"What's funny?" Scott inquired.

"Well, it's just the fun Lucas and I had putting this thing together."

"Tell me about it. The last I saw you, you two were just setting off on this jaunt."

"Well, Lucas found this ship, and she is a beauty but . . ." His chuckle broke into a soft laugh, and for a minute his story was delayed. Then he achieved control. "Anyway, Lucas was feeling pretty good, and we started talking about names for this black pirate's ship and her captain." Now Chris broke into a hearty laugh which he tried to muffle for security's sake.

Scott was smiling broadly in expectation.

"Well . . . come on . . . tell me."

"Listen to this." Chris tried to control his mirth. "What do you think of the *Black Angel* and her

ferocious owner the sinister Captain Gabriel Blanc?"
He had forced himself to sound stern as he repeated
the name, but he was shaking with laughter again
and completely unaware of Scott's open-mouthed
shocked expression.

"It's great, isn't it?" Chris continued to talk. "Can
you picture Lucas dressed like a wild pirate and
being called Captain Blanc?"

"I most certainly can," Scott said, but he began to
comprehend the unbelievability of the situation.
"All this time Captain Blanc was Lucas?"

"That's right."

Now it was Scott's turn to laugh. He leaned against
a tree and gave in to the hilarity of a situation he
could hardly believe. He crossed his arms about him
and bent forward in his glee.

"Scott?"

"You . . . you aren't going to believe this." Scott
gasped. "You are really not going to believe this."
Again he broke into laughter.

"Well, I'm not going to believe it if you don't tell it
to me."

"Lucas Maine ran away from Arianne St. Thomas
and a marriage he didn't want. And . . . and . . ."
He laughed harder.

"Come on, Scott!"

"And Arianne St. Thomas ran from a marriage she
didn't want. She and her brother are Brian Thomas
and Ria, the captain, of the *Swan* and his ques-
tionable mistress."

Chris looked at Scott, who was convulsed with
laughter; then the absolute hilarity of the situation
struck him too, and he began to laugh.

"Ria is . . . is Arianne St. Thomas?"

"Right," Scott replied.

"You mean . . . all this time . . ."

"All this time Ria and Lucas have been man and wife, running away from each other . . . and right into each other's arms. Now who can't believe in fate?"

"Now tell me how you got here," Chris said through the tears of laughter.

"It's . . . it's"—Scott tried to regain some sobriety—"it's near the same story for me. I ran across William and Sophia and made friends. They thought I was a pirate from . . . God!" He laughed again. "The pirate ship owned by Brian and Ria . . . Ria, Arianne St. Thomas." Again laughter overcame him. "Lucas has been caught by his own trap."

"Can you see Lucas, the eternal bachelor, when he finds out?" Scott grinned broadly.

"Right." Chris snickered with devilish pleasure. "The rake no woman could catch, forced into marriage to . . . to the one woman"—he could hardly control his hilarity—"in the world he would really want."

"And he ran." Scott guffawed as he leaned against the tree. "He ran like a scared boy."

"Right into her arms."

"Oh, this is rich," Scott said gleefully. "Do we have the ammunition for some fun later? I can just see Lucas's face."

"It'll probably be the first time any woman has ever given him a genuine surprise." This thought delighted both of them.

"Come on," Chris said, trying to regain control, "we've got to think of some way out of this."

"You're right. I wouldn't miss the looks on Lucas's and Ria's faces when they meet again."

"We must find a way to escape. I, for one, would not want to cross that wilderness by myself. I was totally lost on the way here."

"Our safest bet is to leave by ship," Scott suggested. "But the only ship around is Henri's, so I don't think it's going to be easy."

"Not with old Henri and Dan together. Dan's pretty suspicious."

"He's not a trusting man," Chris agreed. "I have to tell you that he knows more than you think. To keep my skin in one piece I was forced to tell him that I was here because Lucas—Captain Blanc," he corrected with another deep laugh, "is really after Henri."

"And he hasn't told Henri about that?"

"He doesn't trust Henri either. I think Henri was bringing him something pretty special, and if I'm not missing my guess it's guns and ammunition. He made a deal with Henri to slip his loot back across the border to be sold, but I don't think it would take much for Dan to break with him."

"You trust Dan?"

"Yes, to tell you the truth, I do. I don't think he's as black as they'd like to paint him. Besides, he could have turned me over to Henri long ago but he didn't, not even after what happened tonight."

"Henri is an animal, isn't he?" Scott said. "I sure don't think, after tonight, you had best cross his path too often. I have a feeling he's treacherous enough to find a nice quiet way to let these swamps swallow you up."

"You're right there, but after what he's done to Louisa I can hardly stop myself from running a sword through him."

"Let's let the hangman take care of him." Scott put a hand on Chris's arm. "We can prove what's going on if we can get one scrap of paper from the ship he took Louisa from. That and Louisa's testimony should do it."

"We have to agree on some kind of plan."

"Let's wait and watch for a couple of days."

"Good idea. Maybe we can find a better way out of here. I'm not leaving without Louisa."

"I agree. We need her, and we certainly can't leave her to Henri's tender mercy."

"All right then. We can't afford to risk meeting for a while. We'll wait a week and watch. Then we'll meet again."

"Agreed."

"Let's get back. I don't want to leave Louisa alone too long. These drunken sots don't have any qualms about taking what they want."

Scott was quiet for a moment, then his rich chuckle cut the night air. "Chris, you think we ought to invite some of the pirates to the wedding?"

"Maybe Dan McGirtt and his boys." Chris fell in with the idea.

"Yeah." Laughter again built in Scott. "We could each put black patches over one eye."

"One thing is certain, if—when—we get out of this and make contact with Lucas, we'll have to keep this a secret." Chris smiled. "I wouldn't want to spoil all the fun when those two find out just how close they've been all this time. There should be one fine explosion."

"God, the possibilities of this situation are flabbergasting."

"Yes," Chris agreed solemnly, "makes room for some enterprising creativity doesn't it?"

"Considering the success Lucas has had with every woman he's met, it might do his overinflated ego good to find the one who ran from him because . . ." He paused thoughtfully. "How did Ria put it? He most likely has warts on his nose and is short and fat."

"She said that?" Chris laughed.

"And more. The lady was not too pleased at being married off."

"Scott, this situation gets more interesting every minute. I hope we get out of here soon though. I can't wait for the wedding of the year."

"Wedding of the century," Scott countered. "Let's go."

They split up before they entered the camp. Scott went back to the noisy communal hut to glean what information he could, and Chris returned to his hut to keep a close eye on Louisa.

The *Black Angel* moved up the river slowly and cautiously, heading for the place Lucas had marked on the map as his rendezvous point with Henri.

He had no way of knowing that just a few short hours ahead of him the *Swan* was heading in very nearly the same direction.

The undulating river had wide curves; it twisted and wound randomly. At no time could one ship see the other, for when one rounded a bend the other had disappeared from view.

When Lucas finally dropped anchor at the pre-arranged spot he was still unaware that the *Swan* was anchored less than five miles away.

Now that he was forced to wait, he wondered how long it would be before Henri arrived. He smiled grimly. He would be certain to pass on to Henri enough incriminating evidence from the ship he had "attacked" to guarantee that the Frenchman would hang. He was impatient now to make an end to this game. It had lost its luster, and he wanted to put it and the intrusive memories of Ria behind him.

*   *   *

Brian had returned to the original point at which he had promised Scott he would wait. He was sure that soon, one way or the other, Scott would signal his whereabouts or come to the *Swan*.

Once he did, whether or not they could bring Henri to justice, he and Ria were going to leave. He was worried about her. Something within her had changed, and he wasn't sure he liked the change at all. A once laughing and happy girl had become an introspective and quiet . . . woman.

Yes, he thought with anger he tried to contain, Ria had been touched deeply by that conscienceless rake. The man had taken her innocence, Brian knew that, and he had left her vulnerable in a way that was difficult for her to handle.

He mused thoughtfully on Ria's reasons for not wanting to see Lucas pay dearly for what he had done to her. Surely, she could have no feelings toward this man but anger and hatred? Yet he wondered, because for the first time Ria was not confiding in him. He couldn't seem to reach her.

Once the ship was at anchor, Brian went to Ria's cabin. There he found her curled in a chair with an open book in her lap, but something told him she had not turned a page in a long time. She raised her head when he entered. Again, he was caught by the fact that her wide eyes seemed to dominate her face like deep unfathomable purple pools.

"We're at anchor," he said.

"Good," she softly replied.

He could feel her lack of interest and the deep lethargy that clung to her. He prayed silently that Scott would hurry. He wanted to take Ria away, take her home, far from the memories that held her.

He knew she had convinced herself that a loveless marriage was all she had to look forward to, but the thought of her facing years and years of unhappiness was hard for him to bear. He had half made up his mind that even if she didn't care, he might fight to get the marriage annulled. He would take her somewhere else, to some happy place where she might learn to smile again.

"Ria?"

"Yes, Brian?"

"You've been curled up in that chair reading for hours. Come on deck and watch the sunset with me. It's going to be beautiful."

"Brian . . . I don't—"

"Damn it! You just can't shut yourself off like this. I won't let you! Do you understand me! Now put that book away; you haven't been reading it anyhow."

Ria closed the book and rose from the chair, but he could see tears she would no longer shed glistening in her eyes and he felt more miserable than ever. He went to her and put his arms about her.

"I'm sorry, Ria. I didn't mean to shout at you."

"I know. I'll be fine."

"Sure you will. You just have the wind knocked from your sails. You'll pick up the pieces, and I'll help you. Now"—he grinned—"come on deck and get some air . . . maybe . . . if you feel like it, we can talk."

Ria was grateful for Brian. His gentle kindness provided a shield behind which she could recoup her forces.

"I can't think of anything I'd rather do than see the sunset . . . and talk with you."

"I told you, Ria. You'll get over him. Just give it time, and try not to think of him anymore."

Ria smiled and nodded. She went to the deck with him, and they watched the fiery sunset. But despite her attempt to enjoy it, Ria could only feel a sense of emptiness and longing. She contained it well, but Brian sensed it and again he was filled with anger at Lucas and the destruction he had wrought. Of one thing he was sure, he would do what he could to help her forget Blanc . . . and maybe fate would let him run across the man again. This time Ria would not be there to stop him, and he would kill him.

The *Swan* rocked gently in the dusky light. The man who knelt in the heavy underbrush near the river had been watching it since the dying sun had touched it with its final glow. He had seen the man and woman who had stood on the deck together and had been fascinated by her beauty.

When the shadows deepened and he could see no more, he moved away as silently as he had come, walking along the shore until he came to the boat he had kept hidden. He pushed it out into the swift current of the river and began to paddle energetically.

Soon he disappeared into the darkness. He grinned to himself as he skimmed the boat expertly along. He was more than pleased with the news he would carry to Henri Duval.

He had been sent to keep watch for the ship called the *Black Angel*. When it made anchor he was to let Henri know at once. Well, he had seen the ship Henri sought, but he had seen much more than Henri had expected.

Henri had expected one ship on the river, but there were two—two!

To him that meant the possibility of loot. Maybe one ship was a friend of Henri's, but the other could be a prime target.

When he thought of loot he thought of the slim beauty he had seen standing on the deck, and his body reacted violently. He could almost feel her soft skin beneath his hands. Oh yes, if Henri gave the word, he would be the first man aboard and the first to taste the pleasure he knew he would derive from the body of the girl with the sun-touched hair.

He had a great distance to row. It would most likely take him over an hour to get back, but it would be worth it.

Henri was impatient. Surely Blanc would have taken his ship and been back by now. The camp of Dan McGirtt was most certainly not a place where he chose to spend much time. It was too confining for Henri who liked wine, women, and song in abundance.

Besides, he didn't quite trust Dan McGirtt, and he knew damn well Dan didn't trust him. But he didn't care. The two cargoes would make him a wealthy man—those and the ransom he expected to get from Louisa Herald's father.

He felt he had planned well. Once he overtook Blanc's ship and rid himself of her captain, he would have even more profit . . . The only thing that still twisted him inside was his desire to have the beautiful mistress from the *Swan*.

He thought now of Louisa. He had hated her. Maybe because he had not derived the satisfaction he had expected to get from subduing her and forcing her to bow to his will. She is not my kind of woman, he thought. He wanted a woman with fire, like the amethyst-eyed beauty Ria.

Henri slept in his elaborate cabin aboard the *Sea Rover*. He liked luxury, and the only luxuries Dan's camp offered were women. He had come aboard to ease his impatience with bad rum and inadequate feminine company, and had undressed and fallen on his bunk when a rap on the door jolted him awake.

"Blast you, it had better be important," he shouted. "Come in!"

A man stuck his head inside.

"Sir."

"Well, what is it?"

"José is here, sir. He has word of the ship you're looking for."

"Where is he?"

"On deck, sir."

"I'll be right there."

The door closed quickly and Henri rose, dressed quickly, and went on deck to find José.

"So my friend has come."

"Aye, sir. That he has. He is at the big bend in the river. He lays at anchor and waits as you told him."

"He has guards posted?"

"Aye, sir. Several."

"Hmmm. Cautious man, isn't he? Making ready for trouble. Well, we'll go see him tomorrow and finish out our bargain."

"There is more news."

"More?"

"There's another ship on the river."

"Another. What ship? Where does she lie? We were expecting no other ships."

"I think you will be very pleased, my Captain, to hear the name of this ship." José grinned broadly in expectation of his captain's pleasure.

"Well confound you," Henri roared, "what's the name of this mysterious ship?"

"She's the *Swan*, sir."

For several moments Henri only looked at José; then, suddenly, he threw back his head and roared with laughter.

Chapter 27

"The *Swan* is here?" Henri said delightedly.

"Aye, sir."

"And where does she lie?" he asked quickly.

"Between us and the *Black Angel*."

"So," Henri said meditatively, "we could get to her without my dear friend Captain Blanc knowing a thing about it."

"Aye, sir. We could. Shall we take her?" José's anxious attitude drew Henri's close scrutiny.

"You seem to be in a hurry to take this ship. What draws you to her so energetically?"

José's eyes shifted away.

"The truth man, or I'll have you skewered," he threatened.

José smiled ingratiatingly. "The *Swan* has a woman aboard."

Henri's eyes narrowed. "A beauty with golden hair?" he asked.

"Aye."

"So . . . she has found her way back to her ship." He laughed. "And back to me. When you take the *Swan,* I want whoever captains her to be brought to the camp and tossed in with the Americans. I want the woman separated from him immediately and brought directly to my cabin."

José was disappointed. He knew the blond woman was lost to him, but losing her was better than dying for her. Besides, his captain tired of women easily and maybe . . .

"Pick enough men, but don't waken the Americans," he cautioned. "It's best they don't know of this. Not just yet."

"Aye, sir," José said happily.

"Bring the woman to me at once." Henri added, "And make sure that no man lays a hand on her, for if he does I shall cut it off—just before I cut off his head."

"Aye, sir," José said in a sullen voice. He set about spreading the word and collecting men who would do the job well.

The men left the camp in almost complete silence, and neither Chris nor Scott stirred from deep sleep while they did so.

For the first time in several nights Brian slept soundly. Most of the crew did the same, with the exception of the few who were taking their turns at standing guard. None of the men on duty could figure out what they were guarding the ship from with only lush green wilderness about them, so the lapping of the water against the hull and the soft call of night animals lulled them into a careless and relaxed state—too relaxed.

They were set up so suddenly that they stood no chance at all. The sentries were silenced and the attackers went below to finish the job.

Brian had finally sought rest in his cabin, but Ria still paced the deck of hers, restless and full of a strange nervous tension that forbade sleep.

Maybe, she thought, it is because every time I lie down Luke intrudes into my thoughts and my dreams. I resist him by staying away from my bed as much as possible.

As she paced, she passed a mirror that hung on the wall, and her reflection caught her attention. She stopped and moved closer to study her face intently. Yes, she decided, Brian is right. I have changed.

She knew who was responsible for the stronger more self-willed woman she had become. She flushed to know she had learned all the tricks and techniques of a whore while she'd become acquainted with her own passionate abandon. During the short time she'd been with Luke, he had taught her well. But who was going to teach her to smother her own passionate needs? Who was going to teach her not to let memories damn her as she lay in the arms of another man.

She tipped her chin up stubbornly, and a glow of new and fierce determination filled her. The strength she had gained from her experience with Luke, the new brand of independence he had forged in her, would help her survive all the long hours that lay ahead.

She could have broken, but she hadn't. She had scars, and she hoped fervently that the canker of bitterness would remain with him a long, long time.

What kind of a woman am I to become? she wondered. She could not find the will to forgive Luke—not because of the things he had forced her to do, but because of the things she had done of her own accord.

In spite of the weakness in her that she acknowledged, the hard lessons she had learned from him had stood her in good stead. She had learned how to erect a shell around herself and how to withdraw behind it, allowing no trace of emotion to show on the surface. This had become her most trusted form of self-defense. She was no longer the green, wide-eyed girl he had first possessed. She had managed to rise above that, and for the first time she realized she was now a woman who meant to have some command over her future.

But one dark shadow persisted in spreading its wings over her heart.

"Oh, Luke," she whispered, "why do I still want you? Why can't I take you as lightly as you seem to take me?" She did not know. She had to hope time would wash her mind, her body, and her heart clean of him.

Used to the creaking sounds of the ship, Ria must have heard the scuffling sounds for some time before she was drawn from her meditative state.

She listened intently, then heard them again. They sounded almost like bare feet running across the deck.

Intending to go to Brian's room to see if anything was wrong, she went to the door and opened it to come face to face with a grinning José who was holding a bloodied sword in his hand.

He lifted it so the point hovered inches from her, and she tried to contain a gasp of sheer terror.

"Do not be alarmed, lovely one," José purred. "No harm will come to you."

She backed away, trying to smother the scream that began to bubble to her lips.

"Come, come, little one." José chuckled. "No need to be afraid. You must come on deck."

As if to give more force to his words, she felt the ship slowly begin to move.

"Brian!" she cried, as she gazed in shock at the

bloodied blade. "Brian! Where is he, what have you done to him!"

"Nothing little one. He will join you on deck." José's eyes chilled her, and she knew she would prefer to be on deck where the chance of escape was more likely than in this cabin with him.

Without another word, she eased past him and went quickly above. There was no sign of Brian, and for one panic-stricken moment fear choked off her other emotions. Then, when she saw an angry, half-dressed Brian being pushed toward her, she almost fainted with relief.

He came and stood beside her, putting a protective arm about her.

"Are you all right, Ria?"

"Yes." She tried to keep her voice under control, but it cracked with fear. "We're underway. I wonder where those devils came from . . . and where they're taking us," Ria whispered.

"I'd say," Brian replied, "that our good friend Henri might be somewhere near. I recognize the ugly one with the sword."

"Henri Duval!" Ria almost choked on the name.

"I think he's going to get a shock from finding me still alive, and I imagine he'll try to rectify that situation as soon as possible."

"What are we going to do?" she whispered raggedly as she clutched his arm frantically.

"Ria," Brian said, pulling her close so his words would not carry too far, "if you get any kind of an opportunity to escape, take it. You're a good strong swimmer. Even if you must go overboard, do it. Fight the current, hang on to anything. The river will eventually take you out of here. It's a slim chance, but better than what we've got with Henri."

"I can't . . . I can't," she gasped.

"You can!" he declared firmly. "And I want you to promise me if the chance comes you'll take it. If one of us slips through his grasp, that is good."

"I won't leave you."

"You will," he said angrily, "or so help me, I'll push him into killing me now."

"Brian don't—"

"Promise me. Any chance at all . . . *promise*."

"I promise." She said the words only to stop him from carrying out his threat. She had no intention of leaving him. They would face Henri together.

It seemed to take hours before they turned another curve in the river and saw Henri's ship anchored near a makeshift dock that seemed to extend only into wilderness.

"I was right," Brian said. "There's good old Henri's ship. I wonder what he's doing so far upriver?"

"There must be a profit to be made here."

"No doubt."

"Brian . . ." Ria began, but at that moment José observed them whispering. He came to them immediately, grasped Ria's wrist in a painful grip, and dragged her far enough away from Brian so they could talk no more. Brian was enraged and would have leapt on José had not two unwavering blades pressed to his chest brought him to a halt.

Ria jerked her arm from the grinning José who pushed her against the rail.

"Do not force me to prove what I can do to keep you . . . obedient." He laughed. Ria had no way of knowing his threat was a bluff, for José knew his head would be severed from his shoulders should any harm come to her.

She kept silent, but her violet eyes snapped in rage and she drew herself as far away from José as the point of his sword would let her go. It chilled her blood when she saw a glow of brutal satisfaction in his eyes and he said softly: "You are arrogant now, but when Henri is done with you, and I have you, I will show you the many ways I have to tame you. Soon you will not look at me like that. You will learn."

Ria would have snarled a reply that might have destroyed the small amount of self-control José had, but at that moment the ship bumped lightly against the dock and José gripped her wrist and dragged her toward the gangplank.

As she was dragged near Brian, who was being nudged in the same direction, his arms now bound firmly behind him, he called to her.

"Don't forget what I said, Ria."

"Brian—"

"Shut up," José growled. Roughly, he pushed Ria ahead of him, and her chance to speak to Brian was gone.

When Brian last saw her, she was being pushed up the gangplank of Henri's ship. He was then forced to walk the distance to the camp, whose presence took him completely by surprise.

He was even more surprised when he was shoved into one of the huts and he found himself face to face with Scott and Chris who had finally been wakened by the sound of the approaching men.

"What's going on?" a sleepy Scott had asked an only semiawake Chris.

"I don't have any idea. Sounds like a lot of activity for the middle of the night. Someone's coming."

Both men rose from their bunks, leaving Louisa still asleep. Chris had bribed Marco into sleeping in another hut.

The door was opened, and both Scott and Chris

were amazed to see Brian pushed inside and the door pulled shut behind him.

"Well, I'll be damned," Scott said in wonder. "What the hell are you doing here?"

"I might ask you the same thing, but I feel safe in surmising this is McGirtt's camp."

"How did you get caught?" Scott asked quickly.

"Stupidity, I guess. I thought we would be reasonably safe where we were anchored and only set out a few sentries. We were waiting for you."

"We?"

"Ria and I."

"Ria's here too!" Scott's voice now revealed a touch of alarm.

"Yes. Thanks to our dear friend Captain Blanc. If it had not been for him, Ria and I would have been safely on the way home by now. If I live through this, I will one day kill that man if it takes me forever to hunt him down."

Chris and Scott exchanged looks, neither sure if the truth should be spoken under the present circumstances.

"Who's your friend?" Brian looked at Chris.

"Chris Martin, he's . . . he's Captain Blanc's first mate."

Brian's eyes were cold and his face was grim. "I see. You don't choose your company well, Scott."

"Now wait, Brian. There's a lot you don't understand."

"I understand what Captain Blanc is and what he's responsible for."

"You could be wrong." Chris smiled.

"He's right," Scott added. "You're jumping to the wrong conclusion."

"I doubt it. After what Blanc has done to Ria, there's no conclusion too foul."

Scott and Chris shared a look of mutual agreement. They had to tell Brian the truth. If Brian found a way out of this, they didn't want him to leave with murder in his heart.

"Just what is it you think he's done to Ria?" Chris smiled.

His smile did not lessen Brian's anger. With a grim face and a cold, unrelenting voice, he told them of Lucas's kidnapping of Ria and of what he thought of the situation.

"Then," Chris said, "Scott has finally told me that Ria is not your mistress but is actually Arianne St. Thomas . . . your sister."

"Yes, she is."

"Why did you bring her into such danger?"

"One does not 'bring' Ria into anything. She follows her own choosing. She stowed away on my ship. God, I wish she had stayed at home. Even facing a marriage she hated would have been better than what she's been through."

Now, to Brian's irritation, both men were smiling.

"You find her situation amusing?" he said coldly.

"Up until tonight, yes," Scott replied.

"Scott—" Brian's face was now twisted by fury.

"Now wait a minute. Come and sit down. I have a story to tell you. It will change your entire outlook on a lot of things, especially Captain Blanc."

"I doubt if anything could change the way I feel about him."

"Don't say that until you know." Chris laughed.

"Know what?"

"Sit down Brian," Scott urged. "This is going to take a while, and you might find it quite a shock."

Brian sat and looked at both men expectantly.

"Well?"

Both Chris and Scott were grinning broadly as they

again exchanged looks.

"Shall I tell him, or do you want to do the honors?" Chris asked.

"You do it since you're Blanc's first mate." Scott chuckled.

"No, no," Chris chided. "You sailed with Ria and Brian, so you can tell him."

"One of you had best tell me something and very soon before I lose my patience."

"All right," Scott surrendered good-naturedly. "It's best we stop the fun and tell him the truth because we have to pool our resources and find a way out of this for us and for Ria."

Brian leaned forward in anticipation, but as Scott slowly began to talk his eyes grew wider and wider. Shock made him sit straighter and straighter.

"So you see, Captain Blanc is in reality Lucas Maine, and he is now your brother-in-law. And I can add another piece of information. From what Chris has told me and from what I know about Lucas, he's madly in love with Ria. Lucas is not a man who would have behaved as he has unless he wanted her enough to take her from you."

"You mean Captain Blanc is really Ria's—"

"Husband," Chris concluded.

Brian was stunned momentarily. He knew Ria loved Captain Blanc; he had read it in her eyes. But why had he been so brutal, given her up to him so easily?

Then his mind found the truth, and he began to smile. Ria had been so worried about him that she'd been afraid to tell Blanc the truth. Blanc still thought Ria was his mistress and that Ria loved him. He had loved her enough to give her up for her own happiness, to give her to another man.

Brian's scowl vanished, and he began to smile. His

smile disintegrated into a soft chuckle, then to laughter.

"My God," he choked out, "they ran so far to find each other."

"You have no idea what a monster Lucas was when he found himself married off to a woman he'd never seen," Chris said.

"No less Ria." Brian laughed. "She threatened the man with everything from mayhem to murder. You have no idea where her imagination carried her."

"To warts and fat legs." Scott chuckled.

"To say the least," Brian responded. "I heard multiple descriptions of what he must be all the way to St. Augustine."

"Well, we've got to find a way to get out of here," Chris declared.

"Yes, and we've got to get Ria out of here," Brian said quickly. "Henri had her taken to his ship. That beast would go to any lengths to get revenge on Lucas and to force Ria to his will."

"Henri will be occupied for a while. He is waiting for someone and has a plan of some sort. Do you think Ria will be quick enough to handle him for tonight? If so we can get word to her tomorrow," Chris said.

"She's a bright girl. She might get Henri to believe she's surrendered, then try to find her own means of escape," Brian offered worriedly. "Or she's likely to try to kill the bastard. Maybe she'll bargain with him for me. That would stop him only for a short while."

"Well, we have to count on her being clever and level-headed tonight. If she can find a way to hold him off we can find a way to get us all out of here," Scott sounded determined.

Brian felt entirely helpless. He knew he would never be able to get to Henri's ship without being stopped. Chris and Scott had assured him that they were closely watched.

"If Ria wants to see me alive, maybe Henri will send for me just to prove I am. I wish I could just get some word to her. I know she must be frightened to death."

"There's nothing we can do now," Scott declared.

"You're right. We'd be dead before we set foot on his ship."

"We can do nothing but sit here," Brian said helplessly.

"And wait," Scott added.

"And pray," Chris said softly.

"Yes," Brian repeated, "and pray."

The three men were silent now. Never in any of their lives had they felt so impotent.

Henri's ship was only a short distance away, but it might have been hundreds of miles from them. Since no one else would help Ria in any way, at this difficult time in her life Ria would have to rely only on her own resources—one woman against the strengths and skill of a man who knew no mercy.

Ria was dragged up the gangplank to the deck of Henri's ship. She looked about, but there was no sign of Henri. She saw only the lust-filled faces of the men who circled about her. One reached out a hand to touch her, and she struck it away with her doubled fists which were still bound together.

"Keep your filthy hands off of me, you degenerate scum," she cried, a snarl in her voice.

"Feisty one, isn't she?"

A pirate laughed. "Them's the kind makes better beddin'," another declared.

Ria had never been so frightened in her life, but she

would be damned if she would show it.

"Keep your hands to yourselves boys," José said. "You'll get your turn. Captain always takes his first. There's plenty of time."

To Ria's shame, they all laughed. She clenched her teeth. Captain Henri Duval will try, she thought, but as Brian had said, she would find a means of escape . . . any means . . . even death.

José dragged her down to the captain's cabin, opened the door, and gave her a shove, thrusting her inside. Then he pulled the door shut, and she could hear the grating sound of the lock slipping into place.

She stood in the center of the cabin, hands bound before her, and looked around, surprised to find it empty.

Chapter 28

Lucas paced and repaced the deck of the *Black Angel* a dark scowl on his face. He hated the waiting, and he knew why.

Hours and hours of being able to do nothing only made it more difficult to fight memories of Ria. He needed to keep them at bay; they were entirely too difficult to handle yet.

"God damn that man," he muttered to himself. "He should have been here by now."

He knew he had to wait. Henri had to have the evidence on him when he was taken, and this meeting with him was the only way Lucas could see to it that he did. The papers and the identifiable property he had taken from the ship would be enough to hang Henri.

Despite all his efforts, Ria continued to invade both his thoughts and his senses. How cold and angry she had been in their last moments together. Those eyes, he thought bitterly. His violet-eyed witch. He remembered too well the frantic beating of her heart against his chest, like a small bird with fluttering wings trying to escape.

He remembered small, incoherent moans through

parted lips. Ria, siren-nemesis. The kind of woman who could lead any man to destruction. How could she fight and scream her hatred of him at one moment only to yield with such complete abandon the next.

She had eluded him as he had tried to grasp the wisp of magic that was Ria, even when he had managed to force the surrender of her body. If only she had given some sign that she loved him or wanted him. But she had walked from him to Brian as if their nights together had been less than nothing.

Now, quite suddenly, as if the veil of doubt and misunderstanding that existed between them all these weeks were lifted for an instant, he realized he would go on wanting her for a long time.

She had chosen Brian freely, and looking into her eyes in that destructive moment, he had known bitterly that she was no longer his. But this knowledge did not stop the wanting, the gnawing desire that ate at him until he felt hollow and drained.

He had cursed himself, told himself over and over that he had no right to hold her, yet he knew he would repeat what he had done if he had it to do over.

His lips were a thin line and the vein in his forehead was throbbing. Thinking was too impossible to bear. This was an appalling situation, and he felt somewhat like a fly caught in a spider web, unable to flee, and knowing some form of death was coming.

He sighed and made a decision. Giving the order to watch for Henri's arrival, he went back to his cabin. There he took a bottle of brandy and a glass and retreated to his bunk where he lay half propped against the pillow.

There has to be a way to ease Ria from my mind, he

thought as he poured a liberal glass of brandy and swallowed it in two quick gulps feeling the fire of the drink burn his throat. Maybe, at least for one night, he could wash the scent and the touch of her from his mind.

He had always enjoyed women, finding them ornamental and useful, but Ria was so much more to him.

He could sense the resilience in her, combined with pride and indomitable courage. If ever he had met a woman who could match him, stand toe to toe with him in passion and in all else that woman was Ria.

He remembered the last time they had lain on his bunk together. When they had finally slept he had curved his body to hers and drawn the covers over them, thinking how right it felt and how he had grown used to her body against his in the night.

Ria . . . quicksilver lover . . . would he ever be able to get her out of his mind?

He finally, after several drinks, dozed in a semisleep. In fact, the knocking on his door must have been repeated several times before he was actually sure he heard it.

He swung his legs to the floor and sat on the edge of the bunk.

"What is it?"

"Longboat, sir."

"Close?"

"Aye, sir."

"Is it Henri Duval?"

"Looks like him and three or four of his men."

"Send him below, but keep his men on deck," he commanded.

"Aye, sir."

The man departed, and Lucas picked up the half-empty bottle and poured another drink. Then he sat and waited, wondering which was the spider and which the fly.

Soon the handle of the door turned, and the door swung open to admit a contentedly smiling Henri.

Lucas's first impression was that Henri was gloatingly pleased about something. He wondered if Henri believed that he was trapped.

"Henri. You took your sweet time getting here."

"Sorry, my friend. I have had some . . . problems. But there is nothing wrong now. You have taken the ship?"

"I have."

"And her cargo?"

"In the hold."

"The ship?"

"Sunk . . . with all aboard."

"I thought you were the one to suggest we keep and sell the ships?"

Lucas shrugged. "She put up too much of a fight. I was forced to sink her. Besides I began to think of what you said. Maybe witnesses are a bad thing. I can guarantee no one from that ship will ever testify against me."

Lucas echoed Henri's chuckle in a streak of perverse amusement at what Henri thought was truth.

"Now what do we do?" Lucas inquired.

"Tomorrow I will make my ship ready, and the day after that I will meet you here and take the cargo on board. Then we will discuss where our future partnerships will take us."

"Henri," Lucas said mildly. "I don't leave this river until I get an introduction to our friendly banditti. That was part of our bargain. Besides, I need a few more answers than you choose to give."

"Such as?"

"What share of the profit from this cargo goes to me and my men for one thing."

Lucas's eyes were twin shards of wine-gold fire, and for one of the few times in his life Henri began to think he had underestimated an opponent.

"We put the cargoes together, and when McGirtt gets the profit we divide it, captains getting the larger shares of course."

"Of course. Tell me, Henri"—Lucas's voice became pleasantly soft, and had not his eyes reflected the distrust he felt one might have thought he was a businessman conducting an honest discussion—"why can we not meet now? I will just bring my ship up to join yours."

"That would be foolish, my friend. Dan is my friend—not yours. He does not take too well to inquisitive strangers in his camp."

"Then bring your ship here now and we'll put the cargo on board."

"I'm afraid my ship suffered some damage in the battle. She is under repair. It will only take another day. Have patience, my friend. Surely you know I cannot leave the river without passing you."

All of Henri's arguments seemed justified, yet Lucas could not ignore his feeling that Henri certainly wanted him to stay where he was. For some reason he didn't want Lucas near his ship or McGirtt's camp. Lucas wondered why. Obviously Henri had something to hide.

It was most important that he get the evidence aboard Henri's ship. This whole business had to be brought to a head soon, for Lucas had great need to get away from Florida and all the poignant memories the place held for him.

Henri had been watching Lucas closely. He

wanted the cargo he carried and the *Black Angel,* but he didn't want Lucas to find Brian or Ria. He waited, not wanting Lucas to become any more suspicious than he already was.

"All right, Henri. I'll stay put until day after tomorrow. But by then your friend McGirtt had better get moving. I want to be rid of this cargo and on the sea again."

"Ah! He will be ready, as will I. Now I must get back to my ship. I must see to its repairs and to other . . . ah . . . unfinished business."

Lucas walked with Henri to the deck, and saw him and his longboat pull safely away. His every nerve jangled with the premonition that somehow he should be doing something, and with an even stronger warning that Henri was up to something.

He watched the longboat disappear into the night. Maybe, he mused, like it or not he just might pay Henri and his friends a visit the next day.

He went back to his cabin where, over the next three hours he drained the last of the bottle of brandy. He wanted to sleep, but it was next to impossible. Instead he returned to the nearly deserted deck. Not suspecting any trouble from Henri or anyone else, he told the one sentry to go below and to get some sleep.

"I'll stand watch," he said firmly. "I've had enough of my bed for the night."

Lucas noticed a movement that could not have been one of an inanimate object. Someone was clinging to a small piece of wood and thrashing in desperation.

Taken totally by surprise, and not taking time to wonder why any human would be clinging to a log and floating in a treacherous river current, he drew off his boots and jacket, climbed to the rail and dove, cutting the water and absorbing the cold shock of it. Then with a strong stroke he aimed for a spot some distance ahead that would cut across the path of the unfortunate who would surely drown if he missed his target.

Henri reboarded his ship, confident and satisfied. He met José on deck.

"The captain?"

"He's in the hut with the Americans."

"Do you know this fool who tried to take over a ship that belonged to me?"

"I do, Captain. He is the one who captained the ship when it came here."

"Impossible, he is dead!"

"Not so, my Captain. He is very much alive. He and the woman brought the ship upriver."

"Yes . . ." Henri said thoughtfully, "and for a very special reason. Now I wonder if that very special reason has anything to do with the young American who was once an officer aboard this ship. One here, then another here . . . it poses many questions my friend, some of which I can find the answers to and some I think Dan should ask. Yes, maybe we should let him know some of the questions tomorrow. For tonight I have some questions I think the young lady in my cabin can answer."

"She awaits you, my Captain." José grinned.

Henri chuckled and walked with slow measured steps toward his cabin.

* * *

Ria had tried to pull her hands free from the rope that bound them but it was useless. All she had achieved was to rub her wrists sore. She gave up with a half-angry half-anguished cry and sat down on the bunk to await whatever must happen next.

To her it seemed as if she had waited for hours before she heard the footsteps approaching. Slowly, she rose and faced the door.

Henri walked in, smiled, and without saying a word closed the door. He leaned against it with his arms folded across his chest.

"So, we meet again, *ma chère?*"

"Why have you brought me here like this?" she exclaimed as she held out her bound hands to him. "Untie me."

Henri chuckled as he moved toward her, and to her surprise he began to untie the rope. He enjoyed her defiance. It would, he thought, add a little spice to the night's pleasure.

"I am truly sorry, *ma petite*. My men were overzealous in my . . . invitation to have you join me here. I am sorry if you have been uncomfortable."

"Where is Brian?" she demanded, trying to keep some hold on her trembling courage. She knew full well she and Brian would be kept separately, but she wanted to know if he was alive and well. The only thing she knew for certain was that she would have to deal with Henri alone and it would take all the subtlety and self-control she had.

"Ah, your lover. He is well." Henri laughed softly. "Do not look so defiant and angry, *chérie*. He is well and outside of one little mistake"—he gestured to the ropes—"you are well. I have sent for some wine and if you will relax we will have something to warm us."

His casual assurance that she would be more than content to be warmed by his wine and then by him sent a tingle of fear through her. She had to move very carefully for beyond a doubt the handsome, virile, and totally conscienceless Henry was quite capable of raping her.

She could feel his eyes touch her, skim her body with heat.

"Tell me, what are you doing here?"

Ria smiled and shrugged. "Brian thought it expedient that we find a safe place to stay hidden for a while. This seemed to be as good a place as any."

She is lying to me, he thought in amusement. Now why does my captured little dove feel the need to lie? He smiled as if he believed her. He would find out later; now there was this night to taste, and he meant to enjoy it to the fullest.

When the wine was brought, he poured two glasses and walked close to her to hand her one.

He could see her hand tremble when she took it, but her eyes met his and he saw in them self-control and, he thought, defiance.

He did not move away but stood towering above her. Ria's thoughts caught at something that would have taken Henri as much by surprise as it did her. Despite the fact that he was handsome, totally masculine, and most likely possessed more charm than most men . . . still some intangible part of her compared him to Luke and found him wanting, wanting disastrously.

She would never see Luke again, but despite the barriers between them she would have much preferred to be looking up into his gold-amber eyes than Henri's dark ones that glowed with an open lust she could read well.

She sipped a touch of the wine and tried to move away from him, but he put an arm before her to block her.

She stood paralyzingly still, and he could not hear the wild beat of her heart or taste the fear that licked through her.

"My lovely little dove," he said softly, "you have the most remarkably beautiful eyes . . . and that mouth"—his voice lowered—"was meant to be kissed."

She backed up a step, a slow aversion growing in her. She was desperate for she knew she could not bear his touch and if he should kiss her or caress her, she would . . . do what? Kill him, she thought wildly.

He set his untasted wine on a nearby table and moved closer. He was more than satisfied. This one would not run before him. This one would be fire if he could ignite her. He was confident of his prowess, and his face showed it clearly.

"Come, little dove," he said with a coaxing smile, as he reached to put his hands about her waist. "You are a woman meant to be loved."

Words Luke had spoken echoed in her mind. "Don't be afraid of becoming a woman, Ria," he had whispered. But even he had not realized that to him being a woman was enjoying the height of sensuous pleasure while being what Henri wanted in a woman would turn her into a thoughtless mindless slut.

"Henri," she began as casually as her shaken nerves would allow her, "you said Brian was safe. I must know where he is."

"Brian," he said, stopped momentarily by the

swift change of subject. Then he shrugged. "I said he is safe and so he is. He is in Dan McGirtt's camp, with the American who was once his first mate. Strange coincidence, isn't it?"

"Yes," she said. "Strange. But it has nothing to do with Brian. How do I know he is well? He could be dead."

"Dead!" Henri laughed expressively. "Now why should I do the young man any harm?"

Ria's nerves were taut because of the game he was playing with her.

"For the same reason you tried to have him killed in St. Augustine," she said coldly. She watched his eyes narrow and grow cold despite the fact that he retained his smile.

"And so you want your lover back with you."

"Yes."

Henri again came to stand close. There was a brilliant rage in his eyes, and she knew the game was over. He reached out and gripped her shoulders in a painful grasp, jerking her close to him.

"You want him safely back with you," he said softly. "Then you must ask me more nicely. In fact if you want to know where he is, and how he is, you must be a little . . . warmer. I can see in your eyes that you are thinking of fighting me. I wouldn't if I were you."

He took her mouth in a painful savage kiss meant to frighten and subdue her. What it accomplished was to blend her aversion to him, her fear for Brian, and her own fear that she could not escape his grasp.

She pressed her hands against his chest and pushed against him as she struggled to be out of his grasp. "Let me go!"

When she finally broke free, he smiled at the

flush on her cheeks, and enjoyed the rise and fall of her firm breasts against the fabric of her dress. This is going to be a very invigorating night, he thought.

"I have played with you long enough, ma chère," he said softly. "Now I would taste what I've waited so long for."

He grabbed for her, but she twisted away and his fingers, catching at her dress, tore the front. He laughed softly as he continued to stalk her.

Henri was enjoying the chase, sure that eventually he would have his way.

Ria made a dash for the table on which rested several weapons Henri had not thought about. She grasped a thin-bladed knife and turned to face him.

"Get out of my way."

Henri chuckled. "And where do you intend to go, my sweet. On deck to entertain the men? I can assure you, you will not leave my ship and eventually . . . you will come to me."

"I will never do that!" she protested. "I will use this on myself first."

"Ah." Henri laughed again. "I'm afraid I can't allow you to do that. It would be such a waste."

His eyes grew serious now and his smile faded. He started to move slowly toward her.

She held the knife before her, fully intending to use it if she had to.

Several times he leapt toward her in a rapid feint, only to find the point of the knife unmoving. Now only his white smile and the growing lust in his eyes held her full attention. She continued to back away from him. At one particularly quick movement on his part, she backed into the door. When she felt the knob with her hand she realized

Henri had been so sure of himself that he had not locked the door.

She jumped at him, the knife cutting the air, and laughing challengingly, he moved back. But his laughter died as she retreated suddenly, jerked open the door, and was gone. With a black oath on his lips, he followed her.

Once she was on deck, Ria soon became aware of her situation. A guard stood by the gangplank so that avenue of escape was closed to her. Several crewmen were approaching from different directions, and Henri was thundering up from behind her.

Quickly she kicked off her shoes and ran for the rail facing the river. As she climbed over it, a very surprised Henri skidded to a stop several feet from her. Then he smiled.

"How very foolish, my sweet. It seems you are trapped. Certainly a very ignoble death in those waters is not more enticing than the . . . comforts of my cabin. Come down from there before I must come up and get you."

As Henri, a twisted smile on his lips, began to walk toward her, a ripple of laughter arose from his men for they were certain of how the confrontation was going to turn out.

"Never you!" Ria cried. "I will die before I will be dishonored and used by scum like you. I choose the river!"

To the absolute shock of all the men on the deck, she flung the knife aside, turned, and dove into the river's dark current.

Chapter 29

The water closed over Ria as Henri and his men ran to the rail. They arrived at it in time to see her disappear below the surface.

When, after several minutes, she did not reappear, all those watching felt she had gone too far and had paid for it with her life.

Ria was, thanks to Brian, an excellent swimmer. She felt she would have no problem in making her way to shore, but she had not taken into account the powerful and swift current that rushed beneath the surface.

The triumph she had known when she had dived over the rail turned suddenly to terror as the ruthless force of the seemingly tranquil water tore at her, pulling her down and down and down, tumbling her until she lost direction . . . and was desperate for air.

When she finally kicked forcefully enough to break the surface, she found herself caught in a current that carried her downstream at an alarming speed.

After a few moments of panic she began to realize if she could just keep herself on the surface she could make her way back to the *Swan*.

But she knew the frigid cold of the water and the rough ebbing tide might defeat her. Her body already felt like ice, and the current seemed to be getting stronger and stronger. Several times she was tumbled beneath the surface and her lungs were nearly bursting before she could get air. Tiring, she knew if she didn't find something to help support her she would never see the *Swan* or freedom again.

Each time she bobbed to the surface she was weaker, and each time the water drew her under she fought less hard. The river was defeating her. It was ruthlessly going to take her life while giving her nothing with which to fight. It was a huge, swift, rolling monster that was slowly draining her strength.

Again she was drawn beneath the surface, her petticoats and dress were a sodden heaviness that weighted her down. Her fingers, numb with cold, worked at the buttons, but they wouldn't loosen so in a frantic effort she tore at the entwining clothes. Finally she kicked herself free of them. Then, dressed in nothing but a wisp of a chemise she struggled to the surface.

This time, when she broke through, she was blinded by her tangled hair and she was about to lose consciousness when her hand came into contact with a large half-submerged log. She clung to it feebly, knowing she was going to lose her struggle and the river was going to claim her.

When something hard came about her waist, she no longer knew or cared, and when her frantic grasp of the log was forcefully broken, she no longer fought. She had long since closed her eyes and had retreated into shock and forgetful unconsciousness.

*　　*　　*

Lucas had no way of identifying the woman he had found. He was too busy fighting the current and pulling her hands free of the small ragged log to which she clung in panicked desperation.

He knew, of course, that this was a female—and a delightfully rounded one, but he had no time to dwell on that. After he had forcefully loosened her hold on the log, she seemed to lose all the fight left in her. He was, for the moment, grateful that she seemed to have lost consciousness, for he had to use all of his strength to reach the shore. In the shallow water along the bank of the river he rose and lifted her inert form in order to carry her to the bank.

The swift current had carried them some distance downriver from his ship. He could just see the *Angel*'s dark form in the distance. He shook his head at the mad instinct that had sent him diving after this drowning wench—he could have been killed.

Placing her on a grassy bank, he rolled her onto her back, wiped the tangled hair from her face, and waited for a cloud to pass from in front of the moon. When it did, when the white moonlight washed over her features, Lucas received the worst shock of his life.

"Ria!" he gasped. "What the hell! . . ."

She lay still—too still—and for a heart-stopping moment he forgot to think of why she was here and only feared that he might have been too late. He knelt beside her, pressed his hand to her heart, and was rewarded by its slow but steady beat.

Then he rocked back on his heels and looked at her. She was dressed in almost nothing, for the sheer chemise was molded to her body like skin. He rose to lift her gently in his arms.

"You have a lot of questions to answer my sweet, but this isn't the place for you to be waking."

He carried her easily along the bank of the river to where his ship lay. He had to call out from the bank several times, hoping his voice did not carry far enough for Henri's men to hear. Once he'd gotten the attention of one of his men, he had a boat brought ashore and he was rowed by a completely mystified sailor to the side of the *Angel*.

He gave orders for blankets and brandy to be brought to him at once; then he carried Ria to his cabin and gently placed her on his bunk. There was a tinge of blue about her lips and her body had begun to shiver from shock.

When the blankets arrived, Lucas immediately stripped off her wet chemise. He dried her body briskly, trying to renew the circulation to her limbs. Then he wrapped her in blankets, and rubbed her hair dry enough to keep it from soaking the pillow.

That done, he poured some brandy and forced a little of it between her lips. She moaned, but to his distress she did not waken. She only trembled more violently. Her face was so pale it alarmed him, and her body shook so uncontrollably he knew he had to warm her before she became desperately ill.

He couldn't admit to himself that her body, small and helpless, might have undergone a shock from which it might not recover.

He stood and nearly tore his damp clothing from his body. Quickly toweling himself dry, he tore the blankets from her, lay down beside her, and drew the blankets over them both. Then he gathered her shivering body close in his arms, twining her legs with his.

"Ria," he whispered. "Ria love, fight it," he coaxed as his hands caressed her.

Though she seemed somewhat warmer she did not open her eyes, and Lucas thought she was shaking even harder. He continued to rub his hands almost harshly over every inch of her flesh, frightened for the first time in his life as he fought grimly to bring her back from the dark place in which she lingered.

Ria felt warm, so warm. She nestled into the warmth, letting it close about her. Somewhere in the very depths of her she heard a soft coaxing voice, gentle words, almost as if some beloved person was calling to her from a great distance. She didn't know who the voice belonged to; she only knew she wanted to reach out to it, to the wonderful feeling of comfort and security it offered. The fearful cold and pain seemed to have melted away, and she was filled with a sense of peace, as if she belonged in this warmth.

She slipped slowly from shock into body-healing sleep, and only then, after an almost two-hour struggle, did Lucas breathe a ragged sigh of relief and give himself over to the pleasure of holding her in his arms again.

Tomorrow there would be time for questions. Tonight she was safe, she was here, and he could hold her for the few short hours before day broke.

Ria woke slowly, and was so disoriented that she lay very still to try to sort out what had happened.

She did not open her eyes, but slowly and patchily memory returned to her. She had jumped from Henri's ship and had been swept downstream. She knew she was on a ship now for she knew well the comforting rocking.

But there were no other ships on the river, only Henri's and the *Swan*, and she had been swept away from them.

A choking panic filled her as she finally came to believe that somehow Henri had retrieved her from the water and she was again aboard his ship.

She cracked her eyes open slightly, trying to identify the cabin she was in. When the familiarity of it and of the bed she lay in came to her she sat bolt upright, grasping the blanket to her. Some twist of fate had returned her to Luke's bed . . . and she was totally naked.

At that moment the door opened, and Lucas stepped into the room.

"So you've finally decided to wake up? It's nearly noon. I thought you were going to sleep away the day."

"How . . ." she began, but her voice was ragged and hoarse from exhaustion and from the river water she had swallowed. She tried to speak again. "How did I get here?"

"I fished you out of the river." He grinned.

"But . . . how did you get here? You weren't supposed to be here," she finished lamely as he laughed at the inanity of her words.

"And where was I supposed to be?"

The bitter past overcame her. "I had hoped in hell by now," she snapped.

"Now is that a way to talk to a man who has risked life and limb to pull you from the jaws of death? You're not very grateful."

"I have jumped from the pan into the fire," she said in exasperation.

Lucas gazed at her. She was still so damned beautiful. Even her close brush with death had not marred her exquisitely peach-tanned flesh, nor had time let him forget the depths of her amethyst eyes.

She was the kind of woman who could keep a man eternally curious and eternally unbalanced by the raw desire she provoked in him. She was a violet-eyed witch with sharp teeth and claws. He must keep this in mind.

"Tell me," he taunted, "did you jump into the river on purpose or did your lover grow tired of your demanding little body and toss you overboard?" He chuckled, his eyes aglow and as deep and mysterious as she remembered.

"Oh, you are still an arrogant bastard. Damn you. You should have let me drown. That would have been better than being obligated to you."

"My, my, what a little bitch you have become. Bitchiness doesn't suit you, Ria."

"I am what you have made me!"

"Hardly." He grinned. "I would gladly have made you something much more interesting."

"I must get out of here!" she cried. She started to rise from the bunk, but he was too quick for her. She would never know that his alarm at nearly losing her had shaken him.

He pressed her shoulders back upon the bunk, prohibiting any movement.

She wanted to tear at him with her nails until he lost that sarcastic grin.

"Let me go!" Sheer rage made her breathless.

He dropped to the bed beside her, fending her off with a lazy, almost indolent, ease. His grip held her very nearly immobile.

"These temper tantrums have to cease. Now . . . say thank you, Luke, for saving my life."

"Go to hell! If it weren't for you—"

"What would have happened if it weren't for me?"

"Nothing," she said sullenly. "Let me go."

"Say thank you, Ria," he cajoled coolly.

"Thank you," she snarled through gritted teeth. But the snarl was replaced by a cry of deep distress when she realized in the struggle the blanket had slipped away and nothing was between them but the thin fabric of his shirt.

She caught the sudden narrowing of his eyes as they studied her squirming body, heard the soft intake of his breath as his gaze grew warmer.

This time she had no intention of letting him intimidate her. She would match him in any game he cared to play.

"You're much stronger than I, and I know by now it is your way to take advantage of one who's weaker. You will have your way," she grated, "but it will be rape, for I will never surrender to you again. Take what you want."

She forced her body still, as if she would be compliant.

Looking down into her defiant eyes, he had the almost insane desire to strangle her, and he had to remain still for a moment to keep his twitching fingers from her throat.

He released her and rose, and she hastily drew the blanket about her. He stood frowning at her, a muscle twitching in his cheek. Then he turned from her to regain his composure. Finally he stalked across the room and poured himself a drink of brandy. When he turned back, he had himself under firm control.

"Now suppose you tell me why I had to fish you out of the river?"

Ria thought carefully, suddenly realizing a number of things. Brian was still a prisoner of Henri, who might take great pleasure in telling him she was dead, and—she looked at Luke through narrowed eyes—Luke was in a position to help her get him free . . . if she could convince him to do it.

"I . . . I'm sorry. I'm just so upset. I didn't mean to say the things I did. I owe you my life, Luke, and I really am grateful."

"Why is it," he said, "that I trust you less when you're sweet than I do when you're not?"

She wanted to strike him, but she held her snarling retort inside and tried to keep her eyes from revealing her thoughts.

"I'm only telling you that I'm grateful, I'm trying to thank you."

"Well, you're welcome," he replied, but she was aware he was regarding her intently and trying to read the truth in her eyes. He knew damned well something was brewing.

"What were you doing in the river?"

"Trying to escape."

"Who?"

"Henri Duval. He . . . he kidnapped me from the *Swan.*"

"How could he have done that? You and your . . . friend were safe when you left me."

"We came upriver to help a friend. When Henri found us, he seized the *Swan* and took me to his ship. I jumped overboard."

"Then you need not worry. You're safe here. Henri need never know you're here."

She bit her lip and searched for the words she would need, but none seemed to express what she wanted to say. Finally she could only state softly, "Brian is still Henri's prisoner."

Lucas was deathly still as their eyes locked together. Grim amusement twitched the corners of his mouth drawing it into a tight smile that did not reach his eyes.

Otherwise his face remained impassive, but Ria could see by the opacity of his eyes and the white lines about his mouth that he was thinking thoughts that might prove disastrous for her.

"And," he said in a deceptively soft voice, "what

would you have me do about that?"

She licked suddenly dry lips and looked up at him. He refused to see the plea in her eyes, and she could not get past his cold gaze.

"Help me free him."

Lucas remained quiet for a moment for her words had stung him like a whip. Then he threw back his head and roared with laughter.

She felt hatred and despair grow inside her until she was almost overcome with frustration.

"Is a man's death so funny to you!" she cried.

"Tell me, Ria," he inquired coldly, "are you such a fool that you would do anything for this man? Do you love him so much that you would put your life in danger again to set him free?"

"Yes . . . yes. He must be free!"

Again Lucas laughed, a dry brittle sound. "I really find it impossible to believe you have the unmitigated nerve to ask me to rescue your pathetic lover again." He raised an eyebrow at her and drawled softly. "You must be a total fool to love where there is no love in return."

"And what do you give me!" she cried out. "You force me to give in to you. You take what you want with no care or thought for me. What do you promise me, Luke, a life together, a future, any kind of future? No, you are no better than he, so don't try to lay claim to emotions you don't even understand!"

She had the sudden impression that a wall had risen between them, shutting her out. He sounded too studiedly casual as he shrugged and spoke softly.

He calculatedly spoke brutal words to render her almost mindless with anger.

"If it is a bargain you seek, a favor you want, you had best be prepared to pay for what you ask."

Her face flushed and she glared at him. He has no

402

scruples, she thought. She could sense an element of danger in her situation, yet she had little choice. She sucked in her breath as she strove to keep her composure.

"Brian and I will be able to pay whatever price you name," she said, deliberately misunderstanding his intent.

"My dear, Ria"—he chuckled aggravatingly—"I am not making a bargain with him; I'm thinking of making one with you." He shrugged. "If the price is right."

She wondered how violent he would become if she refused to bargain with him, for he looked capable of anything.

Damn her, he thought. She had no right to be so beautiful that he could barely control himself, no right to be so unpredictable. He had half a mind to heed his body's demands and take her with no preliminaries and no promises.

"What is your price?" Her eyes looked challengingly into his, as if she were daring him . . . perhaps she was.

Blast the purple-eyed witch, he groaned mentally.

Ria was infuriated by his smile of amusement. Her pulses drummed and her heart beat so loudly she thought he would be able to hear it.

"No," she said softly. "No, I will not give in to you."

"Fine," he shrugged eloquently. "Your lover can rot in Henri's prison for all I care. When there is no reward why accept the risk?"

"Pirate!" she spat out viciously.

"So I am."

"Depraved animal!"

"Now, Ria—"

"Beast! Bastard! Damn you!"

"I take it you agree to my terms?"

"I don't know what they are!"

"I think you do."

"Tell me."

"You will promise me you will never be his mistress again," he stated clearly.

Since Ria knew there would never be any danger of that, and her response would not be a lie, she spoke quickly.

"I agree."

"And you will remain with me, as my mistress for as long as I choose."

"You are no better than Henri Duval!"

"How do you know?" He laughed. "Have you tried old Henri out?"

"You are a vile beast."

"I'm waiting for an answer."

"Why do you force me to surrender what should only be given?"

Because I can't get over you, he thought miserably. Because I can't wash the memory of your touch from my mind or my body. Because I love you, damn your whore's soul, and I must find a way to get you out of my system. Maybe having you again and again whenever I want will rid me of you forever.

These were the things he felt, but he would never let her use them as weapons against him.

"Make up your mind, Ria. Do I get him free or do we forget it?"

"What do you want of me?" She whispered softly.

The tears glistening in her eyes very nearly weakened his resolve. "I want you as my mistress. I want you in my bed. I've never encountered a witch that satisfies and torments me as you do. I want the same thing from you I have wanted from the start. You play the whore for him, why not for me?"

The words crushed her spirit. Not one word of gentleness or warmth, just a cold demand for her body. Well, if the game were to go that way, she would do what she must to get Brian free.

"I agree," she said softly.

For a moment he stood still, surprised. Then he returned to sit on the edge of the bunk. His eyes blazed down into hers, in them a combination of hate, passion, and desire. Then he spoke roughly.

"Why not make the best of it, Ria? It seems bed is the only place we can keep from killing each other."

She looked up at him, and he said the next words almost as a demand to see if she would keep her word.

"Put your arms around my neck. Let's see if your bargain will be worth the risk."

As a sob broke deep in her throat, she obeyed.

Chapter 30

It simply is not fair, Lucas thought as he bent to take her mouth in an almost savage kiss that bent her head back with brutal force. Ria had to be possessed of some witchcraft. There was a demon within her that laughed in the face of his desire, fleeing before him like a shadow he would forever be unable to grasp.

He was no longer able to think of anything but the need of her, a need that grew as he pressed her soft body to his. He wondered if he would ever be able to belong to himself again, to command his body without Ria coming alive in his thoughts. He heard the soft sound she made as he kissed her ear, her closed eyes, and then, much more gently this time, her mouth.

His hands began to move across her body, his fingers teasing and arousing until she was twisting and turning beneath him, aflame again, desiring release, craving it, whimpering against his mouth while words he would not have spoken at any other time were whispered against her heated skin.

Everything in his mind became jumbled, and he knew only the desire to sink to the depths of her, to seek the satisfaction he knew only she held for him.

She could feel the touch of his hands as he spread her thighs. Then he was hard maleness, driving into her endlessly, demandingly, until she knew nothing but the flood of hot passion that swelled to a crescendo, gathering like a tidal wave, rising, rising . . . then falling from the pinnacle of ecstasy to the depth of reality.

He gathered her close, but deep within him an ache burned like hot coals. She had only given him her body, and only because he had forced her.

He felt the bitter taste of defeat in his mouth, a strange intangible kind of defeat. He knew without doubt he would never again force her to answer his need while her heart belonged to another man.

He would do all within his power to free Brian, but when the pirate was free, if it took all that he had, he would set her free so she might follow the path she chose.

He could not tell her he loved her. It would be useless to do so when she loved Brian so she would go into the very jaws of death to keep him safe. At that moment the blackness of his hatred for Brian was almost smothering.

To Ria's total surprise he rose from the bed, dressed, and left the room abruptly, slamming the door behind him.

In the foulest of moods, he walked up on the deck, and tried to keep his mind from Ria by centering it on a plan to seize the *Swan* and free its captain.

He paced the deck for several minutes, his brows drawn together in a dark scowl. Then he summoned one of his men to him.

"Go and gather some men who don't mind taking a chance or two. I need six volunteers for a mission that might just prove to be dangerous."

"Sir"—the young man grinned—"I'll go round up the other five. I'd like to be the first."

Lucas smiled in return. "Okay you go. Now get the others."

When he was alone again, Lucas gazed thoughtfully upriver, but he was seeing Ria in his mind's eye. He could not believe he was actually going to risk his life and the lives of some of his crew to rescue a man who could walk away with the only thing he had ever wanted so desperately.

With one word he could end this. He could take his ship from the river and leave Brian to his fate. He would be able to take Ria with him if he chose. It would be so easy, he thought. One word to his crew was all it would take and he would be sailing away from this confrontation.

He knew he could bend Ria's passion to his; he had done it before. But with an angry flush, he admitted that she would never forgive him. If he could not reach her now, close as they had been, he would never be able to reach her at all. The ashes of passion would not be enough to try to build a future on.

He thought of his unwanted wife. What did it matter to whom he was married? If he could not be wed to Ria, his wife might just as well be Arianne St. Thomas. He would have to find a way to live without Ria and the breathless passion she brought to him.

But if he closed his eyes when he held another woman in his arms would he be able to deceive her? In fact, would he be able to deceive himself and continue to live with the deception the rest of his life? For his own peace of mind he thrust these thoughts behind him. It did no good to agonize over what could not be changed.

The men he had sent for were coming on deck now, so he put from his mind all thoughts except those concerning his risky plan.

Ria sat motionless on Luke's bunk, the blanket still clutched before her, her eyes on the door he had slammed so forcefully behind him.

Again the paradox that was Luke put her in a state of confusion. He seemed so unstable she could not imagine what was to happen to her next or what path his plans for her might take.

She had asked him to help her save Brian, knowing his hatred of him. It was the only way to get Brian free. What had he expected of her? Why had he looked at her with an anger bordering on violence. He had taken from her all that he wanted; what did her future, or who she spent it with, matter to him?

This time he had wanted raw passion and she refused to believe he could ever want anything else. He had made it very clear that a warm and willing mistress was all he would ever want.

Why then couldn't she control the constricting pain that tore at her heart or the heated tears that she couldn't seem to contain?

Slowly she rose from the bunk. She searched about for something she could wear and found, folded and resting on a small stand, the rolled-up pants and shirt she had worn before. They had not belonged to Luke, so she wondered why he still had them. When she went to get them, she found the ribbon she had tied about her hair neatly folded on top, almost as if someone had taken great care to keep her things safe.

Quickly she dressed and tied back her hair with the small piece of green ribbon. Then she started up on deck to see if she could get Lucas to respond to her request that he help her free Brian.

* * *

For a moment, when Ria appeared in the companionway, she snatched the breath from Lucas and his mind skimmed back to the times she had wandered the deck of his ship just so, half-child, half-woman.

Her eyes met his across the deck, but he abruptly turned his back to her and continued to talk to the small group of men he had clustered about him.

It took her only minutes to realize they were discussing something important. Luke was speaking rapidly while he traced a line on the map he had pressed against the rail. She also knew instinctively that the discussion had something to do with her. The youngest of the group, little more than a boy of eighteen, glanced occasionally in her direction once he realized she was there.

Ria had an intense need to learn whether or not Lucas had decided to help Brian.

She came across the deck, but by the time she reached the men, Luke was already dismissing them.

"We can't make any move at all until after dark. You all know what you have to do."

There was a soft murmur of agreement among the men; then, casting surreptitious glances her way, they moved away.

Lucas walked to the rail and, after folding the map and putting it in the pocket of his shirt, leaned both arms on it and looked out over the rapidly moving river. He was doing his best to keep from acknowledging Ria's presence.

"Luke?" she said softly as she came up behind him.

"What now, Ria?" he said in cold exasperation.

"What are you planning?"

"What makes you think I'm planning anything?" he said, his voice dripping with contemptuous amusement.

"Because," she almost whispered, "I know you."

411

He spun about, and she could not miss his barely controlled fury. He was holding back bitter words with a supreme effort. Slowly he regained a hold on his anger, and then he smiled with a devilish sardonic amusement.

"What is it you think you know of me, Ria?" He laughed. "What is this conniving little brain of yours thinking up?"

"I'm not conniving," she said. "Why do you always think the worst of me?"

"Maybe," he retorted, "because that's always the side of you I see." There was a hardness to his eyes. "And besides, what does it matter what I think of you? You just want your lover back, and you're willing to sacrifice anything or anyone to get what you want."

He watched the color fade from her face.

"You know I've asked myself a million times," he continued as the glow in his narrowed eyes turned to melted gold, "why I don't just throw you overboard like your last lover did. Did you try to get old Henri to give your lover back to you?"

He might just as well have slapped her. She sucked in her breath sharply and her eyes widened at the blow.

"You are insufferable," she cried. "Why do you deliberately twist things and think such hateful thoughts every time I speak? Why must you always treat me like a whore!"

Yes, why? he thought. Why did she of all women have the power to disintegrate every ounce of self-control he had. Why did he want to strangle her with his bare hands at one minute, toss her down on the deck and, beneath the brilliant sun, tear the clothes from her and ravage her the next. Why did he want to erase that vulnerable wide-eyed look from her face

412

and replace it with . . . what?

Ria's thoughts almost paralleled his as she stared at him in disbelief, shocked by his brutal remarks.

"I might ask," he replied coldly, "why you continually act like one. Would you like every man in creation sniffing at your heels like a bitch in heat?"

He saw tears spring to her eyes at this final blow, and when she tried to spin away from him, he caught her arm and pulled her roughly against him.

"Of course," he said with a cold casualness, "you won't forget that we have a bargain?"

"No," she said with scathing disdain. "I could never forget, even though I choose to with every breath I take."

"Don't forget, Ria," he breathed out softly, and he smiled wickedly into her eyes.

She jerked her arm free, but she had no intention of trying to get away from him for she knew he would take great pleasure in stopping her.

Instead she moved to the rail to stand beside him.

He watched her intently. She was beautiful, this girl he had turned into a woman, and she had become more of a woman than he had ever expected. It irritated him that she seemed more desirable every time he was with her.

Ria was well aware that his eyes were on her, but she had no intention of meeting his cold amber gaze again.

"What are you going to do?" she asked.

"I'm going to finish my part of the bargain."

"You're going after Brian?"

"That should please you."

"Henri is dangerous."

"No doubt." He chuckled.

Her eyes registered her anger. "Your arrogant conceit could get you killed," she snapped. The thought of that possibility almost stretched her nerves to the breaking point.

"Well," he said with casual humor, "let's hope old Henri doesn't do me in before I set Brian free. After that"—he shrugged and his smile flashed white against his tanned skin—"if he kills me one more problem will be out of your way. Just think, you'll have no bargain to keep."

She wanted to strike him, to claw the insolent grin from his face, but she controlled that urge because she knew he would take a great deal of satisfaction in subduing her before the entire crew which was now trying to stay out of their captain's vicinity and to appear busy.

"I asked," she said in as cold a voice she could muster, "what you are planning to do?"

As if totally exasperated by her continued pressure he took the folded map from his pocket and again placed it on the rail.

As he placed a finger on the thin line that signified the river, she moved close to his side.

"We're here," he said as he moved his finger to an indentation that indicated a deep curve in the river. Then his finger followed an elongated S up the river before tapping another spot.

"And Henri and the *Swan* are here. I've sent one of the men up to find their exact position. He should be back by nightfall. Anyway we can't move until after dark. We have to wait until early morning and hope Henri and his cutthroats are asleep. I'm going to take over the *Swan* and drift her downriver. We'll cause some confusion and in the chaos I'll slip in and find your . . . friend."

"You."

"Yes, me. Why?"

"You alone?" she could have bitten her tongue at

the snort of half-disgust half-laughter that he gave.

"Ria, it has to be. One man can slip in easier. Besides I need the men to get the *Swan* moving. I stand a better chance alone."

"But if you're caught?"

"I'll be in Henri's tender grasp. I think the man's got me marked anyway."

"Why must you be so careless?" she cried, and now he was surprised by the real fear in her voice. In self-protection he created a misunderstanding. If he hadn't he would have taken her in his arms and kissed away the tears that lingered in kaleidoscopic drops on her cheeks.

"I'm not going to get your lover killed if that's what you're afraid of. I'm not that careless. Don't worry," he said through a grim smile. "I'll bring him safely to your arms."

Of God, she thought, if I were a man I would beat you senseless. But she wasn't a man, and she had only sharp claws with which to rake his arrogance.

"Of course you will," she drawled, favoring him with a haughty sneering smile. "Are you not a man of honor? Of course you'll keep your word. I should not have expected any less of the brave and courageous Captain Blanc—Luke—or whatever your name is. Your conceit is boundless, and if Brian's life were not at stake, I would see you caught and hung for the pirate you are."

"You have developed a nasty tongue since I first saw you, love." He grinned. "You are turning into the perfect pirate's lady. You and your friend should do well together in your chosen professions."

She wanted to throw the truth in his face so desperately that it was on the tip of her tongue. She bit it back with supreme effort.

"You suddenly seem to have lost your sting, Ria.

415

This isn't like you. Can't you even extend a friendly goodbye to me in case you become lucky and I don't return."

For one stricken minute he thought she was going to hit him as he stood, a brilliant flame in his eyes and a jeering half-smile on his lips.

But before she could reply he reached out, gripped her shoulders, and jerked her against him. His arms crushed her to him, his mouth bruised hers in a violent kiss that sucked away all her strength, and his tongue ravaged her mouth, demanding a response she was unable to withhold. Suddenly he freed her as abruptly as he had pulled her into his arms. It took her a moment to retrieve her breath and her wits.

"Go below, Ria," he said softly. "Stay there until this is over." He moved her aside, then walked across the deck and up the steps to the quarter deck, where he stood, back to her, gazing over the river. Ria stumbled to the cabin and closed the door before she released her bitter tears. Why, she thought, does it always have to be this way?

The hours seemed to move so slowly that Lucas found his nerves on edge. He held them in rigid control as he watched the sun touch the horizon, turn the sky a blended pink, blue, and red, then drop below the horizon.

The trees along the bank went from leafy shadow to a black canopy as he was pleased to find the moon would, for a while at least, hide its face behind some clouds.

Later, as he met the small knot of men at the rail, he saw only vague dark forms. It was entirely too dark to see their faces, but he knew the names of those who were to accompany him.

They lowered a boat as soundlessly as possible, then Lucas and his men climbed down a rope ladder into it. Each man sat at an oar, and Lucas sat at the back to steer. They moved silently but swiftly up-river, hugging the shore, occasionally having to bend their heads to avoid the overhanging trees.

It took nearly two hours before they reached the last jut of land that stood between them and Henri. There they found a place where the bank slanted down to the water, and they pulled the boat ashore. That done, they gathered in a small huddle. Here Lucas would give them their final instructions.

"Move slowly and easily across this jut of land. The *Swan* is anchored close to this side of the river. Our friend has made a mistake in not anchoring it close to his ship on the far side.

"I doubt very much if they will be guarding the *Swan* too closely because they don't expect anything. Her crew must still be aboard.

"You're to get aboard and drift her downstream until you get to the *Angel*. Hold her there until dawn. If I'm not back by then, you're to take both ships, and the lady, out of here. Is everything understood?"

"What about you, Cap'n?" one man whispered. "How are you goin' to get out of there?"

"If I have any luck, I'll have a couple of the prisoners with me. We'll hit the water and let it carry us to his boat; then we'll come back to the ship."

"We'll be waitin for ya, Cap'n." A man laughed softly.

"You get the *Swan* and the *Angel* out of there if I don't get back," Lucas ordered, "and on your life don't let anything happen to Ria. I want her protected no matter what happens. Do you hear?"

"Aye, sir," came the soft reply. "She'll be taken good care of."

"Good. Now get going . . . all of you. And . . . good luck."

All of the men vanished into the night except for one slim dark figure that stood a few feet away.

"What's the matter, Tom? You afraid?"

"No." His voice was barely audible.

"Then get going."

"I'm going with you."

"That's not what we planned."

"I don't care what the plan was. I'm going with you."

Lucas knew the voice that whispered from the dark. With a shocked gasp, he almost leapt the distance that separated them, and yanked off the dark hat that had been pulled over what he thought were Tom's eyes.

A mass of golden hair caught the frail moonlight as it tumbled about her shoulders.

"Ria," he groaned in a combination of fear and fury. "What the hell are you doing here?" he hissed.

"As I just said," Ria said calmly, "I'm going with you."

"You can't do that, it's too damned dangerous."

"I'm here," she said with frigid determination. "You can't leave me here alone, and it's too late to take me back. Besides, I won't go."

"You are the most stupid hard-headed female it has ever been my misfortune to run across."

"I know." He heard her soft laugh. "But I'm here . . . and I'm going with you."

At that moment he could have throttled her, but he gritted his teeth instead. He knew there was nothing he could do but take her with him and pray his scheme worked out well. He went to her and took her shoulders, drawing her close to him.

"You must be quiet and careful, understand? If

418

anything goes wrong, run like hell and get back to the *Angel* as fast as you can."

"I will."

"Ria?"

"What?"

"Be very careful."

She was surprised by his deep concern for her safety and by the sudden gentleness in his voice. Then he kissed her, and before she could speak, he pushed her gently toward the boat in which they would cross the river.

She helped him row, and in the silence her thoughts dwelt on the fact that this was one of the first times he had spoken to her gently . . . and had kissed her almost tenderly.

Chapter 31

During the daylight hours, while Lucas had been making plans for Brian's rescue, Scott, Chris, and Brian were trying to find a way out of the dilemma they found themselves in.

Chris had drifted freely about the camp keeping his eyes open, alert for what was going on. In doing so he had found out the exact nature of the "special" cargo Henri had brought to Dan, and he had mentally mapped Dan's entire camp.

The path that led to the river was nearly a mile in length. Huts sat on either side of the widened part of it. Six on the right. One held supplies, four held several men each and one contained the mysterious crates Henri had brought to Dan. Chris had found out what was in them as soon as he'd been able to slip past the guard that was always standing before that hut.

To the left of the path lay five more huts. The first belonged to Dan, William, and John. The next two, close to the first, held several women, camp followers who cared for a multitude of the men's needs. It was in one of these that Sophia slept. Then there was the large meeting hut, where the men congregated almost every night. The last hut, the one closest to the lush growth and to the swamp that encircled the camp, was the one in which Chris, Scott, Brian, and Louisa found themselves.

Scott, too, had a great deal of freedom, and he used it to maneuver within the group of men and seek information.

Louisa was quite willing to stay a prisoner within the hut. Neither she nor Chris wanted her to draw Henri's attention, for at the moment Duval seemed to have lost interest in her and he was quite content to let Chris have her.

Brian was a total prisoner, and had no freedom at all.

"So," Scott said, as they sat about within their hut again discussing any possibility of escape. "The hut is full of arms?"

"Gunpowder," Chris declared positively. "Gunpowder, my friend. It would prove useful to have some if we could figure out a way to get it."

"That's next to impossible." Scott looked thoughtful nonetheless.

Brian was thoughtful too. "It seems there should be a common denominator here somewhere. The *Swan*, a ship we could escape on if we could get to it, and gunpowder that might prove useful, if we could get to it. We have to put those two things together and, with a little ingenuity, find a way to use them."

"Easier said than done, my friend," Chris replied. "We'd have to create a hell of a big diversion to draw that guard away from the gunpowder."

"I can't think of anything that would work. Dan has these men pretty well trained. I just wish—"

"What?" Brian asked.

"I wish Dan would finalize the plans I know he's been working on. If he decided to move we might be able to do something. Then we would only have to contend with Henri," Chris replied.

"I don't think he'd let us live very long once Dan was gone," Brian responded.

Scott looked very serious. "Maybe just long enough to cause him a hell of a lot of trouble."

"Scott . . . Chris," Brian said, "we've got to find out what happened to Ria. She might have gotten around Henri last night, but we have to keep in mind that she is still aboard Henri's ship. I don't intend to try anything that doesn't include getting her away from Duval."

"You don't really think we would let her stay in Henri's hands." Scott was surprised. "For God's sake, Brian, outside of the fact that she's your sister and a gentlewoman"—Scott smiled—"she's Lucas's wife and one day he's going to know. How could we tell him we left her with Henri? If you think we're in a tight spot now, I'd hate like hell to be in that one."

"He's right, Brian. When Lucas finds out who Ria is it's going to be a bad enough situation without telling him Henri's got her." Chris laughed.

"Then we're back to creating some kind of a diversion so we can get to that gunpowder and to Henri's ship."

"Well, I'm going to move around a bit and see if I can sniff out just what Dan is planning and how soon he intends to make a move," Chris said.

Louisa, who had been quietly listening to the conversation, now rose and went over to Chris.

"Do you mind if I walk with you, Chris?" she inquired.

Scott and Brian knew that Louisa had been frightened so badly by Henri that she felt safe only in Chris's presence.

They knew she never slept until Chris returned to

the hut for the night, and they sensed the deep feelings for her growing in Chris. However, they were quite sure Chris would say nothing about them until they found a way to escape their present situation.

They were correct in both assumptions: Chris was drawn to Louisa, and his attachment to her had grown stronger by the hour. But he was afraid she was in no state to handle that, and he didn't want her turning to him out of gratitude and a need for security.

"Of course not." Chris smiled. The entire camp now thought of Louisa as Chris's well-earned possession. None of them cared to cross swords with Chris, not after seeing his expert and rapid disposal of Louie. Chris felt that Louisa was reasonably safe, but she had been through too much to believe it. If his presence gave her some kind of comfort, then he would be content with that . . . for now.

They left the hut and walked slowly down the path toward the river. The green canopy overhead allowed only strands of sunlight through the trees, so the pathway was shadowed and cool.

"Chris?"

"What, Louisa?"

"I'm . . . I'm glad that I'm here with you."

He stopped walking and turned to look at her.

"That"—he laughed softly—"is the craziest thing anyone has ever said. You're glad to be caught in this Godforsaken place with me and the rest of us? We just might not be able to get out of here so easily."

"You will," she said softly. "I know you will."

For a minute they looked at each other; then Chris drew her slowly into his arms and kissed her gently, a soft feather-light touch of his mouth on her trembling lips.

"Louisa, this is no place to talk of the future. Time and circumstances change people. Maybe . . . in a different situation . . . we'll be different. Right now you're grateful, and gratitude is not a thing to build one's life on."

"Do you think I'm a child?" She smiled.

"Not a child"—he smiled in return—"but a lady in distress, and in need of a knight in armor. I just want to make very sure that when the distress is past you don't see the tarnish on my armor and realize you've made a mistake."

"All right, my tarnished knight. But when this is over perhaps we could try to search for Camelot."

He laughed again and took her hand as they continued to walk.

Sophia stood in the doorway of the hut. She had watched the gentle exchange between Chris and Louisa. A shadow crossed her face, reflecting the dark pressure within her. She recognized the exchange for what it was, and again tasted a strange new bitterness she had only known since she had arrived in Dan's camp with Scott.

The differences between her and Scott had not meant much until she had begun to realize that he was becoming too important to her. She was in love with him, and that had never been a part of her plans. She bit her lip reflectively. She knew Scott had wanted to find a way to Dan and she had been the means to it. She also knew that he didn't love her.

But now a new ingredient had been added. The arrival of Louisa and the handsome young captain of the *Swan*.

She was wise to the world of men, and with her freedom to come and go in Scott's hut she knew that if those four weren't planning a method of escape now, they soon would be.

Moving freely among Henri and his men had a profound effect on her also. She was certain it was not Dan and the camp they would be running from, but Henri Duval.

As she walked slowly across the compound she was giving a great deal of thought to how she could help Scott succeed in whatever he planned to do.

Before Sophia could reach Scott's hut she saw Henri and several of his men approaching it. Unobserved, she drifted silently toward the back of the hut, and stood where she could overhear what was going on inside.

Scott and Brian sat together trying to put together the pieces of a puzzle that might give them the key to freeing Brian and Ria. Brian was sure Scott and Chris would be allowed to leave the camp with Dan when Dan chose to go. He also knew that Dan would be leaving very, very soon.

Henri's abrupt entrance surprised Scott and Brian, but in a way Brian was grateful for it. He knew he would not be able to get to Henri so he was glad that Henri had come to him. Brian rose to his feet quickly, but his progress toward Henri was stopped by the sword that was raised between them. Henri took precautions. He smiled benevolently at Brian.

"Do not be so aggressive, my young friend. You are not in a position to behave so."

"Just what 'position' do you think I'm in?" Brian said coldly.

"Not a very good one I would say." Henri laughed.

"I thought we had an agreement, you and I," Brian stated calmly.

"Ah yes, our agreement," Henri said casually. "I find it no longer necessary to deal with you, not as long as I have you, your ship, and—"

"And Ria," Brian grated through clenched teeth. "Where is she? I want to see her."

"I'm afraid that is impossible. There has been a little . . . ah . . . accident."

"Accident!" Brian's heart was thudding. "Just what kind of accident? Damn you, if you've harmed her I'll—"

"You'll do nothing," Henri declared firmly. "I am not responsible for your mistress's stupidity."

Brian stared at Henri, fear gripping him. "What have you done with her?"

"I repeat, I have done nothing. She chose to do harm to herself."

"You're a liar. Ria would not do anything foolish unless you pushed her to it. Is she hurt? Let me see her!"

"That's impossible," Henri said brutally. "She is dead. She chose to kill herself rather than enjoy life as the mistress of Henri Duval. Very stupid."

Brian felt as if he had been struck a mortal blow. With a cry of absolute rage, he leapt at Henri's throat. His hands closed around it and he squeezed, his fury giving him strength. Only the crashing blow that rendered him unconscious saved a very surprised and very angry Henri.

"Get him out of here," he said. "Take him to his ship and lock him below with his men until I can find a very painful way of getting rid of him."

Brian was dragged off, and Henri was left with Scott whose face was pale with anger and whose hand itched to run a sword through Henri's heart.

"You are a damned bloodthirsty bastard," Scott declared in a voice trembling with rage. "Ria would not have killed herself.''

"But it is true." Henri went on to jokingly describe his confrontation with Ria. Then he shrugged. "So she chose the river. Very foolish girl."

"Christ!" Scott groaned. "Did you have to tell him just like that?"

"What does it matter? He will not be alive much longer to worry about it."

"What are you planning?"

"That is not your concern, my friend. You will be making a choice by tomorrow morning."

"What choice?"

Henri roared with hearty laughter. "To leave with McGirtt . . . or to find your way back to St. Augustine alone, through the swamp. You see Dan and I have concluded our business. He is, shall we say, forced to make a move, while I am now in possession of two fine ships that will allow me to retrieve many cargoes from unwary merchants."

"Dan said nothing about moving to Chris or me."

"We are both reasonably sure there is entirely too much between you two," Henri said gently. "I think maybe you have known each other for a long time, and the captain of the *Swan* as well. No, my friend, neither Dan nor I are fools. The three of you work together somehow . . . and the three of you must be eliminated. If Dan is not prepared to do it, I am. So enjoy this night. It just might be your last."

Henri smiled nastily and then left, while Scott sat wondering just how he, Chris, Brian, and Louisa were going to get away.

Sophia's breath caught in her throat. She couldn't let Scott die. The thought of him dead turned her blood to water.

428

She would have to think of some plan by nightfall, or it would be too late.

She nearly ran the distance from Scott's hut to Dan's. Inside, she found Dan, Will, and John bent over a map spread out on the table, and in quiet voices they were deep in discussion.

The three men looked up when Sophia entered.

"Sophia," Will said quickly, "what's wrong?"

"I have to talk to you," Sophia panted. "I have to ask a very great favor."

"Sophia"—Dan smiled—"you have been loyal too long not to be able to ask for whatever you want."

"Is it true that you are giving orders to pack and leave this camp?"

"Who told you that?" Will said quickly.

"I just heard it."

"Henri," Dan said quietly.

"Yes. Henri Duval," she admitted.

"We have to leave Sophia," Dan stated firmly. "It is too dangerous to stay here any longer. Besides, we have the gunpowder we came for. There is no reason to stay."

Will's lips curved in a half-smile. "Is it young Scott you are worried about, Sophia?"

"Yes."

"Don't. Henri has said he will take the men and the woman safely back to St. Augustine."

"Henri is a black-hearted liar!"

"What are you talking about?"

Sophia quickly explained, telling them of the death of Ria and of Henri's plan to kill Scott, Chris, and Brian. She declared that a worse fate was in store for an unsuspecting Louisa.

Dan absorbed this news without changing the expression on his face. He had thought Chris and Scott to be reasonably safe, but he did not doubt

Henri's treachery or Sophia's accuracy in assessing the situation.

"Sophia, bring Chris and Scott to me."

Sophia never questioned him, she just left the hut and ran to find Scott. Chris and Louisa were still out walking around, but Scott was pacing the floor, trying to think of a way to get him and Chris and Louisa away, but he had not yet dealt with how they were going to get to Brian or how was he ever going to tell Lucas about Ria?

Scott spun about when Sophia came in, expectant but not really knowing what was to come.

"Sophia—"

"Scott, Dan would like to see you."

"Now?"

"Yes. He sent me. He has already heard about what has happened to your friend."

"My friend?"

"Brian, the captain of the *Swan*."

"I don't even—"

"Scott, please. There's no time for any more pretending. I know the three of you are old friends. If you want to get yourself and your friends out of here and away from Henri, you had best go see Dan right now."

Scott knew she was right. He didn't even question her. Sophia knew everything. He didn't know how, but he knew she did. She always seemed to have sources. He left the hut with Sophia and they almost ran across the compound. As they entered Dan's hut, several of his men were leaving.

"You wanted to see me?" Scott asked.

"Yes," Dan replied. "Sophia seems to believe you and Chris are in some kind of danger from Henri and that you should get out of here."

It was no time for lies. Dan just might be their only

avenue of escape. Scott began to see that Chris's instincts had been right. There seemed to be many shades of black in men, and Dan's seemed to be the lightest.

"She's right," Scott said, directing a grateful look at Sophia. "Henri wouldn't mind cutting our throats once your protection is gone, and God only knows what terrors he plans for Louisa. He is already responsible for the death of the woman from the *Swan*."

William and Dan exchanged looks, and Dan smiled. "So you were right, Will. I never should have dealt with that scoundrel, but we needed gunpowder."

"I think," Will said in his quiet way, "we have a responsibility to these people. One death is quite enough."

"You're right." Dan turned to Scott. "I cannot leave until late tomorrow, but by then Henri may have arranged some unpleasant destiny for you. So here is what we will do."

Scott bent toward Dan.

"You, Sophia, and three of my men will leave now, before Henri can realize you are gone. You will go back by the same route your friend took here." He smiled at Scott's silence. "Sophia and my men know the way."

"What of Chris and Louisa?" Scott protested. "I won't leave without them."

"I guarantee their safety. They will move in here with me, and I will make sure they are with us when we leave. We will take them to a place from which they can find their way back to St. Augustine."

"And what of Brian?" Scott said stubbornly. "No man should be left in Henri's tender care."

"I will bargain with Henri. He likes a profit better

431

than anything else. I have the means to buy your friend's release."

The men stood looking at each other, Dan waiting and Scott trying to judge the wisdom of trusting Dan.

"I feel that I'm deserting my friends," Scott declared.

"Nonsense. They will be free before you get to St. Augustine. I won't let anything happen to them. It will be much worse should you stay."

"Listen to him, Scott," Sophia urged. "He wouldn't betray you or your friends."

Finally, and to Dan's amusement, he nodded.

"Good. I've already instructed my men. Gather only what you need. You had best be gone soon, for Henri is coming here to make arrangements for the disposal of his cargoes and for our next meeting."

"Dan," Scott said.

"What?"

"They will be safe?" he asked softly. "Chris and Brian, I mean?"

"I'll do all that I can. Who can say what fate will bring? But if it's in my power, they'll be safe."

"Thanks. Dan?"

"Yes?"

"I have to tell you—"

Dan chuckled. "No need to make confessions Scott. None of us is about to meet our Maker, I hope."

"I do have to tell you. When I came here it was to make a connection between you and Henri . . . and to catch you both."

"And you changed your mind?" Dan smiled.

"Henri deserves whatever he gets. You don't. As far as I'm concerned, and I think I can include my friends, we've never seen the infamous Dan McGirtt. I wish you well, Dan, and you have my gratitude."

"Thanks," Dan said quietly. "Go with God, Scott.

We'll do our best to see that your friends join you soon. Don't be impatient. It may take some time."

The two men shook hands, and Scott left with Sophia. He returned to his hut and gathered the few possessions he had.

The men Dan had chosen were already waiting at the edge of the forest when Sophia and Scott joined them.

They waved a quick farewell to Dan and Will and John, who stood before their hut to see the pair left safely.

In a few minutes Sophia, Scott, and the men accompanying them disappeared in the thick green foliage, and once in the wilderness they were safe from Henri's long and vengeful arm.

Sophia strode along beside a very silent Scott. She was very pleased about one thing. For the few days it would take to get to St. Augustine she would have Scott entirely to herself. She knew he was engrossed in his thoughts so she did not speak. There would be time to talk later.

Scott was thinking of the tragedy of Ria's death. He was dreading the effect the news was going to have on Lucas. The couple had never had the time to really know each other, and now they would never have it.

Who can say what fate will bring? Dan had said. Scott was sure this blow of fate would be difficult for Lucas to survive.

Chapter 32

Brian was dragged from the hut, tossed in the bottom of a boat, and rowed to the *Swan*. There he was forced, half-conscious now, into the hold with the rest of his men. Dazed, he rolled from his back and forced himself up to his knees. By the time he could focus his eyes in the dim light, he was already surrounded by his crew which had preceded him to this prison.

"Who is it?" one man said as they moved closer.

"By God!" another exclaimed. "It's the cap'n, right enough. Are ya all right, sir?"

"Hell no," Brian grated out. "My head hurts like the devil. Lately it's been used just a little too roughly. I'd like to have my hands on that bastard's throat."

"He's all right." The speaker laughed. "He's got his temper back, and that's a sure sign he's goin' to be okay."

Now Brian's complete control returned, but when it did a flood of white-hot grief pierced him so sharply he drew a ragged gasping breath.

"Ria," he groaned.

He bent forward until he was nearly doubled in

agony as Henri's words returned to him. *She chose to kill herself.* Henri had let her forfeit her life and had thought it amusing.

His men sat about him in total amazement as he damned Henri Duval and all the man's ancestors to hell. Brian's grief filled the room like an invisible specter, and every man could feel his pain as if it were a live thing.

"Be damned," one man whispered in awe, "the cap'n has gone and lost his senses."

"Cap'n, sir," another ventured, "what's gone wrong, sir?"

"Ria! Ria!" Brian gasped. "She's dead. Henri Duval killed her."

A slow wave of anger rippled through all men present. There was not a man that did not have a special place in his heart for Lady Arianne, the violet-eyed sister of the captain.

"Dead, sir?" The seaman was stunned. "You mean that bloodthirsty son of Satan has—"

"He's killed her." Brian growled low in his throat like a crazed animal. "And I shall avenge her if it takes my dying breath."

"Be ya thinkin' there's a way out of here, lad?" Another voice. "We been tryin' to find one ever since he took the *Swan*."

"There has to be . . . there has to be," Brian declared.

"Ya finds it, Cap'n, and we'll all follow ya. We'll get the bloody monster."

Brian grew silent, but he rose and began to pace the floor, his mind searching for some form of escape.

Chris was surprised to find the hut empty when they returned.

"Stay here, Louisa. I must go and talk to Dan. I have a feeling something has happened that I should know."

"Do you think something's wrong?"

"Yes. I don't believe Brian would be wandering aorund. He's gone and so is Scott."

"Please, Chris, I'd rather be with you. I can't bear being alone in this terrible place."

"All right. Come along. Let's see what Dan has to say."

They walked across the compound together and stopped in front of Dan's hut. Even Chris wouldn't think of trying to go inside without permission. Once it was given they entered. Dan was obviously packing, but he was the first to speak. He answered Chris's unspoken questions immediately.

"We'll be leaving tomorrow. I know you're looking for your two friends. Some of the news is good and some is bad."

"What's the bad?" Chris demanded.

"Henri has taken Brian to the *Swan*."

"Damn the man's soul!"

"But your friend Scott and Sophia are gone."

"Gone . . . gone where?"

"To St. Augustine."

"That's impossible," Chris said.

"Not so. They have some of my men with them."

Chris looked at Dan closely. Then he smiled. "So Dan McGirtt has a soft spot."

"For Sophia, yes. She had been a loyal friend for a long time."

"And Scott? He certainly hasn't been a longtime friend."

"No." Dan chuckled. "But he is a little more than a friend to Sophia. She desired his safety in St. Augustine. She needed only to ask."

437

"I find it hard to believe that Scott would have left Louisa and I."

"He wouldn't."

"But he did."

"No, he didn't. I had to guarantee your safety and the young lady's."

"You guaranteed it?"

"I did."

"Me and Louisa . . . you're going to make sure we get safely out of here."

"Tomorrow . . . when I'm ready to leave."

"I see," Chris said softly. He was thoughtful for some time; then he turned to Louisa. "I think we'd better go back to our hut, at least until we leave here tomorrow."

He took Louisa's arm and started for the door. But both stopped in their tracks when Dan, William, and John all began to laugh at the same time.

Chris turned to face them, and Louisa was surprised at the half-smile that touched his lips and the glow of amusement in his eyes.

"I've won my wager, I believe," Dan said.

"Wager?" Chris replied.

"I assured John that you would not leave your friend in Henri's grip. You have not disappointed me. You do intend to try to get him free, don't you?"

"Any way I can," Chris said quietly.

"Just what do you think you can do?" William inquired.

"I don't know yet. I'll do something. I have to wait until after dark anyway."

"He'll have guards on that ship," Dan challenged.

"I suppose he will."

"But you'll try anyway."

"That I will." Chris chuckled mirthlessly.

"How will you get away?"

"Isn't Brian on his own ship?"

"Yes."

"Then if I have any success we'll just take the *Swan* out of here."

"I see," Dan said thoughtfully. "But you have forgotten something haven't you?"

"What?"

"Your lady," Dan said softly.

Chris looked at Louisa, then at Dan. "I thought it would be safer if she were to stay with you."

"No!" Louisa cried.

"She'll be safe with you, Dan. Henri can't take her from you, and you can see that she gets safely to St. Augustine."

"I won't go without you."

"Louisa, for God's sake listen to reason."

"I am reasonable," Louisa said. "I'm not going to go with Dan. Wherever you go, I'm going with you."

"Damn it!" Chris shouted. "It's too dangerous!"

"Are you going to fight them?"

"Not if I can help it. I'd be outnumbered."

"Then I can move as quietly as you. I won't go with Dan. I'd rather be with you, no matter where it is."

"Let me try to solve this problem." Dan smiled.

"Please," Chris said disgustedly.

"You're going to try to take over the ship after dark."

"Yes."

"If you succeed she'll move downriver. I will send two men with you and two more to take your lady downstream a ways. If you succeed you can pick her up and you both can be gone by morning. If you fail we'll take her on to safety."

"Sounds like the answer we need," Chris agreed. "Louisa, it makes sense. If I can get Brian free, we'll

439

be on our way downriver before daybreak."

"And if you don't?" Louisa's voice was very low. She went to Chris and put both her hands against his chest. "I'm strong, Chris, and I'm not afraid of anything except being separated from you. Let me come with you. I would rather stand beside you than be free . . . and alone."

Their eyes met and held for a heart-stopping moment. He understood completely what she was saying. It was him . . . or nothing.

"All right, Louisa. Win or lose, you're with me. We'll have to wait until just after dark. The guards won't be expecting anything. We'll take the two men Dan offered and"—he smiled—"with a drop or two of your stubborn determination, we'll be on our way downriver by morning."

With a soft laugh, Louisa flung herself into his arms, and Chris held her close.

"Then I suggest you join us in a drink," Dan offered. "You have a few hours' wait so we might just talk a little."

Chris and Louisa sat down with Dan and the others, and waited for the sun to set.

The camp was dark when Chris, Louisa, and the two men Dan had provided made their way toward the river. They moved slowly, for they could not use the direct path but had to make their way through the dense foliage. Once they got to the riverbank they took silent possession of a small boat and pushed it into the river. They dipped the oars without sound and rowed to the *Swan*.

Chris was the first to silently climb over the side. One of Dan's men followed. The third gripped Louisa by the waist and then the ankles, helping her up the rope until Chris leaned down to grasp her hand and pull her aboard.

Once they had gathered in a silent knot on deck, they looked about. What surprised them was not the absence of guards, but the fact that the few Henri had left lay strewn about the deck, unconscious or dead. They moved slowly among the bodies, alarmed but trying to remain in control. Slowly they made their way to the companionway door . . . and there they were met by Brian and his crew who were coming out.

Lucas had left his men to cross the river with Ria and head for Dan's camp. He had told them to move with absolute silence, and they did. They slipped across the jut of land like silent panthers, and when they neared the *Swan* they bent close to the ground along the river, shuffling silently along until they were opposite the ship. They swam to it almost silently and shimmied up the rope that anchored her to the bottom.

They moved slowly and carefully, so much so that the few men Henri had left to guard the *Swan* were taken totally by surprise. Unprepared, some of them were even unarmed. All were rendered unconscious with dispatch; then the attackers moved down into the dark hold.

Quietly, one by one, they wakened the sleeping men. By the time they got to Brian he was already becoming conscious of them.

"Who the hell—" he began.

"Shhh," one of Lucas's men whispered. "We're here to get the *Swan* and you out of here."

"Who sent you?" Brian asked suspiciously.

"Well, mate, we're part of the *Black Angel*'s crew—

Captain Blanc's men."

The seaman's words struck Brian hard. Captain Blanc—Luke—had sent his men, Brian suspected, to rescue Ria, so he would have to tell him that Ria was . . . He didn't want to think of it now, not until he could find Henri, because his rage was too great to control until he found Henri.

"We'd best get on deck and sail the *Swan* out of here," Brian said as he rose.

As a group, the men started for the deck.

When Brian reached for the handle of the companionway door it was suddenly jerked open from above.

No one could have been more surprised than Brian, who had promptly prepared to do battle, when he came face to face with Chris.

"What the! . . ."

"Brian!"

"Chris. What the hell are you doing here?"

"Coming for you." Chris grinned. "What does it look like?"

"It looks like we've been rescued from all directions." Brian grinned too.

"I recognize our crew from the *Angel*," Chris said. He turned to a seaman. "Where is Lucas?"

"He's across the river. He and the lady are goin' into the camp to find him." He motioned toward Brian.

"Lady?" Brian said.

"Aye, sir," the man replied quickly. "The lady from the *Swan*, sir."

"Ria!" Brian cried hopefully.

"Aye, sir. That be her name. She and the cap'n be lookin' for you, sir. The lady wouldn't hear of nothin' else but comin' after you."

"Ria . . . God, Ria," Brian said softly. He was choked with relief. Ria was not dead. Some wonderful twist of fate had kept her alive, twisted her from Henri's arms and carried her to Lucas. He didn't care what twist it was; Ria was alive and that was all that mattered.

"We've got to get this ship out into the current before somebody on Henri's ship gets wise to what we're doing," Chris said quickly.

At that moment Brian took notice of the fact that Louisa was with them. He turned questioningly toward Chris who simply shrugged his shoulders and smiled.

"Stubborn," he said perfunctorily.

"Like most women," Brian declared. "She and Ria should get on very well."

Orders were given in subdued whispers, the anchor was raised, and the ship eased, like a ghost, into the current. No one aboard Henri's ship knew that the *Swan* drifted away from them and disappeared into the night. No sails were raised for the sounds would have carried across the water as a warning of what was happening. It would be morning before anyone noticed the *Swan* was gone.

The *Swan* was a dark shadow now, moving down the river swiftly, flowing with the current. Brian called for the man who had first told him Ria was still alive.

"What's your name?"

"Nate, sir."

"Well, Nate, you said Ria is still alive."

"Aye, sir. She is."

"But Henri Duval told me she was dead."

"Mayhap he thought she be, sir."

"Why?"

"Well, I can't rightly say, but from what I could tell the lady was either pushed or jumped into the river. She was carried down it, and the cap'n jumped in and fished her out."

"That must be why Henri thinks she died. I wonder if he or anyone else even tried to save her."

"I doubt it, sir. Looks to me like she was just left to care for herself as best she could."

"What a blight on humanity he is," Brian said, half to himself.

"Aye, sir. That he is."

"You were sent to get the *Swan*."

"Aye, sir . . . and most important, to get you."

"Me."

"Seems the lady was set on getting you along with the ship. She was the one that put him to it." Nate grinned. "The cap'n . . . well, I kinda think he'd do most anything to please her, even though he'd be the last to admit it. Anyway after he fished her out was when he decided to go after the *Swan* and you, so we kinda thought 'twas her that brought up the idea. She puts great store in you, sir."

Knowing Ria and Luke's situation, Brian was amused by imagining the thoughts that must have been in Luke's mind when Ria had insisted on coming back for him once she was free. In fact now that he knew the truth about Luke, he was looking forward to seeing him and his sister.

He thought of his last confrontation with Luke and winced with remembered pain. Still, he was looking forward to meeting the man he now knew was his brother-in-law and not the pirate he had once believed him to be.

444

"Will we reach the *Angel* soon?"

"Won't be too long, sir."

"I can't wait to thank your captain and to see Ria again."

"'Fraid that will be awhile, sir. 'Spects we'll be there long before they are."

"Before they are?"

"Aye, sir. I'm rightly sure they don't 'spect to be back till near mornin'. You see, sir, they have to come back without a ship. They have to walk a ways to their boat, so it'll take some time."

"Where did they go?"

"To the McGirtt camp."

"If they knew where I was, why did they go to the camp."

"I don't suppose Lucas knew for certain you were on the ship. He most likely thought to make sure wherever you were he would find you," Chris said from behind them. Brian turned to look at him. Louisa was standing close to Chris. "I can't see Lucas planning on doing a job halfway," Chris added.

"I haven't had the chance to become too well acquainted with the man." Brian laughed. "Every time we met there was some kind of a battle. We've threatened to kill each other a number of times."

"Brian, if Lucas and Ria don't find you in the village they'll make their way back pretty quickly."

"I sure hope so."

"Since it looks like we're all going to get clear of this thing, let's not say anything to Lucas about knowing who he is or that he and Ria are married. When Scott can get together with us, it will be a little more interesting."

"You mean let them go on thinking—"

"That you and she were involved."

445

"He's in love with her, Chris?"

"Without a doubt. And her?"

"She's been tied in knots since they've been separated."

"It should be interesting when Captain Blanc and Ria part company and Lucas Maine meets Arianne St. Thomas."

"There's going to be an explosion."

"Personally"—Chris smiled—"I think it's a marriage made in heaven."

"Carved in stone, designed by fate," Brian agreed with a chuckle. "But if Ria finds out I knew and didn't tell her, she'll have my head on a plate."

"She need never know."

"Do you think they might both say to hell with society and stay together. Ria isn't one to toss her family aside."

"I can tell that by the way she's fought for you. Lucas isn't either. That's why I believe Lucas and Arianne will have to meet to resolve things between Captain Blanc and Ria."

"Chris," Louisa said with a half-smile, "this all sounds very interesting and amusing, but I have no idea what you two are talking about. Who are Ria and Lucas?"

"Good heavens." Chris laughed. "I've been so caught up in all this I forgot you didn't know what led up to it. In fact I've never even introduced you two. Brian, this is Louisa Herald, another victim of our dear friend Henri. He took her father's ship some time ago and she became his hostage. For ransom," he added. Louisa cast him a look of affection and gratitude; Brian didn't miss it. "Louisa, this is Brian St. Thomas. He's the brother of Arianne St. Thomas."

Louisa's eyes grew wider as Chris spoke. "You mean they are married and don't even know it?"

"They spent so much time running away from each other they didn't even have time to find out."

"Oh, Chris. That's unfair."

"What is?"

"Not telling her."

"Well, we'll tell them."

"When?"

Both men began to laugh. "I figure the best time is when we introduce them," Chris said.

"Let's do it in a place where we have plenty of room to run," Brian added.

"You two are terrible," Louisa declared, but the sparkle of laughter was in her eyes too.

"Louisa," Brian said, "this is one time I'm going to be able to pay Ria back for all the pranks she has pulled on me, especially for stowing away on my ship when all this started. I do have a little revenge coming. Besides"—his voice gentled—"I know Ria loves him, and I want her to be happy. If they battle now as Ria and Captain Blanc, they might never get together."

"But you're wrong, Brian," Louisa said quietly.

"I am?"

"If your sister is as you say, if she loves this man, then pirate or no, she is going to tell him she loves him before she lets him go. And he won't let her go either without telling her what he feels for her."

"You believe they'll profess their love even if they know there's no future for them?" Brian asked.

"I do," she replied.

The men exchanged glances.

"I wonder," Brian said.

Chris looked thoughtful. "Maybe that would be

best. If they can admit their love as pirate and mistress think of how wonderful it will be when they learn the truth."

"So you are both going to keep the secret." Louisa laughed softly.

"Right," they replied in unison. Then all three laughed.

Chapter 33

The weak moonlight made Luke just a dark form before her, so Ria tried to follow closely. She had lost her sense of direction, and the last thing she wanted was to lose sight of Luke and to be lost in this wilderness.

She had tried to make no sound since they had pulled their small boat ashore and hidden it carefully so a rapid escape would be possible. Now she allowed her thoughts to touch on the broad-shouldered form before her. He had reached out to touch her in that moment before they had started on this mission, and she was trying to understand its effect on her.

Did he really care? She had been nothing but a torment to him, insisting he rescue a man he so obviously hated. They had fought almost from the second they had met, and now she was aggravated by the thought that somehow it could be different. He was risking his life to save Brian. Of course he had demanded something in return, but she wondered if any other man would risk his life at all.

She knew she would never understand him. She also knew their bargain would never be carried through. Once Brian was free, he would get her out of this and Ria, pirate's mistress, would leave Captain Blanc behind. They were worlds apart and their lives would never cross. She could not see Lady Arianne St. Thomas living beside Captain Blanc, pirate *extraordinaire*. Her obligations tied her to another, and she could not ignore those obligations.

This whole affair had started out as a jaunt, an escapade, a way to escape a man she could not face. But it had turned into something much different. She felt the sharp tang of bitterness as she realized the girl who had sought fun, excitement, and escape had changed to a woman who did not know what she really wanted. A page in her life had been written by the man before her, and she would never be able to erase it.

For once, the honesty that was basic to her character forced her to look at what they had shared. Despite their battles, in his arms she had tasted a magic she knew she would never find again. Could she balance that against what pride and family called for her to do?

Could she choose to stay with this man knowing what he was, offering her body to him, knowing that one day he would tire of her and discard her. No! She could not live that kind of life . . . but a small voice deep inside her refused to be silenced and it echoed the call of her wayward body. She sighed deeply.

Lucas heard her ragged sigh and thought he might have been going too fast for her. He said nothing, but he slowed his progress. He shook his head and a grim smile touched his lips. He still could not quite believe he was in this situation, risking his life to find a man who was going to take from him something he wanted.

Yet, to be honest with himself, he had to admit that life with Brian would be better suited to Ria's wanton ways than life with him. Then a thought jangled through him: if she truly was not selective about the men she slept with, why had she run from Henri, almost losing her life to do it?

He would never understand her. But soon it would no longer matter. Once they had gotten the *Swan* and her lover to safety, she would sail from his life just as she had sailed into it. But he knew he would never be the same again.

There was duty. Duty to the woman he had married and never seen. Duty to the family that had given him an honorable name, an education, and love. He couldn't just disregard them as if they had never existed. Ria would be miserable in those circumstances, yet he could picture her in silks and satins. He envisioned her uplifted face as they danced together. He saw her in the midst of society, saw himself being envied by every man present. He turned from the path down which these thoughts were taking him. It could never be, and he had better resign himself to that fact.

They were nearing the dark quiet camp now, and Lucas stopped abruptly just inside the ring of undergrowth that surrounded it. Lost in her thoughts Ria collided with him before she realized he had stopped.

"Shhh," he cautioned angrily.

"Sorry," she snapped. "Why don't you let me know when you are going to stop. Why are we stopping anyhow?"

"Well, I don't think it would be wise to dash into the camp shouting your lover's name, do you?"

"We're there?"

"Yes."

"Now what?"

"You wait here a minute," he said, and he

vanished into the darkness before she could protest. She stood still, trying to listen for his presence, but he made no sound.

To her, the minutes seemed like hours before he suddenly reappeared beside her, causing her to gasp in fear.

"Damn it! Don't do that."

"Stop swearing and keep quiet," he commanded roughly. "It looks like most of the camp is asleep. There's light in only one hut. If you can manage to keep your mouth shut and make as little noise as possible, we'll make our way to it and see if we're lucky."

"Yes, master," she snarled angrily, and was rewarded by his soft chuckle.

This time, as they moved forward, he took her hand, but she refused to admit that its large hard strength gave her a new sense of security.

"There should be guards somewhere," he whispered, "but I'll be damned if I see any."

"What do they have to guard out here?"

Again Lucas laughed softly. "If old Henri were anchored anywhere near me, I'd have half my force posted as guards."

Now they moved very slowly, and she was pleased that he still held her hand. What she didn't know was that her small hand nestled safely in his pleased him as well.

They moved quietly from hut to hut, keeping in the shadows and aiming for the only one in which the soft mellow light of candles glowed.

They were about to approach the lighted hut when again Lucas stopped abruptly. He cursed softly.

"What's the matter?" she whispered.

"The *Swan* was supposed to be across the river from Henri's ship."

"It was."

"Ria, I don't know if my men have had the time to get here."

"What if they haven't?"

"The *Swan* is gone."

She peered around him and her brows furrowed in a deep frown as she scanned the river's edge. Henri's ship was clearly outlined against the night sky, but there was no sign of the *Swan*.

"Your men must have been faster than you figured. Why else would the *Swan* be gone?"

"Maybe you underestimated your lover," he grated out with aggravating amusement.

"What do you mean?" she demanded.

"Maybe he's not as worried about you as you seem to be about him."

"What are you implying?"

"That your friend made a deal with Henri and he's gone. He must have slipped by us in the darkness."

"That's a lie! Brian would never do that!"

"You have that much confidence in him?"

"Yes," she said.

"Well, I don't. We're on a rescue mission that might not only be dangerous but a waste of time."

"No. Brian is here. We have to find him."

"Don't worry," he said firmly. "If he's here I'll find him. Maybe he can explain why his ship's gone and he's still here." He laughed bitterly. "Come on."

Ria was frightened. Why was the *Swan* gone? Did that mean something had happened to Brian? She prayed silently as they slowly approached the lighted hut.

Now they moved one step at a time until they could reach out and touch the side of the hut. They waited, listening intently for any sound coming from within.

The night, except for the sounds of animals

floating on the night air, was quiet. The voice that came from behind them sounded cold and harsh.

"Suppose you both just keep goin' right on in. If you want to talk to Dan why sneak around out here."

They both spun around to come face to face with a rather large man whose gun, pointed at them, seemed even larger.

"I don't know who you are, but Dan don't take well to folks sneakin' around his camp. He's kinda friendly like, and always wants to greet his visitors. Get inside."

The last two words were spoken with such an air of command that Lucas pushed aside his thoughts of jumping the man. He didn't want to get Ria shot.

He put a hand on Ria's shoulder and pushed her ahead of him into the hut before she could give vent to the protest he knew was on the tip of her tongue.

Dan, William, and John sat around a small table, engrossed in the plans they were making. With the gunpowder Dan had now, he was plotting future forays against the plantations that lay along the St. James River and more continual harassment of the outlying areas of St. Augustine in order to further the conflict between the two governors. The three men were totally surprised when Ria and Lucas were pushed inside. They looked up from the papers before them.

"What is it?" Dan asked quickly. "Who are they?"

"I don't know, Dan. I been trailin' 'em all the way in from the woods. They was headed right here"—the big man grinned amiably—"so I just let 'em come till they got here. Then I sort of invited 'em inside so you could ask 'em."

"Thanks, Briggs." Dan turned from the man and

his gaze fastened on Ria and Lucas. "Who are you, and what business do you have here?"

"Our business doesn't really have anything to do with you," Lucas replied. "I take it you are Dan McGirtt?"

"I am. Who are you?"

"My name is Captain Blanc," Lucas replied coolly. He was more than certain Dan had never heard of him before, so he was completely surprised when the three men exchanged glances, then smiled.

"And I take it your name could be Ria?" Dan said pleasantly.

Lucas and Ria frowned at Dan's casual use of her name. It seemed he knew all about her.

"You," he said to Lucas, "are the captain of the *Black Angel*, and if I'm not mistaken you both are looking for someone."

Now Ria was totally aghast. "How do you know all this?"

Dan smiled and then turned to Lucas. "You have, I believe, a friend who has been with us for some time."

"Chris," Lucas said softly.

"Yes."

"Where's Chris now?"

"He left sometime ago to try to take the *Swan* downriver without Henri knowing. It seems there is someone aboard he feels he should rescue from Henri's clutches."

"And you didn't help him?" Ria said coldly.

Dan laughed. "I sent men to help him take the *Swan*. I must not anger Henri. He is my constant supplier of arms, and I need him."

"The *Swan* is gone," Lucas said.

"I know." Dan chuckled. "My men reported that fact to me. I thought everything was over. The person aboard the *Swan* must be very important when so many people come to the rescue. Anyway the ship is freed, and you had best be gone from this camp. We must leave tomorrow and Henri, with the loss of the *Swan*, just might not be as hospitable as I."

"We have a boat downstream a ways," Lucas said quickly. "We'll get back to it right away. If they've taken the *Swan* downstream they're bound to run across the *Angel*. I sent some of my men up here to take over the *Swan*. Maybe good fortune will turn its face my way for a change and they've gotten aboard."

"You had best go before Henri gets wind of anything," Dan declared.

A very familiar voice interrupted their conversation. "I'm afraid it's just a little too late for that."

At the door, Henri and several of his men stood, guns pointed at those in the room.

Henri laughed as Ria gasped and moved closer to Lucas, who, his eyes holding Henri's, put an arm about her and drew her close to him.

"So, my little cat"—Henri smiled at Ria—"toss you in the air and you seem to land on your feet. We have some unfinished business you and I."

"You'd best not lay a hand on her, Henri my friend." Lucas's voice was so cold it was like a knife blade. "It could cost you your life."

Henri laughed delightedly. "You are in a bad position to threaten me. You are the one who might be forfeiting his life. I do believe it is time our partnership is dissolved. I'll let you go back to your ship . . . but you must leave her here."

"Not on your life," Lucas declared. "I don't believe the lady enjoys your . . . ah . . . amorous attention, Henri." His laugh was harsh. "She chose the river instead of you. My, my. You are slipping, Henri old chum."

456

Henri's face grew mottled with black rage.

"Do not worry. The lady will have her mind changed."

"What are you going to do?" Ria cried.

"This is my camp, Henri," Dan said coldly.

"Ah yes, Dan, but you are at this moment greatly outnumbered. By the time you rectify the matter these two will be safely aboard my ship. I would not advise you to try anything. My cannons are expertly aimed at the hut in which you have stored the gunpowder. One shot could blow up this camp and everyone in it."

For a moment Dan was stunned, but he quickly regained his composure. "Surely you are not barbarian enough to kill so many just to have these two."

"He is," Ria said firmly.

"Are you foolish enough to give up the lives of all your people to keep two safe?" Henri inquired casually, but he already knew the answer to that. He could read it on every face.

Dan was helpless, and Lucas knew it. It was too much to ask him to let all his people die for the sake of two strangers to whom he had no loyalty, and whom under better circumstances he might never see again.

Dan turned to Lucas and Ria.

"It's all right Dan," Ria said gently. "We understand. We would not ask such a sacrifice from you."

Lucas felt a distinct urge to clasp Ria tightly in his arms and tell her how proud he was of her courage . . . and how much he loved her. At this moment he felt grateful for the woman she was, and if he had to die, he knew it was better to have loved her than never to have known her.

"You're right, Ria my love," he said as he held

her close.

She lifted her head and her eyes met his. For one fleeting moment she saw a warmth, a tenderness that reached within her and touched a spot that had hungered for so long. If only he had looked at her this way before . . .

The moment passed when Lucas tore his eyes from hers and looked again at Henri.

"We're still alive, and there is always a chance," he said coolly.

"You are still alive, but I intend to remedy that soon," Henri snarled. "Take them to the ship," he commanded.

After Ria and Lucas had been forced from the hut, Henri again looked at a pale-faced Dan.

"You have a choice. Be gone from here by morning, or we will blow you and all your people from the face of the earth." With those words, Henri left the hut.

Lucas and Ria were forced aboard the *Sea Rover* and shoved into Henri's cabin. There they stood for a few moments in total silence. Then Lucas drew a trembling Ria into his arms and held her.

"Don't be afraid, Ria. Rats like Henri can smell fear and they thrive on it. Let's keep our wits. Maybe we can find a way out of this yet."

"Do you think anyone on your ship will come to look for us?"

"Not until at least midday tomorrow," Lucas said cautiously. He didn't want to add that by that time whatever Henri planned to do would already be accomplished.

Ria moved from Lucas's embrace and went to look out over the moon-dappled water.

Lucas stood and watched her in silence, wondering if she was longing for Brian. He wanted to go to her, take her in his arms, and force her to listen. He wanted to tell her that he loved her and wanted her, but before he could speak the opportunity was forever lost. The door opened and Henri came in, with two men.

"Now let us discuss . . . your future." Henri chuckled. "Or, for you, Captain Blanc, what is left of it."

Ria's face blanched, but Lucas just gazed at Henri. A frigid smile drew his lips back, but never extended past them.

"Henri," he said, as if making casual conversation, "do whatever you want with me, but let Ria go. My ship is downstream and"—he hoped he was right—"the *Swan* will stand with her. You don't stand a chance in hell of getting past the two of them."

Henri gazed at Lucas speculatively. "Ah, but I cannot let her go." He smiled amiably at Ria. "As you must already know, Captain"—his voice lowered suggestively—"she is much too enticing a creature not to taste. I'm sure you have already"—he shrugged—"sampled."

Ria made a small sound of anger, and Lucas's eyes grew even colder.

"You are a foul one, Henri old friend." Lucas's voice was brittle with anger. "You should be eliminated for the sake of civilized society."

"Arrogant," Henri hissed. "Let us see if we can take some of that arrogance from you with a whip."

"No! No!" Ria cried.

"Take him on deck," Henri snapped.

The men who had accompanied Henri moved toward Lucas. There was nothing he could do. They were heavily armed and he didn't want Ria to be hurt.

One of the pirates gave Lucas a rough shove toward the door. Ria ran after him, but as she passed Henri he reached out and caught her about the waist.

"No need to run, my sweet. You'll be there to see it, I promise you that. You will see just what his arrogance has brought him."

Ria struggled against Henri's grasp, still trying to get to Lucas.

Slowly, his grip still firm on her arm, Henri made his way to the deck.

Lucas had been taken to the huge main mast. His wrists were tied to it, well above his head. He twisted about, trying to see where Ria was.

She was still trying to free herself from Henri's grasp. Her eyes, wide and full of disbelief, were on Luke.

"Make him ready," Henri shouted.

One man went to Lucas and gripped the back of his shirt. He tore it in two, baring Lucas's back. Then he stepped away and another slowly approached. In his hand he carried a wicked-looking whip. It had a heavy leather-wrapped wooden handle, from which hung at least twenty thin strips each with a small metal ball at the end. Henri meant to punish Lucas as much as possible before he killed him, and he intended to punish Ria by making her watch . . . before he made her submit to his will.

Chapter 34

Lucas pulled against the leather strips that bound his wrists, but his struggles had no effect except to make the strips cut into his flesh until his wrists bled. He could hear the man behind him chuckle softly and slap the whip lightly against his palm.

For a moment fear rippled through him, but then his mind returned to Ria. He had to think of her because he knew Henri planned to beat him until Ria surrendered. Only her submission would bring him the death Henri was sure he would beg for . . . in time.

Henri motioned to one of his men to restrain Ria. Then he moved close to Lucas, so she could not hear the words they exchanged.

"I have a feeling you will be stubborn," he said softly, "that you won't cry out. Maybe you think to be noble for the lady's sake, eh? Well, I will have her. If you could see her eyes now, full of tears. But she is stubborn, like you. So I must make her understand what you will go through if she remains stubborn."

"If you think to have my blessing, Henri, you can go to hell."

"You have given me a great deal of trouble, but in a

few minutes your heroics will be brought to an end."

Lucas did the one thing he knew would enrage Henri and perhaps bring his torture to an end sooner—he laughed.

"Your insolence knows no bounds. We will see who breaks first, you or the lady."

Lucas's muscles strained painfully as he waited for the first blow to fall. He tried to think of some way to break the hold pain would have on him. He began to wonder how much a man was able to endure before he could no longer control his mind . . . before he broke.

He licked his lips and leaned his head against the rough wood of the mast.

"Henri!" he called out.

Henri was again at his side, a smile of satisfaction on his face. "You wish to apologize . . . maybe to beg for a quick death?"

"I want to talk to Ria," Lucas stated firmly.

"You what?"

"I want to talk to Ria."

"And why should I grant that request?"

"Because you're a sadistic bastard and you are probably enjoying all this so you want to prolong it as long as you possibly can." Lucas kept his voice as emotionless as possible lest Henri hear the desire for Ria somewhere in his voice and deny him.

But Henri shrugged. He motioned to the man who held Ria and she was released. When she ran to Lucas's side, he turned his head to look at her.

Her eyes were filled with compassion and pain. Tears streaked her face and she was pale, her eyes like deep violets in her stark face.

"Oh, Luke . . . Luke."

"Don't let him see you like this, Ria. It gives him too much satisfaction."

"I don't care, I don't care."

His feverish skin felt the coolness of her trembling hand, and he knew he could not die before he told her many things—of his regrets and of his love, and of how she had changed hatred to something warm and deep.

"Ria, listen to me. I have to tell you something before it's too late."

"Nothing matters now."

"But it does." He inhaled deeply, realizing the many times he could have told her, times that could have been so beautiful. Again regret chewed at his mind. "Ria, I'm sorry you are part of all this, God, I'm sorry I've hurt you so badly so often."

"What does it matter now, Luke! I don't care about that. If you die . . ." Her words broke into a sob that tore at his spirit.

"Ria," he said gently, "look at me."

Her eyes met his, and she was shaken by the glow of warmth in them.

"I love you, Ria. That's the one and only truth. I love you, and I'd give my life gladly to undo all the harm I've done you. I was stupid not to see what I had when I had it. My jealousy was a two-edged sword. I could not bear the thought of your loving anyone else. I'm sorry."

Her breath caught in her throat, and her heart felt as if a huge hand was squeezing the life from it. But before she could answer, before she could tell him she loved him, Henri had grasped her arm and was dragging her away.

"Enough!" Henri said as he dragged her from Luke. With terror-filled eyes, Ria watched the large muscular man with the whip. His arm rose, and descended, and she could hear the strips whistle through the air. Luke's body jerked under the blow, and Ria felt as if the whip had struck her. She cried out, aware that Luke had not made a sound.

"Shall I give him some time to change his mind, my sweet?" Henri gloated. "Maybe he will not be so brave with the next blow . . . or the next."

"Please," Ria moaned, "let him go. I'll do anything you ask, only let him go."

Lucas again heard the whistling sound of the whip just before it landed, with a sickening force, across his bare shoulders.

The sounds of agony escaped Ria's lips more often than Lucas's as the whip fell again and again. Now his back was a mass of red streaks and small drops of blood formed on each one.

Lucas, who had always had more than his share of pride and arrogance, began to wonder if the next blow would be the one to tear a scream of agony from him.

He centered his mind on Ria and clenched his teeth together.

Ria gripped Henri's arm in a frantic hold. "Henri, no more. Please don't."

Henri caught her chin in a ruthless grip. She was half-blinded by tears, and the pleading in her eyes, to Henri's satisfaction, came from her soul.

"You have finally seen the stupidity of your arrogance."

"Yes, yes," she sobbed.

"And you are more than willing to make . . . ah . . . amends?"

"I will do anything you want, anything; only stop this."

His eyes were cold, but he could not control the surge of desire he had always felt for her. He would have her any way he chose, for as long as he chose.

"Suppose we prove to your friend just how useless

it was to oppose me."

"What?"

Henri took her arm and slowly, dragging her with him, he moved to a place where Lucas could clearly see him.

Sweat glazed Lucas's entire body. He clenched his teeth and cracked his eyes open when the whip did not fall again. Through a mist of sweat and pain he could see Ria and Henri. He blinked as beads of sweat burned his eyes, and tried to focus on them, drawing his mind slowly back to reality. His back burned like a raging fire, but he knew it could have been worse. Was this all Henri planned to do? Would he kill him now?

Ria gazed up at Henri, not caring anymore for anything except putting a stop to Luke's pain.

Henri smiled down into her eyes, feeling more satisfied than he had for a long time.

"And now, my sweet, let us show this very foolish man why all his nobility has been for nothing. Let us show him just who has won, who will command you from now on."

"What do you want of me?" Ria said listlessly. Her eyes were on Luke who seemed to have stiffened and become still.

"You will come to me now, my sweet, and you had best be convincing or the whip will fall again . . . and continue to fall until his body hangs in shreds."

Ria turned to Henri. As if she were no longer part of her body she raised her arms and put them about his neck. Henri waited, he would do nothing to help her. She must surrender completely.

She pressed her body against his and slowly drew his head down to her.

465

This drew a cry of agonized rage from Lucas. "No . . . Ria . . . no!"

Ria tried to close her ears, but the sound of his bitter cry filled her entire body and she knew that once Luke was gone she would find a way to end her life. She would never be a toy for this cruel man.

When Henri's arms encircled her and bound her tightly to him, a seething hatred broiled inside Ria, a hatred so intense that she almost felt smothered by it. But at that moment she noticed something that made her heart leap with excitement. Henri had put his pistol in the sash about his waist. Preoccupied with subduing Lucas and taking his revenge on Ria, he had forgotten.

His arms bound her breathlessly against him. She had to find a way to get the pistol . . . and there was only one way. When their kiss ended, Ria steeled herself for her greatest effort at deception; Luke's life and hers depended upon it. She smiled up into Henri's eyes and forced herself to seem suddenly entranced by his effect on her.

"Henri," she murmured softly. "It seems I have underestimated you."

Henri was not quite sure of this sudden change in Ria, but he decided maybe she was becoming wise enough to desert to the winner once she knew who it was.

Henri's immense conceit would let him acknowledge no other reason. He laughed and drew her close to him again. This time she moved so seductively against him that he lost all reason. She was so amazingly beautiful.

Lucas gazed at them in utter disbelief. The scene played out before him was a worse torture than bearing the cut of the whip.

Henri slid his hands from her shoulders, running

them down her back to caress the soft buttocks that rounded the boy's pants she wore.

Ria retained her smile as she ran her hands over his chest slowly . . . slowly . . . each move bringing her closer and closer to the pistol.

She knew she would have only one chance. If it failed, Henri would never believe her again and his anger would be doubled.

She prayed silently, then she struck. She grasped the pistol, cocked it with her other hand and pressed the muzzle against Henri's stomach in one rapid fluid move.

Henri's smile faded. He would have retrieved himself and laughed at this small ineffectual woman who threatened him if he had not looked into her eyes and seen death. There was no weakness in her. She meant to kill him.

"Henri," she said very softly, "Luke and I have nothing to lose. Our lives would be over anyway, so believe that I have not one regret about taking you with me. I will blow a hole in you now if you don't give the order to cut him down."

As if to punctuate her words she dug the pistol into his stomach and watched with sincere pleasure as his face grew pale and his eyes widened with what she delightedly recognized as fear.

"I said, order him cut down."

"Cut him down!" Henri shouted to a group of very surprised men.

They were quick to follow his orders and cut the bonds that held Lucas's arms over his head.

For a minute Lucas clung to the mast, trying to gather his strength. Then he straightened slowly, still amazed by what had suddenly happened. Had Ria bargained with this monster? Had she offered herself in place of him? He couldn't let that happen.

Slowly he walked toward Ria and Henri who, for a reason he couldn't as yet fathom, had not moved. When he drew near enough, he saw the pistol that seemed to connect Ria and Henri like a metal cord.

"Good God." He chuckled, forgetting now the sharp jabs of pain in his back. He moved to Ria's side and saw that she was very nearly frozen in position. He could read real fear in Henri and he knew the cause of it. Both Henri and Lucas sensed that Ria's fury was building and she was gathering the courage to pull the trigger.

"Ria, back up," Lucas ordered sharply. She jabbed the pistol harder against Henri whose face grew even grayer. He turned to look at Lucas who could see the sweat on his face.

"For God's sake, stop her," Henri gasped.

"Why?" Lucas said calmly. "You most certainly deserve it."

"She is going to kill me," Henri gasped, half in wonder and half in a combination of shock and certainty.

"No, my friend, she's not," Lucas said calmly. As he came up beside Ria, put one arm about her waist, and reached slowly toward the hand that held the pistol. "Let go, Ria," he said softly.

"He deserves to die," Ria whispered.

"That he does, but not by your hand. Let go."

Ria shivered and for a heart-stopping moment both Henri and Lucas felt the taste of death.

"Mother of mercy," Henri whispered.

"That's right, Henri," Ria snarled, "pray."

Lucas had to get the pistol from her for he was as certain as Henri that she intended to fire it.

Lucas took his arm from Ria's waist and slid it up beneath her hair to gently caress the nape of her neck. "Give me the pistol, Ria . . . come on . . . give it to me."

Minutes ticked by. Henri licked lips suddenly gone dry, and his eyes gazed into unrelenting amethyst depths. Then, slowly, her hand relaxed and Lucas grasped the pistol.

Henri knew of Lucas's anger, but he felt more relieved when Lucas held the pistol.

"I don't think any merchant is safe with you roaming the seas, Henri," Lucas said. "It's time we put an end to it. Move ahead of me after you order your men ashore. We have a little something to settle with Dan."

Henri's orders were obeyed and Henri, Ria, and Lucas followed the crew ashore.

If Dan was surprised, he didn't show it. He was still unsure of what Lucas might do about him and his dealings with Henri.

But Lucas had his mind set on making sure Henri was never a threat again, on the sea or anywhere else. When he told Dan his plan, men were ordered to carry it out. Henri and his crew watched what they were doing for several minutes before they realized what was going to happen.

Lucas had not even looked at Henri for quite some time. He turned to him only when Henri protested what was happening.

"You cannot do this!" he shouted.

Lucas had torn off the rest of his shirt and had refused another because his back was too raw. When he turned his gaze on Henri he looked like vengeance itself.

"We can, Henri, and we will. But for you this doesn't mean it's over. We have a score to settle, you and I, and we'll settle it here and now." His voice was

469

so emotionless and final that Henri again became silent.

Several of the crates of gunpowder were carried back to the *Sea Rover* and placed where Lucas had instructed. When the men who had taken it aboard returned and Lucas was sure his orders were completed, he prepared for the final step of his mission.

"Dan," he said, "make sure everyone is back from the dock. When she blows, there will be debris strewn for some distance."

Henri raged, his fury so extreme that he couldn't contain it. He was held where he could watch as Lucas alone walked down to the dock and boarded the *Sea Rover*. After some time he appeared on deck with a small keg of gunpowder in both hands. It had been opened, and he was trailing a narrow stream of the powder as he walked down the gangplank to the dock.

"Damn him! Stop him!" Henri shouted, but no one made a move to do so, and Henri was forced to watch the preparations for the destruction of his ship.

When the flint was struck and the stream of gunpowder was ignited, a waft of gray-white smoke could be seen moving toward the *Sea Rover*.

Lucas ran toward the camp as the gunpowder burnt toward the ship. Lucas had just reached the spot where Ria and Dan stood when an explosion cut the night air. Another followed the first almost immediately; then a third reverberated. Sheets of flame and clouds of smoke rose from the *Sea Rover*.

Only when the flames began to lessen did Lucas turn toward Henri. He was being held by two of Dan's men, but now he stood immobile, a hate-filled glare in his eyes.

Lucas's smile would have chilled the hardest of hearts, but Henri was past feeling anything but murderous fury for the man who had so suddenly snatched from him all he possessed.

"Let him go," Lucas said.

The men holding Henri looked at Dan who nodded silently.

"How well do you get along when you have no one to do your dirty work for you, Henri?" Lucas asked in a quiet voice. "Tell me, do you have the guts to face a man yourself?"

Henri laughed, a harsh bitter laugh. "To face you man to man, yes, I have the courage. But what good is it to fight you for my life. If I win I will lose my life at the hands of your friends."

"This is between you and me," Lucas said calmly. "If you win Dan will give you supplies and a map. You can go your way . . . if you win." Lucas's voice became a cold weapon with which he flayed Duval. "But, Henri old friend, let me tell you what I intend to do to you."

Lucas walked to two of Dan's men and slipped evil-looking bladed knives from their belts. Casually flipping one in his hand he walked toward Henri, and as he walked he talked in a firm and emotionless voice.

He began to explain to Henri, as if he were making casual conversation, the amount of damage he was capable of doing to a man with a knife.

He spoke of castration and disembowelment. He spoke so coldly and so self-assuredly that Henri's face paled and the hand that accepted the knife from Lucas shook.

Lucas backed away from Henri with a sardonic half-smile on his face, and the flame in the depths of his amber eyes scorched Henri's heart.

Lucas assumed a position alien to Henri who was more used to fighting with a sword. The pirate had resorted to a knife only when the odds were more in his favor. Lucas crouched with knees slightly bent and the upper part of his torso leaning forward. He made of his large body the smallest and most difficult target to reach as he held his arms akimbo, the knife suddenly appearing to be an extension of his hand.

Henri licked his lips as he assumed the same position. The dawn was just breaking, and the first rays of morning sunlight glistened off of the blades and were reflected into the eyes of the two opponents. They circled each other slowly, and Ria, watching Lucas, was held motionless by a strong sense of power. He was like a predatory animal. His lips were drawn back from his teeth, and they glistened in a white snarl. His eyes had a feral glow that was instinctive. The desire to kill could be read in every lithe move of his body.

Henri slashed out and Lucas leapt back only to strike like a cobra. Henri felt only a light sting, but a spot of blood touched the white of his shirt sleeve.

He slashed out again and again, but Lucas, like a shadow, was always an inch or so away from the blade.

Long before it became apparent to any of the others, Henri knew that Lucas meant to cut him to shreds before he killed him.

Another touch of the blade, a small nick, enough to bring blood.

"Bastard!" Henri hissed.

"My ancestry is well known to me"—Lucas smiled—"which is a situation you wouldn't know. Most likely your mother was a streetwalker and your father a leprous jayhawk who left you as a package even she didn't want."

There was a roar of rage. Lucas had expected it. His taunts had been intended to provoke it. This time Lucas did not strike lightly and retreat. He sliced upward, opening a cut from Henri's waist to his shoulder.

Henri bellowed like an angry bull and spun about. Lucas had misjudged the speed with which Henri could turn, and as a result he found himself grasped by the wrist of the arm that held the blade. Quickly reacting he gripped Henri's wrist and they strained for supremacy like two titans.

Suddenly Henri thrust his foot between Lucas's, and a sharp cry of fear was torn from Ria as the two men tumbled to the ground. Lucas felt himself falling and tightened his grip on Henri's wrist drawing him down with him. He grit his teeth against the pain as they rolled on the ground, each searching for one moment of weakness in the other that would end the conflict.

Henri found himself atop Lucas who kept the blade of Henri's knife from his throat by only a hair while he tried to jerk his arm free of Henri's grip. The battle now was muscle and sinew against muscle and sinew. It was a soundless struggle, but the foes' eyes were locked.

Slowly . . . very slowly Lucas began to push Henri's hand up and the wicked blade away. Then, suddenly, he thrust Henri from him and both men scrambled to their feet. Henri's clothes were covered with blood, and he gazed into unrelenting gold-amber eyes that asked or promised no quarter.

With a shout of pure fury Henri attacked. He resorted to brute force meant to overpower Lucas. Ria could hardly believe what was happening. Henri charged with a force that would have overcome most men.

It looked to all present as if the battle were decided. Lucas appeared unable to move as he stood, legs spread, and waited.

Henri was almost upon him when, with what appeared to everyone to be only a slight movement executed with a dancer's grace, Lucas stepped aside at the last second and drove his knife in and up.

Henri sagged to his knees, then fell face forward on the ground. The battle was over.

Chapter 35

The waiting had been difficult for Brian and Chris, but they had decided not to move until dawn to make sure they had given Lucas and Ria enough time to return.

They stood on the deck indulging in sporadic conversation, but both kept their eyes on the river, expecting to see the boat that would mean Lucas and Ria were safe.

"Damn," Brian breathed softly. "This waiting is hard."

"I agree. The only thing that gives me any confidence is the fact that Lucas and Ria are together, and he wouldn't do anything to add to the danger she is facing. When he doesn't find you in Dan's camp, he's clever enough to get out of there."

"They should have been back by now."

"They still haven't been gone too long. They'll make it, Brian."

"It will be dawn soon."

"When they get back we're going to face a somewhat difficult situation."

"How so?" Brian turned to him.

"Well, to begin with are you and Ria going to tell

Lucas you are brother and sister?"

"I should think this would be a good time." Brian grinned. "It's gone far enough, and besides, Ria doesn't need my protection any longer."

"Then Lucas and I will go home, and you and Ria will go home," Chris said.

"Temporarily," Brian replied.

"While we can, let's plan what we will do to get these two together."

"I should think the first thing we must do is explain to Lucas's parents and mine just what has transpired. They can insist that Lucas and Ria meet, even if it is just to discuss an annulment. When they do"—he shrugged and laughed—"it's over."

"And they live happily ever after."

"I hope so. They've had a very hard struggle all these weeks. They deserve happiness."

"But when Lucas learns who Ria is, you and Scott and I will probably be in more danger than ever before. We must stand together."

"Are you a coward?" Brian chuckled.

"Have you ever seen Lucas really angry?"

"To tell the truth only once, and he knocked me senseless. At least I can understand the reason for that. It seems he didn't want to kill me."

"Well, he's formidable when he's angry . . . and that's an understatement."

"He certainly can't be any worse than Ria. She has a hell of a temper."

Chris laughed. "Maybe they've met their match. Their marriage should be volatile at least."

"They'll have the damnedest kids," Brian declared.

Chris was about to voice a humorous response when an explosion ripped the night air. It was quickly followed by another and then another.

A sheet of flame leapt into the sky some distance upriver. They exchanged shocked looks as both realized the only place it could have come from.

"Good God," Brian said. "What the bloody hell was that?"

"I don't know what it was, but I sure know where it was."

"Ria. Do you think—"

"I don't want to think. Let's get the *Swan* upriver as fast as we can."

"We'd better be ready to run into Henri."

"We're ready," Chris said firmly.

They wakened the crew and put the ship into motion as rapidly as they could. As they rounded each bend they expected to run into a well-armed Henri, but they didn't. When they did spot the *Sea Rover*, she was a smoldering hulk.

They drew as close to the shore as possible, and surged ashore. The group of people congregated there seemed completely engrossed in something they could not see yet, and their approach was ignored. When they broke through the ring of spectators it was to see Henri Duval lying in a pool of blood and a half-naked bloody Lucas holding a weeping Ria in his arms.

"Ria!" Brian called out. He was overwhelmed with relief at seeing her alive and well.

Ria lifted her head from Luke's chest, and her eyes widened with pleasure.

"Brian," she gasped. She ran to her brother and threw herself into his arms, laughing happily. "Oh, Brian, I thought I'd never see you again! Are you all right?"

"I'm fine, Ria, just fine. But you, you look rather . . . unusual."

"I haven't dressed like this since I used to borrow

477

your breeches to go riding."

Lucas's face was grim when Ria ran from him to Brian. He remembered that he had told Ria he loved her, but she had said nothing. Obviously her emotional involvement with Brian had not changed. It is over, he thought. He had done what he had set out to do. Henri and the threat of his piracy were gone. He had no choice but to go home and make the best of an unwanted marriage.

While Lucas explained what had happened he kept one eye on Ria and Brian. Chris watched his face closely.

"Lucas, for God's sake," Chris said, "go and get her if you want her. Are you going to just give up?"

"She's free to make her own choices," Lucas replied in a deadened voice. "I've interfered in her life enough. I'll not do it again. She's free to do whatever she wants."

Ria had taken Brian's hand, and was drawing him with her as she crossed to where Lucas and Chris stood.

"I think it's time Brian told you how grateful he is for all you've done for me." She smiled at Lucas who refused to respond in kind.

"I don't really need or want his gratitude, Ria. I think you two had best take the *Swan* and go home."

"But Lucas, Brian and I—"

"God damn it, I've taken all of this I care to take. I don't want gratitude; I just want you two out of my life!"

For a moment Ria was speechless. Then she thought Lucas had only said that to make what they were going through less difficult. She finally decided that since they were safe he had returned to his antagonistic hateful ways.

It was Brian who spoke for a stunned Ria.

478

"You have my gratitude anyway, and if you can control that murderous disposition of yours, I can tell you something that will make you grateful to me."

"I doubt it," Lucas snapped.

"Don't speak too soon." Brian laughed. "If I'm not mistaken you're in love with Ria."

For one heart-stopping moment both Chris and Brian thought Lucas might strike Brian. His face was taut, grim, and cold.

"That, my friend," he grated out, "is none of your damned business. I've brought Ria to you, safe, which is more than you have done. In fact I don't think she is any better off with you than she was with Henri. You are too stupid to see what you have!" Lucas's anger, because of his painful back and physical exhaustion, was slowly beginning to get out of hand and he knew it. He inhaled deeply, trying to control the urge to put his knife into Brian and thereby wipe the delighted grin off his face.

Brian had intended to have a little fun with the situation, but the look on Lucas's face was enough to make him realize this was no time for humor.

"She's safe with me," he said gently, "not, I suppose, as safe as she is with you. I love her too, my friend, and have all the years of our lives. You see, Ria is my sister."

Brian began to wonder if Lucas's anger had driven him beyond the point where he was capable of hearing. His face was a total blank. Then the words slowly began to register.

"Sister?" he choked out.

"My sister," Brian affirmed.

Lucas's eyes shifted quickly to Ria's. "You mean . . . all this time . . . you were not—"

"Not his mistress," Ria said softly. Her eyes had

479

softened, and they shone now with the unrestrained love she had held within for so long. "You have been the only man, Luke . . . you will always be the only one."

Lucas could not believe his eyes or his ears. Was his desire for Ria so strong, his misery at the thought of losing her so great, that he was dreaming things he wanted to hear.

"I don't understand . . ." he began. Ria went to him.

"Luke, it was something beyond our help. It was the only way, at first, that Brian could protect me. Later, when I thought . . . well when I felt his life was in danger, I couldn't tell the truth. I was afraid. But it's over now, Luke. There's no need for lies anymore. I can tell you that I love you as you told me when you felt you were about to die. Was that a lie, Luke?"

By the time Ria finished speaking Lucas had already regained his equilibrium. With a half-laugh, half-groan, he reached out to her, and Ria found herself snatched up into arms that felt like oak. Her gasp of surprise was silenced by the hunger of the mouth that claimed hers in a wild, urgent, and most satisfactory kiss.

Lucas had swept Ria up against the breadth of his chest. With his arms about her, and her feet inches from the ground, she could only cling to him and laugh deep in her throat at the sheer glory of knowing their battles were done, the war was ended—Luke loved her.

Brian and Chris stood by, grinning at the total happiness of those two. Even when Lucas reluctantly let Ria slip to the ground again, his arm remained about her waist as if, should he let her beyond his touch, she might disappear and his dream would end miserably as so many had before.

When Lucas faced Brian again, his grin was broad and he extended his hand. "This is the first time I have been able to say that I'm pleased to know you."

"I remember well the last time we met," Brian replied. "You were somewhat . . . violent to say the least." Brian said this with good humor. "At the time you were not too pleased with me," he added.

"I was as jealous as hell," Lucas admitted. "I thought Ria belonged to you. I knew she loved you. I harbored quite a few thoughts of murder myself."

"I thought you might have, but then I didn't always feel magnanimous toward you. Tell me the truth. That day on your ship, you wanted to kill me?"

"You're right there."

"Why didn't you?" Brian asked.

"I'm damned sure you have the answer to that. At the time I thought Ria's happiness was with you."

"So you gave her up."

Ria moved closer into Lucas's embrace, knowing the answer and knowing she would have done the same.

"I want Ria to be happy," Lucas vowed, while his arm tightened about her. The answer was simple and complete.

"From what I hear you two still have a rather large problem ahead of you," Chris put in.

"I don't think any problem can stand between us again. If you are talking about our marriages, they will just have to be annulled or—"

"Or what Luke?" Ria gazed up at him.

Lucas's vision was filled with amethyst eyes. He spoke with certainty. "Ria, nothing is going to stand between us. If he won't let you go, and he would be totally insane if he did, then we will go away somewhere together. Tell me," he said quietly, his eyes searching hers, "would you go with me knowing we could never marry? Knowing that the only future we had would be what we could make for each other?"

"I would go with you, Luke," Ria said without hesitation. "Anywhere you wanted to go. And you? You have the same choice."

"No, Ria." Lucas laughed happily. "I have no choice. If I cannot live with you, I have no life at all."

"I hate to interrupt all this"—Dan chuckled—"but would anybody care to enlighten me as to what is being planned."

Chris responded. "I told you we came here for Henri. He's dead now and the piracy is ended, so I'm sure I can speak for everyone present. We wouldn't mind turning our backs and forgetting we have ever seen Dan McGirtt or known the location of his camp."

"And what of Henri's men?"

"Give them a choice."

"Such as?"

"Joining you or taking a boat downriver to St. Augustine. They can fend for themselves. They're like a snake without its head, nearly harmless."

Dan turned to Lucas.

"We were mounting an offensive to try to rescue you. Would you like to tell me how two people not only got away but captured a ship as well?"

"Two didn't." Lucas chuckled now.

"You're not making sense."

"One did." Lucas went on to explain that it had actually been Ria who had rescued him. "I was tied up when she took over." He grinned. "And for several minutes I was sure she was going to blow him in two."

"I was," Ria put in quickly.

"Well, it's over," Brian said firmly, "and Ria and I have to take the *Swan* and go home. I'm sure our parents are beside themselves with fear and worry over her. I'd like to let them know she is safe."

There was a moment of total silence, for resistance to Brian's plan could be seen on Lucas's face almost at once.

"Can't you go home and speak to them yourself?" Lucas protested. "What needs to be done for Ria's annulment can be handled from America."

"That's not fair to our parents." Brian turned to Ria. "They have a right to see you, to know you are all right. And besides, why should they do something about a marriage you don't want and they do. Unless we're both there to fight for an annulment, Father might just see fit to force you to honor your vows."

"He's right, Luke," Chris inserted quickly. "It's only a matter of a short separation."

"A short separation," Lucas repeated. "What if her father decides there will be no annulment? You know damned well the law would support her father's right to force her to abide by the marriage vows whether she agrees or not. I'm not going to let that happen."

"Luke," Brian said, "if such a thing should happen I, personally, would spirit Ria away and bring her to you. You have my word that I want Ria to be happy and I won't let her be caught in a marriage she doesn't want. You will have your hands full getting out of your own entanglement. It will be hard for Ria if she comes with you as a mistress while you try to rid yourself of a wife. Do you want to put her through that?"

"Damn it!" Lucas said in frustration. He knew Brian was right, but Ria was slipping from his hands before he even had the chance to really know her. "It will be at least two months!"

"What are they compared to a lifetime?" Brian answered.

"Two months is a lifetime, Brian," Ria said. She turned to look up at Luke. "But we can survive that when we have survived so much bitterness and misunderstanding. Luke, soon we'll both be free."

Lucas put both hands on her waist and drew her against him. The look in his eyes almost made Brian and Chris relent and tell the truth, but they restrained themselves. Both wanted the St. Thomases to know their daughter was safe, and both wanted Ria and Lucas to meet on more solid ground.

"Two months, Ria," Lucas whispered.

"I know." Her eyes sparkled with crystal tears. "But I want to be free. I want to belong to you completely."

He sighed, knowing he was defeated. Letting her go, even for a night, was difficult. Mentally he cursed Arianne St. Thomas. Why had her father decided to buy her a husband? And he had the same angry attitude toward his own father for agreeing to an alliance just because he and Reginald St. Thomas had been friends. He intended to make short work of the agreement between the older men and even shorter work of his unwanted, unconsummated marriage.

"Then I guess we should set sail right away. If I wait longer than two months, I will come and drag you away."

"We can take the *Swan* down and anchor her near the *Angel*," Brian said. "It would be better to leave in the morning. Daylight is rapidly fading, and I don't intend to navigate this river in the dark."

"We are going to break camp," Dan said. "By the time you are halfway down the river we will be gone." He extended a hand, first to Chris and then to Lucas and Brian. "It has been, to say the least, an interesting experience meeting you. I suppose our paths will never cross again but"—he laughed—"I doubt if I will forget you."

"While I was in St. Augustine I heard rumor of an amnesty Governor Tonyn was offering for any and all of the banditti," Lucas said. "It means being deported to Cuba or one of the islands, but that's far better than being hunted."

"I know of it, Luke," Dan replied, "but there are circumstances which keep me from accepting the offer. My men are free to make their own choices, but . . . I can't."

"No need to explain to us," Lucas responded. "I just wanted to make sure you knew."

"Thank you. But the choice was made for me a long time ago. Good luck."

Dan, William, and John stood on what remained of the dock and watched the *Swan* move slowly away.

Brian, Chris, and Louisa stood at the rail of the ship and watched their figures recede. Ria stood a short distance away from them in the circle of Lucas's arms.

"Ria . . ."

"Ummm?"

"We're going to be at anchor for the night, and I'd like to spend the time with you. Two months is a very long time, and we have a lot of things to talk about."

"Yes, we do." Ria laughed softly. "We have never really talked to each other, have we?"

"Not really. I can't believe Brian is your brother. Brother!" He chuckled. "I like the sound of that. All this time we've been at each other's throats, misunderstanding, not being able to find any common ground, and all because I was so jealous of him.

Brother," he added softly. "The word has an absolutely fine ring to it."

"I'm sorry it had to be so, Luke. But surely you can understand that Brian was only protecting me."

"Of course I can."

"And you'll have to admit another thing."

"What?"

"I needed to be protected from you too. Your motives weren't exactly"—she shrugged—"honorable, and your opinion of me wasn't the highest."

"That was only self-defense," he admitted. "I just didn't want to believe I was in love with a woman who was in love with someone else. My vanity I guess. I had to fight what you were doing to me with those eyes of yours—they haunted my sleep—not to mention your other physical attributes."

"Ah well, it is all finished. In a month we can be together."

Lucas held her close, aware that there were questions in his mind and in hers. He wanted to know what her name really was, but if he asked her, she would ask him about his; he had to keep his identity secret until he was free to marry her. His station in society forbade him from marrying out of his social class, but once he was free, he would say to hell with what society wanted. He would have Ria, and all the proprieties in the world would never separate them. He knew she would have a very difficult time fitting in with people who would look down their noses at her, but after a while the scandal would die down. They would be happy, he thought, if he had to move heaven and earth to make it so.

The situation was just as difficult for Ria, whose thoughts followed the same path. Her family, with the exception of Brian who had finally accepted Lucas, would most likely be scandalized, as would their friends. To bring home a pirate and fit a man of his wicked ways into society was going to be very hard. But she intended to do battle one way or the other until Lucas was accepted.

So neither spoke of names, and neither was aware that Brian and Chris, who had introduced Louisa only as a gentlewoman caught in a difficult situation, were standing some distance away, enjoying the fact that Ria and Lucas were happy, and aware that they faced a great deal more happiness in the near future.

Ria had already invited Louisa to come home with her, but the young woman had quietly declined. Ria was pleased to find later that Chris was taking Louisa home with him and in the very near future she would be his wife.

The *Swan* made her way downriver slowly and anchored near the *Angel*. Then the five friends ate dinner together. Afterward Ria and Lucas walked the deck alone before he returned to the *Angel*, both very aware that when morning came they would be separated and would not see each other for two long months.

Chapter 36

Lucas and Ria walked the deck slowly, breathing in the fragrances of wild tropical flowers wafting on the warm night air. Brilliant stars and a mellow gold moon lit the night sky, reflecting their glows in the water.

Both were reluctant to part, and both wished this night would end in a much more satisfactory way than separation. However, when the morning sun streaked the sky, they knew the ships would sail.

As they stood by the rail, below them the small boat in which Lucas would return to his ship bumped lightly against the hull of the *Swan*. Lucas turned to Ria and without a word drew her into his arms.

"I have found a lot of things difficult in my life, but this is the worst. We could just go to my ship, leave quietly, and no one would know until dawn."

"And spend the rest of our lives in a like fashion? Neither of us would accept that, Luke. I don't want to run and hide with you. I want to tell the world how proud I am to be your wife and how much I love you. I am no more patient than you, but we must be."

"I know that. I've been telling myself that for days. My mind says one thing," he said quietly as he tipped up her chin to look deeply into melting amethyst eyes, "but my body most certainly isn't listening to logic." He bent his head to taste the heady wine of her half-parted lips.

Slowly he drew her closer; slowly their mouths warmed to the sweet exploration of their kiss.

Slim arms twined around his neck and her body molded to his in the first touch of real surrender he had known. For the first time she came to him without a battle, without the forced seduction that had always preceded their lovemaking. Only this time she was further away from him than she had ever been.

He was stormed by vivid memories. He saw her as she had looked asleep, her eyelids red and swollen from tears he had made her shed. He remembered the silken feel of her hair when, in a wild and passionate moment, she had knelt astride him letting her tresses spill over him. Her tangled strands had veiled her sweat-touched face. He envisioned a quiet moment when passion was done and reality had not yet come to them.

He recalled the fear, tears, and recrimination he had provoked. He felt the old scars, mementos of his desire to possess her, begin to ache again. He remembered vividly the curve of her back pressed closely against him, the heat of it when he had wakened her from sleep to possess her again. He wondered if the scars he had given her would be washed away in the love he had for her.

She was proud. She was strong, and never had she let him truly capture her. He had thrown the idea of love in her face and had accused her of things that deep inside him he had known were not true.

"I can't touch you without wanting you, but you'll have to get used to that because I don't ever expect to stop wanting you, my amethyst-eyed vixen," he declared. "You've driven me half-mad ever since I set eyes on you. I imagine your woman's intuition sensed that I loved you—that I've loved you a long long time."

"Don't you realize," she responded, "that I feel no less desire than you? We are just in an impossible situation."

"I know." He sighed. "So kiss me goodbye, my sweet, and I promise I won't be able to sleep one night until we're together again."

The kiss she gave him did very little to cool his ardor. He had never met with such a wild and intoxicating response. It left him no alternative but to leave her or find a place to freely indulge his urgent passion.

It took more grim determination than Ria would ever know for him to grip her shoulders and hold her away from him.

"I'm leaving this ship now. Remember Brian has promised you will be on the dock in America in two months. Make sure he's not late."

"I'll be there, Luke . . . I'll be there."

He kissed her quickly and climbed down to the boat. As he disappeared in the darkness Ria felt a sudden sense of loneliness; she knew it would not leave her until Lucas held her again. She was so intent on her own thoughts that she didn't hear Brian come to stand beside her.

"He's gone?"

"Yes," she said softly, brushing a wayward tear from her cheek.

This was the closest Brian had come to telling her the truth. He knew the pair had admitted their love for one another as pirate to mistress, but he felt they must meet on safer ground. This is the best way, he thought. But Ria's tears were difficult to handle. Because of them he made a decision that surprised even him.

"Ria . . ."

"What?"

"Why don't I row you to the *Angel?* Why don't you go down the river with Luke? Then you would have some time together."

Nothing in the world could have taken Ria more by surprise. She spun around to look at him, unaware that he had justified what he had just said in his own mind by reminding himself that they were, after all, man and wife.

"Brian . . . I . . . I can't believe you."

"Damn it, Ria,"—he was uncertain of how to make her understand without revealing information that would surely create a storm he was unprepared to handle. "You've been cheated. You love him and he loves you. Maybe . . . well maybe I feel that's enough for now."

Ria couldn't understand this abrupt change in Brian, but she was more than grateful that he was trying to be sensitive to her needs.

"Thank you, thank you," she whispered.

"Let's take the other boat." He laughed. "I'll row you over and then come back. I'll be waiting for you in St. Augustine. We'll make this marriage permanent, legal—and have our parents' blessing. You'll see. It will all work."

She flung her arms about him with a laugh of delight, and he hugged her close, then held her away from him.

"Let's go," he said softly. She nodded.

Brian rowed easily and very nearly soundlessly toward the *Angel.* He held the rope ladder steady and watched as Ria climbed to the deck. Then, with a silent whistle on his lips and satisfaction in his heart, he rowed back to the *Swan*.

Ria had no difficult in finding her way in the semidarkness. She knew the location of the captain's cabin on the *Angel* very well. She moved silently and soon found herself in front of Lucas's door.

She trembled, as if it were the very first time they would be together. Despite the battles they had had in the past, she had found a magic in his arms, a magic for which she would sacrifice anything. The thought that he loved her sent a pleasurable thrill through Ria. He had loved her all the time, from the very first, as she had loved him; but neither of them had admitted it.

For a moment she closed her eyes, her lips curved in a slight smile; then she reached out and turned the handle. The door swung open, and she stepped inside and closed it behind her.

Lucas had boarded the *Angel* in a mood that was a combination of frustration and helpless anger. The anger was directed at himself. Memories of the times he'd shared with Ria were forcing him to see the darker side of being alone.

He remembered his brutality to her, and when he looked at his past behavior, he wondered that she could love him. He poured himself a drink and sipped it while he removed his boots, then he eased off the shirt he had borrowed from Chris, taking care not to let it scratch against his back which was extremely sore and painful.

He went to a small stand where a basin sat and poured into it some water from the container that sat beneath it. He cursed softly. It would be very nearly impossible to soothe the soreness in his back with a cool wet cloth for he couldn't reach that part of his body. He soaked the soft cloth in the water, then lifted it to his shoulder, squeezed it, and felt water run down his back. It was inadequate, but the best he could do to ease his discomfort.

He continued to dip and squeeze until his back felt wet and began to cool. It was still uncomfortable, but he knew there was not much more he could do. He smiled to himself, thinking that Ria's gentle touch would most certainly ease his pain. He chuckled, for he was certain he could most likely forget any amount of pain if he held her in his arms.

He washed his face and arms, lathering them well and then rinsing them with the cool water. Then he reached for a towel that hung nearby, only to freeze into immobility as he heard the door click softly behind him.

He stood erect and turned slowly, but he was unprepared for what he saw.

Ria stood against the door, the most seductive smile he had ever seen on her face, her eyes filled with a warmth that was only a mild echo of what he felt.

For Ria, Lucas was a vision that supplied fuel to the unquenchable need she had for him. Water glistened like drops of crystal and silver on his bronzed skin, and his amber eyes seemed like heated gold as they appraised her.

"Ria?" A soft question, as if he couldn't quite be sure she was really here and not something he had conjured up from his dreams. "What are you doing here? How did you get here?"

"Brian brought me," she replied in a faint whisper.

"Brian . . . he brought you here?" he asked in a disbelieving voice.

"He understands me well. He knew where I wanted to be . . . where I belonged. I'm going at least as far as St. Augustine with you."

Slowly Ria walked across the room. With a tentative hand she reached to brush drops of water from his skin. With a half-laugh half-groan, he reached for her.

"If this is a dream," he said as he bent to kiss her, "I hope I never waken."

The dam that had restrained them, that had held back ultimate giving, broke. Irreparably shattered, it allowed a surge of passion to burst forth and carry them on currents that would never again be harnessed.

Ria's lips parted eagerly beneath his, allowing her tongue to meet with his and linger in a molten embrace.

Then Lucas kissed her eyes, teased her earlobes, brushed his lips across her soft skin, and finally claimed her lips with a kiss so potent it shook the foundation of Ria's world.

He moved leisurely, letting his mouth skim across the softness of her shoulders, as, with gentle hands, he began to remove her clothes. A soft moan of pleasure came from Ria when his lips followed his hands to caress and taste the crest of a passion-hardened breast. His breath was warm and moist against her flesh, and his hot tongue licked her flesh until she felt that a flame teased her body.

His strong hands continued to stroke the length of her, then kneaded her firm buttocks gently while his tongue continued its journey down the valley between her breasts to the soft flesh of her belly. Expertly, he sought the peak of trembling need, his tongue lovingly entering her and laboring skillfully to tantalize her senses.

Her body quivered with delight and her breath grew short, and her eyes were glazed with passion when he rose to immerse himself in their depths. He began to remove his clothing, aware of the heat of Ria's gaze which devoured his iron-muscled body.

She took pleasure in knowing he did not merely seek a lustful release, but that he wanted to be part of her, to give as much pleasure as he took. His hunger for her was evident in his quivering muscles and in the greedy length of the proud erect shaft that spoke of his readiness.

But Lucas had no intention of bringing this blissful time to a quick end. For them, this was a beginning, and he meant it to be perfect. He would not taste her passion for many long days and nights, so he meant to drink deeply of it this night.

He took her hand and slowly drew her with him to the bunk they had once shared in bitterness and anger. Now it would be different. Ria was no longer afraid of opening herself to him and giving completely, for she knew the depth of his passion and sought the depths of his love. They would share, for the first time, the special part of themselves that could be touched by no other.

Ria's amethyst gaze fused with amber gold, in an unspoken message of love and urgency. Lucas's probing eyes caressed each line of her face with an infinite tenderness that set her pulse to beating wildly. Her breath caught, then seemed to increase in a deep throbbing rhythm.

His fingers drifted over her heated flesh with matchless tenderness. Her whole body was quivering in wild anticipation as he drew her down on the bunk beside him, and she drifted to him with half-closed eyes, her hands reaching for him as if they had wills of their own.

He lay beside her, resting on one elbow, his eyes roaming over her body. Then he placed one hand against her cheek and a half-smile tugged his hard rugged mouth. Eyes locked with hers, he traced his fingers lightly down her throat; then very slowly, as his hand captured her firm breast and his fingers taunted it to sensual fullness, his head bent and he took her mouth with his—gently at first, his lips slowly playing across hers. Then passion grew, and she felt his tongue trace the soft pliancy of her lips, teasing her mouth open to accept him more fully. Their tongues met and merged with a remembered need.

The aching need grew to a feverish pitch, but still Lucas made no move to bring it to fruition. Ria's hands now began to touch, to caress, her fingers moving lightly across his shoulders to his chest, then down across his hips and belly, drawing a sharp intake of breath from him.

Her hands found his pulsing shaft, closed about it with a confidence she had not had before. She would make him as much her possession as he had made her his.

Her gentle fingers moved, slowly and easily, until he had to grit his teeth to keep from ravaging her. He might be kissing her almost savagely, but she was triumphant. She no longer doubted his love.

"I didn't think any woman could be so beautiful," he whispered, "or so intoxicating."

The waves of passion were growing higher and higher. He was kissing her again, deeply, breathlessly, and her hands were impatient now. He was excited by the sure knowledge that she was as eager for him as he was for her.

He molded his body against hers, and his hard maleness made waiting no longer possible. Both knew they were at the peak where control was gone. He moved above her.

Ria arched to meet him, wanting to feel his hardness fill her. His movements quickened and she matched her rhythm to his. She could think of nothing now, could merely feel his lips taking her willing ones, sense the heat of him against her avid flesh.

She cried out in blinding ecstatic passion again and again, until his mouth caught her cries and they mingled with his as their bodies mingled. Ria was half-sobbing, and incapable of feeling anything but the white-hot strength-sapping magic that tumbled her senses about like feathers in a hurricane.

Lucas reveled in the way her body surged to meet his, the way her long slim legs clutched him possessively. He braced himself on his elbows so he could see her face when they reached the pinnacle of passion, when her climactic explosion rendered her as much a victim to their mutual bliss as he knew he was.

When it came, it left them both shaken and helpless. Lucas was reluctant to leave her body. He could feel her surround and hold him, and he again cursed the time they would be separated. He turned on his back, slipping his hands beneath her buttocks to carry her with him. She lay atop him, her head resting on his chest and his arm about her.

For long moments they lay so. Until pounding pulses eased, until racing blood slowed.

Finally, Lucas caught her hair in his hand and rubbed it against his cheek inhaling the subtle fragrance of it. He was content when he heard her deep sigh.

"This will most likely be the shortest night of my life," he whispered.

"I, too, will find the hours too fast. Why is it when one finds pleasure the hours always race."

"I would wish the hours of the next month away."

"So would I."

"We wasted so many days." He chuckled softly. "It's your fault, you know. Why didn't you tell me you weren't Brian's mistress?"

"Brian and I had made a bargain. Besides, you were so mean it was very nearly impossible to tell you anything."

"I'll make up for that, Ria. I promise."

"Luke?"

"What?"

"What if . . . what if she refuses to annul the marriage?"

"She can't."

"Why? If you were my husband, I would surely refuse to give you your freedom."

"Well, in the first place there's a little matter of consummation. It never happened, and it's not likely to. In the second place, I have no intention of having any other wife than you."

"But Luke—"

"Ria, we're not continuing this conversation. I have no intention of lying in the arms of the woman I love and talking about my marriage to another woman whom I've never even seen. Besides," he said softly, "there are so many much more important things to be discussed."

She lifted her head to look into his eyes, and saw in them the reflection of her own.

She smiled. "You are right. There is so much more that you have to say to me . . . and you have such a wonderful way of making a point. In fact"—her voice lowered seductively—"I think we're wasting time talking at all when you have other wonderful methods of expression."

He laughed in deep pleasure and kissed her fiercely. Then he caught her face between his hands and drew her lips to his again in a teasing kiss that sent a quiver of breathlessness through her. Would he always be able to ignite her body with a touch, able to wipe every thought from her mind with a kiss? She knew it had been so in the past and would be in the future. It excited her that they would have years together to prove their instinctive need for each other was right.

The night was too short for words, so both surrendered to their returning warmth, grasping for each moment and knowing that dawn was such a short time away.

When dawn did come Lucas was still awake. Ria lay nestled close to him, and his arm held her curved to his body. He didn't want to wake her. For a few minutes he allowed himself the luxury of letting his imagination place them in other circumstances. They were in their own home, and the dawn would not bring separation but the promise of beautiful days together.

He sighed when he felt Ria stir, and looked down as her sleepy eyes opened.

"I'd hold back the dawn if I could."

"The time was much too short, but I'm afraid you are right. We'll have to be leaving soon."

They rose from the bed, both trying to contain words that were useless to utter. Their situations made separation necessary. The trip downriver would be too short.

Again some strange feeling made Ria question Brian's sudden change of heart. He had actually told her to stay with Luke, had given them this time together. It was an extraordinary thing for him to do, and she had the oddest feeling there was something she should have known.

The sails of the *Angel* filled with the morning breeze, and she headed down the river to St. Augustine . . . then home.

500

Chapter 37

The *Swan* reached St. Augustine first, and Brian was pleased with that for several reasons, one being that he and Chris had decided it was too cruel to extend any longer what had started as a joke. He would tell Ria the truth at once. He hadn't thought it would be like this. The deception had started as fun, but it had gotten out of hand.

When Scott and Sophia had made it to St. Augustine, they had returned to Sophia's room and he had begun a daily watch for Brian and the *Swan*.

Sophia, though silent, was well aware that Scott was torn by conflicting desires: to go home, to remain with her, or to take her with him. She knew their situation was impossible. She would never fit into Scott's life, and he could not remain in hers.

Moments after word was brought to Scott that the *Swan* was in the harbor, Sophia returned to the room. She knew at once when Scott turned from the window to look at her that a time for decisions had come.

She walked to him and stood close, but they did not

move to touch each other. Only their eyes met.

"You're leaving," she stated with finality.

"I have just gotten word from Brian. The *Swan* is in the harbor . . . waiting."

"Scott . . ." She whispered his name helplessly.

"Come with me, Sophia."

"I can't do that, you know I can't."

"I know nothing of the sort."

"Scott, that is impossible."

"Why? Unless you don't want to come because you're tired of me."

"Don't." The word choked her. "It is because I care for you that I won't go with you."

"Then I'll stay with you."

"And do what . . . be what? You would be miserable here within a year, and when you looked at me with disgust and anger, I couldn't bear it."

"Sophia, I can't leave you like this."

"We knew it would happen someday."

"Why won't you come with me?"

"Because I could never be anything more than your mistress. For a while we might be happy, but one day you would meet a woman right for you to marry. What would I be then, Scott? Unwanted, and you too kind to tell me so."

"It doesn't have to be that way," he protested.

"But it would. There are some things we cannot change. You and I have no future . . . our lives can never mix. Please, Scott, make it easier for me. Go, before I change my mind and do something we will both regret."

Scott had never felt so miserable. He had tried for days to convince Sophia to come with him. This was his final attempt, and he knew he had no chance to succeed. He would have to leave. As he drew her into his arms to share a final embrace and a bittersweet kiss, he made a silent vow to himself.

When he arrived in England, he would make use of his fortune by setting up a fund which would ensure a constant flow of money to Sophia. She would never want for anything as long as she lived . . . and she would never have to belong to another man unless she chose to. That was all he could do, because it was all she would allow. He knew she might refuse to accept the money, so he said nothing. He wasn't going to give her that chance.

He kissed her hungrily, for he knew it would be a long time before he found such affection again. She returned his kiss with wild passion, wanting to hold him but knowing she had to let him go.

Before he could speak again Sophia, with a heartrending sob, tore herself from his arms and ran from the room. Scott stared at the door a long time, knowing she was gone from his life. She would watch the place, and would not return to the room until he was gone—until the *Swan* was gone.

Slowly he gathered up his few possessions and he left, sadness clinging to him.

The *Swan* left the mouth of the river and entered the bay. Chris and Brian stood at the rail, looking toward St. Augustine, when Brian suddenly stopped speaking in midsentence.

"Brian?" Chris turned to his friend.

"My God, if I'm not mistaken that ship looks familiar," Brian replied. He quickly snapped out an order, and in a few minutes a telescope was brought to him. He held it to his eye and, in a moment, laughed softly.

"Come on, Brian, what is it?"

"We don't have to worry anymore about telling

Ria and Lucas anything. The truth will be out of the bag very soon."

"You're talking in riddles."

"That ship is the *Windward* . . . my father's ship. I'd not be surprised to find my parents are both here. The truth will be out"—he chuckled—"and we had better be able to talk fast—or run faster. There's no way to get around it now: Lucas will have Ria's name in a matter of hours."

Chris groaned. "Tell me, is there a place on St. Augustine where I can hide?"

"Sorry, my friend. We have to face the music and throw ourselves on their mercy."

Chris groaned again, and Brian could have seconded it when he thought of how much mercy he might expect from Ria.

When they docked, Chris and Brian sent word to the *Windward*, and received a message that they would find that ship's owner and his wife at the inn.

Upon arriving there, Brian was welcomed with enthusiasm and immediate questions about Ria. Whatever anger his father had felt had long since been overcome by relief at his children's safety.

Brian told his parents that Ria was well; then Chris excused himself from the reunion, and went to find Scott and to send word to Louisa's father that his daughter was safe.

Once Brian had told his parents everything, they were amazed at the trick of fate that had drawn Ria and Lucas together.

"She still does not know this man is her husband! My God, Brian, your little joke has gone beyond humor."

"I know that, Father," Brian said. "But in the beginning it was just that I wanted them to accept each other for what they were, because they loved each other. Once they did, I felt they would be happier. Then . . . well, it started as a joke, but I can't put a stop to it."

"Well, I can." His father rose. "It's time for us to take Arianne St. Thomas to meet her husband Lucas Maine. Once they are together you'll just have to throw yourself on her mercy."

Brian groaned. "Ria's mercy in this case will be little short of murder."

"Murder well deserved."

"Father . . . uh . . . maybe it's best if you take Ria on the *Swan* and I—"

"Not on your life. You and Ria have pulled tricks on each other all your lives. This time you must pay the price." He watched Brian's misery with twinkling eyes.

"Brian, really," Cecelia St. Thomas said. "I believe this little charade has been carried much too far. How could you let Ria suffer so?"

"Mother"—Brian laughed—"I'd hardly say she is suffering. She's with Lucas."

"But she believes they must be separated for a long time. Oh, Brian, truly I find myself very angry at you. You must repair this damage at once! At once, do you understand me?"

"I readily concur with your mother," Sir Reginald added. "Your actions are reprehensible, young man, and don't look to us for protection. Whatever your sister puts you through, you richly deserve."

"You are both right, and as soon as the *Angel* docks and they come ashore, I'll go and tell her. Then I'll bring them here."

"Very good. See that you do," his father said firmly.

*   *   *

It was a very uncomfortable pair of conspirators that watched for the arrival of the *Angel*. Only when her sails came into view did an idea spring to Brian's mind. It was given birth because of his need for self-defense.

He turned to Chris.

"I'll stay and wait for the *Angel*, but if you want to get us both off the hook, I've got an idea that just might work."

"What is it? I'd rather do anything than face those two and tell them the truth."

"All right, listen carefully . . ."

As Brian began to explain his plan, Chris smiled and nodded his head.

"Sounds great," he said enthusiastically when Brian was finished.

"Good, then you go on and do your part, and I'll stay here and do mine."

Chris set off, and Brian actually felt relieved as he watched the *Angel* approach the dock.

Ria was determined that Lucas Maine would be told the truth upon her arrival home, for she wanted to be free as soon as she possibly could.

The *Swan* bumped lightly against the dock, and Ria stood with Lucas by the rail. Both were reluctant to go ashore even though they saw Brian waiting for them. When her brother greeted her, he took her arm and drew her a little aside. Ria looked up at him, a puzzled expression on her face.

The faint touch of a premonition moved across her mind. Again she felt that ever since the night Brian had told her to go to Luke he had been somehow different. This was unusual, since she and Brian were in the habit of sharing confidences.

Brian put his arm about Ria, but he spoke to Lucas first.

"Luke, our parents are here to meet Ria and me."

"That's wonderful. I can't wait to meet them."

"Well, I have a carriage here, and I'll take you to them straightaway."

Ria was delighted. "I can't wait for Luke to meet Mother and Father. Once they know how much we love each other, they'll understand why my marriage must be annulled."

"There is another thing I must tell you."

"What?" Ria inquired.

"I've explained everything to Mother and Father. They are going to meet us at the church here to discuss your problem with the reverend." Brian could not resist his last little bit of fun. "Father says if you still want the annulment he will start the proceedings at once . . . of course, you must tell him to do so."

"Oh I shall, I shall," Ria cried happily. "Thank you, Brian. I'm so grateful."

"Keep that thought in mind, Ria," Brian said wryly.

They entered the carriage and rode into St. Augustine. Despite Ria's questions, Brian would say nothing more to her except that he knew their parents understood and that she could discuss the situation when they arrived at the church.

Outside the church, Lucas helped Ria from the carriage and then pushed open the large doors so they could walk inside. The interior was dim and quiet, but the small group of people near the front of the church turned when they heard the door open.

It was Ria who moved swiftly down the aisle and threw herself into her mother's arms. After a tearful reunion she kissed her father, still wary of the position he might take.

"Father . . . this is Luke. Luke, my father."

"Yes," Brian added quietly, "our father . . . Sir Reginald St. Thomas."

Scott had found his way to the church quickly after receiving a hastily written note from Chris telling him what was about to occur.

Chris began to smile as did Brian and Scott when they saw Lucas's eyes reflect shock, and the hand he had extended to Arianne's father paused.

"Sir? . . ."

"Sir Reginald St. Thomas," Brian repeated. "Ria's father."

Lucas remained motionless for several moments while Ria looked at both men in surprise. Then Lucas began to smile.

"Sir Reginald St. Thomas . . . Ria's father . . . good God." He turned to Ria. "Love, tell me your full name."

"Does it really matter, Luke?" Ria asked. She feared that her father's presence had brought their situation home to Lucas in a new way.

"Oh yes, Ria my love." Lucas grinned. "It does."

"Arianne . . . Arianne St. Thomas," she said quietly.

Lucas began to laugh; then he lifted Ria in his arms, binding her to him. Ria felt he had suddenly gone mad.

Everyone was smiling now, except Ria who was becoming more puzzled by the minute.

Lucas stopped laughing. "I would be truly miserable if you were to annul your marriage. I think Lucas Maine is the man who should be your husband."

"Luke!"

"No, love," Lucas said quietly, "Lucas . . . Lucas Maine."

"What . . . I . . . I don't . . ." Then Ria's mind began to grasp the situation. "Lucas," she whispered.

He nodded slowly. Then Ria began to laugh. She threw herself again into Lucas's arms.

"Lucas Maine! This is impossibly wonderful. I don't understand, but I don't care," she cried. "It's the answer to a prayer."

"I'll have a lifetime to explain it all," Lucas replied. "But for now let's just celebrate. Ria . . . Ria," he said softly, "all this time you have truly belonged to me."

"Luke—Lucas—I don't know what to call you."

"I'll think of some appropriate words later," he whispered. "For now . . . would husband do?"

"Oh yes," she murmured, as his lips found hers. "Husband would do very well."

Epilogue

Louisa's father came at once after receiving Chris's message, and the reunion was tearful and happy.

The wedding of Chris and Louisa was surpassed only by the wedding of Lucas and Ria, which was attended by two thoroughly forgiven friends and one equally forgiven brother.

The ceremony over, Lucas and Ria set sail on the *Angel* for a destination known only to them. Having promised to be gone no more than three months on their honeymoon, they walked the streets of St. Augustine again, and the beach of Anastasia Island, reliving the past and creating new memories.

Ria lay in Lucas's arms aboard the *Angel* which rode at anchor in Matanzas Bay. The night was one of rare beauty, but Lucas knew a beauty beyond it. Their lovemaking had been extraordinarily passionate, for there were no barriers to their pleasure now and they tasted it fully.

"To think, Ria, that we could have been together from the first, that we were married during all the battles."

"I don't believe I would change it now," she replied, "but I don't believe I could live through it again."

"I was so brutal with you. It is hard to believe you could still have loved me. The only excuse I can make for my ugliness is that I was so profoundly jealous of Brian it was almost impossible not to think of ways to eliminate him."

"Yet you saved him."

"For you."

"When you thought I would go with him."

"Even then your happiness meant more to me than anything in the world."

"Oh, Lucas," she whispered, "you are my happiness. I love you, dear pirate . . . lover . . . husband."

There were no answering words—Lucas had sought her willing mouth with his—and none were necessary for his kiss told her of his love. Ria did not doubt there would be nothing in their future but the wild and tumultuous love they shared.